Pilgrim Pathways

Essays in Baptist History
in Honour of B. R. White

Barrington Raymond White

Pilgrim Pathways

Essays in Baptist History in Honour of B. R. White

edited by
William H. Brackney
and
Paul S. Fiddes
with
John H. Y. Briggs

MERCER UNIVERSITY PRESS
1979–1999
Twenty Years of Publishing Excellence

ISBN 0-86554-687-8   MUP/H507

Pilgrim Pathways:
Essays in Baptist History in Honour of B. R. White
   Copyright ©1999
   Mercer University Press, Macon, Georgia USA
   All rights reserved
   Printed in the United States of America

The paper used in this publication meets the minimum requirements
of American National Standard for Information Sciences—
Permanence of Paper for Printed Library Materials, ANSI Z39.48-1984.

Library of Congress Cataloging-in-Publication Data

Pilgrim pathways : essays in Baptist history in honour of B. R. White /
   edited by William R. Brackney and Paul S. Fiddes.
     pp.   cm.
   Includes bibliographical references.
   ISBN 0-86554687-8 (alk. paper)
   1. Baptists—England—History.   I. White, B. R. (Barrington Raymond).
II. Brackney, William H. III. Fiddes, Paul S.
BX6276.P55   1999
286'.0942—dc21   99-41193
                                                                CIP

Contents

Contributors vii

Foreword .... ix-xii
    William H. Brackney and Paul S. Fiddes

Issues of Baptist Identity

1. Doctrine, Polity, Liberty:
   What Do Baptists Stand For? 1-46
   Alan P. F. Sell

2. "Walking Together": The Place of Covenant Theology
   in Baptist Life Yesterday and Today 47-74
   Paul S. Fiddes

The Baptist Way of Being the Church

3. The Child and the Church: A Baptist Perspective 75-110
   W. M. S. West

4. Life Together in Exile:
   The Social Bond of Separatist Ecclesiology 111-25
   Stephen Brachlow

5. "Sing Side by Side":
   John Rippon and Baptist Hymnody 127-63
   Ken R. Manley

6. The Covenant Life of Some Eighteenth-Century
   Calvinistic Baptists in Hampshire and Wiltshire 165-83
   Karen Smith

History As Biography

7. Another Baptist Ejection (1662):
   The Case of John Norcott 185-88
   Geoffrey F. Nuttall

8. The Contribution of Bernard Foskett 189-206
   Roger Hayden

9. Jane Attwater's Diaries 207-22
   Marjorie Reeves

10. "Active, Busy, Zealous":
    The Reverend Dr. Cox of Hackney 223-41
    John H. Y. Briggs

Crossing Boundaries

11. The Evangelical Revival and the Baptists 243-62
    W. Morgan Patterson

12. The English Baptist Legacy of Freedom
    and the American Experience 263-81
    William R. Estep

13. The Planter Motif among Baptists
    from New England to Nova Scotia, 1760–1850 283-302
    William H. Brackney

14. A. J. Gordon and H. Grattan Guinness:
    A Case Study of Transatlantic Evangelicalism 303-18
    Scott M. Gibson

Barrington Raymond White:
A Bibliography of Printed Works 319-28
   Stephen M. Copson

Contributors

Stephen Brachlow is professor of Church History and Spirituality at North American Baptist Seminary in Sioux Falls, South Dakota.

William H. Brackney is principal of the Divinity College and professor of Historical Theology at McMaster University in Hamilton, Ontario, Canada.

John H. Y. Briggs is principal of Westhill College of Higher Education in Selly Oak, Birmingham.

Stephen Copson is secretary of the Baptist Historical Society (U.K.) and secretary of the Hertfordshire Association of Baptist Churches.

William R. Estep is professor emeritus of Church History at Southwestern Baptist Theological Seminary in Fort Worth, Texas.

Paul S. Fiddes is principal of Regent's Park College and a member of the Faculty of Theology at the University of Oxford.

Scott M. Gibson is assistant dean and assistant professor of Ministry at Gordon-Conwell Theological Seminary in South Hamilton, Massachusetts.

Roger Hayden is general superintendent of the Western Area of the Baptist Union of Great Britain, and lives in Bristol.

Ken R. Manley is the principal of Whitley College in Melbourne, Australia.

Geoffrey F. Nuttall, formerly visiting professor at King's College, University of London, is retired and lives in Birmingham.

W. Morgan Patterson, formerly president of Georgetown College, now serves as visiting professor of Church History at New Orleans Baptist Theological Seminary and other institutions.

Marjories Reeves, Fellow of the British Academy, is honorary fellow of St. Anne's College in Oxford, where she lives.

Alan P. F. Sell is professor of Christian Doctrine and Philosophy of Religion and director of the Center for the Study of British Christian Thought at the United Theological College, Aberystwyth, Wales.

Karen Smith is a tutor in Church History at South Wales Baptist College in Cardiff, Wales.

W. M. S. West was formerly principal of Bristol Baptist College and now resides in Bristol.

Foreword

William H. Brackney and Paul S. Fiddes

Barrington Raymond White was born on 28 June 1934 in the County of Kent, England, the son of Raymond and Lucy White. He took his undergraduate degree (B.A. Hons) in Theology at Cambridge University as a member of Queens College, and then went on to Regent's Park College, Oxford, to prepare for the Baptist ministry and to write a doctoral thesis in Church History (D.Phil.) in the University. He was ordained as a minister in the Baptist Union of Great Britain, and served Andover Baptist Church from 1959 to 1963, leaving to become tutor in Ecclesiastical History at Regent's Park College. In 1972 he was inducted as the twelfth principal of the College at the young age of 38, succeeding the Rev. Professor Gwynne Henton Davies. In 1989 he retired from the principalship to be able to give more time to research, and was elected as Senior Research Fellow in Ecclesiastical History in the College, retiring in turn from this appointment in 1999.

This is the bare outline of Dr. Barrie White's ministerial and teaching career, largely centred upon the life of Regent's Park College in the University of Oxford, but such a list of details gives little hint of the enormous impact he has made personally on the lives of students, scholars, ministers, and members of Baptist churches over the years. As a teacher, he initiated the undergraduate student into his own enthusiasm for Church History, or the story of what he always called "The Great Church," in deliberate contrast to some Baptists whose horizons were limited by the local congregation. In tutorials he was a penetrating questioner, ready to respond with an instant and devastating wit, at his best when a student dared to take up the verbal cudgels with him. He was an influential and conscientious supervisor of graduate students, spending a great deal of his time in bringing the doctoral work of others to fruition, some of whom repay that debt by writing in this present volume. Through his scholarship and passionate advocacy of the subject, he opened up a larger place for the history of nonconformist churches in Oxford, the most Anglican of Universities. The Faculty of Theology in the University honoured him by electing him for a period as the Chairman of the Board of the Faculty, which he presided over with typical aplomb and good humour.

Yet it is as a pastor in the college community that many students will remember him best. His conviction has always been that theology must serve the churches, and on his appointment as Principal he set about the task of widening and deepening the nature of training for Christian ministry in Regent's Park College. Two other projects he initiated were a trail-blazing post in Mission and Lay Training, where a tutor spent two-thirds of his time outside college providing training in the local congregations, and the provision of accommodation on site for married students and their families. Under his Principalship the number of nonministerial undergraduates in college greatly increased, and he saw this as a means of encouraging future leaders in all the Christian churches to grow in faith and service.

Many who read this volume, who were never students at Regent's, will recall Barrie White as a welcoming presence in the Principal's Lodgings at the corner of St Giles and Pusey Street in Oxford. For many travelers and visitors, and for scholars and ministers on sabbatical leave, he opened up his study for discussions of everything from a recent scholarly publication to contemporary politics. His ironic wit and rapier-like questioning often left guests pondering on the direction of his thought, only to be reassured by a sly smile or an outright chuckle.

But it is mainly for his achievements in the area of nonconformist and Baptist history that this present collection of essays honors Dr. White. Here his influence has been wide. In his graduate studies, he re-raised the questions about connections between Baptist, Puritan and Separatist beginnings which had first been posed by Henry M. Dexter and William T. Whitley. He read extensively under the tutelage of Ernest Payne, Geoffrey Nuttall, and his mentor, Norman Sykes, Dean of Winchester. His ground-breaking doctoral dissertation, completed in 1961 and published as *The English Separatist Tradition: From the Marian Martyrs to the Pilgrim Fathers* (Oxford University Press, 1971), created a watershed for new studies, several of which he personally supervised. The distinguished list of theses which were stimulated by his research includes studies of Separatism, Particular Baptist life and theology, and English Calvinism. His own work has become an authority on the question of the linking of Baptist origins to the Puritan Separatist groups of late sixteenth century and early seventeenth century England.

Over a twenty-five year span, Dr. White has also applied his considerable skills as an historian to other key areas. For instance, in the tradition of W. T. Whitley, he published an annotated version of the Particular Baptist Associational records, to 1660. He rediscovered the art and value of historical biography as a clue to the character of English nonconformity, and William Kiffin and Samuel Eaton have been his special interests. His volume on *The English Baptists of the Seventeenth Century* has become a standard work on Baptists throughout that period, and is a notable contribution to the series on the history of English Baptists, which is published by the Baptist Historical Society, and for which he himself was general editor for some time.

Dr. White was elected a Fellow of the Royal Historical Society in 1973, and succeeded Dr. E. A. Payne as president of the Baptist Historical Society in 1981, a position he held until illness caused him to resign in 1993. He has frequently been invited to lecture at seminaries and divinity schools in Europe and the United States of America, often distinguishing himself on these occasions with the production of new scholarly work. He reckoned it was his duty, while principal of Regent's, to respond to requests to attend or preside over the installation of new presidents and deans of theological institutions, though this was sometimes at his own inconvenience. He has also played a notable part in the work of the Commission on Baptist Heritage of the Baptist World Alliance.

In presenting these essays in honor of Dr. Barrie White, his students and friends have selected a variety of topics which are divided into four sections, reflecting his own concerns. In the first section, "Issues of Baptist Identity," Alan Sell assesses contemporary issues of Baptist identity in light of historic patterns and transatlantic treatments, while Paul Fiddes makes anew the case for the role of covenant in Baptist congregational and denominational life. Section two, "The Baptist Way of Being the Church," contains four essays: Morris West surveys the problems and development of a theology of children among English Baptists; Stephen Brachlow focuses his attention on social relationships among the Separatists as a pattern for later Baptists; Ken Manley tells the story of John Rippon and the rise of Baptist hymnody as an indicator of Baptist piety; and Karen Smith looks closely at the internal life of Baptists in Hampshire and Wiltshire in the eighteenth century, with implications for the present. Because Dr. White's interest in biographical figures was so keen, section three is devoted to that approach: Geoffrey Nuttall recovers an obscured seventeenth century Baptist, John Norcott; Roger Hayden looks at Baptists in the Bristol tradition, particularly Bernard Foskett; Marjorie Reeves gives an insight into the manuscript diaries of Jane Attwater, whose family documents are a special asset of the Angus Library; and John Briggs details the life and outreach of the esteemed Francis A. Cox, minister at Hackney, denominational educator and voluntarist. In the final section, three North Americans look at the application of Baptist principles in their contexts: Morgan Patterson discovers anew the influences of the eighteenth century revival brought forth by Methodists upon the Baptist community in England; William Estep reviews the legacy of religious freedom inherited by the American Baptists from their English ancestors; William Brackney demonstrates the connections between the New England Baptists and the frontier community in Nova Scotia; and Scott Gibson relates the ministry of Boston's A. J. Gordon with that of H. Grattan Guiness in Britain, together creating a nexus of evangelical work.

It has been a matter of sadness for Dr. White, his family and his colleagues, that in the last eight years illness has held him back from the vigorous activity that characterized the largest part of his working life, and has prevented him from further scholarly publication. His friends admire the courage with which he has faced his limitations, the positive spirit and interest in others that he brings to any meeting, his persistent wit and his undimmed skills of verbal interplay. He continues to serve on the Council of the Baptist Historical Society and to reside in Oxford, with his wife Margaret, as Principal Emeritus of Regent's Park College.

In the preparation of this volume the editors wish to thank several persons: Ardele Stokell and Terri Galan who typed various parts of the manuscripts, David Stephens at McMaster Divinity College who assisted with electronic transfers of details, and of course Cecil Staton and Marc Jolley at Mercer University Press. A generous grant from the Foundation in England assisted in the publication, and McMaster Divinity College kindly made available funding for technical services.

The Editors

Doctrine, Polity, Liberty: What Do Baptists Stand For?

Alan P. F. Sell

> In writing upon the theological beliefs for the English Baptists of this century, I do not intend to pen a word as the advocate of a party, or set down a sentence with a grain of personal bias.[1]

If John Clifford felt it necessary to introduce his 1888 study of Baptist theology in this vein, how much more ought a friendly Reformed observer of Baptists to endorse such words—especially since I am ambitious enough to rove over four centuries, not one. The operative word is, of course, "intent," and it is always possible for results to belie intentions. Be that as it may, it is not my purpose to produce one more tract of "the Dippers Dipp'd" variety. Indeed, baptism is not the main focus of this paper, for until the harvest of the dialogues between Baptists—Reformed as well as others—is safely gathered in, there is not much more to be said upon that hoary topic.[2] The concern here is not with Baptists *vis-à-vis* other Christian traditions; rather, I am interested in the attitudes and antics of Baptists among themselves regarding three of their historic concerns: doctrine, polity, and liberty. Were this not such an auspicious

---

[1] John Clifford, "Baptist Theology," *Contemporary Review* 53 (1888): 503. For Clifford (1836–1923), see the *Dictionary of National Biography* (hereafter *DNB*).

[2] Only the most daring ecumenist would predict when the harvest referred to will be in. For while, when responding to the World Council of Churches' document, *Baptism, Eucharist, and Ministry*, the Council of the Baptist Union of Great Britain and Ireland declared, "It would seem that any further work on baptism could usefully be done only in the wider context of Christian initiation"—the very suggestion proposed in the international Baptist-Reformed dialogue of the 1970s—Ernest A. Payne's restrained words of forty years ago have subsequently lost none of their force: "Since the formation of the Baptist World Alliance, it is the stricter wing of the Baptist movement which has, on the whole, been dominant." The continuing positive work of such Baptists as W. M. S. West, and J. H. Y. Briggs, and such thoughtful contributions as that of M. J. Quicke should not, however, be overlooked. See *Baptism, Eucharist, and Ministry. The Response of the Baptist Union of Great Britain and Ireland to the Faith and Order Paper No. 111 of the World Council of Churches* (London: Baptist Union of Great Britain and Ireland, 1985) 3, cf. 1.3; *Baptists and Reformed in Dialogue* (Geneva: World Alliance of Reformed Churches, 1984); Ernest A. Payne, "Baptist-Congregational Relationships,," *The Congregational Quarterly* 33/3 (July 1955): 225; M. J. Quicke, "Baptists and the Current Debate on Baptism," *The Baptist Quarterly* (hereafter *BQ*) 29/4 (October 1981): 153-68.

volume my contribution might have been adorned with the title "Baptists through the Keyhole." As it is, the second part of my heading suggests that, as in other communions (for I am the last to adopt a "more-ecclesiastically-purer-than-thou" posture), Baptist trumpets have on occasion, on the issues under review, made not uncertain sounds, but a number of different certain sounds, some of them discordant. On one issue, however—establishment—Baptist trumpets, like those of others in the line of Old Dissent, are nowadays decidedly muted, if not altogether silent. This is my justification for turning Henry Cook's bold title, *What Baptists Stand For* (1947), into a question.

This preamble may conclude with one procedural point and one statement of the obvious. First, we shall have more than enough material to consider if we confine ourselves to soundings taken within the English Baptist heritage, and no disrespect to Baptists elsewhere is implied by this restriction. Secondly, there is unavoidable artificiality in attempting to treat doctrine, polity and liberty *seriatim*, for Baptist polity has been determined by the Baptist doctrine of the Church, doctrine which has required liberty for its articulation and expression, and implies a theory of church-state relations. In fact, the organs of polity—church meeting, association—have stated those doctrines commonly believed and, in some instances, required to be believed. Nevertheless, in the interests of clarity of exposition, we shall attempt to deal with one matter at a time.

I

We may permit a Congregationalist to erect the poles between which our discussion of Baptist doctrine will oscillate. In one place P. T. Forsyth declared, "There must surely be in very positive religion some point where it may so change as to lose its identity and become another religion."[3] Elsewhere he warned, "Where you fix a creed you flatten faith."[4] Here was aptly posited that tension between clearly defined doctrinal identity and liberty of conscience which Baptists of various stripes have experienced through the centuries. Thus, for example, on the one hand those General Baptists who devised *An Orthodox Creed* (1678) declared that "The three creeds, viz. Nicene creed, Athanasius's creed,

---

[3] P. T. Forsyth, *The Principle of Authority* (1913) (London: Independent Press, 1952) 219.

[4] P. T. Forsyth, *Positive Preaching and the Modern Mind* (1907) (London: Independent Press, 1964) 141.

and the Apostles creed, as they are commonly called, ought thoroughly to be received, and believed."[5] On the other hand, the Western Association, which at its inception embraced a few General Baptist churches, entrusted "every church to their own liberty, to walk together as they have received from the Lord."

However, in the wake of the debates over the Trinity and subscription fueled by both Anglican Samuel Clarke's *The Scripture Doctrine of the Trinity* (1712) as well as the Salters' Hall conference of 1719, the Association, subsequent to its re-formation in 1722, heeded a letter prepared by Bernard Foskett, from the Broadmead church, Bristol. This letter urged that every member church would "in their Letter every year signify their approbation of" the *Second London Confession* of 1689, and requested members to affirm the Trinity and to deny "the destructive and corrupt principles of the Arminians . . . and of the Antinomians."[6] With reference to the same confession, the Particular Baptist John Collett Ryland signed a Circular Letter to the Northamptonshire Baptist Association in 1777 in which the ministers and messengers remarked, "Our confession of faith, and our catechism for the instruction of our young people, are published to the world; and from these glorious principles we hope you will never depart: if you should, you will not longer be churches of Christ, but synagogues of Satan."[7]

These random examples drawn from the two major classical streams of English and Welsh Baptist witness will suffice to justify E. A. Payne's remark, "It is a mistake to suggest that [the earliest Baptists] eschewed

---

[5]*An Orthodox Creed, or a Protestant Confession of Faith, Being an Essay to Unite and Confirm All True Protestants in the Fundamental Articles of the Christian Religion, against the Errors and Heresies of Rome* (London, 1697) art. XXXVIII; in William L. Lumpkin, ed., *Baptist Confessions of Faith*, rev. ed. (Valley Forge PA: Judson Press, 1969) 326.

[6]Caleb Evans, "Records of the Western Association," MSS at Bristol Baptist College, 7; J. G. Fuller, *A Brief History of the Western Association, from Its Commencement, about the Middle of the Seventeenth Century, to Its Dvision into Four Smaller Ones—the Bristol, the Western, the Southern, and the South Western—in 1823* (Bristol: I. Hemmons, 1845) 30. See further, Roger Hayden, "The Particular Baptist Confession of 1689 and Baptists today," *BQ* 32/2 (1988):403-17. For Foskett (1685–1758), see Norman Moon, *Education for Ministry. Bristol Baptist College 1679–1979* (Bristol: Bristol Baptist College, 1979) 108 and passim; Alan P. F. Sell, "Philosophy in the Eighteenth-Century Dissenting Academies of England and Wales," *History of Universities* XI (1992) 101-102.

[7]*The Beauty of Social Religion; or, the Nature and Glory of a Gospel Church, Represented in a Circular Letter from the Baptist Ministers and Messengers, Assembled at Oakham, in Rutlandshire, May 20, 21, 1777*, 7. For Ryland (1723–1792), see *DNB*.

credal statements or objected to creeds and confessions."[8] It remains only to add that in addition to proclaiming their doctrines and indicating to churches and members what the doctrinal parameters were, the early confessions served the apologetic purpose of countering those who maliciously attributed to Baptists view which they did not hold and Münster-like aspirations which they did not share, and of demonstrating Baptist loyalty to the faith of the ages. Thus, the Particular Baptists' London Confession of 1644 was

> Presented to the view of all that feare God, to examine by the touchstone of the Word of Truth: As likewise, for the taking off those aspersions which are frequently both in Pulpit and Print, (though unjustly) cast upon them.[9]

Similarly, the *General Baptist Standard Confession* of 1660 was

> Set forth by many of us, who are (falsely) called Ana-Baptists, to inform all Men (in these days of scandal and reproach) of our innocent Belief and Practise; for which we are not only resolved to suffer Persecution, to the loss of our Goods, but also Life itself, rather than to decline the same.[10]

Apologetics apart, what happened when, as in other traditions, some Baptists deemed others to have overshot the rigorist or libertarian doctrinal markers? Let us recall some incidents drawn from the several streams of Baptist witness, all of which will encourage reflection upon the ever-present question of the permissible degrees of doctrinal tolerance within the church.

Although there is a long prehistory of unorthodoxy—especially Socinian—concerning the Trinity and person of Christ,[11] and although John Smyth "flirted with Anabaptist Melchiorite Christology that Christ received his second flesh but not His first flesh from Mary"[12]—a position repudiated by Thomas Helwys and his supporters[13]—we may set out from the General Baptist Matthew Caffyn (1628–1714).[14] Sent down from

---

[8]Ernest A. Payne, *The Fellowship of Believers, Baptist Thought and Practice Yesterday and Today*, enlarged ed. (London: Carey Kingsgate Press, 1952) 103.
[9]Lumpkin, *Baptist Confessions of Faith*, 153.
[10]Ibid., 224.
[11]E.g., see H. John McLachlan, *Socinianism in Seventeenth-Century England* (London: Oxford University Press, 1951).
[12]James R. Coggins, "The Theological positions of John Smyth," *BQ* 30/6 (April 1984): 255.
[13]See Lonnie D. Kliever, "General Baptist Origins: The Question of Anabaptist Influence," *Mennonite Quarterly Review* 36 (1962): 293.
[14]For Caffyn, see *DNB*. This article, by Alexander Gordon, is supplemented by his

Oxford circa 1624 for advocating Baptist views, he farmed at Horsham, where he joined the General Baptist movement. He was cordially welcomed by the minister, Samuel Lover, whom he succeeded in 1748,[15] and was instrumental in founding a number of other churches in Sussex and Kent. Alexander Gordon writes:

> Caffyn was an intrepid man in the advocacy of Baptist views, but in the expression of his own peculiar sentiments he was exceedingly cautious; he published nothing which could be laid hold of, and I believe I must add that the was purposely ambiguous when attempts were made to bring him to book.[16]

It appears that until 1653 Caffyn maintained orthodox trinitarian convictions, but thereafter he embraced an unorthodox Christology. Gordon came across Christopher Cooper's scarce volume, *The Vail Turn'd Aside* (1701), which recounts Caffyn's addressing a large assembly in London, declaring that the second person of the Trinity was changed into flesh and literally died. This, said Caffyn, had been taught to him by a man wearing a leathern doublet, who approached him at Horsham Fair. Whereas Cooper, casting his net wide, supposed that "some evil spirit in human shape appeared to deceive him, or else the craft of some intriguing Jesuit or popish friar, or one of the Arian stamp sent by the whore of Babylon." This is on the basis that Caffyn adopted in 1661 the anthropomorphic line that God takes human, or similar, form and is not omnipresent. Gordon conjectured that the teacher was a Muggletonian. Gordon ruled out the possibility that Caffyn was influenced by Socinianism on the ground that he expressed no sympathy with that party; and sought to convert its members to his own position.[17] Rather, his Christology had a Melchiorite ring to it, which appealed to a number of General Baptists as it had already done to the continental Anabaptists.

Melchior Hoffman argued that "the whole seed of Adam . . . is cursed and delivered to eternal death."Accordingly, if Jesus Christ took on this accursed flesh, then "redemption has not yet happened."That is to say, "if it should be established that Christ's flesh was Mary's natural

---

"Matthew Caffyn and General Baptist latitude," *The Christian Life and Unitarian Herald* (5 Nov. 1892): 531-32.
  [15]John J. Evershed, "A Short Account of the Free Christian Church, Billingshurst," repr. from *Transactions of the Unitarian Historical Society* (October 1949): 2-3.
  [16]Gordon, "Matthew Caffyn and General Baptist latitude," 531 (c).
  [17]Ibid., 531(c)-32(a).

flesh and blood, we would all have to wait for another redeemer, for in such a one we could get no righteousness."Rather it was the eternal Word who became incarnate.[18]

How do such views measure up against the Christology of the Standard Confession?

> We Believe . . . III. That there is one Lord Jesus Christ, by whom are all things, who is the only begotten Son of God, born of the Virgin Mary; yet as truly *David's* Lord and *David's* root, as *David's* Son, and *David's* Offspring, Luke 20.44., Revel. 22.16, whom God freely *sent into the world* (because of his great love unto the World) who *as freely gave himself a ransom for all*, I Tim. 2.5,6. *Tasting death for every man*, Heb. 2.9. *a propitiation for your sins; and not for ours only, but also for the sins of the whole World*, 1 John 2.2.[19]

Here is a tapestry of selected biblical texts which clearly sound the note of general redemption and are but vaguely Christological in any technical sense. William Lumpkin, a Southern Baptist, noting that "In clarity and definiteness of statement it hardly matches the Particular Baptist Confession of 1644," generously suggests that "The poor arrangement of subjects might indicate that the document was drawn up hurriedly"[20]— certainly the drafters were urgently wishing to remove grounds of persecution. The fact remains that, since little concerning Christ's nature was specified, or precluded, a General Baptist of Caffyn's persuasion enjoyed a good deal of doctrinal freedom, while devotees of heresy trials were deprived of effective ammunition. So it proved. At Aylesbury in 1672 Caffyn was charged with blasphemy by the General Baptists of Buckinghamshire.[21] He agreed that saying the eternal Word could die was blasphemous, and confessed his puzzlement concerning Christ's person. Utterly dissatisfied with Caffyn's prevarications on the matter, Thomas Monk, the messenger for Buckinghamshire and Hertfordshire, published *A Cure for the Cankering Error of the New Eutychians: Who (concerning the Truth) Have Erred; Saying That Our Blessed Mediator Did Not Take His Flesh of the Virgin Mary* in the same year. At the Assembly of 1673

---

[18]See Walter Klaassen, ed., *Anabaptist in Outline* (Kitchener ON: Herald Press, 1981) 27-28; translated from F. O. zur Linden, *Melchoir Hoffman: Ein Prophet der Wiedertaufer* (Haarlem: De Erven F. Bohn, 1885) 441-43.

[19]Lumpkin, *Baptist Confessions of Faith*, 225.

[20]Ibid., 221.

[21]As early as 1659 Caffyn had been one of George Fox's targets in *The Great Mistery of the Great Whore Unfolded*, published during that year.

Caffyn sought to clip Monk's wings by bringing a charge—apparently ethical—against him, but this failed; neither was there a further attempt to denounce Caffyn's teaching. Monk was undeterred. In fact, along with a group of fifty-four, like-minded General Baptists from Buckinghamshire, Hertfordshire, Bedfordshire, and Oxford, he published the *Orthodox Creed* in 1679.[22] Echoing biblical and patristic authors, they declared:

> We confess and believe, that the Son of God, or the eternal word, is very and true God, having his personal subsistence of the father alone, and yet for ever of himself as God; and of the father as the son, the eternal son of an eternal father; not later in the beginning. There was never any time when he was not, not other in substance . . . not a metaphorical, or subordinate God; not a God by office, but a God by nature, coequal, coessential, and coeternal, with the father and the holy ghost. . . . [T]he second person in the sacred Trinity, took to himself a true, real, and fleshly body, and reasonable soul, being conceived in the fulness of time, by the holy ghost, and born of the virgin Mary, and became very and true man. . . .[23]

In article XXXVIII they reproduced the Apostles, Nicene, and Athanasian Creeds in full, and expressed their wish that these be "catechistically opened, and expounded in all Christian families, for the edification of young and old, which might be a means to prevent heresy in doctrine, and practice, these creeds containing all things in a brief manner, that are necessary to be known, fundamentally, in order to our salvation."[24]

At the General Baptist Assembly of 1691 Caffyn, his orthodoxy challenged by Joseph Wright, the messenger from Maidstone, renewed his subscription to the 1660 Confession, but two years later Wright brought a charge of heresy against him at the Assembly in London. The allegation now was that he was a follower of John Weller, who taught that the Word was a creature and Christ's body the created Word "turned into flesh"—a Melchiorite-cum-Arian concoction. As put by the churches of

---

[22]For Monk and the other signatories, see Arnold H. J. Baines, "The signatories of the Orthodox Confession of 1679, *BQ* 18 (1957–1958): 35-42, 74-86, 122-28, 170-78.

[23]Lumpkin, *Baptist Confessions of Faith*, 299-300.

[24]Ibid., 326. In which connection A. C. Underwood has a curious phrase. Having noted the inclusion of the creeds in the Orthodox Confession, and the injunction that they be taught, as something which "would surprise most Baptists," he continued, "There is a return to true Baptist principles in the article on Liberty." See A. C. Underwood, *A History of the English Baptists* (London: Baptist Union Publication Department [Kingsgate Press], 1947) 107. This would appear by implication to sanction that leap from the New Testament to the Reformation, which would deprive Baptists of a good deal of their doctrinal inheritance.

the Northern Association (that is, by churches of the Buckinghamshire, London, and Essex areas), the question's being "Audibly read was universally owned to be an error in the Terms stated.""Whereupon "Bror Smart charging Bror Caffin with owneing the last aforemenconed Ques. Bror Caffin was acquitted by far the greater part of the Assembly."[25] The more orthodox General Baptists of Buckinghamshire and Northamptonshire continued to agitate for a further trial, and at the Assembly of April 15, 1698, the questions of:

> Whether the father Distinct or Seperate from the Word and the Holy Host [sic] is the Most High God . . . our Lord Jesus Christ is a God only by Deputation as Magistrates and Judges are . . . the body of our Lord Jesus Christ Consisting of flesh blood and bones is not of the same substance as ours (to Wit) Mankind[26]

were answered in the negative. The same Assembly heard a communication from Northamptonshire as well, one accusing Caffyn of holding that "the Son of God or the word was not of the Uncreated Nature & substance of the Father neither of the Created Nature & substance of his Mother." The representatives agreed, with one exception, that such teaching was erroneous, and determined that "Matthew Caffin shall be admitted to a faire Tryall in our Next Assembly And in the meantime that timely notice thereof be given unto him."[27]

The trial took place at the Assembly in May 1700. A group of messengers laid the following statement before the Assembly:

> That Christ as he was the word is from the Beginning But in Time that word tooke not on him the Nature of Angells but he took on him the Seed of Abraham & as such is Emmanuell God with us or God manifest in the flesh & he is the word is one with the ffather & the Holy Ghost & as he was God manifest in the flesh so is he Jesus that Tasted Death for Every Man And further whereas that have been & yett are Debates about the most High God wee Conceive he is one Infirmative Unchangable & Eternall Spiritt & Incomprehensable Godhead & doth Subsist in the father ye word & the Holy Ghost.[28]

---

[25]W. T. Whitley, ed., *Minutes of the General Assembly of the General Baptist Churches in England* (London: Baptist Historical Society, 1909) 40.
[26]Ibid., 53.
[27]Ibid., 53-54.
[28]Ibid., 66-67.

During the course of the meeting, it was "Agreed that the Defence Bror Matthew Caffin made in the Assembly and his Acknowledgment was in the satisfaccon of the Assembly."[29] Once again, as Gordon noted with pleasure, "the General Assembly deliberately endorsed latitudinarian opinions in the article of the Trinity and the Incarnation."[30] It passed "the very first formal resolution of tolerance for heterodox opinions on the subject of the Trinity, that was ever passed by any Nonconformist union of congregations, in other words, by any cooperating religious body in this country."[31] *The Moderate Trinitarian* (1699)—a plea for doctrinal tolerance by Daniel Allen, Caffyn's friend—was influential in securing this result. Meanwhile, in 1696, a more orthodox General Association had been constituted over against the General Assembly—not, indeed, that it was so orthodox as to risk Calvinism. On the contrary, it disciplined and dismissed Joseph Stennett of Paul's Alley church, London, for erring in that direction, whereupon he associated with Particular Baptists."[32] In 1704 the breach between Association and Assembly was temporarily healed on the basis of a book entitled *The Unity of the* Churches as well as six agreed articles. But when at the following Assembly all representatives were required either to assent to the contents of the book without question or forfeit the right to membership of the Assembly, a breach ensued and another Assembly was constituted.[33]

From the orthodox side, as Robert Torbet points out, the ministers Richard Allen, Benjamin Keach, Mark Key, and Shad Thames had deserted the General for the Particular Baptists between 1679 and 1689.[34] Churches as well as individuals were affected: the General Baptists were

---

[29] Ibid., 67.

[30] Gordon, "Matthew Caffyn and General Baptist Latitude," 532(b).

[31] Alexander Gordon, *Addresses Biographical and Historical* (London: Lindsey Press, 1922) 141. Cf. idem, *Heads of English Unitarian History* (London: Philip Green, 1895) 30. Gordon notes that the Assembly's significant stand for tolerance "is very often forgotten. It is sometimes forgotten by Baptists, as well as by those who are not Baptists" (*Addresses*, 141). Whether or not they forgot it, Whitley, Underwood, and Torbet, authors of standard Baptist histories, do not mention it.

[32] For Stennett (1633–1713) see *DNB*.

[33] See Whitley, ed., *Minutes of the General Assembly of the General Baptist Churches in England*, xx-xxiii.

[34] Robert G. Torbet, *A History of the Baptists* (Valley Forge PA: Judson Press, 1950) 64. For Keach (1640–1704) see *DNB*. See further Raymond Brown, *The English Baptists of the Eighteenth Century* (London: Baptist Historical Society, 1986) ch. 2.

excluded by the Particulars at Smarden, Kent, in 1706;[35] at Cranbrook there were three varieties of Baptist causes in 1716; while in 1728 a group of General Baptists of the Folkestone-Hythe church seceded to form a Particular church, which associated with fellow believers in Canterbury. Michael Bligh left Bessels Green General Baptist Church to form a Particular cause at Sevenoaks in the 1740s, while in 1762 Henry Booker, influenced by George Whitefield's teaching, began to preach in such a way as to displease the General Baptists of Ditchling, with the result that he was ejected and founded in 1763 a Particular Baptist church, Wivelsfield (where he was born). In the following year a former minister at Ditchling, John Simmonds, was called as pastor.[36] He soon disputed with his fellow preacher, Booker, and appeared to take an Arian line. He brought a case against booker to the church meeting in March 1767, but the church sided with Booker, and in June, "Agreed to silence John Simons from preaching in our meetings by the Consent of the Church untill Such time as Reconciled with the Church."[37] Conversely, in October 1793, nineteen members of the Particular Baptist church at Bond Street, Brighton, who had been led by one of their number, William Stevens, to embrace the views of the Universalist Elhanan Winchester, were excommunicated, constituted a General Baptist church, and eventually opened their own building in New Road in August 1820.[38]

---

[35]See Brian A. Packer, *The Unitarian Heritage in Kent* (London: London District and South Eastern Provincial Assembly of the Unitarian and Free Christian Churches [Incorporated], 1991) 10. Anon., "Baptists in the Weald," *BQ* 2 (1924–1925): 374. Those described as "semi-unitarians" of Biddenden, Fritteden, and Headcorn seceded from the Smarden church in 1677.

[36]Frank Buffard, *Kent and Sussex Baptist Associations* (privately published, 1963) 27-28; Ralph F. Chambers, *The Strict Baptist Chapels of England. II. The Chapels of Sussex* (privately printed, n.d.) 15-16.

[37]*A Transcription of the Church Book of Wivelsfield, 1763–1817*, by Leonard J. Macguire (privately published, 1984) 10-11. It would appear that R. F. Chambers, *Sussex*, 16, errs in dating this dispute 1765. The minutes make clear that the church was in close touch with Dr. John Gill throughout its several early upsets.

[38]Philip Huxtable Bliss, "A Brief History of the Six Member Churches of the Sussex Unitarian Union," presidential address to the General Baptist Assembly (1968), typescript, 11; *The Unitarian Heritage*, Sheffield (1986) 58; John Rowland, *The Story of Brighton Unitarian Church* (London: the Lindsey Press, 1972) 5. The historian of the Strict Baptist chapels simply records that Thomas Vine, called to the pastorate of Salem, Bond Street, in 1790 "proved unfaithful, and after three years the church asked him to resign, which he did, and left, taking with him some of the members and weakening the church." Chambers, *The Strict Baptist Chapels of England. II. The Chapels of Sussex*, 19.

With the passage of time the General Baptists—apart from those evangelical Arminians who joined Dan Taylor's New Connexion of 1770[39]—inclined more and more to Unitarianism, so that by the year 1846 Beard could note twenty-four Unitarian Baptist churches among the "Anti-Trinitarian Congregations and Ministers in England and Scotland," and five in Wales. The majority of these were in Kent and Sussex.[40] Such a doctrinal change played into the hands of C. H. Spurgeon who, with a flourish of splendidly ironical rhetoric, declared:

> Now, we know, at the present time, certain ancient chapels shut up, with grass growing in the front of them, and over the door of them is the *name Unitarian Baptist* Chapel. Although it has been said that he is a benefactor of his race who makes two blades of grow where only one grew before, we have no desire to empty our pews in order to grow more grass. We have in our eye certain other chapels, not yet arrived at that consummation, where the spiders are dwelling in delightful quietude, in which the pews are more numerous than the people, and although an endowment keeps the minister's mouth open, there are but few open ears for him to address.[41]

It is more than likely that Spurgeon here committed the fallacy of incomplete enumeration, for very rarely is doctrinal change alone sufficient to decimate a church; it is evev possible that it had nothing to do with the decline in the church concerned, in which case he has committed the fallacy of the false cause. Moreover, the implication that only churches in the Arminian-Arian-Unitarian line could flounder (and some of them did not, while new General Baptist chapels were opened at Cranbrook in 1807, Headcorn in 1819 and Dover in 1820[42]) needs seriously to be questioned. J. M. Cramp's mournful eulogy, "The loss *of life* followed the obscuration *of light,"* can be shown to apply equally (and just as misleadingly) to some Particular Baptist causes.[43] As a

---

[39]For Taylor (1738–1816), see *DNB*. The New Connexion severed its link with the General Baptist Assembly when in 1802 the latter body admitted a universalist church having unbaptized members in its midst. See "Baptists in the Weald," 380.

[40]J. R. Beard, ed., *Unitarianism Exhibited in Its Actual Condition* (London: Simpkin, Marshal, 1846) 330-37. For the parallel story of Presbyterianism in England, see Alan P. F. Sell, *Dissenting Thought and the Life of the Churches. Studies in an English Tradition* (Lewiston NY: Edwin Mellen Press, 1990) ch. 5.

[41]C. H. Spurgeon, *An All-Round Ministry. Addresses to Ministers and Students* (1900) (London: The Banner of Truth Trust, 1960) 94-95. For Spurgeon (1834–1892), see *DNB*.

[42]See Brian A. Packer, *the Unitarian Heritage in Kent*, 15.

[43]J. M. Cramp, *Baptist History: From the Foundation of the Christian Church to the Present Time* (London: Elliot Stock, 1871) 434.

Baptist writer has said, "if the General Baptist churches were often liable to heresy, the Particular Baptists were liable to immorality, and again and again ministers gave scandal."[44] Thus the church which Daniel Gillard began at Hammersmith "had to dissolve, owing to his conduct."[45] Underwood, among others, have named the doctrinal cause "antinomianism,"[46] and for practical antinomianism David Crosley reigned supreme in Baptist demonology (though he did manage—or, rather, was enabled—to end his days as "a trophy of grace").[47]

Less morally scandalous heresy also beset Particular Baptists. A fairly mild, yet significant form of this is seen in the Somerset Confession of 1656, whose principal architect, Thomas Collier, was the lay apostle to the West country.[48] Under challenge from the Quakers, the Baptists wished to demonstrate that their doctrine was Calvinistic and not out of accord with that of the framers of the London Confession of 1644, as well as to dissuade those who forsook sound doctrine "under glorious notions of spiritualness and holiness."[49] Noting that "The Calvinism of the Western Association was not of a rigid type," Lumpkin suggested that a further objective may have been to enable Particular and General Baptists of the region to stand together, the first Baptist confession to attempt this.[50] Alexander Gordon declared:

> [I]t is remarkable that this confession, while strongly affirming the Calvinistic doctrine of election , is absolutely silent on the Trinity, the eternal sonship, the co-equality of the Father and Son, and the satisfaction of divine justice by the death of Christ.[51]

These points must be conceded, though Gordon does not wish to build an argument on silence. He further records that at first he was

---

[44]Anon., "Baptists in East Kent," 186. One could wish, however, for more evidence to justify the "again and again." Cf. my comment against W. T. Whitley in *The Great Debate. Calvinism, Arminianism, and Salvation*, Studies in Christian Thought and History (Worthing: H. E. Walter, 1982; Grand Rapids MI: Baker Book House, 1983) 46.
[45]Ibid., 187.
[46]A. C. Underwood, *A History of the English Baptists* (London: Baptist Union, 1947) 128.
[47]See further Frederick Overend, *History of the Ebenezer Baptist Church Bacup* (London: Kingsgate Press, 1912) pt. 2, ch. 1; cf. W. T. Whitley, *Baptists of North-West England* (London: Kingsgate Press, 1913) 83.
[48]For Collier (fl. 1691) see *DNB*.
[49]Epistle dedicatory.
[50]Lumpkin, *Baptists Confessions of Faith*, 201-202.
[51]A. Gordon, "Unitarian Baptists," *The Christian Life* (28 January 1988): 45(a).

disinclined not to take the omissions as implying denials on the ground that the Confession does affirm in article XIII, "We believe that Jesus Christ is truly God. . . . " But Gordon, following William Grigge, came to the conclusion that these words refer to Christ's office, not to his essence, and hence,"The confession is one which, so far as its Christology goes, an Arian might subscribe. . . . We must now add to the tale of Baptist heretics not alone Collier himself, but the sixteen churches whose representatives pledged themselves to his confession."[52] I see no necessity to follow Gordon's reading of article XIII, but am convinced that there are doctrinal silences at the places specified which could only hinder the objective of demonstrating agreement with the London Confession, and might indicate either inner-Baptist ecumenical concern or doctrinal hesitancy at crucial points, or both.

Particular Baptist associations, no less than those of the General Baptists, reveal a propensity for division on doctrinal grounds. The Norfolk and Suffolk Association of Baptist Churches, founded in 1771, entrusted to George Wright of Beccles the task of writing its 1829 "Circular Letter." Wright's Letter was discussed at the Annual Meeting of the Association at Stradbroke in June of the same year, and a controversy erupted. Wright feared that Arminian teaching was infiltrating the churches, and that this led to "the concealing of the discriminating doctrines of the Gospel in the public ministry." While Wright did not point a finger in any specific direction, it became clear that he and his followers could no longer live within the original Association. Accordingly, at Grundisburgh in September 1829, the New Suffolk, and Norfolk Association (now the Suffolk and Norfolk Association of Strict Baptist Churches) was constituted in order "to preserve in an Association of Baptist Churches in this County, the doctrine of the Cross, uncorrupted by a system which can rest on no basis but that of General Redemption and Universal Salvation."[53] By contrast the New Association staunchly denied, "that saving faith is the duty of all men."[54]

---

[52]Ibid.
[53]See Wolstenholme, *These Hundred and Fifty Years. A Commemorative Momento [sic] of the Suffolk and Norfolk Association of Strict Baptist Churches, 1830–1980* (1980) 3; John Doggett, "Having obtained help of God . . . , " *Grace Magazine* no. 140 (January 1983): 1.
[54]W. Reynolds et al., *Circular Letter to the Baptist Churches of Suffolk and Norfolk* (Grundisburgh, 1829) 2.

But with the reference to universal salvation and duty of faith, we come to one of two further inner-Baptist doctrinal disputes—one coming down from the eighteenth century, the other from the nineteenth. The first concerned the obligation to, and the manner of, preaching the Gospel, and the question of whether all hearers of the Word have a duty to receive Christ. The second concerned the doctrine of the eternal generation of the Son. In both cases, it is the Calvinistic Baptists who were involved.

Evidence has already been adduced to show that both Particular and General Baptist churches could suffer decline. Such statistics as are available suggest that, whereas there were some 220 Particular causes in England in 1715, by 1750 the number had dwindled to about 150. As with General Baptists and other Old dissenters, the causes of this decline were various: local factions and party spirit, demographic changes, torpor after the heady pre-Toleration days of struggle for Baptist identity among them. Nor can we rule out the possibility that scholastic Calvinism purveyed in sufficiently deadening ways may stifle zeal. We must not, however, commit Spurgeon's fallacies in reverse. That there was decline—and that many Particular Baptist pastors lamented "the decay of practical and vital godliness"[55]—cannot be denied. Happily, by 1798 Particular Baptist churches numbered 361, and of these, 320 had pastors.[56] Why the reversal of the downward trend? In a word, evangelization. Though we should dishonor the memory of Alvery Jackson, Benjamin Beddome, and others who in the earlier years of the eighteenth century were no strangers to revival in their pastorates if we were to a paint too gloomy of those decades, it cannot be denied that when Baptists—like others—caught the missionary spirit, their strength at home increased and their theology underwent a subtle change. That some resisted the change is clear from the disputes of the time.

---

[55] Benjamin Wallin, *The Christian Life. In Divers of Its Branches, Described and Recommended* (London, 1746) 2:ix. Perhaps, therefore, Kenneth Dix exaggerates the contrast between the Particular Baptists and others: "For the PBs the eighteenth century was not at any point a period of disaster, as it was for both the General Baptists and the English Presbyterians." See his "Particular Baptists and Strict Baptists. A Historical Survey," *The Strict Baptist Historical Society Annual Report and Bulletin* 13 (1976): 4-5.

[56] See K. Dix, "Particular Baptists and Strict Baptists," 5, citing John Rippon, *The Baptist Annual Register* (1798): 1-40. See further on the declension and the statistics, Michael A. G. Haykin, " 'A Habitation of God, though the Spirit,' John Sutcliff (1752–1814) and the Revitalization of Calvinistic Baptists in the Late Eighteenth Century," *BQ* 34/7 (July 1992): 304-19; idem, "The Baptist Identity: A View from the Eighteenth Century," *Evangelical Quarterly* 67 (1995): 137-52.

To a considerable extent the disputes revolved around the question of the free offer of the Gospel, and the question of to what extent sinners had a duty to respond positively to it. A focal point of the Baptist debate in the mid-eighteenth century was the teaching of John Brine and John Gill, both of whom had been influenced by John Skepp's book of 1722 (behind which stood the Independent Joseph Hussey's *God's Operations of Grace but No Offers of Grace* [1707], which Gill republished in 1751):[57] *The divine energy: or the efficacious operations of the Spirit of God in the soul of man, in his effectual calling and conversion: stated, proved and vindicated. Wherein the real weakness and insufficiency of moral persuasion, without the super-addition of the exceeding greatness of God's power for faith and conversion to God, are fully evinced. Being an antidote against the Pelagian plague.*

In the meantime, Matthias Maurice of Rothwell had published *The Modern Question* (1737), in which he proclaimed the duty of those who heard the Word preached to close with Christ. Gill and Brine stoutly denounced this teaching, fearing the encroachment of Arminian universalism. Gill was widely understood not "to address unconverted sinners, nor to enforce the invitations of the gospel,"[58] and Spurgeon, while noting that some of Gill's utterances on practical godliness had prompted an hyper-Calvinist to charge him (of all people!) with Arminianism, nevertheless declared that this theology, together with that of Brine, "chilled many churches to their very soul, for it has led them to omit the

---

[57]Skepp had preceded Brine at Curriers' Hall. See further on this entire subject, Alan P. F. Sell, *The Great Debate*, ch. 3. For Gill (1697–1771) and Brine (1703–1765) see *DNB*. For Hussey (1659–1726) see Geoffrey F. Nuttall, "Northamptonshire and the Modern Question: a Turning Point in Eighteenth-Century Dissent," *Journal of Theological Studies*, n.s. 7 (1965): 101-23; idem, "Cambridge Nonconformity 1660–1710: from Holcroft to Hussey," *The Journal of the United Reformed Church History Society* 1/9 (1977): 241-58; Sell, *The Great Debate*, 52-54.

[58]Walter Wilson, *The History and Antiquities of Dissenting Churches and Meeting Houses in London, &c.* (London, 1808) 4:222. Cf. Cramp, *Baptist History*, 443: Gill "abstained from personal addresses to sinners, by inviting them to the Saviour, and satisfied himself with declaring their guilt and doom, and the necessity of a change of heart. It is not surprising that the congregation declined under such a ministry." Gill, however, did rather more than Cramp suggests but, no doubt, not as much as he would have liked. For Maurice (1684–1738) see *The Dictionary of Welsh Biography* (London: Honourable Society of Cymmrodorion, 1959); Thomas Rees, *History of Protestant Nonconformity in Wales* (London: Snow, 1883) 302-305; G. F. Nuttall, "Northamptonshire and the Modern Question"; Sell, *The Great Debate*, 59, 78-79.

free invitations of the gospel, and to deny that it is the duty of sinners to believe in Jesus."[59]

Some recent Baptist scholars have sought to temper this doleful estimate of Gill. Southern Baptist Thomas J. Nettles has gone so far as to claim that Gill believed that all people were under obligation to repent of sin, and that all hearers of the gospel had a duty to believe it.[60] But this would seem to allow the pendulum to swing too far in the opposite direction, for while Gill could insist that, "The gospel of salvation ... declares ... that whoever believes in [Christ] shall be saved: this is the gospel every faithful minister preaches, and every sensible sinner desires to hear,"[61] on other occasions, especially when in polemical, anti-Arminian, mood—against Whitby, for example—Gill wrote in terms which are too definite to admit of misinterpretation: "I know of none [i.e. texts of Scripture], that exhort and command all men ... to repent, and believe in Christ for salvation." Again, he denied that,"God calls all those to faith and repentance, and conversion, who have a knowledge of the divine will, a sense of sin, a dread of punishment, and some hopes of pardon: for the devils have all these but the last, whom he never calls to faith and repentance."[62] Positively, he contended for prevenient, enabling grace: "Men are required to believe in Christ, to love the Lord with all their heart ... to keep the whole law of God; but it does not follow that they are able of themselves to do all these things."[63]

Whatever the final judgment on Gill and his fellow High Calvinists (and we should not assume either that they saw exactly eye-to-eye on all points of doctrine,[64] or that their views necessarily precluded cooperation

---

[59]Susannah Spurgeon and J. W. Harrald, eds., *C. H. Spurgeon's Autobiography* (London: Passmore and Alabaster, 1899–1900) 1:310.

[60]Thomas J. Nettles, *By His Grace and for His Glory. A Historical, Theological, and Practical Study of the Doctrines of Grace in Baptist Life* (Grand Rapids MI: Baker Book House, 1986) 107. Timothy George is somewhat more cautious. See his paper on Gill in Timothy George and David S. Dockery, eds., *Baptist Theologians* (Nashville TN: Broadman Press, 1990) 93.

[61]John Gill, *A Complete Body of Doctrinal and Practical Divinity* (1839) (Grand Rapids MI: Baker Book House, 1978) 2:668.

[62]John Gill, *The Cause of God and Truth* (repr.: Grand Rapids MI: Sovereign Grace Publishers, 1971) 167(a), 179(a).

[63]Ibid., 35(a). For a recent study of Gill's preaching, see Peter Naylor, *Picking up a Pin for the Lord. English Particular Baptists from 1688 to the Early Nineteenth Century* (London: Grace Publications, 1992) ch. 11. For Daniel Whitby (1638–1726), see *DNB*.

[64]Indeed, John Johnson's hyper-Calvinism was too much even for Brine. Johnson, raised a General Baptist, became minister at Byrom Street Particular Baptist chapel,

with ministers on the opposite side of the argument[65]), there can be no doubt that many felt that the gospel was being proclaimed in a stultifying manner. This was unquestionably Andrew Fuller's view, and he expected a far from easy ride in challenging the practice of his elders. As he confided to his diary in October 1784, "I feel some pain at the thought of being about to publish on the obligations of men to believe in Christ, fearing I shall hereby expose myself to a good deal of abuse, which is disagreeable to the flesh."[66] But publish he eventually did, and in the *Gospel Worthy of All Acceptation* (ca. 1785), he countered the opinions of Gill and Brine on duty faith,[67] and boldly proved,"that faith in Christ is the duty of all men who hear, or have opportunity to hear, the gospel."[68] He thereby gave impetus both to the modern missionary movement, and also that gradual softening of the sharper edges of scholastic Calvinism which was eventually to facilitate the union of the majority of the Particular Baptists with the evangelical Arminians of the New Connexion to form the Baptist Union.[69]

That the Strict and Particular Baptists who could not take this road were not immune to internal doctrinal differences is clear from the continuing strife engendered by the "duty faith" question.[70] The line derived from Gill, Brine, and others, reinforced by the powerful views of such an

---

Liverpool, in 1741, seceding with his followers in 1747 to form a new denomination, the Johnsonian Baptists, which were represented in northwest England in East Anglia. For Johnson (1706–1791) see *DNB*; Raymond Brown, *The English Baptists of the Eighteenth Century*, 86.

[65]E.g., as Kenneth Dix properly reminds us, Joseph Stennett sat with both Brine and Gill on the Baptist board. See "Particular Baptists and Strict Baptists," 3. On the other hand, John Stevens, author of the anti-Fuller work, *Help for the True Disciples of Immanuel* (1803), made his witness in noncooperative isolation. See anon., *Memoirs of Mr. John Stevens* (London, 1848) 31; Robert Oliver, "John Stevens. A Forgotten Leader," *Grace Magazine* no. 149 (November 1983): 2-7.

[66]John Ryland, *The Work of Faith, the Labour of Love and the Patience or Hope Illustrated in the Life and Death of Andrew Fuller* (London, 1816) 206. For Fuller (1754–1815) see *DNB*; Sell, *The Great Debate*, 83-87, 93-94, 130-33.

[67]See *The Complete Works of the Rev. Andrew Fuller* (London: Holdsworth and Ball, 1831) 2:26, 50-59, 67.

[68]Ibid., 22ff.

[69]See Ernest A. Payne, *The Baptist Union. A Short History* (London: Carey Kingsgate Press) 1958.

[70]See Robert Oliver, "The significance of Strict Baptist attitudes towards duty faith in the nineteenth century," *Strict Baptist Historical Society Bulletin* 20 (1993); Sell, *The Great Debate*, 93-94, 129-30, 133.

Independent as William Huntington,[71] was, as we have seen, evidenced in the declaration of the New Association of Norfolk and Suffolk of 1829, and reached its terminus (I say neither "nemesis" nor "fruition") among the Gospel Standard Baptists, whose leaders were William Gadsby; John Warburton; John Kershaw; the erstwhile Anglican, J. C. Philpot; and James Wells of the Surrey Tabernacle.[72] The comment on Gadsby is applicable to them all: "Mr. G. always considered, and often stated publicly, that Andrew Fuller was the greatest enemy the church of God every had, as his sentiments were so much cloaked with the sheep's clothing."[73] Not surprisingly, article XXVI of the Gospel Standard Baptists stated, "We deny duty faith and duty repentance—these terms signifying that it is very man's duty to spiritually and savingly repent and believe. . . . [W]e reject the doctrine that men in a state of nature should be exhorted to believe in or turn to God." In 1878, after lively discussion, four new articles (XXXII–XXXV) were added, the burden of which was:

> That for ministers in the present day to address unconverted persons, or indiscriminately all in a mixed congregation, calling upon them savingly to repent, believe, and receive Christ, or perform any other acts dependent upon the new creative power of the Holy Ghost, is on the one hand, to imply creature power, and, on the other, to deny the doctrine of special redemption. (article XXXIII)

A fresh lease of life was given to the controversy when, in 1921, William Wileman (1848–1944), who had been associated with the *Gospel Standard* committee and magazine at the time the added articles were devised, published a critique of the articles and of the motives of those who framed them. J. K. Popham, editor of the *Gospel Standard,* reprinted his

---

[71]For Huntington (1745–1813), see *DNB*; W. Huntington, *The Kingdom of Heaven Taken by Prayer* (1784) (Redhill: Sovereign Grace Union, 1966); T. Wright, *The Life of William Huntington, S.S.* (London: Farncombe, 1909).

[72]For Gadsby (1773–1813) see *DNB*; Sell, *The Great Debate*, passim. For Warburton (1776–1857) see *Mercies of a Covenant God. Being an Account of Some of the Lord's Dealings in Providence and Grace with John Warburton, Minister of the Gospel, Trowbridge* (1837) (Schwengel PA: Reiner Publications, 1971). For Kershaw (1792–1870) see *John Kershaw. The Autobiography of an Eminent Lancashire Preacher* (1870) (Sheffield: Gospel Tidings Publications, 1968). For Philpot (1802–1869) see J. H. Philpot, *The Seceders*, 2 vols. (1930–1932); for Wells (1803–1870), see *A Concise Account of the Experience of James Wells* (London: C. J. Farncombe, 1840).

[73]*A Memoir of the late Mr. William Gadsby*, in Gadsby's Works I (1870) 33n.

earlier defense of the articles, and pieces on either side of the argument still appear from time to time.[74]

Turning with some relief from the Baptists' anxieties over duty of faith and the free offer of the Gospel, we come to our second example of an inner-Calvinistic-Baptist doctrinal dispute: that concerning the eternal generation of the Son; and we may be brief. From time to time during the eighteenth century, the doctrine surfaced that Christ's sonship is a function of his human nature, not his divine; hence, the second person of the Trinity is not eternally Son (though, oddly, the first person is eternally Father). In the early years of the nineteenth century the Calvinistic Baptist pastor John Stevens embraced this teaching, to the consternation of other pastors. He further taught that Christ's human soul existed prior to the incarnation, and that any reference to a preexistent Son must refer to Christ's humanity as yet to be enfleshed.

These and opposing views began to spread, but it was J. C. Philpot who brought the debate out into the open with an article in the *Gospel Standard for 1844*. In the previous year Charles Waters Banks had founded *The Earthen Vessel* and while he himself upheld the doctrine of the eternal generation of the Son, he permitted alternative views to be published in his journal, and his successor editors either did not accept the doctrine or did not declare themselves upon it. In a subsequent article, Philpot set out to refute the view that the doctrine was (in words drawn from *The Earthen Vessel* of November 1860) "a piece of twaddle," "a metaphysical conceit," etc., etc.—"as if the true and proper Sonship of Jesus, as the only begotten of the Father, were a lying tale."[75] The

---

[74]See further, S. F. Paul, *Historical Sketch of the Gospel Standard Baptists* (London: Gospel Standard Publications, 1945); B. A. Ramsbottom, *The History of The Gospel Standard Magazine, 1835–1985* (Carshalton, Surrey: Gospel Standard Societies, 1985) 60-61; J. K. Popham, "Preaching the Gospel," *The Gospel Standard* (December 1906); idem, "An Address to the Unconverted and Such as Have No Distinct Knowledge of God or of Themselves," *The Gospel Standard* (January 1908); idem, "An opening word," *The Gospel Standard* (January 1926), wherein he defends the view that the Gospel Standard Baptists "are a definite, distinct, and separate body, or denomination," 9; William Wileman, "The Secret History of the Four 'Added' Articles: 32, 33, 34, 35," *The Christian's Pathway* 26 (November 1921): 206-10; B. J. Honeysett, "The Ill-fated Articles," *Reformation Today* no. 2 (Summer 1960): 23-30, repr. as *How to Address Unbelievers* (n.d.). For James Kidwell Popham (1847–1937), see B. A. Ramsbottom, *The History of The Gospel Standard Magazine, 1835–1985*, 191-204.

[75]Repr. in J. C. Philpot, *The True, Proper, and Eternal Sonship of the Lord Jesus Christ, the Only-Begotten Son of God* (Harpenden: Gospel Standard Baptist Trust, 1962; [1]1861) 84.

longevity and disruptiveness of the dispute is shown in the fact that in 1926 J. K. Popham could say regarding Philpot's case, "From that day to this the breach has remained open, and the two parties have been known as the "*Gospel Standard*" Churches and the "*Earthen Vessel*" Churches, respectively, and as holding the exact opposite views on that fundamental doctrine."[76]

So concerned were the *Gospel Standard* leaders to preserve the purity of proclamation of their denomination that in 1926 they determined that only those preachers who upheld the agreed doctrinal petitions and submitted a satisfactory account of their call to preach should have the pulpits of *Gospel Standard* churches opened to them. This policy drew fire from a number of quarters, not least from some pastors and preachers sympathetic to *Gospel Standard* views. Alfred Dye, for example, strongly objected to a list of approved preachers:

> To me a Committee in London or elsewhere proposing Rules and deciding cases belonging to any Church or minister is too near a relation to *a Jewish* Sanhedrim [sic].And indeed there must be something radically wrong when *more* than *three* parts out of the four of Churches and ministers in the G. S. Connection are not seen upon the List of Supplies; and the fact is, so many stringent Rules betray *weakness* and not *strength*.[77]

The illustrations provided of inner-Baptist doctrinal debate, though necessarily selective, invite a few reflections. First, it has become clear that within the English Baptist tradition(s) a variety of positions have been adopted on fundamental Christian doctrines. If the old General Baptists emerged from the Caffyn case as those most tolerant of views they would not formally endorse, the *Gospel Standard* Baptists exemplified the most rigorist posture *vis-à-vis* doctrines and interpretations deemed by them essential. To recall Forsyth's poles from which I set out, if the Arminians were keenest not to flatten faith, the *Gospel Standard* leaders were most anxious not to forsake the faith for "another gospel."

Secondly, we have seen that in Baptist circles, the "faith once delivered" has, as far as its doctrinal expression is concerned, undergone changes in a number of directions. Not only did many General Baptists become Unitarians, and many Particulars become hyper-Calvinists (if

---

[76]Philpot, "An Opening Wrd," 13. See further on this doctrinal (and journalistic) maze, Paul, *Historical Sketch of the Gospel Standard Baptists*, ch. 5.

[77]A. Dye, letter to the editor, *The Christian's Pathway* 31 (1926): 42. See further Alan P. F. Sell, *Alfred Dye, Minister of the Gospel* (London: Fauconberg Press, 1974) ch. 5.

those proclaiming at least doctrinal antinomianism, or denying "duty faith," may thus be designated), but the converging center parties, which came together in the Baptist Union, could do so only on the basis of a measure of Calvinist-Arminian accommodation. The extent of this is clearly seen if we juxtapose examples of regional and national affirmations. In 1779 the Kent and Sussex Association of Particular Baptist Churches declared:

> We, the ministers and messengers of the Baptist denomination representing our respective churches, holding the Doctrines of personal election, particular redemption, effectual vocation and the final perseverance of the Saints, being met together at Ashford in Kent this second day of March 1779 have entered the several churches we represent into an Association.

In 1904, following the union nationally of the Particular with the New Connexion Baptists, the Kent and Sussex Association revised its terms of membership in doctrinally significant ways, providing:

> That this Kent and Sussex Association consist only of Evangelical Churches practising believer's baptism, and whose doctrinal basis includes the Divine authority of the Holy Scripture, the Doctrine of the Trinity, the Divine abhorrence and punishment of sin, the deity and the atoning sacrificial death of Christ, regeneration by the Holy Ghost, justification by faith and the obligation to live a righteous and godly life.[78]

As for the national General Union itself, although its founding doctrinal basis of 1813 had been Calvinistic in tone, its revised constitution of 1832 specified its first objective thus: "To extend brotherly love and union among the Baptist ministers and churches who agree in the sentiments usually denominated evangelical." This facilitated the entry of the New Connexion churches into the Union. As Ernest Payne remarked, "Fullerism" had provided a bridge between the Particular Baptist churches and those of the New Connexion of the General Baptists."[79]

I cannot find, however, that English Baptists have engaged in corporate reflection upon what might be called a doctrine of doctrinal development, which would do more than simply assert the fact of doctrinal modification (even if only of expression rather than of substance—a big "if"), but seek to explain it and consider what possible criteria there

---

[78]See Frank Buffard, *Kent and Sussex Baptist Associations*, 50: 123-24; E. Bruce Hardy, "Association life in Kent and Sussex, 1770–1950," *BQ* 27/4:173, 181.
[79]Payne, *The Baptist Union*, 61.

might be for justifying it. In this Baptists are by no means alone, and I shall revert to this point in the conclusion of this paper. Similarly, the status of confessions of faith might be thought to require theological consideration. For example, there is on the face of it a great gulf separating the position of the *Gospel Standard* Baptists from Henry Cook, who declared, "Membership in the Church of Christ is not restricted to those who worship in a specified way or accept a detailed theological creed; it is available for all who look to Christ as their Saviour and, like Peter, make to Him the great Confession."[80] The operative word, of course, is "detailed," and Cook seemed to have the New Testament on his side with his implication that church members comprise those who are babes on milk and older hands on strong doctrinal meat.

But what of those who speak officially in the name of the Gospel? This was a particular concern of the *Gospel Standard* Baptists, and it is a question which many mainline denominations answer in a vague way, if at all. To pose the question in another way, did Ernest Payne sufficiently guard his flank when, with reference to the growth of Fullerism between 1780 and 1830, he asserted that apart from the Strict Baptist churches,

> The main stream of Baptist life was . . . to be found in those fellowships which had learned the dangers of heresy hunting and had come to believe in a more liberal and tolerant attitude, fellowships which had recognized that a profession of orthodoxy in belief is no guarantee of the fruits of the Spirit?[81]

Of course, to profess orthodoxy is not necessarily to display the fruit of the Spirit. No doubt heresy hunting is a messy pursuit, and tolerance within the Church is essential, but Payne raised the question, which he did not there address, of the permissible degrees of tolerance within the church. He appeared to be sailing close to Forsyth's liberal pole, and perhaps needs to be balanced by the protest of Joseph Angus: "We must have beliefs or we are not Christians. We must have beliefs—great principles of truth and life—or we cannot have Christian churches."[82] Or, as Forsyth himself put it, "[A] Christianity which would exclude none has no power to include the world."[83]

---

[80] H. Cook, *What Baptists Stand For* (London: Carey Kingsgate Press, 1947; 1964) 60.
[81] Payne, *The Fellowship of Believers*, 104.
[82] J. A., (?) *Freeman* (13 April 1888).
[83] P. T. Forsyth, *The Work of Christ* (London: Independent Press, 1938) 62.

Thirdly, it is interesting to note a matter over which Baptists *en bloc* have *not* seceded from one another, namely, the authority of Scripture. It may be that those who might have seceded on this issue were already in one of the more conservative groupings of Baptists. However that may be, we do not have in England the situation which prevails in Canada, for example, where the *raison d'être* of the Fellowship Baptist denomination over against the Baptist Convention of Ontario and Quebec is the former's requirement of belief in biblical inerrancy.[84] Conversely, there is some evidence to show that if a secession did not occur among the most numerous body of Baptists, conservative attitudes to Scripture, which came to the fore within the Baptist Union during the Downgrade Controversy of the 1870s, coupled with the strength of Unitarian views among the old General Baptists of Kent and Sussex, thwarted the attempts of Henry Solly and his New Connexion colleagues John Clifford and Dawson Burns to bring the old General Baptists into the Baptist Union.[85]

Finally, we have seen that Baptists of all persuasions have historically been more than willing to state the belief commonly held among them in confessional form, and they have at times required subscription to their confessions. They have not, however, spoken in terms of the utility of confessions as "guardians" of the faith. In this connection Robert Hall's outburst against an Anglican author enshrined the Baptists' typical position:

> It is with peculiar effrontery that this author insists on subscription to articles as a sufficient security for the purity of religious instruction, when it is the professed object of his work to recall his contemporaries to that purity. . . . A long course of experience has clearly demonstrated the inefficacy of creeds and confessions to perpetuate religious belief. Of this the only faithful depository is, not that which is "written with ink," but on the "fleshly tables of the heart.[86]

We have further seen that Baptists have been willing to dissent from those deemed to be in error, and on occasion have disciplined them. It

---

[84] See James A. Beverley, "Tensions in Canadian Baptist Theology, 1975–1987," in Jarold K. Zeman, ed., *Costly Vision. The Baptist Pilgrimage in Canada* (Burlington ON: Welch Publishing Co., 1988) 223-24.

[85] See Ian Sellers, "The Rev. Henry Solly and the General Baptists," *Transactions of the Unitarian Historical Society* 19/3 (April 1989): 195-96.

[86] Olinthus Gregory, ed., *The Works of Robert Hall, A.M.* (London: Henry G. Bohn, 1850) 4:62. Hall here reviews *Zeal without Innovation* (1808). For Hall (1764–1831), see *DNB*.

must, however, be said that Baptists do not seem to have propounded a clear theology of the practice of doctrinal discipline as it concerns the relations between assemblies or associations, local churches and individuals. Time and again the practical result of doctrinal difference has been secession—as if to say that when the doctrinal crunch comes, the will of the disaffected concerning doctrine takes precedence over the obligation of maintaining wider fellowship. But this brings us to polity.

II

It would be a serious mistake to suppose that among Baptists (or among heirs of Old Dissent generally) polity is to doctrine as rules are to constitution. On the contrary, the polity is doctrinal; it is ecclesiology. In particular, it is a churchly working out of such interrelated themes as the covenanted saints of God, the regenerating power of the Spirit, and the Lordship of Christ. General, no less than Particular Baptists have classically been in accord on this matter. Thus to John Smyth, Jesus Christ was,"the only King, Priest, & Prophet of his Church,"[87] and Smyth's repeated citing of Matthew 18:20, "For where two or three are gathered together in my name, there am I in the midst of them," clearly indicated his understanding of the saints as visibly gathered by and under Christ. This lofty theme has been transposed into a lower key by the time we reach Joseph Angus in the nineteenth century. Admittedly, he was replying to Thomas Chalmers's defense of church establishments, but at the head of a chapter,"Of the principles and prospects of the voluntary system," he invoked Locke on the church as,"a voluntary society of men, joining themselves together of their own accord, in order to the public worshipping of God, in such a manner as they judge acceptable to him and effectual to the salvation of their souls," and argued that voluntaryism is consistent with Scripture, and "sufficient under the blessing of the Divine Spirit, to secure the maintenance and ultimate diffusion of truth."[88] However, in a subsequent work Angus denied that Christian voluntaryism is "the authority of self will," and argued for the theocratic nature of the

---

[87] W. T. Whitley, ed., *The Works of John Smyth* (Cambridge: Cambridge University Press, 1915) 2:471.

[88] J. Angus, *The Voluntary System* (London: Jackson and Walford, 1839) 178-79. It should not be overlooked—though it often is—that Locke was not unaware of the divine initiative in calling out the church. See Alan P. F. Sell, *John Locke and the Eighteenth-Century Divines* (Cardiff: University of Wales Press, 1997) ch. 5. For Angus (1816–1902), see *DNB*.

Church, whose members are "the sons and daughters of the Lord Almighty."[89]

In the mid-twentieth century we find Arthur Dakin asserting the Lordship of Christ in no uncertain terms:"The true head of the church is the Lord Jesus Himself, who through the Holy Spirit makes His will known as the members seek it."[90] Henry Cook concurred: "The Church . . . is 'the holy society of believers in our Lord Jesus Christ which He founded.' But its relation to Him is more than historical; it is experimental, and He still is what He always was, the Church's Founder, Guide, and Controller."[91] Never one to pull his punches, Cook proclaimed that,"Baptists are High Churchmen in the best and truest sense of that much-abused term."[92] Against this background, let us briefly investigate the place of church meeting and associations in Baptist life and experience.

Consistently with the intention of honoring,"the crown's rights of the Redeemer" in his Church, both Strict Baptists and those in fellowship with the Baptist Union of Great Britain have, in recent years, made clear statements concerning the nature of church meeting. For the former, "When the church meets to make decisions, the object is not primarily to discover the majority opinion, but rather to discover the mind of Christ."[93] The Baptist Union adopts trinitarian phraseology:"The church meeting is the children of the Father; meeting together in the presence of the Spirit; and seeking together the mind of Christ."[94] Many older writers concur. Dakin, for example, asserted that "the [church] meeting is emphatically a meeting under God,"[95] but at the same time he declared that, "it is clear that the government of a Baptist church is on democratic lines."He went on to point out that, "the democratic government in a Baptist church is very different from all forms of democracy which visualize nothing beyond purely human judgment and debate, not to say

---

[89]Idem, *Christian Churches* (London: Ward, 1862) 19.
[90]A. Dakin, *The Baptist View of the Church and Ministry* (London: Baptist Union 1944) 21.
[91]Cook, *What Baptists Stand For*, 34.
[92]Ibid., 32.
[93]*We Believe. A Guide for Church Fellowship* (Devizes, Wilts: National Assembly of Strict Baptist Churches, 1974) 40.
[94]John Weaver, *Baptist Basics. The Church Meeting* (Didcot, Berks.: Baptist Union, n.d.) col. ii.
[95]A. Dakin, *The Baptist View of the Church and Ministry*, 23.

contention."⁹⁶ For this reason a number of writers warn of the danger which lurks in the term "democratic"—as if the objective were simply,"one person, one vote—and government by the majority."Thus, in a statement of 1948, the Baptist Union Council affirmed that

> The church meeting, though outwardly a democratic way of ordering the affairs of the church, has deeper significance. It is the occasion when, as individuals and as a community, we submit ourselves to the guidance of the Holy Spirit and stand under the judgments of God that we may know what is the mind of Christ.⁹⁷

This seems strikingly different in tone—and far less anthropocentric—than H. Wheeler Robinson's exposition of 1927, which was reissued two years before the Council's document was published: In church meeting "all the members of the Church are at liberty to speak on matters affecting its common welfare, but the control of the meeting is naturally in the hands of the 'deacons' and the minister who presides."⁹⁸ From the other side of the Atlantic, Robert G. Torbet waxed lyrical about Baptist democracy: "The democratic principle is at the heart of Baptist polity and largely explained the tremendous popularity and appeal of the denomination in the development of the religious life of the United States."⁹⁹ Well might the saints tremble, as many of them are doing. The cautionary word uttered by John W. Grant to Congregationalists applies: "Congregationalists have been under constant pressure to apply to their Church life the secular forms of their own ideas. The original desire to spiritualize the nation has tended to secularize the Church."¹⁰⁰ Small wonder that A. Gilmore bluntly declared, "The Church is not, and must never be regarded as, a democracy, for the power is not in the hands of the *demos* but of the *christos*: it is a Christocracy."¹⁰¹

---

⁹⁶Ibid., 25.

⁹⁷*The Baptist Doctrine of the Church* (London: Carey Kingsgate Press, 1948) 3.

⁹⁸H. Wheeler Robinson, *The Life and Faith of the Baptists* (London: Carey Kingsgate Press, 1946; ¹1927) 88.

⁹⁹Torbet, *A History of the Baptists*, 487. There is a lament concerning the more baneful influence of the corporate model on church life, as well as a defense of church meeting, in Alan P. F. Sell, *Commemorations. Studies in Christian Thought and History* (Cardiff: University of Wales Press and Calgary AB: University of Calgary Press, 1993) ch. 14. There is even, at note 4, a mild rebuke on a different matter addressed to the recipient of this festschrift. How grace prevails!

¹⁰⁰John W. Grant, *Free Churchmanship in England, 1870–1940* (London: Independent Press, n.d.) 87.

¹⁰¹A. Gilmore in *The Pattern of the Church. A Baptist View* (London: Lutterworth

Who are they who thus gather? The classical confessions have been interestingly ambiguous on the matter. According to the London Confession of 1644, the

> Church, as it is visible to us, is a company of visible Saints, called & separated from the world, by the word and Spirit of God, to the visible profession of the faith of the Gospel, being baptized into that faith, and joyned to the Lord, and each other, by mutuall agreement, in the practical enjoynment of the Ordinances, commanded by Christ their head and King.[102]

The Particular Baptist Somerset Confession of 1656 agreed that, "it is the duty of every man and woman, that have repented from dead works, and have faith towards God, to be baptized." By so doing, they are "planted in the visible church or body of Christ . . . who are a company of men and women separated out to the world by the preaching of the gospel."[103] In its rambling and more polemical way, the General Baptist Standard Confession of 1660 concurred:

> XI. That the right and only way, of gathering Churches . . . is first to teach, or preach the Gospel . . . then to *Baptise* (that is in English to *Dip*) in the name of the Father, Son and Holy Spirit, or in the name of the Lord Jesus Christ;[104] such only of them as profess *repentance towards God, and faith towards our Lord Jesus Christ.* . . . And as for all such who preach not this Doctrine, but instead thereof, that Scriptureless thing of Sprinkling of Infants (*falsely called Baptisme*) whereby the pure word of God is made of no effect, and the New Testament way of bringing in Members, into the church by regeneration, cast out . . . all such we utterly deny. . . .
> XII. That it is the duty of all such who are believers Baptized, to draw nigh unto God in submission to that principle of Christs Doctrine, to wit, Prayer and Laying on of Hands. . . .
> XIII. That it is the duty of such who are constituted as aforesaid, to *continue stedfastly in Christs and the Apostles Doctrine, and assembling together, in fellowship, in breaking of Bread, and Prayer.* . . .[105]

These three Confessions agreed that the way into the company of the visible saints—God's covenanted churches[106]—was by baptism, and to

---

Press, 1963) 143.
   [102]Lumpkin, *Baptist Confessions of Faith*, 165.
   [103]Ibid., 209.
   [104]An alternative, this, which did not escape the notice of the Unitarian Alexander Gordon. See his "Matthew Caffyn and General Baptist latitude," 531 (c).
   [105]Lumpkin, *Baptist Confessions of Faith*, 228-29.
   [106]For the theology of, and examples of, local covenants see Charles W. Deweese, *Baptist Church Covenants* (Nashville TN: Broadman Press, 1990).

this the General Baptists added prayer and the laying on of hands. But, strangely, in the London [Particular] Confession of 1677 the link between baptism and church membership was not clearly established. Chapter XXVI contained fifteen paragraphs "Of the Church" in which baptism is not mentioned, while Chapters XXXVIII and XXXIX on baptism required believers to be baptized as a sign of their engrafting into Christ, but did not relate the ordinance to church membership.

A century later, in a context in which they were convinced that, "there is a very criminal inattention to [church fellowship] amongst professors of Christianity, and even among Protestant Dissenters of our own denomination," John Collett Ryland and his Northamptonshire colleagues declared in 1777 that

> A Church of Christ is a peculiar society of gracious souls, who are called out of a state of sin and misery by the almighty Spirit of God, associated by their own free consent to maintain the doctrines of grace—to perform gospel worship, and celebrate gospel ordinances, with the exercise of holy discipline to the glory of the divine perfections, and to promote their own usefulness and happiness in time and eternity. . . . They are, or ought to be, real believers in the Lord Jesus Christ, with the exercise of true repentance towards God. They are distinguished from all other men by three great characteristics, (viz.) Their convictions, their faith, and their new and divine nature.[107]

We thus have oscillations in Baptist circles between those, like the Strict Baptists, who would make believer's baptism a term of membership and of communion, and fence the Lord's Table against all not thus baptized; those who, like eighteenth century Benjamin Wallin, believed that believer's baptism and congregational church fellowship were "necessary to [Christianity's] Growth or Continuance in any Place; so that every Method taken to promote or revive it, which doth not include and insist on a Conformity to this Gospel Institution, is essentially deficient";[108] those like H. Wheeler Robinson who can say that "Entrance into the Church is regarded as distinct from baptism, though in practice it is usually combined with it";[109] and those who with John Clifford denied

---

[107] *The Beauty of Social Religion*, 2, 3.
[108] Benjamin B. Wallin, *The Folly of Neglecting Divine Institutions. An Earnest Address to the Christian, Who Continues to Refrain from the Appointments of the Gospel*, 2nd ed. (London, 1758) v.
[109] Robinson, *The Life and Faith of the Baptists*, 84n.2.

that the acceptance of candidates for baptism had anything to do with the church.[110]

Into the tangled web of Baptist history concerning the debates over open versus closed membership and (which is not the same) open or closed communion we cannot here enter. Suffice it to say that in their most recent statements on the matter, Baptist Union writers are not, perhaps, as consistent as an interested enquirer might wish. Thus, while Paul Beasley-Murray boldly affirms that, "Baptism is the normal way of entry into the church.... Baptism is God's way for you to join the church," David Coffey, while noting that, "For some people it is a natural progression to move from commitment to Christ confessed in believer's baptism to commitment to Christ expressed in membership in the local church," and while answering those who do not or cannot see the connection between the two, does not explicitly justify the connection theologically along the lines that to be baptized *is* to be a member of the church. While W. M. S. West has reassured Baptists that there is "a growing body of opinion which recognizes that [the procedure of baptismal classes and the place of church meeting in decisions concerning those who are to be baptized] must have a basic principle for action that baptism makes a person a member of the Church,"[111] the optional possibility continues to hover. One wonders whether Baptists are tempted to believe that baptized non-members (to me a contradiction in terms) can be catholic Christians "in general" without the requirement and the challenge of anchorage within a local group of visible saints,[112] or whether there is an implied concession to open membership—perhaps on ecumenical grounds—in which case there needs to be a follow through regarding the several "moments" of Christian initiation, of which the baptism of infants might be one.

Lest it be thought that Strict Baptists alone may appear to be the rigorists of the Baptist family where matters of church membership are concerned, we may note in passing that, as their Standard Confession made plain, the old General Baptists required new members to receive the laying on of hands. They were more restorationist at this point and others than some of their contemporary Particular Baptists were concerning believer's baptism as a prerequisite of membership and communion.

---

[110]See Briggs, *The English Baptists of the 19th Century*, 136.
[111]West in Gilmore, ed., *The Pattern of the Church*, 34; cf. 3.
[112]Paul Beasley-Murray, *Baptist Basics: Believers' Baptism*, col. iv; David Coffey, *Baptist Basics. Church Membership*, col. i.

Thus, for example, the Horsham General Baptist church was founded as a "Six-principle" cause, membership of which required (in accordance with Hebrews vi:1,2) repentance from dead works, faith towards God, baptism, the laying on of hands, and belief in the resurrection of the dead as well as eternal judgment. When in 1818 it was

> Resolved that the Church return to its original mode of admitting members; viz., by baptism and the Laying on of hands, henceforth no person shall be admitted to the church without complying with his mode; and that those friends who have hitherto been admitted without the Laying on of Hands . . . can no longer be considered as members unless they choose to submit to the rite . . .

a rift developed between the Horsham members and those who lived at Billingshurst. The latter protested against the dismission of thirteen members of their branch "without any charge being made against their moral conduct," and the result was that they constituted themselves as a separate church.[113] Other issues could cause similar disturbances. When John Stanger arrived among the General Baptists of Bessels Green in 1769 (where the rite of foot washing was observed until 1785), he caused a split in the church, not least because "he was a Calvinist, in favor of Singing and Catholic Communion." The fact that his preaching was "tedious and tautological" may also have had something to do with the breach.[114]

In all parts of the English Baptist tradition, the duties of church meeting are similar: members are to be received and, where necessary, disciplined; ministers are to be called and officers appointed; the needy are to be supported, premises maintained, relationship with like-minded believers elsewhere developed, and specific questions such as the introduction of singing and organs, or the anointing of the sick determined. In the early days members would sign the covenant, and the question of relations with the state would sometimes loom large. In 1764 the Yorkshire and Lancashire Association of Particular Baptists gave advice concerning matters with which church meetings might deal: the truths of the gospel, specific passages of Scripture, cases of conscience, the discussion of sermons—but none of this in such a ways to "glide into a light

---

[113] Emily Kensett, *History of the Free Christian Church Horsham from 1721 to 1921* (Horsham: Free Christian Church Public Library, 1921) 103-105.

[114] Packer, *The Unitarian Heritage in Kent*, 31.

and frothy conversation" or beget dullness.[115] Latterly, questions concerning mission, education, and ecumenism have found their way onto the agenda of church meetings. Underlying all has been the doctrine of the priesthood of all believers—at its best rightly construed to denote the corporate priesthood of the gathered saints, not the sanctification of the aspirations, whims, or prejudices of every individual member.[116]

But for all the theory, in practice church meeting is admitted to have declined in attendance and significance in many churches. R. C. Walton lamented that, "In the great majority of our churches [the] exalted view of the nature of the church meeting has been almost entirely lost, and with it has gone one of the most important characteristics of the Baptist community."[117] All through this century writers have been speculating upon why this might be. H. Wheeler Robinson spoke of "the rivalry of other forms of organization . . . Christian Endeavour Societies, Young People's Guilds, and the like, together with the very large number of special organizations not linked to any one Church, yet drawing their supporters almost exclusively from the Churches."[118] Henry Cook questioned "whether our present system is really suited to some conditions. It does wonderfully well in suburban districts where get a good community of middle-class people. But what about the mission field? What about slum areas?"[119] Ernest Payne observed that "Changed social conditions and habits have made it more difficult to secure a large attendance of members at a midweek meeting. The two World Wars accentuated these developments. So did the growth of a more centralized denominational organization."[120] For his part, B. R. White, calling "a spade a spade," has pointed to the dissuasion that in church meeting and Association alike, "the 'boredom quotient' is about 95%"—a view endorsed by Alistair Campbell.[121] The latter, though not opposed to church meeting as such, questions whether the institution should any longer be deemed "the test of loyalty and the badge of identity." It is not simply that many local churches are finding other ways of expressing, "the

---

[115]See Raymond Brown, *English Baptists of the 18th Century*, 88-89.
[116]Cf. West in Gilmore, ed., *The Pattern of the Church*, 46-47; N. Clark in ibid., 106.
[117]R. C. Walton, *The Gathered Community* (London: Carey Press, 1946) 130.
[118]Robinson, *The Life and Faith of the Baptists*, 90.
[119]Cook, *What Baptists Stand For*, 82-83.
[120]Payne, *The Fellowship of Believers*, 105.
[121]B. R. White in David Slater, ed., *A Perspective on Baptist Identity* (Kingsbridge: Mainstream, 1987) 25; cf. ibid., 35.

Scriptural principle of every member ministry," it is, *inter alia*, that,"The Church Meeting cannot be proved from Scripture to have existed in any form recognizable to us, let alone be shown to have obtained everywhere or have been laid down by the Apostles."[122]

Clearly, the questions of the locus of authority and the validity of restorationism lie beneath this remark, which appears in a discussion pamphlet offered by conservative evangelical Baptists. I should simply enquire, "Is there a more fitting way for those called to be saints to pray about, and deliberate upon, their witness and mission than to gather regularly and expectantly for this purpose?" While agreeing with Brian Haymes that,"It is [Christ's] presence and not the specific organization that makes the Church the Church,"[123] we may nevertheless ask, did not Baptist (and Congregational) forebears do something of value when they "completed" Reformed ecclesiology by including the ministry of the whole people of God in their deliberative aspect; and could not this experience put flesh on the bones of an ecumenical ecclesiology which affirms the importance of this ministry, to which some polities pay little more than lip service?[124] These questions press if Baptists still intend to regard the local church as comprising called, regenerate, baptized, covenanted saints who, by virtue of their local enrolment, are members of the Church catholic.[125]

I do not suggest that the perceived inadequacies of church meeting are the only counterproductive factors in facilitating the offering of the Baptists' ecclesiological gift.We may ask, for example, how are Baptists to relate convictions on polity still shared by many of them to the predilection shared by some of them for church growth? This may be

---

[122]Campbell in *A Perspective on Baptist Identity*, 35. It would be utterly undiplomatic—even evidence of an unsanctified mind—to mutter, "A fortiori, neither can Southern Baptist boards!"

[123]In Keith Clements et al., *A Call to Mind. Baptist Essays towards a Theology of Commitment* (London: Baptist Union, 1981) 59.

[124]E.g., see the opening paragraphs of the chapter on "Ministry" in *Baptism, Eucharist, and Ministry* (Geneva: World Council of Churches, 1982).

[125]"Covenanted" is perhaps the operative word at this point. One suspects a situation among (at least) British Baptists similar to that manifested by Congregationalists, namely, that in the wake of the Evangelical Revival the emphasis in many places switched from "covenant" to "conversion," so that the church came to be regarded not so much as God's corporate election of grace, but as an aggregate of saved individuals. In Congregationalism there is a decided tailing off of local covenants from about 1830. See Sell, *Dissenting Thought and the Life of the Churches*, ch. 1.

especially a problem for Baptists in North America and Korea, where local Baptist churches of twenty to forty thousand members are not unknown, whose ministers know personally only a number of the deacons. One can, no doubt, have evangelical meetings—even worship—on such a scale, but can one have gathered churches of like size? It would seem that a church meeting of such numbers is impossible to organize if not fearful to contemplate—certainly if the words of Thomas Helwys' confession are still thought to have significance:

> The members off everie Church or Congregacion ought to knowe one another, that so they may performe all the duties off love towards another both to soule and bodie. . . . And therefore a Church ought not to consist off such a multitude as cannot have particular knowledg one off another.[126]

Long before the modern church growth movement was launched, a correspondent in *The Patriot* in January 1866 declared that "a chapel of over a thousand seats was a denial of basic nonconformist principles."[127]

While taking full account of these points, may it not also be that, just as secular democratic ideas have done their eroding work, so, too, has a feeling of embarrassment felt in many quarters. Is there an unease about the clash between the inherited doctrine on which so much Baptist polity turns, namely, that there is a distinction of eternal significance between those who are in Christ and those who are not, and the perceived need to reach out to other Christian traditions, and to do right by members of other faiths and of none? It is not only members of established churches who need to ask, "Who is A Christian?" Robert Hall drew the distinction plainly enough: "Congregations are the creatures of circumstances; churches the institution of God."[128] What Southern Baptist Charles Deweese has written of Baptists in the United States would appear to have wider application: "A dilemma facing contemporary Baptists in America

---

[126]Lumpkin, *Baptist Confessions of Faith*, 121. The insistence that "the belief that Jesus Christ is not only Lord over all the congregation, but exercises his reign through that whole community, not just certain designated members of it" is said to be a conviction "which cannot be jettisoned without a radical departure from the meaning of 'Baptist' in this country." See Paul S. Fiddes et al., *Bound to Love. The Covenant Basis of Baptist Life and Mission* (London: Baptist Union, 1985) 7. In the same volume is found Roger Hayden's defense of church meeting, 34-35. For Helwys (?1550–1616?), see *DNB*.

[127]See Briggs, *The English Baptists of the 19th Century*, 13.

[128]Gregory, ed., *The Works of Robert Hall, A.M.* 4:296.

is how to reconcile mounting trends toward an uncommitted membership with doctrinal statements that require a committed membership."[129]

I cannot claim to have read every piece of Baptist writing on the church meeting, but in what I *have* read, the connection between church meeting and worship has only rarely been drawn. There is, for example, the suggestion by A. Gilmore that, "the chief responsibility of the church meeting is to complete the liturgy by planning the social life of the church (*koinonia*), together with the church's witness (*marturia*) and service (*diakonia*),"[130] but the worship-church meeting relationship merits fuller exposition, for the idea that the saints who sit under the Word and gather at the Lord's Table then become the church *meeting*, under the Lordship of Christ, in order to determine how the gospel received is to be proclaimed where God has placed them, is too important to be played down. The idea facilitates witness to the fact that just as in worship Christ is proclaimed as Lord, so too is he proclaimed in church meeting, which then takes on its true character as a credal assembly. A related point is that the one presiding at church meeting should normally be the minister—not a businessperson "good at meetings"—for just as he or she is called to lead the church to the throne of grace in worship, so the minister is charged to lead the church to seek the mind of Christ in church meeting.[131]

Experience suggests that if there is not a strong sense of church locally, it is difficult to see how there can be mutuality between the local church and the wider denominational associations, since the latter will find an ecclesiological void, and attempts to develop relationships will be vitiated. On the other hand, there may be a strong, but narrow sense of local church autonomy of the kind which justifies B.R. White's useful observation: "Across three and a half centuries, if Baptists have had to choose between the independence of the local church and cooperation in fellowship with an association, they have chosen independence."[132] Arthur

---

[129]Deweese, *Baptist Church Covenants*, vii.

[130]Gilmore in *The Pattern of the Church*, 148; cf. Clark in ibid., 108-109.

[131]I was therefore surprised to read the following in the statement on church government of a Reformed Baptist church (even though a plurality of elders, each having different gifts, is envisaged) "The elders or church officers call all meetings of the church. . . . They will also appoint a chairman for each meeting." See *Reformation Today*, no. 82 (November–December 1984): 37. For a discussion of church meeting in Congregationalism and its heirs, see Alan P. F. Sell, *Commemorations*, ch. 14.

[132]White in Slater, ed., *A Perspective on Baptist Identity*, 20.

Dakin, while granting that the idea of setting out from the local church is "fundamental to Baptist polity and cannot be departed from without abandoning the essential Baptist position," had to admit that "this it is that creates some of our present difficulties."[133] Among these are the parochialism and isolationism against which Henry Cook warned.[134] Such is the force of the individualism flowing down from the nineteenth century that Baptists who have fallen into these traps would, no doubt, be surprised to be told by William Lumpkin (another Southern Baptist) that "Baptists were never independents, strictly speaking,"[135] and they would find it hard to accept Whitley's assertion that, "Baptists from the beginning sought to maintain sisterly intercourse between local churches; they never thought that one church was independent of others."[136] There can be no doubt that the classical confessions, both Particular and General, bear Whitley out—and Ernest Payne, too:

> [F]rom the seventeenth century Baptists have regarded the visible Church as finding expression in local communities of believers who constitute themselves by the election of officers, the observance of Baptism and the Lord's Supper, and Christian discipline, and who find an extension and expression of their life in free association, first, with other churches of their own faith and order, but also with all other groups of Christians loyal to the central truths of the apostolic Gospel. This, in outline, is the Baptist doctrine of the Church as visible. It is something very different from the exaggerates independence, self-sufficiency and atomism which have sometimes been favored of recent days.[137]

The Baptist Council statement of 1948 underlined the point: "Gathered companies of believers are the local manifestation of the one Church of God on earth and in heaven."[138] All of this in line with the London Confession's assertion that

> although the particular Congregations be distinct and severall Bodies, every one a company and knit Citie in it selfe; yet are they all to walk by one and

---

[133]Dakin, *The Baptist View of the Church and Ministry*, 5. Beware N. G. Wright's significant misquotation of Dakin: "Baptists start all their organization from the local church and it is this which causes our difficulties." See his " 'Koinonia' and Baptist Ecclesiology," *BQ* 35/8 (October 1994): 365.

[134]Cook, *What Baptists Stand For*, 79-80.

[135]Lumpkin, *Baptist Confessions of Faith*, 172.

[136]W. T. Whitley, *A History of British Baptists* (London: Charles Griffin, 1923) 86.

[137]Payne, *The Fellowship of Believers*, 36-37; cf. West in Gilmore, ed., *The Pattern of the Church*, 42-43.

[138]*The Baptist Doctrine of the Church*, 2.

the same Rule, and by all means convenient to have the counsell and help one of another in all needfull affaires of the Church, as members of one body in the common faith under Christ their onely head.[139]

The *Second London Confession* agrees that the local churches "ought to hold communion amongst themselves for their peace, increase of love, and mutual edification." It then proceeds immediately to say, however, that messengers to assemblies "are not entrusted with any Church-power properly so called; or with any jurisdiction over the Churches themselves, to exercise any censures either over any Churches, or Persons; or to impose their determination on the Churches, or Officers."[140]

The General Baptists who composed the Orthodox Creed of 1678 were even clearer that at assemblies "the churches appearing there by their representatives, make but one church, and have lawful right, and suffrage in this general meeting, or assembly, to act in the name of Christ." Then, in a manner consistent with the rigorism concerning polity which we earlier noted, they stated,

> To such a meeting, or assembly, appeals ought to be made, in case of any injustice done, or heresy, and schism countenanced, in any particular congregation of Christ, and the decisive voice in such general assemblies is the major part, and such general assemblies have lawful power to hear, and determine, and also to excommunicate.[141]

If it appears that these General Baptists did less than justice to church meetings, the Particular Confessions seem to have left the associations toothless. They had no church power. Indeed, Ryland and the Northamptonshire ministers and messengers did not mention them at all in their Circular Letter of 1777. But, according to B.R. White, fellowship was an obligation:"Fellowship is the lifestyle of the gospel. *Inter*dependence is the mark of the converted—the search for independence was Adam's sin."[142] The question thus presses: If local church power leads to a breach of fellowship, how are matters to be restored? It would seem that Baptists have not always clearly articulated the practical ways by which the mutuality which they profess as between local church and wider association is actually to be achieved.[143] Doctrinally, the point may be expressed in

---

[139]Lumpkin, *Baptist Confessions of Faith*, 168-69.
[140]Ibid., 289.
[141]Ibid., 327.
[142]White in Slater, ed., *A Perspective on Baptist Identity*, 29.
[143]Even Gilmore is deficient at this point. See *The Pattern of the Church*, 149-54.

terms of pneumatology. Can it be supposed that the Holy Spirit who addresses the local church meeting through the Word is powerless to fulfil a similar function in assemblies? If not, then in cases in which the local church and the assembly are out of accord, and on the assumption that the Spirit does not speak with a forked tongue, there needs to be a process of mutual discussion in a spirit of humility and prayer, in the hope that differences may be resolved. Certainly there is something worryingly casual about H. Wheeler Robinson's matter-of-fact assertion that "local Churches join or withdraw from [associations] as they see fit,"[144] especially if there is truth in the Orthodox Creed's declaration that churches represented at assemblies "make but one church." A more recent writer, Brian Haymes, is quite clear on the matter: "When we gather as local congregations, Associations or in Denominational Assembly we meet as those whom God has gathered together in communion with Christ."[145]

III

I turn finally to liberty. We have seen that on matters of doctrine and polity, Baptists have believed a number of different things, and that there have been varying degrees of tolerance amongst them. Some have sailed closer to rigorism, others to a freewheeling liberty of thought, but all would agree that the church, as Church, possesses God-given liberty as over against any powers which would curtail or stifle its spiritual freedom. The negative implication of freedom for Christ, is freedom from the world (in Separatist parlance), and from a coercive state (in the language of Old Dissent). The conviction was classically expressed by the General Baptists. In the one hundred *Propositions and Conclusions* (1612) of the Smyth party in Amsterdam, the draft of which had been written by its recently deceased leader, we read:

> 84. That the magistrate is not by virtue of his office to meddle with religion, or matters of conscience, to force or compel men to this or that form of religion, or doctrine: but to leave Christian religion free, to every man's conscience, and to handle only civil transgressions (Rom. Xiii), injuries and wrongs of man against man, in murder, adultery, theft, etc., for Christ only is the king and lawgiver of the church and conscience (James iv.12).[146]

---

[144]Robinson, *The Life and Faith of the Baptists*, 91.
[145]Haymes in Clements et al., *A Call to Mind*, 67.
[146]Lumpkin, *Baptist Confessions of Faith*, 140.

Thomas Helwys was even more pointed:

> Our lord the King is but an earthly King, and he hath no authority as a King but in earthly causes, and if the Kings people be obedient and true subjects, obeying all humane lawes made by the King, our lord the King can require no more: for mens religion to God is betwixt God and themselves; the King shall not answer for it, neither may the King be iugd betwene God and man. Let them be heretikes, Turcks, Jewes or whatsoever, it apperteynes not to the earthly power to punish them in the least measure.[147]

In succession, and on similar lines, came Leonard Busher's *Religion's Peace* (1614), John Murton's *Objectives Answered* (1615) and *An Humble Supplication* (1626), and Roger Williams's *The Bloody Tenent of Persecution* (1644). In making this protest, the early seventeenth-century Baptists stood alone among what might (anachronistically) be called the mainline Old Dissenters.[148]

Although the early English Baptist confessions are unanimous on the necessity of spiritual freedom, they were nevertheless couched interestingly varied terms. The authors of the London Confession, while granting that "a civill Magistrate is an ordinance of God set up by God for the punishment of evil doers, and for the praise of them that doe well," nevertheless reserved the right to continue witnessing faithfully should magistrates turn adverse, "And thus wee desire to give unto God that which is Gods, and unto Caesar that which is Caesars."[149] The *Second London Confession* followed the same general line, though the absence of a declaration of intent to stand against erring magistrates is noteworthy, and was probably owing to the desire of the authors not to incite further persecution and to encourage thoughts of toleration in their opponents. The General Baptists' *Standard Confession* of 1660 showed no such inhibitions—and this is surprising in view of their desire to demonstrate that all rumors aligning them with Munster and other disturbing agents are wide of the mark. They granted that there ought to

---

[147]Helwys, *A Short Declaration of the Mistery of Iniquity* (1612), 69.

[148]The Independents were quite happy to be the established church in Massachussetts, and in England they did not turn their thought seriously towards toleration until it became clear during the Westminster Assembly that if they did not they would lose out to Presbyterianism. See further, Robert S. Paul, *The Assembly of the Lord. Politics and Religion in the Westminister Assembly and the 'Grand Debate'* (Edinburgh: T. & T. Clark, 1985) 31-467. Some Presbyterians hoped for an establishment along their favored lines of polity as late as the early years of the eighteenth century.

[149]Lumpkin, *Baptist Confessions of Faith*, 169-71.

be civil magistrates—and that they were to be submitted to—but they gave notice that

> In case the Civil Powers do, or shall at any time impose things about matters of Religion, which we through conscience to God cannot actually obey, then we with *Peter* also do say, that we ought (in such cases) to obey God rather than men; *Acts* 5.29 and accordingly do hereby declare our whole, and holy intent and purpose, that (through the help of grace) we will not yield, nor (in such cases) in the least actually obey them; yet humbly purposing (in the Lords strength) patiently to suffer whatsoever shall be inflicted upon us, for our conscionable forebearance.[150]

On the basis of the foundations laid, it will now suffice if we take soundings in subsequent centuries. When in 1772 a bill to repeal the law requiring nonconformist subscription to Anglican articles was defeated in the House of Lords, one bishop only voting in favor, Robert Robinson apostrophized thus:

> Christian liberty! Thou favorite offspring of heaven! Thou firstborn of Christianity! I saw the wise and pious servants of God nourish thee in their houses, and cherish thee in their bosoms! I saw them lead thee into public view; all good men hailed thee; the generous British Commons caressed and praised thee, and led thee into an upper house, and there . . . there didst thou expire in the holy laps of spiritual lords![151]

Five years later, Ryland and his Northamptonshire colleagues made it clear that those who comprise the Church were

> Very much distinguished from the merely civil and political societies of this world, by the spiritual nature of their constitution, the privileges they enjoy, the officers they appoint, the worship they perform, the rules they observe, the head they obey, and the great and noble ends they pursue, which are abundantly superior to all the designs of the political societies of this world.[152]

Increasingly, Baptist heat was turned upon the establishment principle as such: "Turn a Christian society into an established church," warned Robert Hall, "and it is no longer a voluntary assembly for the worship of God; it is a powerful corporation, full of such sentiments and passions,

---

[150]Ibid., 233.
[151]*Miscellaneous Works of Robert Robinson, Late Pastor of the Baptist Church and Congregation of Protestant Dissenters, at Cambridge* (Harlow: B. Flower, 1807) 2:182-83. For Robinson (1735–1790), see *DNB*.
[152]*The Beauty of Social Religion*, 3.

as usually distinguish those bodies; a dread of innovation, an attachment to abuses, a propensity to tyranny and oppression."[153] He elsewhere argued that, "A full toleration of religious principles, and the protection of all parties in their respective modes of worship, are the natural operations of a free government; and everything that tends to check and restrain them, materially affects the interests of religion."[154]

In 1843 the Kent and Sussex Particular Baptist Association rather missed the point as they glanced north to Scotland. They unanimously resolved to endorse the action of those Free Church people who had seceded from the Church of Scotland in that year, but seem not to have grasped the fact that the Free Church of Scotland staunchly maintained (and its remnant still maintains) the establishment principle, regarded itself as the Church of Scotland (Free), and believed that the *Church* "came out"—mainly over the question of the patronage system which permitted the intrusion of nonevangelical ministers into pulpits against the will of the people. But at least the Kent and Sussex Baptists reaffirmed their own view of church-state relations.

By the end of the nineteenth century, the cry was a "free Church in a free state," and Baptists and others worked for this, their ardor increased by perceived injustices in the field of education—a long story which cannot now detain us. Suffice it to say that none worked harder for what he regarded as the proper freedoms of both Church and state than John Clifford:

> Our fathers suffered and fought for what they described as "the crown rights of King Jesus." This is—be it believed or be it scorned—this is the real force at the heart of the agitation for Disestablishment or Disendowment. In that unselfish and sublime aim lies its unsubduable strength; from thence it draws its patience, its quenchless enthusiasm, and its assurance of final success.[155]

From Clifford's day to the 1950s, the case was made in these terms with some, but by no means all, remembering what Clifford here seems to have forgotten, namely that in addition, "our fathers"—consistently with their view of a regenerate church—had serious reservations concern-

---

[153]Gregory, ed., *The Works of Robert Hall, A.M.*, 3:145. Cf. Sell, *Dissenting Thought and the Life of the Churches*, 638-39. This is from *An Apology for the Freedom of the Press and for General Liberty* (1793; repr. 1831).
[154]Ibid., 12.
[155]J. Clifford in *The Contemporary Review* 67 (March 1895): 454-55.

ing the established Church, to whose communion services regenerate and unregenerate alike could come on nonbiblical grounds.

At the end of the nineteenth century, Principal William Edwards adduced no fewer than fifty arguments favor of Nonconformity, many of them standard, but some of them idiosyncratic, for example: "As the Welsh especially are a nation of Nonconformists, the presence of the Establishment is an anomaly and a grievous injustice."[156] The Welsh Nonconformists have their reward.

The middle years of the twentieth century saw a flurry of literary activity by Baptists on the establishment question. The classical position on the matter was reiterated, though in modern accents, but as to what should be done about the problem, some were more cautious than others. In 1944 Arthur Dakin explained that

> The gathered church distinguishes itself sharply from every form of national or state church, and from every sort of church where the basis of membership is birth privilege of any kind. Those who adhere to the gathered-church idea cannot allow that a person is of necessity a member of the Christian Church because he happens to be born in a so-called Christian country, or for that matter in a Christian family.[157]

As he reflected on the establishment issue, Henry Cook concluded that the underlying vital question is

> What is the Church? And how is it constituted? The State Church or Church State assumes that membership in the one is coterminous with the other, and "converts" are made by the fact that they are born and then baptized. But this is fundamentally wrong. The Church, Baptists believe, is a society freely constituted by the free acceptance on the part of men and women of the free grace of God, and unless there be a "willing covenant" there cannot be the entrance into the holy society we call the Church.

Freedom from an unregenerate Church was implicit only in the remarks of both Dakin and Cook.

Four years later the Baptist Council expressed itself on the general question of Church and state, without reference to the establishment, thus:

> Our conviction of Christ's Lordship over His Church leads us to insist that churches formed by His will must be free from all other rule in matters relating to their spiritual life. Any form of control by the State in these

---

[156] William Edwards, *A Handbook of Protestant Nonconformity* (Bristol, 1901) 226. See further Sell, *Dissenting Thought and the Life of the Churches*, 646-48.

[157] Dakin, *The Baptist View of the Church and Ministry*, 15-16.

matters appears to us to challenge the "Crown Rights of the Redeemer." We also hold that this freedom in Christ implies the right of the church to exercise responsible self-government. This has been the Baptist position since the seventeenth century. . . .

This freedom, however, has not led to irresponsibility in our duties as citizens. We believe it is a Christian obligation to honour and serve the State and to labour for the well-being of all men and women.[158]

By far the most sustained and perceptive treatment of the entire question of Church and state was that by Henry Townsend, principal of Manchester Baptist College, which was published in 1949. He set out from the assertion that,"The Bible ascribes absolute authority to the transcendent Lawgiver, Who revealed to Moses, the prophets, and finally through Jesus of Nazareth, the ethical standards of righteousness and love. In the New Testament Jesus Christ is Lord—a term signifying His unique ethical authority over his followers."[159] Townsend pointed out that Jesus distinguished sharply between God's kingdom and that of earthly governments, and taught that, as citizens, his followers should "obey authority except when it clashed with loyalty to Himself."It was a sad day for the Church when the Empire of Constantine entered into official relations with it, for

> The World entered the Church as it had never done for three hundred years; and ever since the fourth century its presence in the church has been the bane of the Christian religion. It was, and is still, a departure from the spiritual independence of the Church. . . . When it has suited their mutual interests, mostly financial and entirely worldly, the Church and State have flirted with each other, and both have suffered; the betrayal of Christ and the Gospel lies at the Church's door, and such betrayal cannot be divorced from the demonic forces which have swept over the world in these latter days.[160]

These forthright words did not, however, imply the absolute ignoring of the church by the state, and *vice versa*. On the contrary, "The State makes the laws, must administer justice and restrict evil doers. The function of the Church is to preach the gospel in the State, to leaven society, and to educate the people in Christian principles, until they elect men to rule who will make laws approximating to the Christian ethical ideal."[161]

---

[158]*The Baptist Doctrine of the Church*, 7.
[159]H. Townsend. *The Claims of the Free Churches* (London: Hodder and Stoughton, 1949) 196.
[160]Ibid., 197.
[161]Ibid., 199.

Townsend is unflinching:"National Churches have arrested the universal ideas of the New Testament, and have thereby de-Christianised the idea of God which was revealed by Jesus."[162] We shall not expect him to endorse the arguments of those in the Church of England who appeal to the utility of the establishment, and he does not: "The whole argument from Free Church history is a protest against the complacency of the principle of the utility of the Establishment."[163] He allies himself with the Puritans, who, "regarded the alliance of Church and State as a betrayal of the Gospel and a hindrance to the spiritual growth of the nation," declaring that,"the dread of the loss of endowments keeps the Church in bondage to the State: the proposals for her independence confirm this statement."[164] In answer to Archbishop Garbett's claim that the Church of England,"has in practice freedom which is hardly equaled by any other church or sect," Townsend points to the way in which the church cannot without recourse to Parliament legally determine its worship, appoint its senior officers, change its statement of doctrine, or amend its constitution.[165]

Three years later, as if to dampen down any seditious thoughts which Townsend's robust argument might engender, Ernest Payne was found reaffirming the classical position on *the Free Churches and the State*, but he advised that the time was not ripe for the Free Churches to press for the disestablishment of the Church of England (a) because "We are obviously in a dangerous transitional period in regard to the theory and activity of the State"; (b) because "A sharp church conflict would seriously endanger" growing inter-Church confidence; and (c) because "it would be disastrous at the beginning of a new reign to embark upon a religious controversy which would inevitably be complicated, prolonged and embittered, and which would, equally inevitably, involve the status and powers of the Crown."[166] Payne denied that his position entailed repudiating "the historic witness of the Free Churches." Rather, he appealed for Anglicans and others, "to think a little more, and learn a

---

[162]Ibid., 200.
[163]Ibid., 208.
[164]Ibid., 210-11.
[165]Ibid., 211. He quotes, C. Garbett, *The Claims of the Church of England* (London: Hodder and Stoughton, 1947) 182.
[166]E. A. Payne, *The Free Churches and the State* (London: Independent Press, 1952) 28. Repr. in idem., *Free Churchmen Unrepentant and Repentant* (London: Carey Kingsgate Press, 1965) ch. 5.

little longer, before we commit ourselves to an entirely new religious settlement in this country."[167]

As already hinted, forty years on the situation is significantly changed. To use the words of the 1593 Act Against Puritans, if Baptists are not (necessarily!) "seditious sectaries and disloyal persons,"[168] it is equally clear that such relative youngsters in our land as Methodists and Muslims, Sikhs and secularists—and many others—are not so to be labeled either. But their presence calls into question any lingering establishment theology to the effect that to be English is to be a member of the Church of England, and that not so to belong implies subversion at best and treachery at worst. Moreover, many parish churches are *de facto* gathered (and often highly eclectic gatherings at that), while many gathered churches, as we have seen, sit more loosely to the principle of the regenerate saints than once they did.

Further, at a time when the monarchy is under review—by everyone from the royal household to writers in the tabloid press;[169] and when nationalisms are rapidly developing across Europe—some of them highly dangerous—the churches might be thought to have a prophetic and a genuinely ecumenical word to speak. The fact that older religious disabilities have almost entirely vanished, and that Nonconformists are no longer thrown into prison or killed, should make it easier for the underlying theological questions to be amicably discussed, and for the necessary reconciliation of memories to take place. We do not need to be so blunt as Forsyth, from whom I set out: "What we protest against is not the abuses but the existence, the principle, of a national Church."[170] We need not sound so complacent as H. Wheeler Robinson who, in 1927, wrote, "While Baptists still feel that the 'establishment' of one religious denomination above all others is an anomaly under present conditions [what an astounding qualification!], they are probably less disposed today to promote political action for its removal, and prefer to leave this, in the interests of religion, to the more or less inevitable course of events,

---

[167] Ibid., 29.

[168] Gee and Hardy, *Documents Illustrative of the History of the English Church* (London: Macmillan, 1896) 492.

[169] The tabloid breast-beating over the question whether Prince Charles, because of his divorce, his flirtation with New Age thought, and the like, is fit to be the next temporal head of the Church of England represents a sublime missing of the point.

[170] P. T. Forsyth, "The Evangelical basis of Free Churchism," *The Contemporary Review* 81 (January–June 1902): 693.

within and without the Anglican Church."[171] And we ought not to sound as triumphalist as Henry Cook:

> [T]he Free churches are a recognized power in the religious life of the nation. The Church of England itself is conscious of the chains that bind it, and the Liberty and Life movement under the late Dr. Temple has done much to create a desire for a larger freedom. That cannot, however, fully come until the gilded bonds of the Establishment are broken, and the Church of England itself becomes a Free Church.[172]

It is not necessary for the Free Churches to agitate for disestablishment [173]; that will come about, if at all, when the Church of England itself seeks it. But all the pertinent issues might be raised in a wide-ranging ecumenical discussion in England and in Europe (for the Lutheran and Reformed establishments, though different, are also being urged to examine themselves) of the theological basis of church-state relations as Christianity's third millennium approaches. There are signs that such a discussion is already in its early stages,[174] and one wonders how much part Baptists (and, indeed, other Old Dissenters) will wish to play in it.[175]

To end, as I began, with some poles: at the 250th anniversary of the Great Ejectment of 1662, the Baptist Alexander Maclaren bequeathed agenda, begged questions, and implied rebukes in all directions:

---

[171]Robinson, *The Life and Faith of the Baptists*, 134.

[172]Cook, *What Baptists Stand For*, 209.

[173]And republicanism has never been regarded by most Dissenters as the necessary consequence of their theological stance. On the contrary, time and again they have professed loyalty to successive (not always very helpful) monarchs. Consider this, for example, from a John Collett Ryland and his Northamptonshire colleagues: "[W]e do not judge ourselves independent of civil government, as we are members of society: no, sirs! We are so far from assuming independence on [*sic*] the good old British constitution, that we will dare to affirm, no men in England, or in the world, are better friends to such civil government that we are, and desire always to be." See *The Beauty of Social Religion*, 7.

[174]See Sell, "Called to be one: Decision Making in Our Churches, Including Matters of Faith. A Report," *One In Christ*, 32/1 (1996): 82-83.

[175]I have no means of predicting what role the Free Church Federal Council might play in such discussions. It is surely concerned with Church-state relations, but its membership is diverse, and its young members did not, for the most part, find their origin in matters ecclesiological, neither have they the stimulus of martyrs, or such long memories of civil and religious disabilities. Since I should not wish to encourage others to do what I am not prepared to do myself, I may, perhaps, mention a few attempts made to increase the visibility of a question the consideration of which I believe to be an urgent matter: *Dissenting Thought and the Life of the Churches*, ch. 22; *Commemorations. Studies in Christian Thought and History*, ch. 4; "A Renewed Plea for 'Impractical' Divinity," *Studies in Christian Ethics* 7/2 (1995): 68-91.

The future of England will be to that Church which shall know how to reconcile most perfectly the rights of the individual and the power of society; the claims of free thought and the claims of dogmatic truth. A Church on the so-called multitudinist theory will not do it; for of the two terms of the antithesis it reduces one, the element of dogmatic truth, practically to zero. An Established church, be-articled, and be-liturgied, and be-bishoped, will not do it. Narrow Dissenterisms will not do it. But Churches which take the Bible for their creed, and Christ for their sole master, and all their members for brethren, ought to do it. They may do it if they will be true to themselves, to their principles, to their ancestry. Shame on them if they fail.[176]

IV

From this necessarily selective consideration of varied Baptist positions on doctrine, polity, and liberty, there arise three urgent questions of ecumenical significance: How are we to understand the development of doctrine in relation to degrees of tolerance within the Church? How may we best articulate a theology which will clearly relate the several foci of churchly life? Which theology of Church-state relations will most adequately facilitate the Church's mission as Christianity's third millennium dawns? Is it too much to hope that Baptists will be among those who will urge these questions upon us?

If and when the churches pay substantial ecumenical attention to these questions, in relation both to their several heritages and to what our forebears would have called "the needs of the hour," they would do well to have the devoutly majestic words of the "Epistle Dedicatory" to the Particular Baptist Confession of 1644 ringing in their ears:

> [W]e confess that we know but in part, and that we are ignorant of many things which we desire and seek to know: and if any shall doe us that friendly part to shew us from the word of God that we see not, we shall have cause to be thankful to God and them.[177]

---

[176]Alexander Maclaren, "Fidelity to Conscience," in *The Ejectment of 1662 and the Free Churches* (London: National Council of Evangelical Churches, 1912) 34. For Maclaren (1826–1910), see *DNB*.

[177]Lumpkin, *Baptist Confessions of Faith*, 149.

"Walking Together": The Place of Covenant Theology in Baptist Life Yesterday and Today

Paul S. Fiddes

Baptists have never been much interested by historic moments and places in their story. They do not readily look back to an Augsburg or a Dort, or even to a Chalcedon. It seems to be a mark of Baptist life to adapt to the present and constantly seek to reinvent itself, which at best can be seen as openness to the Spirit of God, and at worst, as a neglect of the lessons which the Spirit has wanted to teach the church during its history. But if one place and time were to be fixed upon as formative for Baptist Christians, it might well be at Gainsborough near Lincoln in 1606 or 1607, when a congregation of English Separatists made a covenant together. As William Bradford recalled years later in North America, the members

> joyned themselves (by a covenant of the Lord) into a Church estate, in the fellowship of the gospell, to walke in all his wayes, made known, or to be made known unto them, according to their best endeavours, whatsoever it should cost them, the Lord assisting them.[1]

They were not yet a Baptist church, but within a year the part of the congregation that gathered in Gainsborough would be in exile in Amsterdam with their pastor, John Smyth, and within two years would have adopted the practice of believer's baptism. Some members of the church would return to England in 1611 with Thomas Helwys as their pastor to found the first General Baptist church on English soil. The other part of the original covenanting group, who worshiped in Scrooby, were to follow their fellow believers to Holland, though not into similar Baptist convictions. From their church in Leiden, served by John Robinson as its pastor, many of them would sail for America on the Mayflower and contribute to the story of Congregationalism in New England.

This covenanting at Gainsborough was a defining moment. It exemplified the continuity between Baptists and the earlier movement of separ-

---

[1]William Bradford, *History of Plymouth Plantation*, vol. 1, 1620–1647 (Boston MA: Massachusetts Historical Society, 1912) 20-22.

atism from the newly established Church of England. Its language reflects the Separatist heritage, from Robert Browne onwards, of conceiving covenant in two dimensions at once, vertical and horizontal; that is, the church was gathered by the members' making a covenant or solemn agreement *both* with God *and* with each other. There is the characteristic pledge "to walk in the Lord's ways," which reaches back to the earlier congregational covenant of the Separatist church led by Francis Johnson,[2] and forward to the many covenants of local General and Particular Baptist churches form the late seventeenth century onwards.

Significant as well is the openness to the future, expressed in the phrase "to be made known to them," which recalls a similar "further light" clause in the covenant of Johnson's church ("all ways . . . whether as yet seen or not"),[3] and the later much-celebrated saying of John Robinson that "the Lord has more truth and light yet to break forth out of his holy word."[4] In a recovery of interest in the theme of covenant among British Baptists in our own time, a good deal of stress has been laid on the openness to the unknown that is implied by the metaphor of "walking together." The image is a dynamic one, of pilgrimage and process, and its use by some modern Baptists has been influenced by "theologies of hope" which have stressed that God's promise opens up a future with a quality of newness which constantly challenges the institutions of the present with the unexpected.[5] The openness of "walking together" on the way of trust in covenant has thus also been contrasted with the more closed boundaries of a confession of faith. So the concept of covenant has been appealed to in our day not only as a means of understanding the nature of the local congregation, but also in support of

---

[2] See the account by Henry Ainsworth, *The communion of saincts* (Amsterdam: 1615) 340.

[3] F. Johnson, *An inquirie and answer of T. White* (1606) 35. This, however, is a negative reference to discerning evil ways. Ainsworth's account (previous note) is more positive, referring to "paths of God as he shall teach them."

[4] From notes of Edward Winslow on John Robinson's parting speech to those leaving his Leyden congregation to sail on the *Mayflower* in 1620.

[5] See, e.g., Richard Kidd, "The Documents of Covenant Love" in Paul S. Fiddes et al., *Bound to Love* (London: Baptist Union, 1985) 43-44; Brian Haymes, "Covenant and the Church's Mission," ibid., 66-72; Richard Kidd, ed., *Something to Declare: A study of the Declaration of Principle Jointly Written by the Principals of the Four English Colleges in Membership with the Baptist Union of Great Britain* (Oxford: Whitley Publications, 1996) 12-16, 24-25, 31-32; Paul Ballard, "Baptists and Covenanting" in *Baptist Quarterly* (*BQ*) 24/8 (1972): 377-78.

the risks of ecumenical partnership, as a theological basis for association between churches, and as a way of conceiving identity as a union of churches on a national level.

All this may seem a great distance from Gainsborough. If the seed is present in the phrase "to be made known," it must be confessed that the search for future guidance in that turbulent period often led to the growth of dissension rather than mutual trust. The two parts of the original covenanting group were to be alienated from each other on the issue of believer's baptism, and John Smyth's congregation was to split over the issue of whether, having adopted believer's baptism, it should apply to join the Mennonites. The congregation led by Francis Johnson, already in Amsterdam when the Gainsborough-Scrooby groups arrived, was not only divided on its reaction to John Smyth's self-baptism, but was rent internally over the matter of the interpretation of Matthew 18:17 regarding church discipline. From the perspective of the present day, however, it may be a source of encouragement that both paedobaptists and believer-Baptists share a common story in the covenant of Gainsborough. It is as we are willing to discern obedience to the ways of the Lord in the two somewhat different paths taken thereafter by Congregationalists and Baptists that we may learn to "walk together" in the wider ecumenical context of the present day.

These opening remarks should already have made clear that this essay is not intended to be limited to a strictly historical study. The place of covenant in the thought of English radical Puritans and Separatists in the late sixteenth and early seventeenth century has already been considered in a number of modern studies;[6] a pioneering work in this area was *The English Separatist Tradition* by B. R. White,[7] in whose honor this essay is written, and notable further works were published by two of his doctoral pupils at Oxford, R. T. Kendall[8] and Stephen Brachlow.[9] White's thesis that Separatist theologies of covenant were central to John Smyth's

---

[6]See Perry Miller, *The New England Mind* (New York: Norton Press, 1939); David Zaret, *Heavenly Contract: Ideology and Organization in Pre-Revolutionary Puritanism* (Chicago: University of Chicago Press, 1985) 106.

[7]B. R. White, *The English Separatist Tradition. From the Marian Martyrs to the Pilgrim Fathers* (London: Oxford University Press, 1971).

[8]R. T. Kendall, *Calvin and English Calvinism to 1649* (Oxford: Oxford University Press, 1979).

[9]Stephen Brachlow, *The Communion of Saints: Radical Puritan and Separatist Ecclesiology 1570–1625* (Oxford: Oxford University Press, 1988).

thought has been subject to some criticism,[10] but I believe that my present essay will offer support for his account. However, I am concerned not only with the origins of the covenant tradition among Baptists in their early days, but with its development in the next two centuries, its widespread demise in the nineteenth century, and its resurgence among us in the last two decades. Nor will these be simply historical reflections; instead, I hope to show that a renewed theology of covenant will be fruitful for several concerns that face Baptists in the context of the "interchurch process" and the secular culture of today, and especially through the tendency of covenant towards openness to others and the whole of creation.

Indeed, one of the attractions of the concept of covenant for early Baptists was that it provided a larger sense of identity to those who had separated from the national church; in answer to those who accused them of losing continuity with the Catholic (i.e. universal) church, it enabled them to claim a continuity with the whole covenant people of God throughout the ages. This is the spirit of the covenant of New Road Baptist Church, Oxford, made in 1780 when it reformed a church life which was already more than a century old, daring to call itself a "Protestant Catholic Church."[11] It is also, I believe, the spirit of my predecessor and friend, Dr. White, to whom I am deeply indebted for his witness to the Catholicity which rightly belongs to Baptists as a part of the "Great Church" of Jesus Christ.

1. The Meaning of "Covenant"

When Stephen Brachlow at North American Baptist Seminary refers to the "rich texture of Puritan covenant theology,"[12] he has in mind a complex relationship between unconditional and conditional understandings of the covenant relationship between God and human beings. He rightly protests against a too simple polarization, as if it were only the *most* radical of Puritans who took a conditional view of the covenant, insisting that it would be invalid unless the conditions of ethical obedience to God's laws were fulfilled, especially in the area of church discipline.

---

[10]See James R. Coggins, "The Theological Positions of John Smyth," *BQ* 30/6 (1984): 247-59.

[11]Printed in W. Stevens and W. W. Bottoms, *The Baptist of New Road, Oxford* (Oxford: Alden Press, 1948) 25.

[12]Brachlow, *Communion of Saints*, 34.

This was certainly the view of Separatists such as Robert Browne, Henry Barrowe, and Francis Johnson, and was later the view of Baptists such as John Smyth and Thomas Helwys. For them, therefore, the covenant relationship between God and the national English Church was broken and void. However, Brachlow observes that radical Puritans who remained within the establishment could take a conditional view when it suited their argument in urging internal reforms within the church. William Perkins, for example, could define covenant as "[God's] contract with man concerning the obtaining of life eternal, upon a certain condition."[13] But Puritans such as Perkins could equally lay stress upon the unconditional aspect of the covenant when opposing separation from the established church, and especially when seeking to counter the case for believer's baptism. Separatists such as Johnson could also appeal to the unconditional nature of the covenant when opposing the adoption of believer's baptism by fellow Separatists, arguing that infant baptism was analogous to the everlasting covenant of grace made with Abraham "*and his seed for ever.*"[14]

Here Brachlow ventures to take issue with B. R. White, who had suggested that the conditional view of the covenant among Separatists was a departure from their Calvinistic Puritan tradition. Brachlow notes that the ambiguity between conditional and unconditional aspects was already present in Puritan thought, and that this mirrors the tensions within the Old Testament itself in its account of covenant, containing as it does both unconditional forms (notably the covenants with David and Abraham) and conditional ones (especially the covenant made through Moses).[15] We shall return to this issue when considering the relation between covenant and salvation, but for the moment we need to put it in a wider context of meaning. We can observe at least four threads of significance of the term "covenant" within the cloth of English Puritan and Separatist theology. Failure to identify these will undoubtedly lead to confusion in any discussion, as will failure to notice where they are woven together in a harmonious pattern or even into a single multiple-stranded thread.

---

[13]William Perkins, *A Golden Chaine* (Cambridge, 1591) 31, as quoted in Brachlow, *Communion of Saints*, 33.

[14]Francis Johnson, *A Brief Treatise against Two Errours of the Anabaptists* (Amsterdam, 1609) 17. On this issue, see Stephen Brachlow, "Puritan Theology and General Baptist Origins," *BQ* 31/4 (1985): 187-89.

[15]Brachlow, *Communion Of Saints,* 4-13, 34-40.

In the first place, "covenant" refers to an eternal "covenant of grace" which God has made with human beings and angels for their salvation in Jesus Christ. John Calvin was influential in developing this idea, which for him included the restriction of the covenant to the elect.[16] Again, from Calvin comes the belief that there is only one eternal covenant, but that it takes a different form of application or dispensation in the two eras of the Old Testament and the New Testament. Under either testament the covenant is made through Christ as mediator, but under the old Christ is present in shadowy types, whereas he is fully manifested in the new.[17] So John Smyth began his discourse on *Principles and Inferences concerning the Visible Church* with the definition:

> Remember that there be alwaies a difference put betwixt the covenant of grace; and the manner of dispensing it, which is twofold: the form of administring the covenant before the death of Christ, which is called the old testament; and the forme of administring the covenant since the death of Christ which is called the new Testament or the kingdome of heaven.[18]

Smyth goes on immediately to say that his treatise on the nature of the church which follows was actually concerned with the "dispensing of the covenant" since the death of Christ, a point we shall return to in a moment.

Second, the divine covenant could refer to a transaction between the Persons of the triune God, in which the Son is envisaged as consenting to the will of the Father to undertake the work of the salvation of the elect. While Calvin depicted the atonement in Christ as a transaction in which the Son satisfied the justice of the Father, he only hinted that this might be regarded as a *covenant* relationship between the two persons. This idea was fully developed by seventeenth-century Calvinist theologians, and was embodied in the Westminister Confession. Thus, while the Particular Baptist "London Confession" of 1644 referred only to "the blood of the everlasting covenant," the Second London Confession of 1677/89 specified the eternal covenant as being "a transaction between

---

[16]E.g., Calvin, *Institutes of the Christian Religion*, trans. H. Beveridge, (London: James Clarke, 1949) vol. 1, 2.vi, 293-98; vol. 2, 3.xxi, 208-11.

[17]Calvin, *Institutes*, vol. I, 2.x, 85, 391-96; cf. John Gill, *Complete Body of Doctrinal and Practical Divinity* (1770). *A New Edition in Two Volumes* (repr.: Grand Rapids MI: Baker Book House, 1978; = London: 1795/1839) vol. 1, bk. 2, 308.

[18]John Smyth, *Principles and Inferences concerning the Visible Church* (1607); printed in W. T. Whitley ed., *The Works of John Smyth*, vol. 1 (Cambridge: Cambridge University Press, 1915) 250.

the Father and the Son about the Redemption of the Elect."[19] In his treatise on the Covenant, *The Display of Glorious Grace* (1698), the Baptist pastor Benjamin Keach regarded the "federal" agreement between the Father and the Son[20] as the primary meaning of the covenant of grace. In the "Holy Covenant" between the Father and the Son, "Jesus Christ struck hands with God the Father, in behalfe of all God's Elect."[21] So Keach agreed with those theologians who maintained that:

> Christ is the covenant primarily . . . with Christ the covenant was made as with the chief Party; with Believers it was made in subordination to him; with him it was made at first Hand, with us at second Hand.[22]

In the later higher Calvinism of John Gill, the covenant between the Father, Son, and Spirit has become virtually the *only* meaning of the covenant of grace. The elect participate in the benefits of this transaction, but it is not *made with* them even in the secondary way envisaged by Keach, since Gill found no mutuality of conditions or reciprocal freedom in the relationship between God and creatures.[23] Instead, Gill portrayed a scene in the heavenly council in which the covenant is made, which—though colorful—holds just a touch of bathos (and at least a passing resemblance to a Baptist church meeting!):

> In the eternal council [Jehovah] moved it, and proposed it to his Son, as the most advisable step that could be taken to bring about the designed salvation, who readily agreed to it, and said, *Lo, I come to do thy will, O God*, Heb.x.7, from Psalm x1.7,8; and the Holy Spirit expressed his approbation of him to be the fittest person to be the Saviour, by joining with the Father in the mission of him. . . . The pleasure and satisfaction the three divine persons had in this affair, thus advised to, consulted, and approved of, is most clearly to be seen and observed at our Lord's baptism.[24]

Third, the term "covenant" could refer to an agreement God makes corporately with his Church, or with particular churches. For instance, a radical Puritan who remained in the established church, Thomas Cartwright asserted against the Separatists that God's covenant with the

---

[19] In William Lumpkin, ed., *Baptist Confessions of Faith* (Valley Forge PA: Judson Press, 1959) 260.
[20] Benjamin Keach, *The Display of Glorious Grace, or, The Covenant of Peace Opened. In Fourteen Sermons* (London, 1698) 285.
[21] Ibid., 243.
[22] Ibid., 294, quoting "a worthy writer."
[23] Gill, *Body of . . . Divinity*, vol. 1, 2, 309.
[24] Ibid., 305.

Church of England remained unbroken, despite disobedience over matters of church order: "The Lord is in covenant; this he does to our assembly in England, therefore they are the Lord's confederates."[25]

When portraying the covenant bond between God and his people as organized into the form of a society or institution (the "church estate"), writers tended to appeal to the covenant formula of God with Israel—"I will be their God and they shall be my people"—and its forms in the New Testament referring to the church.[26] At first this may seem identical with the first meaning, the covenant of grace with the elect, but there are subtle differences in the ways the idea of the covenant was handled. For instance, Calvin could envisage God's making a "general covenant" with Israel as a nation, while bestowing on the elect only the "Spirit of regeneration, by whose power they persevere in the covenant even until the end."[27] He then drew the parallel with the church of Christ as a way of explaining how some *seem* to be in covenant relationship with God and yet fail to persevere. Again, and rather differently, some who thought that the covenant bond between God and his elect stood unquestionably firm could still debate the question as to whether it had come to an end with a particular church.

Of course, this complicates the issue as to whether the "covenant" was unconditional or conditional upon obedience; what covenant is in mind? In his answering the question as to how a church "must be planted and gathered" under the lordship of Christ, Robert Browne clearly set out a conditional view of the covenant bond, with two sides to it:

> (36) First, by a couenant and condicion, made on Gods behalfe. Secondlie by a couenant and condicion made on our behalfe. . . . The couenant on Gods behalf is his agreement or partaking of condicions with us that if we keepe his lawes, not forsaking his gouernment, hee will take us for his people, & blesse us accordingly. . . . (38) What is the covenant or condicion on our behalfe? We must offer and geve up our selues to be of the church and people of God.[28]

---

[25]Cit: Brachlow, *Communion of Saints*, 47.
[26]Second Cor. 6:16-18, Heb. 8.10, quoted by John Smyth, *Paralleles, Censures, Observations* (1609) in *Works* 2:386-87.
[27]Calvin, *Institutes*, vol. 2, 3.21, 210-11.
[28]Robert Browne, *A Booke Which Sheweth the Life and Manners of All True Christians* (Middleburgh, 1582); repr. in *The Writings of Robert Harrison and Robert Browne*, ed. A. Peel and L. Carson (London, 1953) 254-56.

But this discussion is not explicitly related to the eternal covenant of grace in Christ, so we do not know whether Browne thought that this was conditional as well; rather Browne was immediately concerned with the nature of the local congregation as being under the direct *government* of Christ, and obliged to keep his laws. If we were to attempt to systematize these two uses of covenant, we might envisage the first as God's agreement with the invisible church of the elect, and the third as God's partnership with a particular, visible church, whether local or national.

But there are dangers in being *too* tidy. Keach and Gill referred to those who try to distinguish between a "covenant of redemption" and a "covenant of grace," the first being the covenant in which Christ achieved peace with God in eternity, and the second which was "made with the elect, or believers, in time."[29] Both Keach and Gill protested with some justice that there can be only one gracious covenant of God. Perhaps it is better to see the Puritan, Separatist, and (later) Baptist theologians as registering an ambiguity, or mysterious area, when the eternal decree of God actually takes form in time and space, and to this recognition of mystery I intend to return.

The fourth sense of covenant has already been implied in our consideration of Browne's account. That is, "covenant" can refer to the agreement undertaken and signed by church members when a particular local church was founded, and subsequently by new members upon their entering it. It seems that the early Separatist churches associated with Browne, Barrowe, Johnson, and Smyth were constituted through such a covenanting, and Smyth defined a church by this way of gathering it: "A visible communion of Saincts is of two, three or more Saincts joyned together by covenant with God & themselves. . . . "[30] That he envisaged a literal act of covenant-making is clear from his assertion that

> The outward part of the true forme of the true visible church is a vowe, promise, oath, or covenant betwixt God and the Saints. . . . This covenant hath 2 parts. 1. Respecting God and the faithful. 2. Respecting the faithful mutually.[31]

---

[29]Keach, *Display of Glorious Grace*, 212; Gill, *Body of . . . Divinity*, vol. 1, bk. 2, 311.
[30]Smyth, *Principle and Inferences*, in *Works*, 252.
[31]Ibid., 254.

Typical phrases in such covenants express the twofold dimension of a contract made by the members both "vertically" with God and "horizontally" with each other: members promise to "give themselves up to God" *and,* likewise, to "give themselves up to each other"; to "walk in the ways of the Lord" *and* to "to walk together"; to obey the "rules of Christ" *and* to "watch over each other." These covenants were common among the Congregationalist descendants of the Separatists from the early decades of the seventeenth century onwards, and Geoffrey Nuttall well expresses the advantages of what was a physical as well as a spiritual act:

> The drawing up of a covenant and the committing of it to writing added to its solemnity; while the appending of the signatures (or marks) of those who entered into it both underlined its binding character and satisfied their self-consciousness as individuals.[32]

Covenant-making like this appeared rather rarely after Smyth among churches that required believer's baptism for membership,[33] until the last years of the seventeenth century, when the publication of their church covenants by both Benjamin and Elias Keach (father and son) seem to have exercised a considerable influence on Baptist practice. These covenants from Horsley Down and London respectively (both published in 1697) were often copied or modified, and the popularity of making church covenants among both General and Particular Baptists increased to the extent that when the church at Downton, Wiltshire, was reestablished in 1793, it assumed that the making of a covenant was "the usage of all organized Churches of the faith of Jesus Christ";[34] it employed Keach's model. John Gill asserted that baptism in itself did not make someone a member of a church, but only "mutual consent and agreement, in their covenant and consideration with each other."[35]

It was probably, in fact, the adoption of believer's baptism as the moment of entry into the local church that diminished the usage of a written covenant among Baptists for a period in the seventeenth century. The part of John Smyth's Amsterdam congregation that had returned to London in 1611/1612 with Thomas Helwys as their pastor certainly re-

---

[32] Geoffrey Nuttall, *Visible Saints: The Congregational Way 1640–1660* (Oxford: Basil Blackwell, 1957) 78.

[33] Those who accepted both infant and believer's baptism often seem to have had covenants, e.g., the church at Hitchin.

[34] See the unsigned article "Church Covenants," *BQ* 7/5 (1935): 231.

[35] Gill, *Body of . . . Divinity,* vol. 2, bk. 4, 565-67.

placed entry to membership by covenant promises by entry through baptism. Among Particular Baptists in London, Hanserd Knollys in 1645 refuted the charge that his and other independent churches required potential members to make a covenant. Knollys was not only himself opposed to this practice for having no foundation in Scripture, but insisted that none of the churches he knew in London that practiced the baptism of believers "make any particular covenant with Members upon admittance."[36]

In accord with this, the *London Confession* of 1644—of which Knollys was one of the signatories—made no mention of gathering a church through a covenant, nor was there any such explicit reference in any of the seventeenth-century Baptist Confessions of Faith, Particular or General. However, the definition of a church in the 1644 Confession echoed the same covenant ideas that had been expressed in Separatist church covenant-making, following quite closely in wording the *True Confession* of 1596, which had been issued by Johnson's church. The visible church was defined as

> a company of visible Saints, called & separated from the world . . . being baptized into that faith, and joyned to the Lord, and each other, by mutuall agreement, in the practical injoynment of the Ordinances, commanded by Christ their head and King.[37]

There was typical covenant thought in the language of being joined to the Lord and each other "by mutual agreement," as in the next article which spoke of being under the direct government of Christ, and being given "his promises, and . . . the signes of his Covenant." This is a *concept* of a local covenant, entered by mutual consent and carrying obligations between members, which goes beyond the general theological idea of a covenant between God and his church (the third meaning I have distinguished above). The language of "walking together" also regularly appeared in early Baptist confessions,[38] including the *Second London Confession* of 1677/1689, which echoed the wording of covenant promises when it stated that members of the church "do willingly consent

---

[36]Hanserd Knollys, *A Moderate Answer unto Dr. Bastwick's Book; Called, Independency Not Gods Ordinance* (London, 1645) 13-14.
[37]Art. XXXIII, in Lumpkin, *Baptist Confessions*, 165.
[38]E.g., *Faith and Practice of Thirty Congregations* (1651), art. 52 in Lumpkin, *Baptist Confessions*, 183; *The Midland Association Confession* (1655), art. 15, in Lumpkin, 199; *The Somerset Confession* (1656), art. XXIV, in Lumpkin, 209.

to walk together according to the appointment of Christ, giving up themselves, to the Lord & one to another."[39]

Therefore, for most of the seventeenth century Baptists clearly thought of the gathering of the local church in covenant terms, even if they did not have the "outward form." As John Fawcett was to put it at the end of the next century,

> it is the custom in many of our churches to express this [covenant or mutual compact] in writing . . . though this circumstance cannot be thought essentially necessary to the constitution of a church.[40]

2. The Relation between the Eternal and the Local Covenant

Having picked out four separate threads of the Puritan-Separatist tapestry of covenant thought, we can now see more clearly how they are woven together. It is no accident of words that the very same term "covenant" is used for the mutual agreement of church members and the eternal decree of God, that is both for the local and eternal covenant. Some modern writers seem to assume that it *is* merely coincidental,[41] and James Coggins, a Canadian Mennonite Brethren editor, argues explicitly that the covenant ecclesiology of John Smyth "should not be confused with Calvinist covenant theology."[42] He considers that the difference between the idea of an eternal covenant of God with the elect and a "covenant among individual men and women" is too great for them to be brought together. Here he takes issue with B. R. White, who gave Smyth credit for originality in fusing the two together, maintaining that "it seems that for him, in the covenant promise of the local congregation the eternal covenant of grace became contemporary and man's acceptance of it was actualized in history."[43]

White further points out that the relation between the local covenant bond and the eternal covenant offered to all humankind will be analogous

---

[39]Chap. XXVI, in Lumpkin, 286.
[40]John Fawcett, *The Constitution and Order of a Gospel Church Considered* (Halifax, 1797) 12.
[41]See Roger Hayden, "The Particular Baptist Confession 1689 and Baptists Today," *BQ* 32/8 (1988): 413: "in the local church, covenant *signified something different*" (from the Covenant of Grace).
[42]Coggins, "Theological Positions of John Smyth," 249.
[43]White, *English Separatist Tradition*, 128.

to the relation between a particular local congregation and "the invisible company of all God's elect." This means, I suggest, that a Baptist ecclesiology built on the concept of covenant must take a strong view of the Church Universal. The Universal Church cannot be just an adding together of many local communities—as Baptists have sometimes depicted it; rather, there is a universal reality which *preexists* any local manifestation of it, as God's eternal covenant with humankind preexists the local covenant bond. Covenant and Catholicity belong together.

A dislocation between the covenant of the local church and the eternal covenant of grace is encouraged by the secular use of "covenant" to mean nothing more than a voluntary society, and I intend to discuss this further below. Thus, Baptist Unions in Europe which actually use the biblical word for "covenant" in their titles—for example, *Förbundet* in Sweden and *Bund* in Germany—have had little or no theological reflection on the relevance of covenant theology to fellowship at Union level. Since the word "covenant" is used for many secular organizations, it has become a dead metaphor. I suggest that the theological "depth" of the concept of covenant needs to be recovered, that is its rooting in the life and mission of the triune God, and that the witness of Separatists and early Baptists can prompt us to do this.

If we refer to the four meanings of covenant I have isolated above, then it becomes clear that Robert Browne brought the third and fourth together. God's making of covenant with his church is simultaneous with the making of covenant *by* the church. Local covenant-making is not merely a human enterprise, a promise by believers to be faithful; it is also God's gracious taking of the church "to be his people," and God's "promise to be our God and Saviour."[44] Thus the ambivalence between the divine and the human making of covenant which White finds original to Smyth was already present in Browne. It is indeed embedded in the Separatist (and later, Baptist) conviction that through covenant a local community is under the direct rule of Christ, and so has been given the "seals of the covenant"—that is, the power to elect its own ministry, to celebrate the sacraments of baptism and the Lord's Supper, and to administer discipline (the authority to "bind and loose").

Smyth, however, used expressions which drew the first meaning of "covenant" more clearly together with the third and fourth than in

---

[44]Browne, *A Booke which sheweth,* in *Writings,* 37-38, 254-56; cf. *A True and Short Declaration* (1583?), in *Writings,* 422-23.

Browne. As I have already noted, he evidently intended his treatise on the nature of the church to be a working out of the "ordinances of Christ for the dispensing of the covenant since his death," and this is the eternal covenant of grace "established by the blood of Christ." God's part in the "vowe, promise, oath or covenant" of the visible church is "to give Christ" and "with Christ al things els."[45] Through the covenant bond, "the Lord chose us to be his," and "by vertue of the covenant God made with us . . . God is our God & our Father, only in Chr[ist] & through him: & al the promises of God in Christ are yea and Amen."[46] When Coggins maintains that "Smyth hardly ever discussed covenant theology at all," he misses the significance of the Scripture references which Smyth attached to such statements as: "Unto whome the covenant & Christ is given, unto them al the promises are given"[47] or "God with them maketh his covenant, & they are his sonnes & daughters, & he is their Father."[48] Texts like 2 Corinthians 1:20, Galatians 3:14-16, and Hebrews 8:10 are exactly those which would be appealed to in any discussion of the eternal covenant of grace made through Christ as mediator. In sum, when the church makes its covenant promise it receives "the promise" of God"[49] and the covenant of grace was understood in Calvinist tradition precisely as God's promise to humankind: "We say the Church or two or three faithful people Separated from the world and joyned together in a true covenant, have both Christ, the covenant, & promises."

We notice the easy slipping from one sense of "covenant" to another; those who are joined in [church] covenant "*have* the covenant [of grace]." The way that these aspects of covenant are connected is not, of course, worked out systematically, and it remains tantalizing not only in Smyth, but in the later model covenant of Benjamin Keach at Horsley Down (1697). This began with the pledge

> to give up ourselves to the Lord, in a Church state according to the Apostolical Constitution that he may be our God, and we may be his People, through the Everlasting Covenant of his Free grace, in which alone we hope to be accepted by him, through his blessed Son Jesus Christ, whom we take to be our High Priest, to justify and sanctify us.[50]

---

[45]Smyth, *Principles and Inferences*, in *Works* 1:254.
[46]Smyth, *Paralleles,* in *Works* 2:387.
[47]Ibid., 2:389.
[48]Ibid., 2:386.
[49]Ibid., 2:403.
[50]Keach, *The Glory of a True Church, and Its Discipline display'd* (London, 1697) 71.

In this drama of the "solemn covenant of the church," the members were not just recalling that they *had been* included in God's eternal covenant, but also envisaged themselves as somehow entering it at that very moment. How is it possible to square this with Keach's (moderate) Calvinism? There is a clue in an extended quotation from Isaac Chauncey which Keach included in *The Display of Glorious Grace* to support his argument that the "covenant of redemption" was the same as the covenant of grace. "Church Covenants" are said to "add nothing to this Grand covenant," but as "an accomplishment of the promise" they are an occasion for the believer to "enter personally into this Covenant," "embracing" and "laying hold of it." On God's part the church covenant can be understood as "renewings of the same Covenant without changing the Covenant."[51] The author (quoted and warmly approved by Keach) thus placed the covenant of the local church in a line of succession of renewings of the one Covenant of grace with "Adam, Noah, Abraham, Isaac and Jacob etc." In another sermon in the collection, Keach found baptism and the Lord's Supper to be other places where the taking of the sinner into the Covenant of Grace was "renewed and confirmed" by the Spirit.[52]

Shortly, we shall consider the implication of this theology of covenant renewal for the nature of salvation, but we should note that the later high Calvinism of John Gill showed no interest in linking the "Covenant of grace" with the church covenant. Gill's locking up of God's covenant-making within the Persons of the Trinity resulted in a view of the local church covenant which was modeled thoroughly on a secular contract of mutual human obligations; "like all civil societies" the union between members was made by "voluntary consent and agreement" in which they "propose themselves to a church."[53] Gill notably refrained from using the traditional phrase "give themselves up to God" in this discussion, urging only that members "give themselves up to the church."

By contrast, Smyth and Keach, at two ends of a century, offered a dynamic account of participation in God's covenant of grace thorough mutual covenant-making. There is also the theological potential here for developing a link with the second meaning of covenant explored above—the covenant within the very life of God—and extending it beyond the

---

[51] Keach, *Display of Glorious Grace*, 211.
[52] Ibid., 285.
[53] Gill, *Body of . . . Divinity*, vol. 2, bk. 4, 566-67.

decree of atonement. That is, we might conceive of the local fellowship of believers as participating within the inner communion of the triune God. In our time this kind of development of the theme of covenant has been made by the theologian Karl Barth, who stood in the tradition of John Calvin and yet made the doctrine of electing grace more dynamic than in the thought of the great Reformer.

In the first place, Barth did not envisage the eternal covenant decision of God as an absolute decree, but as identical with the actual working of God's word in history;[54] therefore, God's sovereign election happens *here and now,* in interaction with those who hear the word, which is nothing less than "the Person of God speaking." This means that God's election is understood as a grace that enables the human response of "yes" to God's "yes" to us, rather than as a static "double decree" in which some are destined for salvation and others for damnation. In the second place, Barth envisaged a "double covenant" made by God the Father; as the Father makes covenant of love eternally with the Son, so he intends that there should be a covenant in history with created sons and daughters. In one movement of grace, God elects both the divine son and human children as covenant partners.[55] We know this because the Person of the eternal Son is inseparable from the human person of Jesus of Nazareth. So our covenant with God, freely given by him in grace, is inseparable from the covenant made within God's own communion of life in which God freely determines to be God.

This is the kind of theological depth to the concept of covenant that should be particularly congenial to the Baptist tradition of a church gathered by covenant. It has, indeed, recently been employed in some British Baptist writing[56] and been adduced in aid of resisting any reduction of a covenant bond to a mere "strategic alliance," a union only for the sake of performing certain tasks, or making economies, or providing

---

[54] Karl Barth, *Church Dogmatics*, ed. Geoffrey W. Bromiley and Thomas F. Torrance (Edinburgh: T. & T. Clark, 1936–1977) II/2.175-94.

[55] Ibid., II/2.161-65.

[56] See Paul S. Fiddes, "Church, Trinity and Covenant: an Ecclesiology of Participation," in E. Brandt, ed., *Gemeinschaft am Evangelium. Festschrift für Wiard Popkes* (Leipzig: Evangelisches Verlagsaustalt, 1996) 37-55; Hazel Sherman, "Baptized in the Name of the Father, the Son, and the Holy Spirit," in Paul S. Fiddes ed., *Reflections on the Water* (Oxford/Macon GA: Regent's Park College/Smyth & Helwys Publishing, 1996) 110-14; *Transforming Superintendency. The Report of the General Superintendency Review Group presented to the Baptist Union of Great Britain Council* (London: Baptist Union, 1996) 9-13.

resources.[57] It draws attention to the "ontological" element in covenant, the dimension of sheer being which underlies any doing. Thus our mission to the world shares in the mission of the Father who eternally "sends forth" the Son.

3. The Covenant and Salvation

Church covenant-making, we have observed, uses at least the *language* of conditionality. That God's covenant might be conditional on human obedience is obviously a modification of Calvin's thought, where God's covenant with his elect must be one of unconditional grace, and thus based on a "limited" atonement which includes only the elect. But a powerful motivation for a conditional approach to covenant thinking was the issue of assurance that haunted the Puritan mind, prone to despair in the face of a predestinarian God; how could a believer be sure that he or she was indeed one of the elect and part of God's covenant? Calvin himself had appealed simply to the existence of faith as assurance enough, but English Puritan theology followed the trend that sought to find more visible evidence of election, that is in the living of a life that was obedient to the commandments of God recorded in the Scriptures.[58]

This stress on personal obedience, often called "experimental Calvinism," converged with an interpretation of the second commandment that identified idolatry with any humanly devised worship and ministry, and with a portrayal of Christ as the new Moses, giving rules for the government of his church. As the earliest systematic theologian of Puritanism, Dudley Fenner, expressed it, faithful obedience to the commandments of Christ about the ordering of his church brought God's people "into a covenant of life and blessedness."[59] Into this constellation of ideas the Separatist added one further belief: the covenant of God with the church meant that each local congregation was under the direct rule of the covenant-mediator, Christ, without any external ecclesiastical authority. The result of this conjunction of beliefs and anxieties was that discipline of members and true church order was regarded as a mark of salvation, assuring the believer of election within the covenant.

---

[57] See R. Kidd, ed., *On the Way of Trust* (Oxford: Whitley Publications, 1997) 22-27.

[58] This trend was notably promoted by Theodore Beza. R. T. Kendall, in his *Calvin and English Calvinism*, considers whether the form it took in Puritan England was in accord with Calvin's own theology.

[59] Fenner, *A Briefe Treatise upon the First Table of the Lawe* (Middelburg, 1587) D.1.; cit: Brachlow, *Communion of Saints*, 36.

By contrast, those who wanted to stress the unconditional nature of the covenant developed a scheme of biblical history in which a "covenant of works" had been replaced by the "covenant of grace."[60] The original covenant of works made with Adam and Moses, they asserted, was indeed conditional, but because it had been broken, it had been replaced by a new unconditional covenant of grace, first made with Abraham. This sequence could be appealed to in the cause of maintaining that God's covenant with the national Church in England stood firm, while those who wanted to introduce a conditional aspect into God's covenant were accused of falling back into the old "covenant of works," and of trying to establish salvation by their works.

A conditional view of the covenant, dependent on human obedience for its continuance, was certainly conducive to emerging Arminianism, with its stress on human free will and the possibility of refusing the grace of God. It is not surprising to find these elements in John Smyth's later thought, and then in the ensuing General Baptist tradition. Strictly speaking, from a Calvinist—and a Particular Baptist—perspective, good church order was necessary for salvation only in the sense that having it demonstrated one's already existing election. But there were already signs of convergence between the two approaches in Baptist thinking of the seventeenth century, in the commonly held convictions that (a) the initiative of God's grace was necessary to get any human response started (though for Arminians it could be declined), and (b) that a visible response of faith was necessary to actualize the covenant relationship here and now. With regard to the first, the General Baptist *Orthodox Creed* of 1679 affirmed that

> Justifying faith is a grace, or habit, wrought in the soul by the holy ghost, through preaching the word of God, whereby we are enable to believe . . . and wholly and only to rest upon Christ.[61]

With regard to the second aspect, we find the Particular Baptist theologian Benjamin Keach arguing that while a covenant agreement existed between God and the elect by eternal decree, it is only when by the Spirit we "choose Jesus Christ as the only Object of our Affection"

---

[60]First propounded by the Heidelberg Calvinist theologians, Ursinus, Olevianus, and Zanchius.

[61]Art. XXIII, in Lumpkin, *Baptist Confessions*, 314.

that "we enter into an *actual* Covenant with God," and "the Reconciliation becomes mutual."[62]

I suggest that the very act of making or assenting to the church covenant constantly moved participants toward a *blend* of Calvinist insistence upon the enabling grace of God and Arminian affirmation of "choosing" Christ. The act surely reminded them of the initiative that God takes in making covenant, as well as requiring them to make their own personal response. The two sides of this mystery of divine grace and human freedom were also, of course, kept in balance by the act of believer's baptism. On the one hand, this was a "seal" of the covenant given to the church by God; on the other, the Separatist insistence on the assent of the congregation to "the covenant betwixt God and the Faithful made in baptisme"[63] led for Baptists to the unsuitability of infants for baptism since they were—in the words of John Smyth—"unable to enter into the New Testament by sealing back the covenant unto the Lord,& consenting unto the contract."[64]

There was then a trajectory already in place which Andrew Fuller adopted toward the end of the eighteenth century in his brand of "evangelical Calvinism," which liberated many Particular Baptist churches for an era of mission. A belief in limited atonement had not extinguished a concern for evangelism altogether, but it had certainly had a dampening effect. Now Fuller's theology provided a spark for the reignition of a passion for proclaiming the Gospel, by proposing that while only some people were elected to salvation, all people had the positive *duty* to turn to Christ in faith. While he provided a technical means of holding the two propositions together by appealing to Jonathan Edwards's distinction between a general atonement and a limited redemption, this abstract theology was surely not what provided the motivation for mission. Rather, people were gripped by the twin truths that God's grace alone *enabled* response, and that human beings were *obliged* to make that response. The word "duty" picked up all the echoes of a conditional covenant, and it is not surprising that Fuller had to devote a section in his book, *A Gospel Worthy of All Acceptation*, to refuting the charge that duty belonged to a "covenant of works," which had nothing to do with salvation.[65]

---

[62] Keach, *Display of Glorious Grace*, 282.
[63] Smyth, *The Character of the Beast* (1609), in *Works* 2:645.
[64] Ibid.
[65] Andrew Fuller, *The Gospel Worthy of All Acceptation*, 2nd ed. (London, 1801) 112-

But the practice of church covenant-making did not only preserve the mystery of grace and freedom. I suggest that it also imprinted on Baptist minds the sense that salvation was not merely a point, but a process or a story. In the terms used by Benjamin Keach, the eternal covenant was "actualized" when someone "embraced" or "laid hold" of Christ ("when God gives Christ to a Sinner, the whole Covenant is performed to that Person"),[66] and this actualizing of the covenant in conversion was then "renewed" in the event of church covenant-making, as it was also in the acts of baptism and the Lord's Supper. This story of eternal purpose, temporal actualization, and renewal is the story of a "Pilgrim's Progress" in John Bunyan's allegory, the Pilgrim enters the earthly journey of faith through the narrow gate of conversion, but it is only later by a wayside cross that "his burden loosed from off his shoulders and fell from off his back."[67] This reflects the typical Calvinist stage of inner assurance, but it also fits with the Baptists' placing of assurance in the context of covenant-making and baptism.

Embedded in a covenant theology is, therefore, a theology of renewal of salvation, which is, of course, also a strong Old Testament (and especially Deuteronomic) concept. Perhaps this is why in our modern age the movement of charismatic renewal, with its emphasis upon further stages of filling with the Holy Spirit beyond conversion, has had such a powerful influence on Baptist life in England. The idea that salvation is a story or journey should also help Baptists to enter ecumenical conversations in which questions of salvation, faith, and sacraments are at issue; for instance, the recent report of a working party of *Churches Together in England* on the nature of baptism, written with strong Baptist representation, found common ground in conceiving Christian initiation as a process, within which baptism has a place.[68]

4. The Covenant and Voluntary Societies

The mutual and conditional nature of covenant has often been underlined in Baptist history by comparing it with various kinds of contracts in society which require free consent, and the covenanted community has,

---

14.

[66] Keach, *Display of Glorious Grace*, 296.

[67] John Bunyan, *The Pilgrim's Progress*, ed. R. Sharrock (Harmondsworth: Penguin Books, 1965) 70.

[68] *Baptism and Church Membership with Particular Reference to Local Ecumenical Partnerships* (London: Churches Together in England, 1997) 13, 17-19, 29.

likewise, often been designated as a "voluntary society." The most influential definition of the church as a voluntary society was offered by John Locke, in the context of his view of human society as bound by a voluntary "social contract" or a series of interlocking contracts. In his *Letter on Toleration* (1689), he wrote that

> [A Church] is a free and voluntary Society . . . no Man is bound by nature to any particular Church or Sect, but he joins himself voluntarily to that Society in which he believes he has found that Profession and Worship which is truly acceptable to God.[69]

William Brackney, who has written extensively on voluntarism as a characteristic of Free Church life, believes that in offering this definition Locke was already "well immersed in the Nonconformist theory of the church as a voluntary society," and was "reflecting fourscore years of evolution of churchmanship and dissent."[70] Secular models for voluntary societies, Brackney points out, were available from 1550 onwards with the development of joint stock companies for trading, and from these emerged in 1649 the "New England Corporation," which existed solely for the religious purpose of mission among the North American Indian population. This lasted only for the period of the Protectorate, but the Nonconformist "New England Company" existed from 1660 to 1776 as a royal chartered corporation combining trade and evangelism.

It might then be argued that the covenant principle in the local church was essentially the principle of voluntarism, developed from both the mutualist aspects of the biblical covenant and secular models of contract. Not only the language of voluntary consent found from Browne onwards, but also explicit analogies drawn between covenant and voluntary societies, might be brought in support of this view. Smyth, for instance, compared the local church covenant with the kind of corporation referred to above: "As the charter of a corporation is from the King & al the offices have powre from the corporation, so the Church hath powre from Christ, & the Eldership from the church."[71]

---

[69] John Locke, *A Letter Concerning Toleration* (London, 1689) 10.
[70] William Brackney, *Voluntarism: The Dynamic Principle of the Free Church* (Wolfville NS: Acadia University, 1992) 16. In his *Christian Voluntarism: Theology and Praxis* (Grand Rapids MI.: Eerdmans, 1997) 33-49, Brackney asserts that voluntarism itself is a gift of God and in no way diminishes the church's dependence upon God's sovereignty and grace.
[71] Smyth, *Paralleles*, in *Works* 2:391.

In the expanded version of Keach's *Baptist Catechism,* made by Benjamin Beddome (1752), the church was called "a voluntary society," to which was attached the Scripture reference 2 Corinthians 8:5, containing the phrase often employed in church covenants: "They gave themselves to the Lord and to us by the will of God."[72] We have already noted Gill's stressing that the union between church members is "like all civil societies, founded . . . by consent and covenant." In the nineteenth century, Joseph Angus wrote a prize essay on *The Voluntary System,* in which he quoted Locke's definition of a church with approval, urged the analogy of free trade, and described believers gathering together as "form[ing] a voluntary religious society for the double purpose of obtaining mutual instruction and comfort and of propagating their faith."[73]

But for all this, voluntarism can encompass only one dimension of relationships in the local church when they are conceived in *covenant* terms. Mysterious as it is, the link between the church covenant and the covenant of grace means that human consent is inseparable from God's initiative in making the covenant in the first place, and offering to remake it when it is broken. Thus Baptist confessions of faith have usually held together the voluntary "gathering" of the church with its being "gathered" or called together by Christ as the covenant-mediator. The *Second London Confession* (1677/89), for example, described believers as "consent[ing] to walk together *according to the appointment of Christ;*" churches, it affirmed, were "gathered by special grace . . . according to His mind."[74] The modern English statement, *The Baptist Doctrine of the Church* (1948), declared that "churches are gathered by the will of Christ and live by the indwelling of his Spirit. They do not have their origin, primarily, in human resolution."[75]

From a covenantal perspective, it is thus positively misleading to call a local church a "voluntary society." According to the covenant theology of the early Separatists, because the local church was under the direct rule of Christ, all members shared in that ministry of "kingship," and so had the right to exercise judgement by "watching over" the spiritual health of

---

[72] Benjamin Beddome, *A Scriptural Exegesis of the Baptist Catechism* (London, 1752) 162.

[73] Joseph Angus, *The Voluntary System* (London, 1839) 191. Later, however, in *The Christian Churches* (London, 1862), Angus called the Christian church a "theocracy."

[74] Arts. XXIX-XXXI, in Lumpkin, *Baptist Confessions,* 318-19.

[75] Repr. in Roger Hayden, *Baptist Union Documents* 1948–1977 (London: Baptist Union, 1980) 6.

each other and withdrawing from a church where the covenant was broken.[76] This rooting of freedom in the rule of Christ is quite different from Locke's principle of marketplace choice, in which a religious person joins with others for worship "in such a manner as they judge acceptable to [God] and effectual to the Salvation of their Souls."[77] Similarly, the freedom of a local church from external ecclesiastical government because it is under the rule of Christ, differs from Locke's notion that a church as a voluntary society has the freedom to make its own rules and prescribe its own membership qualifications.

It was essentially the latter view of self-government (also held by Angus)[78] to which Joseph Kinghorn appealed in the nineteenth century dispute over closed and open communion, maintaining that "if persons ask for admission into any voluntary society they must submit to its terms," in this case, believer's baptism as a qualification for coming to the Lord's Table.[79] Robert Hall's reply returned to earlier Separatist and Baptist principles, rooting the nature of consent in "the fundamental laws of Christ's kingdom"; he argued that "there is little or no analogy" between a church and a "voluntary society" in the matter of membership, since "human societies originate solely in the private views and inclinations of those who compose them" whereas "the church is a society instituted by Heaven."[80]

Although Kinghorn believed that the entrance qualification for communion derived from the "founder" of the society, Christ, he still stood under Hall's censure of envisaging the church as a voluntary society "organized with a specific view to the propagation of some particular truth." For Hall, all Christians are under the rule of Christ in the sense that they belong to the spiritual kingdom which is the Body of Christ, and so the Table should be open to them.

In what Hall is opposing we can see the heritage of Gill's separation of the local covenant from the eternal covenant of grace. Ironically, although this secularizing of the church covenant as a voluntary society was

---

[76] E.g., see Browne, "An Answere to Master Cartwright" (London: n.p; n.d.) in *Writings*, 465-66.
[77] Locke, *Toleration*, 9.
[78] Angus, *Voluntary System*, 191.
[79] Joseph Kinghorn, *Baptism, a Term of Communion at the Lord's Supper* (Norwich: Bacon, Kinnebrook, 1816) 61; cf. 81-82.
[80] Robert Hall, *A Reply to the Rev. Joseph Kinghorn*, in O. Gregory, ed., *The Works of Robert Hall*, vol 2, 2nd ed. (London, 1833) 473-75.

in the cause of preserving divine sovereignty, it could lead to a demise of the concept of covenant altogether, since it could then be simply *replaced* by voluntarism. In his study of the English Baptists in the nineteenth century, John Briggs at Westhill College, Birmingham, judges that the theology and practice of covenanting declined because the image of a community held in covenant seemed too self-enclosed and privatized in an age when churches were working together in mission agencies, associations, alliances for social reform, and interchurch movements for education and health.[81] Here he builds on the insight of W. R. Ward that "the Sunday School open to all rather than the covenanted meeting of baptized saints was the sign of the times . . . the kingdom of God seemed delivered over to associational principles."[82]

Ward thus discerns that there was an "empirical and pragmatic spirit embodied in the associations." However, I suggest that the covenant concept, when grounded *theologically*, is itself thoroughly open to the associating of churches together in the widest forms of cooperation. It is true that the voluntary principle of consenting to work together for a particular task was (and indeed remains) the key element in certain larger groupings in which Baptists participated from the seventeenth century onwards, and increasingly in the nineteenth century: examples are centralized funds such as the Particular Baptist Fund, Trusts such as those for theological education, and agencies such as the Baptist Missionary Society, the Bible Society, and the Sunday School Union.[83] But there is a danger in supposing that the relating of *churches* together in regional associations and in a national Union will *also* be driven by the voluntary principle. This was indeed the view of Angus,[84] who painted a picture of churches coming together under some common direction as a matter of "expediency" in order to "extend their usefulness," but the logic of Separatist and early Baptist thought seems to have been more similar to that of Robert Hall. That is, if a local church is under the direct rule of Christ as King, then it is necessarily drawn into fellowship with all those who are under Christ's rule, and so part of his Body. The *London Confession* of 1644

---

[81]J. H. Y. Briggs, *The English Baptists of the Nineteenth Century* (London: Baptist Historical Society, 1994) 15-20.

[82]W. R. Ward, "The Baptists and the Transformation of the Church, 1780–1830," *BQ* 25/4 (1973): 172.

[83]See William H. Brackney, *Christian Voluntarism in Britain and North America* (New York, 1995) 27-45.

[84]Angus, *Voluntary System*, 191-93.

depicted the associating of churches in the Body of Christ, and while it did not explicitly use the word "covenant," it followed the *True Confession* of 1596 in using the covenant language of "walking together":

> And although the particular Congregations be distinct and severall Bodies, every one a compact and knit Citie in it selfe; yet are they all to walk by one and the same Rule, and by all meanes convenient to have the counsell and help of one another in all needfull affaires of the Church, as members of one body in the common faith under Christ their onely head.[85]

The freedom of a local church from external ecclesiastical authority is, therefore, based neither in Enlightenment concepts of the freedom of the individual, nor in the self-regulation of a voluntary society, but in the Lordship of Christ. It follows that whether covenant is an exclusive or inclusive idea depends upon how the rule of Christ in the church and the world is to be understood. In the turmoil following the English Reformation, it was inevitable that Baptists understood the scope of Christ's rule to run in a fairly narrow way, but some recent English Baptist writing has taken up a wider vision of the rule of Christ in reviving the covenant concept; it has urged that if the local church meeting aims to find the mind of Christ for its life and mission, it should be equally anxious to discover how churches in assembly find his mind. For example, a recent report of the Baptist Union of Great Britain has proposed that British Baptists take a creative step beyond the explicit definitions of their predecessors by treating the Union itself as a covenant relationship.[86]

Associations and Unions of churches are thus not merely task-oriented, but means of exploring the purpose of God in his world. Further still, Baptist churches and Baptist associations should be eager to discover how assemblies of other denominations, gathering under the same rule, discern the mission of God as well as their place in that mission. It is apt that a number of Baptist churches in Wales (though not the Union itself) have been able to participate in the ecumenical *Covenanted Churches in Wales*; unlike a similar, but unsuccessful attempt at covenanting between denominations in England in the mid-1970s,[87] the Welsh Covenant avoided both the language of "organic union" and the setting of a date for

---

[85] Art. XLVII, in Lumpkin, *Baptist Confessions*, 168-69.
[86] *The Nature of the Assembly and the Council of the Baptist Union of Great Britain A report presented to the Council of the Baptist Union, 1994* (London: Baptist Union, 1994) 11-17.
[87] *Visible Unity: Ten Propositions* (London: The Churches' Unity Commission, 1976).

structural unity. Instead, it declared that "we do not yet know the form union will take" and echoed earlier covenant documents in expecting that "God will guide his Church into ways of truth and peace."[88] This openness in walking together has also been the spirit of the more recent "Inter-Church Process" or "Churches Together in Pilgrimage" in Great Britain as a whole, in which the Baptist Union of Great Britain is a partner.[89] The language of covenant was, however, strangely not used in the foundation document for these ecumenical instruments.

5. Covenants and Confessions

Considerable reference has already been made in this essay to confessions of faith, in which Baptists have sought in the past both to explain their beliefs to those outside their own fellowship and to provide a tool for teaching those inside it. Often a Church Book will contain both a confession and a form of covenant, adjacent to each other. The confession might be compiled by the minister of the church or, among Calvinistic Baptist churches, the Particular Baptist *Confession* of 1677/89 was frequently used or modified. When Benjamin Keach, for example, published the covenant of the church at Horsley Down, it was bound with a version of the 1689 *Confession*. Sometimes, but it seems not always, the potential member was asked to sign assent to a confession as well as to the covenant.[90]

Appeal has recently been made to this relationship between confession and covenant to propose the adoption of a modern statement of faith by Baptists where one does not exist (for example, in Britain). Some have urged that if we are to develop the concept of covenant as a basis for the association or union of churches together, then a confession of faith is needed as a basis for the covenant. It is said that the "cooperation" expressed by a covenant requires a "commitment to shared understanding of the essential Gospel, as expressed in the Confession."[91] But, as a

---

[88]Text of the Welsh Covenant in *Not Strangers but Pilgrims. The Next Steps for Churches Together in Pilgrimage* (London: British Council of Churches, 1989) 74-76. See further, Paul Ballard, "Baptists and Covenanting."

[89]See the "Swanwick Report," in *Not Strangers but Pilgrims*, 9-15.

[90]So at Alcester, e.g., as cited in Roger Hayden, "Particular Baptist Confession 1689," 414.

[91]Ibid., 415. The adoption of a Confession has also been urged by George Beasley-Murray, "Confessing Baptist Identity," in David Slater, ed., *A Perspective on Baptist Identity* (Kingsbridge: Mainstream, 1987).

notable English proponent of this view, Roger Hayden of Bristol, judges the past situation, "There was an ambiguity about the link between the confession of faith adopted by a church and its covenant document."[92] While the two might be adjacent, the one was not included in the other. Moreover, the difference in nature between them becomes especially clear when we consider the theological depth of covenant, which is more than an expression of human "cooperation" or mutual duties; it is nothing less than a participation in the eternal covenant of grace.

Covenant is about relationship and trust, about "walking together," which is in some mysterious way a part of the very journey of salvation. As we have seen, covenants predated confessions and were deeply bound up with the nature of the church as existing under the government of Christ. Although some have regretted that the "basis" of the Baptist Union of Great Britain and Ireland adopted in 1903 (revised 1938), was a simple three-point declaration rather than something like the 1689 Confession, others have recognized in it the character of a covenant.[93] The first clause, which affirms the final authority of Jesus Christ and the liberty of each local church to "interpret and administer his laws," precisely takes us back to the image of a church's agreeing to walk together under the rule of Christ. The next two clauses briefly set out the nature of this walking together by affirming believer's baptism and the necessity of world mission, and the three together follow the structure of the commission of the risen Lord in Matthew 28:18-20.

The creation of modern confessions of faith provides useful—and perhaps essential—tools for teaching and communicating our faith to others and ecumenical relationships. But if we are to learn from, and yet not be bound by our past, I suggest that a theological and practical distance be kept between confessions and covenants; confessions should be regarded as the *context* for covenant-making, but never *required* as the basis for "walking together." As argued by the authors of a recent study of the *Declaration of Principle*, "in the making of covenant, be it at Sinai, Calvary or in the present day, the text is always subordinate to the relationship."[94] In short, there is an openness that belongs to trust which covenant can encourage.

---

[92]Ibid., 414; cf. Hayden, "Baptist, Covenants and Confessions" in Paul S. Fiddes et al., *Bound to Love*, 26-28.
[93]See R. Kidd, ed., *Something to Declare*, 15-16, 24-25
[94]Ibid., 25.

Covenant was an idea that gripped the minds and imaginations of our predecessors in the early days of Baptist life. It belonged to the quest for assurance of salvation in an age of religious anxiety. It provided a sense of identity, claiming continuity with the whole covenant people of God in the universal Church. It gave expression to a spirit of renewal, with political and social implications as people looked for the remaking of a broken covenant between God and his Church in England. It also gave a sense of empowerment, for people in a covenant relationship with God under the direct rule of Christ were thereby liberated from ecclesiastical authority, free to call their own ministry and celebrate the gospel sacraments. Covenant aroused enthusiasm because it offered the possibilities of assurance, renewal, continuity, and power. The concept's popularity declined in the nineteenth century, because it could no longer be connected with these aspects; in an age of mission and interchurch ventures, it seemed only to denote a community closed in upon itself and upon a narrow definition of its membership.

But, as we have seen, the inner dynamic of covenant is precisely in the direction of openness, toward the goal expressed in the biblical account of the "everlasting covenant between God and every living creature of all flesh that is upon the earth" (Gen. 8:16). In our age, the making of covenant can accord with a culture which lays stress upon the virtues of openness to others and to the future. At the same time, covenant expresses a necessary closure, in commitment to God and in faithfulness to God's purposes.

The Child and the Church: A Baptist Perspective

W. M. S. West

I

On 5 September 1524, Conrad Grebel, leader of the Zurich radical reforming group, wrote to Thomas Müntzer, the German radical, indicating his group's intention on biblical grounds of moving from the practice of infant baptism to that of believer's baptism. In so doing, they recognized that the question of the child and the church needed to be confronted. Their answer was clear and simple:

> We hold that all children who have not yet come to the discernment of good and evil and have not yet eaten of the tree of knowledge, that they are surely saved by the suffering of Christ, the new Adam . . . but they are not yet grown up into the infirmity of our broken nature—unless indeed it can be proved that Christ did not suffer for children.[1]

What the Zurich Anabaptist group subsequently did about their children—apart from refusing to baptize them—is not clear, but we do know that on 16 January 1525, Balthasar Hubmaier, who shared Conrad Grebel's view, wrote from Waldshut to Oecolampadius, a reformer in Basel, describing his practice concerning infants:

> Instead of baptism, I have the church come together, bring the infant in, explain in German the gospel, "they brought little children" (Matthew 19). When a name is given it, the whole church prays for the child on bended knees and commends it to Christ, that he will be gracious and intercede for it. But if the parents are still weak, and positively wish that the child be baptized then I baptize it; and I am weak with the weak for the time being until they can be better instructed.[2]

How far the sixteenth-century Anabaptists are directly related to the English Baptists of the following century remains still an open question. Nevertheless, when John Smyth and his group of English Separatists

---

[1]*Spiritual and Anabaptist Writers. Documents Illustrative of the Radical Reformation*, ed. George H. Williams and A. M. Mergal, Library of Christian Classics 25 (London, 1957) 81. Original letter in Stadtsbibliothek St. Gall, band XI, 97.

[2]George H. Williams, *The Radical Reformation*, 135.

broke with the Anglican Church, including its practice of infant baptism, they realized also that the issue of the child and the church needed to be addressed.[3]

What was to be the status of children, vis-à-vis the believing Christian community? Smyth's answer, like that of Conrad Grebel, was seemingly simple, even if rather more theologically refined. He drew a distinction between sin as a *state* and sin as an *act*. Although Smyth is seen as a pioneer of the General Baptists, there was sufficient Calvinism in his thought to cause him what Michael Walker called "a partial agnosticism" as to the status of infants.[4] If an infant were elected, then baptism could not affect the issue one way or another until election could be made sure and evidenced; only then could baptism be administered.

Smyth's colleague, Thomas Helwys, in his *A Short and Plain Proof That No Infants Are Condemned*,[5] developed the distinction between original and actual sin. But sin is not solely a matter of individual responsibility, for all of humanity has been affected by the sin of Adam. But "by grace Christ, hath freed Adam, and in him all mankind from that sin of Adam." Helwys stressed that sin is a personal responsibility, but also that the death of Christ is for all. Christ's death is as far-reaching in its effect as was Adam's sin. An infant outside the sphere of moral responsibility—and therefore, outside the sphere of consenting sin—is within the salvation won by the second Adam.[6] Smyth and Helwys both appear simply to have "written large" the basic statement in Grebel's 1524 letter.

Later in the seventeenth century, Thomas Grantham, the General Baptist Messenger, returned to the theme in his *Christianismus Primitivus*.[7] He used as the representative figure of the covenant the concept of Christ as the New Adam. God had made a covenant with Adam (Genesis 3:15) that had never been repealed. All infants, therefore, regardless of parentage, were members of the Church by virtue of that covenant. According to Grantham, humankind did not stand outside the

---

[3]See esp. Michael J. Walker, "The Relation of Infants to Church, Baptism and Gospel in Seventeenth Century Baptist Theology," *Baptist Quarterly* (hereafter *BQ*) 21 (April 1966): 242-62.
[4]Ibid., 246.
[5]Ibid., 247.
[6]Ibid.
[7]T. Grantham, *Christianiamus Primitivus* (1678), 2nd treatise, pt. II 3.

Body of Christ waiting to be gathered in. It is the Body of Christ *out of which* persons could sin themselves in the years of responsibility.[8]

Thus, Grantham did not recognize any difference in status between the children of believers and those of nonbelievers. All benefitted from the work of the Second Adam, and likewise, all belonged to the invisible Church, but all required conversion and faith to enter the visible Church through the visible act of baptism.

At the same time, however, Grantham went on to maintain that the children of believers stood in a particular relationship to the visible church, a relationship of prayer and pastoral concern. Upon parents is laid the responsibility of bringing up their children in an atmosphere of family devotion. Grantham acknowledged that the children of believing parents are in a particular way "related to the visible Church, being in a more visible state of Beatitude as being given to God in the Name of Christ from the womb."[9]

A second, separate strain of Baptists with Calvinist views which emerged in London about 1616 faced the same issues. For them, the child and the church were closely related to the concept of the covenant. Israel was elected to be the people of God, and so the Church consisted of the elect whom God has chosen by His grace. Children have a place in that covenant. The old covenant prefigured the new. For Calvin, this meant that, just as circumcision was the visible sign of entry into the old covenant, so infant baptism was the sign of entry into the new.

The Particular Baptists, however, took issue with Calvin's interpretation. They did not deny that there was continuity between the old and new covenants, but they claimed that the old had to be interpreted in light of the new. Christ was the expositor of Moses, not vice versa. Infant baptism made "the Old Testament expound the new, whereas the new should expound the old: Christ should and doth expound Moses."[10]

Furthermore, while acknowledging the continuity of the covenants, they also drew attention to the discontinuity. The community of old covenant was a racial group, while the new covenant community was a

---

[8]T. Grantham, *The Controversie Concerning Infants Church Membership Epitomized* (London: n.p., 1680) 46. See Walker, op.cit., 249.

[9]*Christianismus Primitivus,* Bk. II, Sect II 5,6. See Walker, "The Relation of Infants to Church, Baptism and Gospel," 250.

[10]Paul Hobson, *The Fallacy of Infant Baptism Discovered* (London: n.p., 1645) 11.

multiracial group called out of all the nations by grace. Response to that grace was by faith leading to baptism and entry into the Church.

Nevertheless, the Particular Baptists also recognized that the infants of believers stood in a particular relationship to the Church. John Tombes described the children of believers as being "born in the bosom of the Church, of Godly parents, who by prayers, instruction, example will undoubtedly educate them in the true faith of Christ." [11]

What then of the status of infants? Michael Walker, formerly at Cardiff, described the view of the Particular Baptists as one of "optimistic agnosticism."[12] Christopher Blackwood writes:

> The Scripture has not revealed to us anything clearly concerning the salvation or damnation of infants. . . . It is most likely that infants, as well as others, are saved by the presentment of the satisfaction of Christ to God's justice for overall sin.[13]

Evidence is scanty as to how far the seventeenth century Baptists practiced any form of service for the child. On the basis of the blessing of children by Jesus, Grantham stated that the children of believing parents were "devoted to God by the prayers of the Church . . . and accordingly we do dedicate (them) to Him from the womb."[14] Paedobaptists, he suggested, "should do to their infants as Christ did to them which were brought to him, either by praying for them themselves or by presenting them to Christ's Ministers that they might do it for them in the most solemn manner."[15]

Clear evidence for some such practice is found in Bristol. In 1642 during the Civil War, Thomas Ewins had come to Bristol with his congregation from Llanvaches, in Monmouthshire. He came to exercise a wide preaching and teaching ministry, which occasionally included the church at Broadmead. Ewins recounted an occasion when a "Godly" woman, one at whose husband's house the church often used to meet, "was delivered of a child" and invited the church to meet at her house to render praise to God:

---

[11] John Tombes, *Examen of the Sermon of Mr Stephen Marshall about Infant Baptism* (London: n.p., 1645) 32-33.

[12] Walker, "The Relation of Infants to Church, Baptism and Gospel," 258.

[13] Christopher Blackwood, *The Storming of Anti-Christ* (London: n.p., 1644) 11.

[14] *Christianismus Primitivus*, bk. II, 6.

[15] Ibid.; see Walker, "The Relation of Infants to Church, Baptism and Gospel," 250.

> Now when the church was met she decided that her children might be presented to the Lord by prayer, both that which she then lay with, and one more the age of two years . . . the like was done again about two years after when the Lord gave her another child, and as I have known it done in Wales.[16]

Ewins went on to suggest that any "Godly" woman who has a child should present herself with her child in the Church, so that God may be praised, and her child presented with prayer in dedication to God. The name of the child should be declared by the parents and the child's name should be entered

> into the book where the names of the congregation are written together with other dedicated children as the Children of the Church who upon occasion may be mentioned to the Lord as the seed of the faithful, that when the children come to age, and the Lord shall give them to profess Faith in Christ, and that they do believe with all their hearts as Acts 8:37 they may then be admitted to the Ordinances of Christ, both Baptism and the Lord's Supper as believers were in primitive times.[17]

Thus, the return to the practice of believer's baptism on the basis of biblical practice and theology led the seventeenth-century Baptists to face two connected issues relating to the children and the Church. The first was the status of the child theologically. This involved:

1. the claim that there is a distinction between sin as a state and sin as an act
2. the inclusion of children in the salvation achieved by Christ as the representative New Adam
3. for Particular Baptists, the inclusion of the children of believers in the New Covenant in Christ
4. for the General Baptists, the claim that the children of believers are in a more visible state of Beatitude.

The second issue was the need for a Service for Children, certainly of the "Godly," in the midst of the congregation, which would include prayers of thanksgiving, a prayer seeking God's blessing on the child, the naming of the child, and the inclusion of the child's name in the Book of

---

[16]*The Records of a Church of Christ in Bristol, 1640–1687*, ed. Roger Hayden (Bristol: The Record Society, 1974) 53.

[17]Thomas Ewins, *The Church of Christ in Bristol* (1656) 64a, quoted in T. L. Underwood, "Child Dedication Services amongst British Baptists in the Seventeenth Century." *BQ* 23 (October 1969): 165-69.

the Congregation. The intention was that, being now the children of the Church, prayer would subsequently be offered regularly on their behalf in the anticipation that the process would lead to baptism, membership of the visible Church, and admission to the Lord's Supper.

Thus, it is evident that there was ample support within early Baptist experience for seeing the child and the Church as an essential issue in Baptist life and thought.

II

Relatively little research has been done thus far on Baptist attitudes and thought concerning the child and the Church in the eighteenth, and much of the nineteenth century. Two isolated references may be mentioned which indicate that the issue was still alive.

On December 4, 1753, there were twenty-three signatures to the new church covenant of Westgate Particular Baptist Church in Bradford. The seventh clause of the covenant read, "And as we have given our children to the Lord by a Solemn Dedication, so we will endeavour through divine help to teach them the way of the Lord and command them to keep it, setting before them a Holy example worthy of their imitation and continuing in prayer to God for their conversion and salvation."[18] While there is no certainty that the "Solemn Dedication" was one special occasion which took the form of a formal act of worship, the phraseology of the clause tends to suggest that this was the most natural interpretation of its meaning.

Adam Taylor, writing of the General Baptists, mentioned the "Barton Preachers," an evangelical group who adopted the sentiments of the Baptists in 1755. In turning from infant baptism to believer's baptism, the group continued to bring infants to the Church for blessing.

> They brought their infants in the time of public service, to the minister; who, taking them in his arms pronounced an affectionate benediction on them using . . . Aaron's words, from Numbers 6:24-27 . . . suitable admonition to the parents and earnest and affectionate prayer for them and their offspring concluded the solemn and interesting transaction.[19]

In the final decades of the nineteenth century, however, the issue clearly reemerged in Baptist thought and practice. In 1858 John Clifford,

---

[18]Covenant quoted in *BQ* 19 (July 1962): 289-91.
[19]Adam Taylor, *History of English General Baptists* (London: T. Bore, 1818) 180, vol. 2, 29-30.

age 22, settled at Praed Street Chapel in London. Charles Bateman, writing in 1904, commented:

> His (John Clifford) belief in immersion does not prevent his adopting a Dedication Service in addition. This he uses because of the fact that many of his people—like Congregationalists—desire to associate their children with the church and seek its prayers, just after their birth. He has told me that at first his wife and himself, when they settled at Praed Street, visited the homes of the members and there conducted the Dedication Service. He afterwards found that the Church, which is of a cosmopolitan character and includes Methodists and Congregationalists, as well as Baptists, desired a public service so that the members could take part in it.[20]

When Charles Williams of Accrington produced *The Principles and Practices of the Baptists* in 1879, there was mention of a dedication service, even though he discussed the Baptist view of the status of the child. When the second edition was published in 1903, a dedication service was included, but the author felt it wise to include what he called "a word of explanation" as to its purpose.[21] This suggested that it was something of an innovation. Williams wrote:

> Many families desire more than individual thanksgiving for preserving the life of the mother and for the child. Not unnaturally they wish their pastor to lead them alike in praise for the preservation of life and for the gift of life and in prayer for the mother and her babe. In the circumstances certain Baptist ministers accept the invitation to be present at a family service for this purpose.[22]

A form of service was suggested which contained a number of biblical texts, including Psalm 103:1-5 and 13-14; Psalm 127:3-5a; Deuteronomy 6:4-7; Mark 10:14-16; a selection from 1 Samuel 2 and 3; Isaiah 40:11ff. The rubric which followed the suggested Scripture said "The Service should close with praise for "goodness and mercy" shown to the mother, and with prayer in which the child is consecrated to the service of the Saviour and is commended to His guardianship and guidance."

---

[20] Charles T. Bateman, *John Clifford: Free Church Leader and Preacher* (London: National Council of the Evangelical Free Churches, 1904) 77.

[21] Charles Williams, *The Principles and Practices of the Baptists*, 2nd ed. (London: Baptist Tract Society, 1903). For this particular reference and for other help in this section of my article, I am grateful to Anthony Cross, who is engaged upon significant research on baptism amongst Baptists in the twentieth century.

[22] Ibid., 113.

In 1905 the Kingsgate Press published *A Manual for Free Church Ministers*, compiled by G. P. Gould and J. H. Shakespeare.[23] It began the pattern of Infant Dedication, which became increasingly used in Baptist churches during the first half of the twentieth century. The opening rubric stated, "The Dedication Service usually follows the regular Morning Service." The meaning and intention of the dedication was threefold:

> . . . to give thanks to God for the precious gift of the child,
> . . . to bring the child to God as an act of consecration,
> . . . to take solemn vows to train the child in the "fear and nurture of the Lord."

Scripture passages should be read from Old and New Testaments. These echoed those suggested by Charles Williams and are followed by a suggested brief address in which the child is described as one "coming out of the unseen; born into a redeemed world; for whom the Saviour died; and called, therefore, by divine mercy to the inheritance of eternal life." The parents are reminded that "You are entering on a solemn responsibility, too great for any to bear alone . . . you will need continual grace and wisdom to guide the child into the ways of truth and goodness."

Reading the second half of the address, one cannot help but be struck by the recurring emphasis on the discipline of the life opening up for the child of ninety years ago:

> These little hands will, perhaps, in days to come, have to bear heavy burdens; these little feet may have to read a hard way. But at least it is possible for you in these early years to soothe and gladden, to cheer and bless. We do not travel far in life before we learn that all our joy is touched with pain and that sorrow sometimes strikes us through our tenderest and holiest relationships.[24]

There followed a prayer to God—the Source of all life—for the home, the parents, the child, particularly that "this child may be brought to know and love Thee in Jesus Christ and may yield to Thy governance and find delight in doing Thy will." The service concluded with the parents standing and being asked the child's name, and the minister's pronouncing the Blessing from Numbers 6:24-26, followed by the Grace.

---

[23]*A Manual for Free Church Ministers*, compiled by G. P. Gould and J. H. Shakespeare (London: Kingsgate Press, n.d. but 1905). The final section contains eight hymns judged suitable for the various services contained in the *Manual*. The suggested hymn for the Dedication is "Standing Forth on Life's Rough Way."

[24]Ibid., 36.

There was no mention of the minister taking the child into his own arms. This practice was not universally accepted. That there were those who viewed Dedication Service as unscriptural—and therefore, undesirable—was evidenced from a discussion in 1908 in the correspondence column of the *Baptist Times & Freeman*.[25]

By 1911, however, *The Fraternal*, the magazine of the Baptist Ministers Fraternal Union, published a "Form of Service for the Dedication of Infants" by J. H. Rushbrooke.[26] An editorial footnote cautiously recorded that it was published "At the request of several brethren, as a form which has, in some degree, commended itself in use, and may possibly be suggestive to those who are instituting similar services. Criticism or correspondence upon the subject will be welcomed." It is worthy of note that the editor was none other than J. H. Rushbrooke himself!

The introduction to Rushbrooke's Service Order is important in that it introduced not only the significance of the service for the child and its parents, but also "for the members of the Christian Society with which these are associated and the congregation now present." For as closely and personally as the service concerned the parents and the children, "*it could have no rightful place in the public worship of God at the accustomed hour of common praise and prayer unless it likewise concerned the Church which has its home here*" (my italics). Thus, the ecclesiological dimension of the Dedication Service was deemed an essential element. Indeed, the Church of Jesus was the instrument of the Kingdom of God:

> the representative of the Lord Jesus Christ, charged with the continuance of His work in His spirit, and therefore bound to adopt His attitude towards all, including those who, by reason of their tender age, are not yet consciously His disciples and are incapable of receiving baptism upon a profession of personal faith.[27]

After reading Mark 10:13-16, the minister stated "the congregation assembled today, a portion of the Church of the Lord Jesus, express in His name His welcome of the little children" and continues "the family of aspect of our Church life is prominent in this dedication service."

In this context, the church gathered in worship was bound to the family and child at the center of the service. But the dedicatory act was

---

[25] *Baptist Times and Freeman* (7 August 1908) 556.
[26] *The Fraternal* 5/2 (June 1911): 42-47.
[27] Ibid., 43.

personal to the family in their thanksgiving, recognition of their responsibility, and need for Divine help. After further exhortation and Scripture quotation, the parents were invited to stand as the minister said, "And I ask all present, who desire to express the welcome of Christ to this little one and to associate themselves with these parents in thanksgiving and in prayer likewise to rise in their places."[28] A prayer then followed, ending with the Blessing from Numbers 6:24-26, and then a hymn and the Benediction. The editorial request for criticism or correspondence seemed not to have produced any response. But looking back now, we can see that this form of Rushbrooke's was a further significant step in the developing pattern of the Dedication Service.

Clearly there was a gradual process of acceptance amongst Baptist churches of a Dedication Service. But many still doubted. Their hesitation sprang from the lack of clear biblical evidence for such a service and a fear of its being in any way viewed as related to infant baptism. In 1915 Mrs. Charles Brown penned "A Plea for the General Adoption of an Infant Dedication Service in Our Churches":

> It seems astonishing that we consecrate marriage and death by religious services, yet when children are born to us, because we do not hold baptism to be appropriate, we have in the past dispensed with a religious service altogether.

She pointed out the pastoral need and evangelical opportunity of such services: "Dedication Services furnish a real opportunity for reaching the hearts of parents at a time when they are especially tender and susceptible of influence."[29]

But doubts remained. In 1925, in the series "A Baptist Apologetic for Today,"[30] Spurr wrote, "It is only within recent years that the solemn service of the Dedication of Infants has come into use amongst us. And there are still many who look askance at it." Spurr's contribution was titled "Our Present, Positive Message." He argued that discipleship is the fundamental condition for church membership, and on the basis of this concept, talked about the position of the child of Christian parents:

> And just as every English child is treated as a potential citizen so every child of Christian parents should be treated as a potential citizen of the

---

[28]Ibid., 46.
[29]*Baptist Times and Freeman* (30 July 1915).
[30]*Baptist Times* (5 November 1925).

Kingdom of God. Many Baptists have failed to grasp this elementary truth. They have treated their children as "outsiders" waiting for the mysterious breath of God to quicken them. If we are to take Christ seriously, we ought to dedicate our children. Dedication, however, is not baptism and ought not to be confounded with it. . . . When the child is grown and educated in the things of Christ, then the heart being willingly surrendered to Him, is the time for Baptism. . . . Baptism should respect discipleship and discipleship alone. The infant dedication and a later ratification in baptism (my italics) is on the lines of the New Testament.[31]

Here was a Baptist in 1925 who began to argue along the lines for what today is called "Christian Initiation." He went on to suggest that for some paedobaptists, infant baptism was nothing more than infant dedication, so he argued that this line of thought should be persistently taught to our own people. But we ought also to witness this to our fellow Evangelicals who confound dedication and baptism. So, "why not retain the dedication and defer the baptism until it becomes an intelligent act on the part of the subject?"[32] The apologetic for Infant Dedication was finally beginning to acquire an ecumenical edge.

The Baptist response accepted at the 1926 Baptist Union Assembly to the "Appeal to all Christian People," issued by the 1920 Lambeth Conference, contained no such courageous edge. In fact, it limited its words on the child and the church to safer parameters:

In our judgement the baptism of infants incapable of offering a personal confession of faith subverts the conception of the Church as the fellowship of believers. We recognize that those concerning whom Jesus said "Of such is the Kingdom of Heaven" belong to God, and believe that no rite is needed to bring them into relation with Him. But many of our Churches hold services at which infants are presented, the duties, privileges and responsibilities of parents emphasized, and the prayers of the Church offered for children and parents.[33]

The following year M.E. Aubrey, the Secretary of the Baptist Union, produced through the Kingsgate Press *A Minister's Manual*, which contained orders of service for various occasions.[34] The order for the dedica-

---

[31] Ibid., col. 1.
[32] Ibid., cols. 1 and 2.
[33] E. A Payne, *The Baptist Union: A Short History* (London: Carey Kingsgate, 1959) app. IX, 280-81.
[34] *A Minister's Manual*, M. E. Aubrey, comp. (London, n.d. but 1927). In the compiler's note, Aubrey acknowledges help from members of the Baptist Union Publication's Committee and from Principal Wheeler Robinson for his suggestions relating to the dedi-

tion of infants contains Scripture readings from Deuteronomy 11:18-20 and Mark 10:13-16. These are followed by an explanation which spoke of the parents' bringing the child to "present him before God and His Church" in order to witness their consecration to their part in the life of the child, as well as to the high and sacred task of parenthood.

The claim of the child in a Christian home upon the prayers and service of the Church was acknowledged. "We welcome him as the Saviour, who is Lord of the Church, welcomed little children in the days of his flesh." In so doing, "we declare the claim of the Church of God upon the lives of those whom He has given to Christian parents." Thus parents and Church should labour together so that "in the fullness of time and in years of understanding this child may be brought into the fellowship of those who serve and follow Christ." Questions were then asked of the parents relating to their acceptance of their responsibilities as parents to nurture the child involving their own lives of example and the ordering of their homelife so "that this your child shall at all times be surrounded by holy living and Christlike example." The minister took the child in his arms; pronounced the child's name and then the Aaronic blessing before returning the child to the Father. The congregation was invited to join in the welcome of the Church to the child, and to unite with the parents in prayer of thanksgiving by standing in their places. There then followed a prayer and the benediction. The dedication service usually was held, Aubrey suggested, immediately after the hymn following the Sunday morning sermon.[35]

This timing became widespread and remained so until the 1950s. It was far from ideal, particularly in the days of half hour morning sermons, as personal memories of the late 1920s and early 1930s confirm. The result was delayed Sunday dinners and a rush to return in time for afternoon Sunday School.

Three years after Aubrey's Manual, the Carey Press at the Baptist Mission House produced *The Call to Worship* by David Tait Patterson.[36] His order for the Dedication of Children was quite close to that of Aubrey, but made no mention of the timing of the service. It contained, however, no explanation of the service, but suggested that the minister

---

cation of infants.
[35]Ibid., 18. Aubrey's *Manual* ran to a second (enlarged) edition.
[36]*The Call to Worship*, compiled by David Tait Patterson (London: Carey Press, 1930). There was a second edition in 1931 and a revised edition in 1938.

should do so in his own words. Patterson suggested also that the service might begin with the singing of a children's hymn. Memory suggests that this was usually "God who hath made the daisies"—with its refrain: "Suffer the little children / And let them come to me."

There was no suggestion, however, of congregational involvement and response—but the final rubric stated, "The child's name should be entered on the Cradle Roll of the Church."[37] Reading the two services now leads to an impression that whilst Aubrey's was a service assuming a close connection of the parent(s) with the church—Tait Patterson's was rather more open for what might be called potentially "missionary" enterprise with parents more loosely connected with the Church. Those were the great days of uniformed Youth Organizations which attracted large numbers of children, many from nonchurch families.

By the end of the 1930s the practice of infant dedication appears relatively widespread amongst Baptist churches. As we have seen, its growth was due to parental pressure and the need for the Baptists to have some ceremony to balance the almost universal practice of infant baptism amongst all other Churches. There seems not to have been very much theological consideration given to its meaning. The generalization of the 1926 response to Lambeth, mentioned earlier, was accepted without further questions about its ecclesiological implications being asked. That infant dedication had such implications was implicit in Rushbrooke's and Aubrey's involvement of the church membership and explicit in Spurr's idea of the ratification of infant dedication in baptism.

In 1932 a special committee was set up to discuss union between Baptists, Congregationalists and Presbyterians. As we have noted, John Clifford's experience had indicated that a dedication service for infants might have had some positive contribution to make to Free Church relations. But the issue was not discussed at any depth and the general tone of the committee's "Report to the March Council of the Baptist Union" in 1937 was rightly described as "negative."[38]

But, so far as infant dedication was concerned, things were soon to change. Typically of Baptists, with pastoral practice well established, the necessity eventually became accepted of discovering what, if any, was its theological and particularly its ecclesiological basis. Like Conrad Grebel 400 years previously, twentieth century Baptists who rejected infant bap-

---

[37]Ibid., 149.
[38]Payne, *The Baptist Union: A Short History*, 199.

tism now came to realize that they had to think through their theology of the child—which meant, of course, discussing their theology of what it is to be human.

If we look for a beginning of such thinking, we can do worse than note George Beasley-Murray's article in the *Fraternal* of April 1943.[39] Starting from the question of a Lambeth woman to her Baptist friends, "Why don't you baptize children, the same as other churches?" and with the answer: "Oh, there's not much difference, only we give 'em a dry christening." Beasley-Murray went on to point out that Baptists should at least be aware of the theological issues which the practice of infant dedication raised and which on the whole thus far in the twentieth century had gone unanswered. In fact he might have added that thus far, they had been rarely raised. He pointed out that the importance of infant baptism in the Early Church was due to the prevalent notion of original sin which led to the assumption that a child was a fully constituted sinner, responsible for his/her sinful state, and so liable to the penalty of eternal damnation. To this view Augustine added "that the wills of all actively cooperated with that of Adam in his transgression, hence all were equally guilty."[40]

Beasley-Murray suggested that whether or not Baptists held to the reality of original sin, few would maintain that the concept included guilt. Sin is not reckoned when there is no law, i.e. when it is not realized that deeds committed are wrong. After considering the question of whether an infant is naturally a "child of God," he went on to suggest that children entered (became members of) the Kingdom of God in the same way that they entered His family—by faith. Thus the years prior to baptism as a believer were preparation for this event.[41]

The purpose of dedication, therefore, was to mark the beginning of such a process. Its meaning was threefold:

- a setting apart of *a child* by its parents for the "nurture and admonition of the Lord"
- a setting apart of *themselves* to the task of making a disciple
- a united seeking by the *assembled congregation* of the blessing of God on the infant.

---

[39] G. R. Beasley-Murray, "The Church and the Child," *The Fraternal* (April 1943): 9-13

[40] Ibid., 9-10.

[41] Ibid., 12.

Beasley-Murray concluded, "Our Service, then is a fitting introduction of a child to the community of believers in Christ. It is a practical remembrance of an unchanging invitation, 'Suffer the little children to come unto me.' "[42]

In April 1945, another distinguished Baptist scholar, Professor H. H. Rowley of Manchester, wrote an article in the *Baptist Quarterly* titled "The Origin and Meaning of Baptism."[43] Toward the end he turned his attention to the practice of infant dedication. He argued strongly in its favor and that it should have some clear and defined context which he was not afraid to call "sacramental." His concern was that at the moment "the services at which infants are brought to the House of God are still too sporadic and casual and are commonly given too shallow and too private a meaning. They are not regarded as a part of our denominational witness and practice, normal throughout the denomination."[44]

Rowley agreed that while the practice of Infant Baptism had little to commend it, "we should recognize the truth it has striven to preserve. For there is room for a sacrament fraught with grace for the child, in its infancy." This is, however, *not* New Testament baptism. Yet something more than a dedication service is called for. The child cannot make vows.

> But the parents can and should undertake in solemn vows to bring up their child in the nurture and fear of the Lord. . . . If the vows are made and kept the child will indeed be blessed. We should cease to speak of it as an Infant Dedication service. It should be a service when the parents dedicate themselves to the sacred obligations of parenthood.[45]

But this was not all.

> It should be a service in which the Church is more than a witness of the parent's vows but a sharer in those vows and in the responsibilities for their fulfilment. It should be a sacrament of the Church and the Church in sharing in it should recognize the child as the child of its fellowship, in whom it henceforth will take an interest.[46]

In this case, the service was for Christian parents only. "If this service is regarded as a Christian sacrament, it should be a sacrament for

---

[42]Ibid., 13.
[43]H. H. Rowley, "The Origin and Meaning of Baptism," *BQ* 11 (January–April 1945): 309-20.
[44]Ibid., 320.
[45]Ibid., 319.
[46]Ibid.

Christians."⁴⁷ The Church should keep a register of the children as the children of its fellowship and feel that it is involved in the fulfilment of the vows. Rowley argued that the statistics and care of children whose parents have solemnly undertaken the vows at such a service are of greater significance than total statistics of the vague category of Sunday School Scholars.⁴⁸ It can be said that implicit in such a viewpoint was the concept of the "catechumenate," which was to be advocated twenty years later and was to reappear fifty years into the 1990s.

Rowley's final point related to antipaedobaptism. It is not good enough to say that infant baptism was not what the New Testament said about baptism. The task of Baptists was to show another and better way of recognizing the worth of children to God and their relationship to the Church:

> If Baptists can make this service normal throughout their fellowship and can fill it with richer meaning and ensure that it shall be taken seriously by parents and Church alike, they can make of their witness something more than the antipaedobaptism with which they are too commonly associated.⁴⁹

For Baptists this was to be a very big "if" indeed. But Rowley's point was entirely valid and Baptist hesitations to heed it adequately can make them their own worst enemy in failing to proclaim a credible theology of the child and the church.

III

The first two decades after the Second World War saw British Baptists striving one way and another to come to theological and liturgical terms with the infant dedication service. Early in 1946, R. L. Child, then Principal of Regent's Park College, Oxford, produced a document which he entitled *The Blessing of Infants and the Dedication of Parents*.⁵⁰ In a very brief foreword, he spoke of "the rapid spread of such service and the need for a brief statement . . . calling attention to the theological and practical issues involved."

After a brief historical note, Child went on to justify the service. If Baptists reject infant baptism as unscriptural, then we must be clear why

---

⁴⁷Ibid., 320.
⁴⁸Ibid.
⁴⁹Ibid.
⁵⁰R. L. Child, *The Blessing of Infants and the Dedication of Parents* (London: Kingsgate Press, 1946) a pamphlet of twelve pages.

our practice is based on biblical principles. He suggested the following reasons:

- The service affirms the truth that all life is a gift of God and that the birth of a little child is a revelation of God's love and goodness to be received with thanksgiving and praise. Within this thanksgiving is included "preservation of the mother in childbirth."
- The service expresses the value which our Lord set upon one individual human life from its earliest beginnings.
- The service brings to a focus both the responsibilities and the resources of parenthood in Christ.
- The service emphasizes the part played by the Christian community in the development of personal faith in Christ.[51]

These reasons were clearly in line with biblical thought and they were "theological" very much in the pastoral sense. They did not, however, grapple with the issues which our seventeenth century forebears faced and which were raised again by Beasley-Murray's 1943 article. For these "reasons," Child argued for a pattern of worship along the lines of M.E. Aubrey's *A Minister's Manual* and suggested a better title might have been "The Blessing of Infants and the Dedication of Parents."

In dealing with the implications of the service, Child argued that it should be primarily for Christian parents but, at the same time, remembering that pastorally no request for the service should be turned down simply because parents are not church members. The request itself should be taken as an "evangelical" opportunity. Even then, if the parents appeared insufficiently responsive to the claims of Christian commitment, some sort of blessing and prayer could be offered within the home.

Child's final point was to become increasingly significant. "The service really requires us to revise our whole conception of the relation of the Church to the homes and families connected with it. . . . It cannot be denied that in too many of our churches the Sunday School is still regarded as a separate organization . . . existing alongside the Church." He called on his readers to seize the opportunity of the "popularity in our churches of the new service for infants," to put the Christian nurture of our children on a more satisfactory footing.[52]

What Child did not do in suggesting the title, "Blessing of Infants" was to indicate what he meant by the word "blessing." To some Baptists,

---

[51]Ibid., 5-7.
[52]Ibid., 11.

probably too many, such language sounded like sacramentalism. Few had been able to agree with Rowley's statement of a year earlier that "there is room for a sacrament fraught with grace for a child in its infancy."

In March 1948 the Baptist Union Council approved a statement titled "The Baptist Doctrine of the Church."[53] It was a succinct and comprehensive document which has not yet been superseded. Within the section on the sacraments, after sentences relating to believer's baptism, the statement continued:

> Thus we do not baptize infants. There is, however, a practice in our churches of presenting young children at a service of public worship where the responsibilities of the parents and the church are recognized and prayers are offered for the parents and child. Baptists believe that from birth all children are within the love and care of the heavenly Father and therefore within the operation of the saving grace of Christ; hence they have never been troubled by the distinction between baptized and unbaptized children.[54]

This was a statement relating to children upon which most Baptists could unite. But, of course, it begged a number of the theological and ecclesiological questions involved. The origin of this statement was to meet a request from the Continuation Committee of Faith and Order which was engaged in preliminary preparations for a World Conference on Faith and Order held eventually at Lund, Sweden in 1952. Amongst the subjects to be discussed were "The Nature of the Church," "Intercommunion," and "Ways of Worship." It was at this Conference that the participating churches moved beyond the methodology of comparing their views and listing their agreements and disagreements to an attempt to seek an ecclesiological unity by reflection upon the common biblical basis of the Faith belonging to all traditions.[55]

The result was a growing consideration of baptism as a symbol of unity, of our being "one in Christ" whose body the Church is. An ongoing theological commission on Christ and the Church was set up which, as it developed over the years, found itself more and more involved with the question of baptism. Gradually as the sources were studied and early tradition examined, the Baptist position on believer's

---

[53] Reprinted in Payne, *The Baptist Union: A Short History*, app. X, 285-91.
[54] Ibid., 288.
[55] *The Third World Conference on Faith and Order—Lund 1952*, report, ed. Oliver S. Tomkins (London: World Council of Churches, 1953) 15-16. See also my article on the fortieth anniversary of Lund: "Swedish Milestone in Road to Unity," *Baptist Times* (13 August 1992).

baptism came to be seen, not as an aberration of the minority, but as a practice universal in the first century and very common through into the fourth. When others took believer's baptism seriously, Baptists felt required to reconsider their attitude towards infant baptism and their own understanding of the relationship between the child and the church.[56] The Commission Faith and Order paper No. 31 for 1960 contained the statement:

> We believe that the controversy between the advocates of adult and infant baptism is not a mere confessional controversy but must be seen in a context which makes apparent its true theological implications.[57]

No longer could the infant dedication question be taken on its own and answered solely in the pastoral context. Now it was necessary for it to be seen within the total ecclesiological context of entry into the Church. The outcome was that from the mid 1950s until the end of 1966, the theological issues linked with the child and the church discussion came more to the fore in English Baptist thought and writing.

There was considerable literary activity on baptism in the immediate postwar years. Other Churches considered the question and not least the Church of England and the Church of Scotland, both of which produced significant reports. Within the British Council of Churches, its own Faith and Order group were at work upon the question of "Christian Initiation" as a process. Baptist writers joined the discussion, amongst them R. E. O. White, G. W. Rusling, Stephen Winward, George Beasley-Murray, Neville Clark and Alec Gilmore, to name but a few.

Before we go on to consider what they had to say on the subject, two other contextual factors should be mentioned. First, the Liturgical Movement, was a worldwide ecumenical enterprise but fostered and developed in England by the Joint Liturgical Group. Amongst other things, it challenged participating denominations including Baptists to rethink their patterns of worship, asking searching questions about the whys and wherefores of current worship practice. Naturally baptism and Eucharist could not escape some scrutiny and now, linked with the former for Baptists,

---

[56]See *Baptists in the Twentieth Century*, ed. K. W. Clements (London: Baptist Historical Society, 1983) containing my article "Baptist in Faith and Order," a study in Baptismal Convergence, 55-75.

[57]*Faith and Order Commission Pager 31: Minutes of the Faith and Order Commission, St. Andrews*, 122-23.

was the service for infants, its form and place in the worship, and its meaning.

The other factor was the widespread enthusiasm for "Family Church," triggered by publications such as R. J. Gouldman's book, *Readiness for Religion*,[58] in which he sought to define in children's development the "personal religious stage," and N. A. Hamilton, with his theoretical and practical publication, *Family Church in Principle and Practice*.[59] This latter publication recognized the truth that during the late 1950s and early 1960s afternoon Sunday School was on the decline due in part to changing Sunday "habits" of the nation with growing mobility of families with their cars and the increase in Sunday "secular" activities. It was this afternoon Sunday School decline which caused many Baptist churches to face the question seriously of the child and the church. Thus the seven years from 1959—1966 were productive years of Baptist work in this topic. There is limited space here to draw attention to some of these contributions.

In 1959 *Christian Baptism*[60] was published by the Lutterworth Press. This was a comprehensive symposium by ten Baptist ministers dealing with the development of Christian Baptism from biblical time to the present day. The concluding chapter was by Neville Clark on the "Theology of Baptism." He argued for a clear distinction to be made between the children of a "believing" family and the children of "unbelievers." "The former belong to the sphere of the Body of Christ; the latter belong to the world which is marked with the seal of redemption and the humanity which, by incarnation, the Son has brought into union with Himself."[61]

Believers have responded to the Gospel, therefore their children will be specially related to the Body of Christ. But this relationship arose not so much from God's dealing with sinful humankind, but rather from the fact of Christian marriage and the gracious Christian influences which will be the experience of the child in that home. As baptism was not at issue for this child, there was no question here of "*insertion* into the

---

[58] R. J. Goldman, *Readiness for Religion* (London, 1965).
[59] H. A. Hamilton, *Family Church in Principle and Practice* (Wallington: R.E.P., 1963).
[60] *Christian Baptism*, ed. A. Gilmore (London: Camelot Press; Philadelphia: Judson Press, 1959). See also A. Gilmore *Baptism and Christian Unity* (London, 1966) esp. chap. 6 on "Baptism and the Child" for a comment on the views of Clark and others.
[61] Gilmore, *Baptism and Christian Unity*, 321.

Body of Christ," but there was a serious question of *relationship* to the Body of Christ grounded in the "one flesh union" of two of its members. This should be marked by a "solemn ritual" adapted from Christ's blessing of infants. The rite is not concerned with human vows, but was concerned with the recognition and declaration of an act of God by which a child has been specially related to the redeemed community and with the claim and demand "which that *opus dei* imposes upon church and parents alike."[62] Baptists, Clark believed, must face up to their persistent myopia in respect of the prevenience of grace.

R. E. O. White in the same volume dealt with baptism in the Synoptic gospels and expressed the view that "in none of these utterances (of Jesus) does the crucial question of the child's relating to the Kingdom of God explicitly arise . . . so far as his recorded words take us, the question is left open." They are undoubtedly within the love of Christ but "their entrance into the divine Kingdom and initiation into spiritual life is a wholly different matter, and far from indisputable."[63] The following year White confirmed his view that "so far as the child is concerned," responsibility came with rational and moral apprehension; until it shall place itself outside that sheltered sphere, "*the child is safe within the love that saves*" (my italics).[64]

In the same year, 1960, G. W. Rusling contributed a very significant article to the *Baptist Quarterly* with the title "The Status of Children."[65] In this he suggested that the Baptist argument against infant baptism was not over "the fact that the paedobaptist finds a place for the child in the life of the Church but that he wrongly transfers to the beginning of life the rite which belongs to the New Birth . . . and makes assertions . . . which distort and confuse the doctrine of the Church and Sacraments."[66]

Rusling's work pleaded for the rediscovery and restoration of the catechumenate. A child of Christian parents will be under the influence of parents, home and Church. He/she will be in the process of being "instructed" in the Christian Faith. All this happens already to Baptist children. "What we have not done is to make allowance for the idea of it in our theology of the Church." The church's ministry of evangelism

---

[62]Ibid., 323.
[63]Ibid., 103.
[64]R. E. O. White, *The Biblical Doctrine of Initiation* (London: Hodder & Stoughton, 1960) 122.
[65]G. W. Rusling "The Status of Children," *BQ* 18 (April 1960): 245-57.
[66]Ibid., 245.

and reconciliation in its response to our Lord's commission to make disciples required a catechumenate in its midst.[67] Although unbaptized the catechumens were in a *creative relationship* with the Body of Christ, Rusling admitted that such a usage of the term and concept did not strictly follow the usage of the early Church, but suggested that the word "catechumen" could properly be used for the children which we have in mind. He went on to argue that the catechumenate should not be limited to children of believing parents—just as Sunday Schools were not limited. Both categories shared the love of God and both have been born into a world for which Christ died.

J. O. Barrett in 1960 published a pamphlet, *Your Child and the Church*.[68] This was addressed to parents, explaining that Baptists do not christen children nor did they ask for godparents. The responsibility for giving a child a Christian upbringing rested firmly on the shoulders of the parents themselves. Barrett suggested an order of service which was brief and to the point. After Scripture sentences the minister indicated that all are gathered at the request of the parents to give thanks for the birth, to unite the prayers of congregation and parents for the guidance and strength of God in the responsibilities of parenthood and to ask God's blessing upon the child. There was then an acknowledgment of the claim of the child upon the prayerful interest and service of the Church and a statement about the partnership of Church and parents, to the end that the child will "freely choose the service of Christ and the fellowship of His people."[69] The parents were asked two questions, the first relating to their gratitude to God in acceptance of responsibility for the child, and the second inviting them to promise to surround the child by Christian example and influence. The minister took the child and pronounced the Aaronic blessing before inviting the congregation to stand with the parents for a prayer. After the Benediction, the parents were given a certificate to mark the occasion.

There follow two sections of explanation. The first had to do with the meaning of the service enlarging upon the content of the promises made and the part played by the Church and parents together. For Christian parents this was an opportunity for the opening of a new chapter in Christian living, for parents who had not yet made any profession of faith

---

[67] Ibid., 247.
[68] J. O. Barrett, *Your Child and the Church* (London: n.p., 1960).
[69] Ibid., 7.

it was a time to ask themselves about their response—parenthood is a God-given opportunity for them to enter upon the Christian life. The second part was pastoral in character and expanded upon the meaning of the words "A Christian Upbringing."

Probably the most influential Baptist publication of 1960 was *Orders and Prayers for Church Worship: A Manual for Ministers*,[70] compiled by Ernest Payne and Stephen Winward. This manual became widely used and helped to draw to the attention of the Baptist ministry some of the thinking of the liturgical movement. It figures significantly in any consideration of Baptist worship in the twentieth century. The order for the dedication of children did not differ in general from that of Barrett, although it is slightly longer and included most significantly the involvement of the congregation in affirming (by standing in their places) a positive response to a question, part of which read:

> Do you as members of the Church acknowledge, and accept the responsibility, together with the parents, of teaching and training this child that being brought up in the discipline and instruction of the Lord . . . he may be led in due time to be made a member of this Christ's Church.[71]

This sounded like support for the concept of a catechumenate.

While it may be said that Barrett's pamphlet and the *Minister's Manual* both begged the theological question, their orders of service were an attempt to take seriously the growing number of requests being made pastorally of Baptist ministers to do "something for the baby." That was certainly the experience of the present writer, then in a pastorate at St. Albans, where such requests were frequent. In 1960 he had submitted an article to *The Fraternal* on the "Child and the Church," which was published in January 1961.[72] Its emphasis lay upon taking seriously the church's part both in the dedication service and in subsequent concern for the child pastorally and in developing discipleship. The article argued that the dedication service was the point at which the church, which was the sphere in and through which the saving of grace of Christ is made known

---

[70]*Orders and Prayers for Church Worship: A Manual for Ministers*, compiled by Ernest Payne and Stephen F. Winward (London: Carey Kingsgate Press, 1960). Stephen Winward, who was a distinguished Baptist liturgiologist both in theory and in his practice at Highams Park Baptist Church, London, produced in the same year a brief order entitled "Dedication of Your Child," the pattern of which is largely followed in the *Manual*.

[71]*Orders and Prayers*, 126.

[72]W. M. S. West, "The Child and the Church," *The Fraternal* (January 1961): 15-19. See also *The Patterns of the Church*, ed. A. Gilmore (London, 1963) 14-21.

in the world, became operative in the life of the child. Concern was expressed that the Sunday School in Baptist churches has often operated as though it ran parallel to the church rather than as part of it. Thus the dedication service was the occasion of relating the child to the church at the commencement of a *continuing* relationship which should be effectively monitored pastorally as the child moved on through adolescence towards baptism and church membership. To this end, it was suggested that the church's response to the question asked of it by the minister should not have been only the standing of the congregation for prayer, but also the verbal response from a church representative, whether church secretary, Sunday School superintendent, Cradle Roll secretary or whoever. It was important that person stands *alongside* the parents throughout the service.

The article continued with a reminder of the importance of bridging the gap between the dedication service and the age of commencing Sunday School or Family Church. There was a plea for one person in the church life (whether the Cradle Roll secretary or not) to have responsibility for maintaining contact with the family and child. This was particularly so when the parents are not fully committed to the life of the church. The writer concluded by suggesting that the syllabus of the Sunday School needed reexamination and set out some suggestions for the content of such a syllabus. This is to be based upon the premise of the "Sunday School as the church in embryo" with the children developing their understanding of the Faith until the day when they are reborn into the fellowship of believers—the church. "In this sense baptismal classes commence in the beginners department and continue throughout the Sunday School."[73] This teaching will seek to show the child its place in God's purpose in history and the church's obedient role in that purpose in guiding the child towards Christ and baptism.

What is again being described implicitly is the pastoral and evangelical imperative for the concept and practice of the catechumenate. George Beasley-Murray in 1966 explicitly supported the catechumenate idea. At the end of an article entitled "Church and Child in the New Testament,"[74] he had a section on the "Care of Children by the Church" in which he wrote: "The secret appears to me to lie in the catechumenate or, in

---

[73] West, "The Child and the Church," 18.
[74] G. R. Beasley-Murray, "Church and the Child in the New Testament," *BQ* 21 (January 1966): 206-17.

modern terms, in an adequate system of Christian education."[75] In a masterly summary he had earlier shown how the catechumenate developed from New Testament teaching into a rigorous school of faith with baptism as its climax. "Its abolition after the Constantinian settlement when the masses swept into the Church and infant baptism became the accepted practice was of untold loss to the Church."[76] What is more, baptism should not mark the end of a child's Christian education but simply an interruption for an occasion for a response to God's grace which has been presupposed throughout the process.

On the theological question of the relation of children to God, Beasley-Murray commented:

> In my judgement we must have the candour to admit that the Bible gives us too little data to enable us to define with precision the relation of children to God just as it has given us too little information to state with confidence how the parents of most of them—the pagans who have never heard the Gospel, stand in relation to God.[77]

Some may have argued (and may still do so) that the children are guilty for their condition as the children of Adam, while others have claimed that children are in redemptive solidarity with Christ the Second Adam until they fall out of it through their sin. Yet it seems wiser to admit the limits of our knowledge. Because of this limitation, and most particularly because God is gracious towards all children, the Church should provide effective Christian nurture and instruction which is comprehensive in every sense hence the catechumenate.

IV

At the suggestion of the Young People's Committee,[78] the Baptist Union Council in November 1963 appointed a small study group to prepare a statement on the Baptist view of the relation of the child to the Church. It was urged that such a statement was greatly needed, first as a basis for denominational policy, both national and local, in respect of children and young people and also to contribute to the current ecumenical discussion

---

[75] Ibid., 217.
[76] Ibid., 215.
[77] Ibid., 213.
[78] The Minutes of the Young People's Department Committee meeting residentially at Dagnall Street Baptist Church, St. Albans on 7-8 June 1963 reveal that the relevant suggestion was embodied in a resolution to the Baptist Union Council following discussion on a paper prepared by Bernard Green.

of Christian initiation and the doctrine of the Church. Its terms of reference were fourfold. The group was instructed to consider the relation of children and the Church in the light of

- the nature of the Church as a redeemed community and a fellowship of believers
- the continuing mission of the Church towards those who are outside and those who, although uncommitted to Christ, are already involved in the life of the Church
- the different environments in which children of Christian and non-Christian parents are brought up
- the lack of recent study on theological and practical questions concerning children which Baptists are being asked in ecumenical discussion.

The report was presented to the meeting of the Baptist Union Council held on March 8, 1966 under the title The Child and the Church.[79] Its contents were reported in the *Baptist Times* of March 10th,[80] which went to print prior to the Council debate on March 8th. Geoffrey Rusling, Vice Principal of Spurgeon's College, was Chairman of the group and Harry Mowvley, who had had valuable and effective experience of Family Church at Cotham Grove Baptist Church in Bristol, was Secretary.

Whatever else may be said about the report, it tackled head on the issues raised by its terms of reference not least the theological implications. No summary of it can do it full justice for the issues are many and complex. We content ourselves, therefore, first by indicating its structure and then by drawing out certain salient points.

The structure of the report is as follows.

A. *Reasons for the Study*
 1. Denominational.
    a. Church Practice
    b. Church Doctrine
 2. Ecumenical
B. *The Child and God*
 1. God the Creator
 2. The Nature of Men and Work of Christ
 3. The Covenant
    a. The Prevenience of Divine Grace
    b. The Solidarity of the Family
 4. Christ and the Children

---

[79]Published subsequently as *The Child and the Church—A Baptist Discussion* (London, 1966).
[80]*Baptist Times* (10 March 1966).

C. *The Child and the Church*
      1. The Catechumenate
      2. Children of Believers and Nonbelievers
   D. *The Child as a Person*
   E. *The Child and the Parents*
   F. *Implications for Church Practice*
      1. Church and Home
      2. The Dedication Service
      3. Young People's Organizations and the Church
      4. Educational Approaches
      5. Evangelism and Children
      6. The Pastoral Responsibility of the Church
      7. Family Church and Sunday School
      8. Baptism and Church Membership

As can be seen implicitly and up to a point explicitly, the doctrines of the Church, Man, Salvation and the Sacraments came under scrutiny. In addition, a whole range of pastoral issues were raised. Whatever else the report illustrated, it made clear that discussion about the child and the church cannot be carried on without involving the whole gamut of Christian life and thought. Among the specific conclusions reached are the following.

1. Baptists have rejected the idea of infant baptism without facing squarely the problem created by the rejection of it.
2. To ask questions about the status of the infant or the child "does not invalidate the theology underlying believer's baptism; rather we would say that theology obliges us to enquire further concerning the questions with which it does not itself deal."[81]
3. As a denomination we have hitherto tended to over simplify our doctrine of the Church as a fellowship of believers. While children are not of the fellowship of believers they are in fellowship with believers.

   We cannot rightly think of the living Church simply as a fellowship of believers. To risk an impersonal metaphor, that makes it as a garden considered apart from the nursery in which plants are being raised. In the history of the Church the classic name for that nursery is the catechumenate and the Church which is involved in the Lord's mission to the world always has her catechumenate and cannot be fully understood or comprehensively described without it.[82]

   The conversion theology which dominates baptist doctrines of baptism and the Church is, in itself, silent about the infant.[83]

---

[81]*The Child and the Church*, 11.
[82]Ibid., 9.
[83]Ibid., 11.

4. The report goes on to discuss the biblical doctrine of Man and claimed that simply to speak of the human race as fallen, in isolation from the work of Christ, is to violate the witness of the New Testament.[84]

The group, however, could not wholly resolve the tension which existed amongst the seven members between two views of the work of Christ. All believed that the work of Christ was for all, 1 Timothy 2:6, "Christ gave Himself as a ransom for all" but the tension arose as to how that work of Christ was to be appropriated. All agreed that repentance and faith are essential for the salvation set forth in baptism, but while some group members regarded this as the response by which a person becomes what he is through his solidarity with Christ, others said that the response was a transition to becoming what he may be. This tension reflected that of the seventeenth century Baptist which we have previously noted.

5. The report maintained that the children of believers and nonbelievers belong together in the catechumenate. It suggested that towards the children of nonbelievers the Church should act in the place of parents in giving the children a Christian upbringing. The dedication service is one of thanksgiving, the making of promises and offering of prayer for the blessing of God.

While clearly included are the children of believing parents if other parents persist in their desire for a service in the Church and in making their promises then they should be allowed to do so. In this case the partnership with the parents in the Christian education of the child is paramount and presents an opportunity of mission towards the home.[85]

6. An effective development of the catechumenate may result in more baptisms of children in the early teenage years. This is to be acknowledged and indeed welcomed. It is vital that all candidates of whatever age on baptism should be welcomed immediately into Church meeting and given the opportunity of learning in practice the full responsibilities of Church membership.

There is a remarkable silence in Baptist records as to the reception of and the debate upon this Report in the Council on March 8th. The *Baptist Times* made no mention of it in subsequent reports of Council. The minutes of the Council carried no report of the debate at all and simply recorded the following resolution:

---

[84]Ibid., 14. On this doctrinal point, and others, a group of Baptists, the Radlett Fellowship, published in 1967 a very critical response entitled *The Gospel, the Child, and the Church*. See *Baptist Times*, 3 August 1967, reviewed by W. W. Bottoms, "Child and Church Report Criticized."

[85]*The Child and the Church*, 34.

> That the Council thank the Committee for its report and believing that it deals with matters of great importance within and outside the denomination, whilst not necessarily committing itself at present to all the views expressed requests the Secretary to negotiate with the Carey Kingsgate Press regarding its publication so that it can be subsequently circulated to the Churches for study.

Ernest Payne, in his brief introduction to the printed report, wrote, "The Council made clear that it was not at this stage necessarily committing itself to all the views expressed."[86] He went on to mention the term catechumenate as "unfamiliar to most Baptists" and in the way the report presented it as "not exactly corresponding to the early Church or Reformation usage of the word." He drew attention to the tension in the group on the issue of salvation reflecting the two streams of theology which have always been present in the denomination. Some readers also, Payne thought, might, at any rate at first, react against the idea that the customary Baptist definition of the Church as a fellowship of believers requires supplementing. He added, "there are other matters which will not necessarily command agreement."

Council members who were present at the debate thirty-one years ago appear united in the "haziness" of recollection of the debate. All agree that it centered around the concept of the catechumenate which was vehemently criticized by some Council members. The Council also reflected the tension within the group on the issue of redemption.

What has largely been overlooked is that there were five recommendations attached to the Report. These were not included in the printed version and, so far as the present writer is aware, are not recorded anywhere apart from the minute book of the Baptist Union Council. The first one called for the appointment of a full time qualified educational specialist by the Union. The fourth asked for the publication of a pamphlet giving guidance on the dedication service. The other three deserve full quotation:

> 2. That any further statement of the Baptist doctrine of the Church should not only define the Church "theologically" as a "fellowship of believers," but also take full account of the catechumenate including children found to be within the sphere of the Church life and inseparable from it in practice.

---

[86]Ibid., 4.

3. That the Baptist Union through its representatives seek to initiate a study of the theology of childhood in the Faith and Order Commission of the World Council of Churches.
5. That the Council should take all possible steps to encourage Churches to take full responsibility for all work among children so that separation between Church and children's work be brought to an end and children taught and nurtured within the Christian community.

These recommendations were referred for further consideration to the General Purposes and Finance Committee. Remarkably, there appears to have been no further action taken upon them. At least, there is no record at all of these resolutions in the minutes of the General Purposes Committee nor of the Young Peoples Department Committee. The rest appears to have been silence.

At the time a number of significant issues were occupying the attention of the Baptist Union. The 1964 Report of the Commission on the Associations was still being absorbed. The issue of "Baptists and Unity" was under discussion. The November Council of 1966 received a full report on the State and Mission of the Denomination. Conversations proceeded between the Baptists and the Churches of Christ, and the Carey Kingsgate Press faced financial difficulties. The Denomination was also in the process of seeking a successor to Ernest Payne who was due to retire in 1968. On top of all this, Ernest Payne had a second coronary attack on March 30th and was out of action for several months.

It may be suggested that the group was given potentially too wide a remit. This resulted in their having to deal, in limited space, with a variety of difficult questions to some of which the Bible gives no definite answers. This was a recipe for division within a denomination as diverse as the Baptists. Certainly the Report was too challenging and risky a document with which to face the Council. At that point in time the denominational boat could not wisely be rocked further.

But this is not to say that all was lost. Like many other reports to the Council, some of the suggestions of *The Child and the Church* have been assimilated over subsequent years into denominational life. Children have been accepted more and more as, in a proper sense, belonging to the Church and this has included raising the question of their presence at Communion services. Baptist worship has reflected this. The infant dedication service has become integrated fully into the context of Sunday morning worship. It has also remained generally practised in the midst of a growing diversification of Baptist worship. Ecumenically now the practice of the blessing of infants in place of infant baptism has increased in a number of paedobaptist Churches. There is a growing recognition on all sides that discussions on Christian Initiation in general and of baptism and church membership in particular must include consideration of the practice and ecclesiological implications of such a service.[87]

In 1980 the Baptist Union published *Praise God*,[88] which was a collection of resource materials for Christian worship compiled by Alec Gilmore, Edward Smalley, and Michael Walker. It contained a service entitled "Infant Dedication and Thanksgiving," which sought to recognize the variety of parents seeking such a service. The compilers stated their aim as seeking

- To combine a variety of diverse elements, assuming that the user will select what expresses the emphasis he wishes to make.
- By pastoral initiatives to encourage freedom to act according to pastoral wisdom and Christian welcome.

Eleven years later another worship manual was published entitled *Patterns and Prayers for Christian Worship*.[89] This was instigated by the General Purposes and Finance Committee of the Baptist Union of Great Britain, because of the development of a growing variety of practice in Baptist worship. The chairman of the compiling group was Bernard Green. By now the title suggested for the service for infants was "Infant Presentation." Once again what was suggested reflected the wide use of such services and continuing variety of understanding on the part both of Churches and parents involved. In fact, two alternative patterns of worship were suggested.[90] The first was entitled "The Presentation of Infants" and contained thanksgiving, promises by parents and Church and blessing of the child. The second was called, "The Blessing of Infants" and was intended for those parents who wish to give thanks for the child, but have no evident Christian commitment. The form of the promise relates simply to teaching the child "a good and true way of life." There was a blessing of the infant but no participation by the congregation. This

---

[87]See *Louisville: Consultation on Baptism* (Louisville, 1980) Faith and Order Paper 97, esp. 15, 18, 19, 105, and 106, and *Baptism, Eucharist, and Ministry* (Geneva: World Council of Churches, 1982) Faith and Order Paper 111, esp. 2-3.
[88]*Praise God*, compiled by A. Gilmore, E. Smalley, and M. Walker (London: n.p., 1980) 129-36.
[89]*Patterns and Prayers for Christian Worship* (Oxford: Oxford University Press, 1991).
[90]Ibid., 109-18.

latter service was a pastoral response to a nonbelieving family's request for "something to be done for the baby."

Ecumenically, a Baptist liturgy for children has become growingly accepted as normal Baptist practice. Following on the 1982 Lima, Peru convergence document *Baptism, Eucharist, and Ministry* from 1982, the Faith and Order Commission published *Baptism and Eucharist: Ecumenical Convergence in Celebration*.[91] Within this volume there are two Baptist contributions on Infant Dedication. The first is the already mentioned Order suggested in *Praise God*, the second is unattributed and is headed, "A Baptist Service of Thanksgiving on the Birth of a Child," which emphasized that it was an integral part of Family worship with the whole church family present. It followed the pattern of thanksgiving and promises taken by parents and Church, but the questions to the Church were specifically addressed to a lay representative of the Church who responded on behalf of the gathered congregation.[92] In 1994, Churches Together in England encouraged the setting up of a Working Party on Baptism and Church Membership. The Working Party, which included Baptists, reported in 1997 on a range of issues. A number of recommendations were made, including one on the place of children in the Church:

> We recommend that the renewed concern about the place of the child in the church with the Christian nurture of children and whole catechetical process should be tackled by churches working together.[93]

Within the body of its report, the group commented:

> Because of their understanding of the character of faith and church membership, Baptists do not consider it appropriate to baptize infants, but that does not mean that they regard the children of believers as being outside the household of God. Baptists believe that their ceremony of infant presentation and blessing signifies that such children belong to the Church.[94]

---

[91]*Baptism and Eucharist: Ecumenical Convergence in Celebration*, ed. M. Thurian and G. Wainwright (Geneva: World Countil of Churches, 1983) Faith and Order Paper 117.

[92]Ibid., 73-74.

[93]*Baptism and Church Membership*. Churches Together in England (Publications) (London: Baptist Union, 1997) 17. Earlier, in 1973, a working party on "The Child and the Church" had been set up by the Consultative Group on Ministry Among Children of the British Council of Churches. Eventually the Working Party produced a "consultative document" *The Child and the Church* (London: British Council of Churches) which does not significantly deal with the fundamental theological issues involved.

[94]*Baptism and Church Membership*, 17.

The most recent basis for such a claim by the Working Group is to be found in a 1996 discussion document issued by the Doctrine and Worship Committee of the Baptist Union of Great Britain under the title of *Believing and Being Baptized: Baptism, So-Called Rebaptism and Children in the Church*.[95] The final four sections (X-XIII) deal with the question of children and the Church. After a paragraph summarizing the present practice of "infant presentation," which very much reflects that reached by Baptists in *Patterns and Prayers for Christian Worship*, the comment is made that "many Baptists will regard the act called baptism administered to infants in other churches as actually having the same kind of meaning as infant presentation."[96]

It is admitted that Baptist understanding of the relation of the child to God and the church has often been vague and that it still needs a great deal of theological reflection and clarification. There are those Baptists who believe that children share the fallen and sinful condition of all human beings, but that they are not reckoned as guilty until they reach an age when they can make truly moral decisions for themselves. Others affirm that being in Adam is not the only truth about human beings; they are also in Christ—the New Adam who has died and been resurrected with resultant reconciliation with God. Children, therefore are within the saving work of Christ until they reject or accept it for themselves by their responsible acts and choices. But many, possibly the majority of Baptists, have not developed any theological theory about the salvation of young children, but appeal to the mystery of the love, justice and mercy of God.

The document then goes on to pick up an idea suggested in the 1966 "Report on the Child and the Church," namely that, prior to the moment of personal faith and acceptance of Christ and the responsibilities of membership of the covenant community, no one can be said to be a "member" of the church, the Body of Christ. Nevertheless "children may be said to be "in" the Body in the sense that they are enfolded and embraced by it." Such imagery is further developed by the group and the conclusion suggested that

> We can develop the image of the Church as a Body in order to understand the inclusion of children who are not yet members. . . . From the New

---

[95]*Believing and Being Baptized: Baptism, So-Called Rebaptism and Children in the Church* (Didcot: Baptist Union, 1996).
[96]Ibid., 39.

Testament also we might think of the Church as the "household of faith" as a space in which people can dwell in different ways. Because children are not yet "members," should not mean for Baptists that they are excluded from the Body or outside Christ.[97]

There is a further significant contribution to our subject as the group makes an attempt to give clearer definition to the meaning of the blessing of children in the service of infant presentation. The blessing it is suggested has a threefold significance. It is first a proclamation of the gospel, for the child shares in the blessing of being in a world in which Christ has risen and in which the grace of God already abounds. Secondly, the blessing is a prayer for the child that he or she will grow in the knowledge of Christ, and in due time come to a personal faith in him and be made a member of the Church through believer's baptism. Thirdly, in uttering this blessing, the church accepts the child into the orbit of its influence. This is the orbit of God's gracious influence. This is true for all children whether their parents are believers or not. Therefore the act of blessing should not be restricted to Christian families.[98]

As the twentieth century comes towards its close, it is encouraging that the influential authors of this report make this appeal:

> In particular, we make a plea for Baptists to think more seriously about the place of children in the church; we urge that the act of "presentation and blessing of infants" among Baptists be understood more clearly as a part of the journey of growing relationship with God.[99]

V

In an attempt to take seriously these concluding words of *Believing and Being Baptized*, and also as a foundation upon which to build Baptist thought and practice into the next millennium, we would suggest the following conclusions from our study of the child and the church in the present century.

1. The controlling conviction is that the baptismal theory and practice of the bible and early Christian centuries is that of believer's baptism. We are baptized on profession of faith into the Body of Christ, the Church. This has been the Baptist belief and tradition from the very beginning. It is now widely accepted ecumenically as the convergence document *Baptism,*

---

[97]Ibid., 43-44.
[98]Ibid., 46-47.
[99]*Believing and Being Baptized*, 48.

Eucharist, and Ministry attests.[100] It provides the context for Baptist theory and practice concerning the child and the church. Ecumenically, the more seriously Baptists take infant presentation then the more effective they will be in proclaiming the truth of believer's baptism and the more seriously they will be taken by their ecumenical partners.

2. It follows that the responsibility of membership within the Church, the Body of Christ belongs to the baptized believers. But it does not follow that, therefore, children are excluded from any significant relationship with the church, the Body of Christ. As the 1966 Baptist Report notes, children can be in the church without being of the church. This viewpoint is echoed in the 1996 Baptist Report.[101] This is in no way an artificial distinction. As serious students of the bible will know, prepositions are crucial in determining theological meaning.

3. The question of the status before God of such children has been, as we have seen, a divisive issue amongst Baptists form the seventeenth century to the twentieth. The reason for this, however, is that we are given no clear scriptural guidance to decide the matter. There have always been Baptist writers from John Smyth to George Beasley-Murray who have preferred an agnosticism on this issue. But all are agreed that such children are within the love and grace of God as reflected in the incarnation, life, death, resurrection and ascension of Jesus. If this be so, it is proper Christian obedience to act positively towards all children.

    The distinction between the children of the believing and the nonbelieving parent has also produced much discussion. Here again, it may be suggested that Scripture does not pronounce definitely on such a distinction. Of God's purpose children are born members of the human race. The belief or nonbelief of their parents does not affect their status of thus being born. The most recent thinking among Baptists cautions on discrimination against the child on the basis of the parents' belief or nonbelief.[102]

4. Such openness presumes, indeed, "optimistic" agnosticism, but it makes far more Christian sense viewed pastorally and evangelically. There is clear evidence that such practice in the longterm facilitates the working of God's gracious salvation to many a child and its parents. In any case, on what grounds has the church any right to bolt the door against a seemingly genuine doorstep request for admittance, help and guidance?

5. The method by which requests for infant presentation are granted will always be a matter of pastoral discretion. For the children of church families it is straight forward. For the children of other families it will involve discussion, explanation and assurance about the seriousness of the request. It can be useful for the minister to have a representative pastoral

---

[100] *Baptism, Eucharist, and Ministry*, 4.

[101] *The Child and the Church*, 9; *Believing and Being Baptized*, 41-45.

[102] *Believing and Being Baptized*, 47. See also my article "Infant Presentation: An Affirmation of God's Love," *Baptist Times*, 18 July 1991. Such a view in no way denies the *privilege* of being born into a Christian home.

support group to share in this matter. This is not to erect a barrier but to make straight the way. How far the church will be reactive or proactive to this pastoral opportunity will be a matter of individual decision. What is essential is that the family is clear that the service of infant presentation is not simply a one-off day of name giving and family celebration but a longterm commitment to relationship of home to church and church to home.

6. The pattern of the infant presentation service itself has been discussed already, involving as it does welcome, thanksgiving, responses by parents and church and the act of blessing. On the basis of what we are suggesting, the question as to whether the alternative service of "The Blessing of Infants" will ever be used, remains open. It can be used as a "halfway" house. But if infant presentation is to be taken as seriously liturgically, theologically and pastorally as we believe it should, then the "Blessing of Infants" service would still require some form of subsequent presentation with responses as and when the relationship prospers.
7. The final point must relate to the follow-up to Infant Presentation. The Church has accepted the child into the orbit of its influence. He/she belongs in the Church. It is not enough only to present a certificate and write the child's name in a book or inscribe it on a Roll. The Church must accept its responsibility, it must have also people and structures to ensure that that responsibility is carried out.

The word "catechumenate" may not be widely acceptable to Baptists for reasons which are not always clear. But the concept of it must be. Church growth comes about as much by the gradual incorporation of families into its life as by sudden conversions. But as plants need nurturing, so do families—be they one parent or two. The pastoral care and interest of the church is crucial. This is so whether the child is born into a Christian home or not. In all these ways the child will grow into the church, coming to believer's baptism and into the saving relationship of Jesus Christ as a member of His church.

The authoritative exhortation comes from Christ. It was He who said, "Let the children come to me; do not try to stop them; for the Kingdom of God belongs to such as these."

Life Together in Exile: The Social Bond of Separatist Ecclesiology[1]

Stephen Brachlow

Among the more than forty English congregations in late sixteenth and early seventeenth-century Holland that Keith Sprunger has identified in his book, *Dutch Puritanism*, only a handful were comprised of those impatient Puritan dissenters known as Separatists.[2] Disillusioned by repeated Puritan failures to secure sufficient reform in the established church, these former Puritans had moved beyond Puritanism by their decision to abandon entirely the English parochial system and form alternative, covenanted congregations of their own devising.[3] Harassed, imprisoned, and—in the case of at least three Elizabethan Separatists—executed for their nonconformity, most Separatist congregations that had briefly flourished in rural English market towns and villages, or in the urban religious underworld of London, eventually fled in fear to the Netherlands.[4] Favorable economic conditions and a policy of religious toleration among the Dutch had made the "Low Countries" an attractive haven for English dissenters of all stripes during the Elizabethan and early Stuart period.[5]

---

[1] This article is a revision of an unpublished paper presented at the Sixteenth Century Studies Conference, Atlanta, 24 October 1992.

[2] K. L. Sprunger, *Dutch Puritanism: A History of English and Scottish Churches of the Netherlands in the Sixteenth and Seventeenth Centuries* (Leiden: E. J. Brill, 1982) 29-34, 45-70, 134-41.

[3] Patrick Collinson has recently described Separatism a form of "puritanism beyond puritanism" in his "Critical Conclusion" to *The World of Rural Dissenters, 1520–1725*, ed. Margaret Spuffred (Cambridge: Cambridge University Press, 1995) 395.

[4] The execution of Greenwood, Barrowe, and Penry in 1593 are well known; John Copping and Elias Thacker were burned by the authorities for merely distributing Brownist propaganda. B. R. White, *The English Separatist Tradition* (London: Oxford University Press, 1971) 44, 89-90; and Albert Peel, *The Noble Army of Congregational Martyrs* (London: Independent Press, 1948) 30-32.

[5] James R. Coggins, *John Smyth's Congregation: English Separatism, Mennonite Influence and the Elect Nation* (Waterloo, Ontario and Scottdale PA: Herald Press, 1991) 44-46. Traffic between English Puritans and Dutch Calvinists was frequent via scholarly exchanges, which also made the Netherlands an attractive environment and a natural destination for English Calvinist refugees. See Anthony Milton, *Catholic and Reformed: The Roman and Protestant Churches in English Protestant Thought 1600–1640*

From the perspective of whether or not these exiled Separatist congregations succeeded in surviving the pressures of refugee existence, in the majority of cases they were failures. At best, one or two congregations—such as Francis Johnson's "Ancient Church" in Amsterdam, which spawned the first experiment in English Baptist polity under the leadership of John Smyth—and John Robinson's Leyden congregation that led to the Mayflower adventure of 1620 managed to survive intact for a decade or so. But more often than not, Separatist communities in exile found themselves hopelessly shattered and divided within a few years, if not months, of their arrival in Holland.[6] Not infrequently these schisms arose over what appears now to be petty, but often bitter, internal quarrels concerning manners and apparel, or over what A. L. Rowse once characterized as being "the useless fooleries" of scholastic differences in the finer points of sixteenth century ecclesial and theological debate.[7] Free of the confrontational religious context of England, in which they had initially come into existence largely in opposition to the corrupt and undisciplined assemblies of the parish system, and where they were often harassed by English prelates and Puritans alike, exiled Separatists often turned against one another.[8] Congregational schism was so common to

---

(Cambridge: Cambridge University Press, 1995) 397.

[6]Robert Browne's short-lived Separatist experiment in the early 1580s in Middleburg disintegrated after a little more than a year over quarrels between Browne and his colleague in ministry, Robert Harrison. The "Ancient Church" suffered multiple fractures during the stormy years of its ascendancy in Amsterdam between 1593 and 1610. See White, *English Separatist Tradition*, 49-50, 95-103, 142-55.

[7]A. L. Rowse, *The England of Elizabeth* (London: Macmillan, 1950) 387. Michael E. Moody has explored the dysfunctional side of Separatist congregational life in several studies. See his "A Critical Edition of George Johnson's *A Discourse of Some Troubles and Excommunications in the Banished English Church at Amsterdam 1603*" (Ph.D. diss., Claremont Graduate School, 1979); "Trials and Travels of a Nonconformist Layman: The Spiritual Odyssey of Stephen Offwood, 1564–ca. 1635," *Church History* 51 (1982): 157-71; "The Apostasy of Henry Ainsworth: A Case Study in Early Separatist Historiography, *Proceedings of the American Philosophical Society* 131 (1987): 15-31; " 'He was not long faithful': Thomas Settle (1555–1622) and Elizabethan Separatism," unpublished paper read at the Sixteenth Century Studies Conference, Atlanta, 24 October 1992.

[8]As Collinson observed about fractious tendencies in exiled separatist communities, "If there were no longer any enemies without, it was necessary to reproduce them within." Patrick Collinson, *The Puritan Character: Polemics and Polarities in Early Seventeenth-Century English Culture* (Los Angeles: William Andrews Clark Memorial Library, 1989) 32.

the Separatist experience in exile that it became a fairly easy target for their many adversaries within the established church.[9]

While the small, sectarian flame of these few Separatist congregations thus burned only briefly—either as hunted congregations driven underground in England or as religious refugees in the Netherlands—the congregational ecclesiology they forged in the crucible of their life together in hiding and in exile nevertheless illuminated a path that led to future significant denominational developments in Old and New England. As B. R. White maintained in *The English Separatist Tradition*, the polity of seventeenth century Baptists and Congregationalists on both sides of the Atlantic owed a considerable debt to the ecclesial vision first articulated in the literature of Elizabethan and early Stuart Separatism.[10]

Certainly, one of the salient features of Separatist polity was the priority they ascribed to the social bond of congregational life. In contrast to the radical individualism that Robert Bellah and others have observed in so much of post-Enlightenment religion in the industrialized West, the early congregationalism of English Separatism emphasized the communal nature of Christian discipleship.[11] As Geoffrey Nuttall observed some years ago in his now classic study of early Congregationalism in England, *Visible Saints*, "few groups . . . rival the early Congregationalists in their conscious and explicit emphasis on "one another" in fellowship." Their corporate focus was not, Nuttall maintained, "only a "note," or characteristic, of the church but a sine qua non, a necessity of the church's existence."[12]

Writing from exile in Amsterdam, Henry Ainsworth made social solidarity a central theme in his devotional treatise, *The Communion of*

---

[9]This was especially true for disaffected Separatists such as Christopher Lawne, a former member of the "Ancient Church" who returned to communion with the Church of England. Lawne argued that internecine conflict in Separatist congregations proved the illegitimacy of what he called "that impure sect" in *The Prophane Schism of the Brownists Discovered* (London, 1612). A year later, Lawne published a second expose of his former coreligionists entitled, *Brownisme Turned the Inside Outward* (London, 1613), in which he highlighted the inconsistencies he saw between Separatist profession and practice. See Peter Milward, *Religious Controversies of the Jacobean Age: A Survey of Printed Sources* (Lincoln and London: University of Nebraska Press, 1978) 59.

[10]White, *English Separatist Tradition*, 164-69.

[11]Robert N. Bellah et al., *Habits of the Heart* (Berkeley: University of California Press, 1985) 152-53, as discussed in Stanly Grenz, "The Community of God: A Vision of the Church in the Postmodern Age," *Crux* 28 (1992): 19-26.

[12]G. F. Nuttall, *Visible Saints: The Congregational Way 1640–1660* (London: Oxford University Press, 1957) 71.

Saints, published in 1607. In his exposition of the Christian life, Ainsworth reminded the gathered saints of the Separatist "Ancient Church," where he was the teaching minister, that "[we] should not live alone, or asunder by ourselves, but join together, and so entertain and nourish a loving and holy communion one with another, in the unity of the faith and Spirit, by the bond of peace. For man is made a sociable creature."[13]

The collective orientation in the congregational ecclesiology of Separatism was fostered in a variety of ways. This essay will explore three of them: first, the role of the church covenant in creating community; second, the communal significant of placing the locus of authority in the gathered people; and third, the way in which congregational discipline was intended to maintain social cohesion.

1. The Church Covenant

The most distinguishing characteristic of Separatist ecclesiology was their use of the church covenant. The covenant provided, in the words of the Separatist John Smyth, the "true form" of a church estate,[14] and therefore, functioned as the organizing and uniting implement of congregational life.[15] The source of the church covenant idea in Separatist ecclesiology has never been entirely clear to historians of the tradition.[16] One of the earliest possible examples of its use in English dissent appears to have been in the Marian underground congregation meeting at Stoke, in

---

[13]Henry Ainsworth, *The Communion of Saints* (Amsterdam, 1607; repr. 1615) 315.

[14]John Symth, *The Works of John Symth*, ed. W. T. Whitley (Cambridge: Cambridge University Press, 1915) 1:270.

[15]R. Tudor Jones, "The Church Covenant in Classical Congregationalism," *The Presbyter* 7 (1962): 10. Typically, Separatists like John Robinson understood that baptism was therefore subsequent to the covenant, being neither the basis for the formation of a church community nor essential to the constitution of a true church. See Timothy George, *John Robinson and the English Separatist Tradition* (Macon GA: Mercer University Press, 1982) 230; and E. Brooks Holifield, *The Covenant Sealed: The Theology of the Sacraments in Puritan New England* (New Haven and London: Yale University Press, 1974) 64-66.

[16]Champlain Burrage, e.g., assumed Anabaptist influence, but offered no conclusive evidence in *The Church Covenant Idea: Its Origin and Development* (Philadelphia: American Baptist Publication Society, 1904) 42-44. Much of the scholarly interest in Separatist covenant theology has centered on their mutualist interpretation. See John F. H. New, *Anglican and Puritan: The Basis of Their Opposition, 1558-1640* (Stanford CA: Stanford University Press, 1964) 94-95; Richard L. Greaves, "The Origins and Early Development of English Covenant Thought," *Historian 31* (1968): 31; White, *English Separatist Tradition*, 54-56.

Suffolk, whose members, "giving their hands together," entered into a covenant with each other not to attend the Roman services of their parish church.[17]

The concept of the church as covenanted community moved to the center of Separatist ecclesiology, as B. R. White has so persuasively demonstrated in the writings of Robert Browne, the first Separatist to write at length on the subject.[18] From Browne on, the covenant served the Separatists as an instrument which separated true saints from the world and bound them together in corporate obedience to the ways of God. Francis Johnson explained that members of Separatist congregations made their covenant "unto the Lord, and one with another, to walk together in the truth of the Gospel . . . and therefore to forsake and avoid whatever is there against [the gospel]."[19] The Separatists who met at Scrooby Manor and in nearby Gainsborough, and who eventually coalesced around the leadership of John Robinson and John Smyth, initially became a formal Separatist congregation when they took a covenant vow together in 1606. According to John Murton's account of the event, "there was first one stood up and made a covenant, and then another, and these two joined together, and so a third, and these became a church.[20] William Bradford's more familiar description of the founding of the Gainsborough-Scrooby congregation by covenant, in which he participated, indicated that "the Lord's free people joined themselves (by a covenant of the Lord) into a church estate, in the fellowship of the gospel, to walk in all His ways made known, or to be made known unto them, according to their best endeavors, whatsoever it should cost them."[21]

Thus, through the ritual of the church covenant, a social—as well as a theocentric—bond was formally established.[22] By means of the church covenant, the gathered folk were formed by the Holy Spirit into an organic community of, in the words of John Robinson, "spiritually hewn and lively stones," who, by virtue of their covenantal relationship, were

---

[17]White, *English Separatist Tradition*, 9.

[18]Ibid., 56.

[19]Francis Johnson, *An Inquirie and Answer of T. White* (Amsterdam, 1606) 19.

[20]John Murton, *A Description of What God Hath Predestined concerning Man* (n.p., 1620) 4.

[21]William Bradford, *Of Plymouth Plantation*, edited by Samuel Eliot Morison (New York: Knopf, 1952) 9.

[22]Larzer Ziff, "The Social Bond of the Church Covenant," *American Quarterly* 10 (1958): 454.

now "orderly laid, and couched together," united together by a bond of close fellowship, interdependence, and shared love.[23] That which formed the communal bond among the gathered saints was not, they believed, merely their mutual willingness to form a covenant community of believers who shared similar interests and commitments. Rather, they believed that their life together was created by the unifying presence and power of Christ, made known to them in and through the covenantal relationship they had embraced with one another in faith. Their sense of Christian community was centered around the experience of the one who, through the agency of the Holy Spirit, had called them out of their separate ways in the world and into the spiritual communion of a covenanted community. So the act of covenanting, they believed, had formed them into an entirely unique, divinely blessed community by virtue of Christ's spiritual presence in their midst.[24] Thus, Robinson defined the church as "they with who[m] the Lord makes his covenant to be their God, and to have them his people, to dwell amongst them as in his temple, which [people] have right to the promises of Christ, and to his presence."[25] Henry Ainsworth agreed that the gathering together of the saints in covenantal relationship was not merely a "bare assembly," but a holy fellowship united in spiritual communion by the Spirit of God. Through the covenant bond, Ainsworth said, "the servants of Christ . . . are so built and coupled together by faith that they grow into a holy temple in the Lord, to be the habitation of God by the Spirit."[26]

2. The Locus of Authority

The spiritual source of Separatist congregationalism arose, then, from the presence of Christ, who became known to the gathered saints through their mutual obedience to the terms of the church covenant. Their communion with Christ in and through the gathered community also provided

---

[23]John Robinson, *A Justification of Separation from the Church of England* (Amsterdam, 1610) 135, 212, 480.

[24]In this sense Separatist covenant theology embraced notions of spiritual presence that Paul Fiddes at Oxford has noted in the New Testament concept of a covenant community, in which the "early Church did not simply believe that they were copying Jesus, but that his personality was present with their community in the form of the Spirit of God, shaping personalities, creating them anew according to his image." Paul S. Fiddes, "Covenant—Old and New," in Paul S. Fiddes et al., *Bound to Love* (London: The Baptist Union, 1985) 18-19.

[25]Robinson, *Justification of Separation*, 134.

[26]Ainsworth, *Communion of Saints*, 318-19.

the source of their congregational understanding of the locus of ministerial authority. Smyth made it clear that Christ's "ministerial power" in the ecclesia did not depend upon a succession of a ministerial elite, as he understood the episcopal structure of the established church in England required. Instead, the gathered members of a true, visible church derived the authority and power for ministerial discipline "immediately from heaven" through the instrument of the covenant: "Unto whom the covenant is given unto them the power of binding and loosing is given."[27]

The egalitarian inclination of Separatist views on ministerial authority was also expressed by Robert Browne, who explained that Christ provided the gathered people, not the prelates or presbyters, with the power of ecclesial government. The congregation, therefore, acted as proprietors of Christ's own ministerial power. As such, Separatist ecclesiology elevated rank and file members to the status of "prophets, priests, and kings." In the language of seventeenth century social structure, congregational members thus formed a spiritual "aristocracy" of those to whom Christ had directly conveyed the authority, power, and privilege "to execute the Lord's government." When, for example, Browne's congregation was initially organized in Norwich in 1580, it was agreed that the members of the congregation possessed the right to "protest, appeal, complain, exhort, dispute, [and] reprove" the ordained shepherds of their flock as they saw fit under God.[28]

At the same time, it is important to recognize that in the highly stratified climate of Elizabethan society, where a clear hierarchy of social rank was widely considered necessary to the well-being of the social order, Separatist propaganda carefully curbed the more radical egalitarian tendencies of their convictions by insisting that the government of the people should be exercised only "in due order."[29] This proviso allowed room for a legitimate use of ministerial authority by ordained officers, who were granted responsibility by the congregation for shepherding the community through their role as interpreters of Scripture. The Separatists believed this proviso should have assured their critics that the democratic drift of their polity would not degenerate into the kind of populist revolt and social anarchy that most Protestants feared in the radical ecclesiology of

---

[27]Symth, *Works*, 2:389, 529, 548.
[28]Robert Browne, *The Writings of Robert Harrison and Robert Browne*, ed. Albert Peel and Leland H. Carlson (London: Allen and Unwin, 1953) 428-29.
[29]Ibid., 429.

the Anabaptists, with whom the Separatists were often associated by their many detractors in Elizabethan and early Stuart England.[30]

Despite the many attacks by Separatists on what they perceived to be the "unwarranted" and unscriptural power of the prelacy in the English church, there thus existed a residual clericalism in their own polity through the distinction Separatists drew between the possession and the use of ministerial authority. The congregation, down to the "meanest member of the body," as one Separatist put it, possessed the power for ministry as an immediate donation of Christ, while the use of that same power was to be exercised only by the elders of the congregation.[31] Neither side of this equation necessarily dominated the other in separatist polity. Rather, the two stood—theoretically—in a balanced, Aristotelian form of equilibrium. Thus, it would be unfair to the real complexities of their ecclesiology to assume, as many of their contemporary opponents did, that Separatists advocated a simple, majority-rule, democratic polity. On the contrary, the Separatists endeavored to uphold a Calvinist veneration for ecclesial order through the executive role they accorded an ordained ministry while, at the same time, recognizing that the locus of authority was firmly rooted in the gathered community.[32]

Nonetheless, given the hierarchical context of ecclesial and political thought in the Elizabethan establishment, the democratic edge of the Separatist paradigm provided the radical dynamic of their polity and offered ordinary Puritan saints a significant and unaccustomed voice in church affairs. Thus the Separatist *Apologie* of 1604, determined that all public church actions should be administered by the officers, but only in so far as the officers did so "with the knowledge, presence, approbation and consent" of the gathered congregation.[33]

This Separatist affirmation of collective decision making, which applied to all major church actions—from the reception of new members and the election of officers to the practice of communal discipline—was the primary reason for another emphasis peculiar to Separatist ecclesiolo-

---

[30]Henry Ainsworth, *An Animadversion to Mr. Richard Clyftons Advertisement* (Amsterdam, 1613) 58.

[31]Robinson, *Justification of Separation*, 133.

[32]Stephen Brachlow, *The Communion of Saints: Radical Puritan and Separatist Ecclesiology 1570–1625* (Oxford: Oxford University Press, 1988) 174-85.

[33]Henry Ainsworth and Francis Johnson, *An Apologie or Defence of Such True Christians as Are Commonly (But Unjustly) Called Brownists* (Amsterdam, 1604) 64.

gy: the size of a congregation.³⁴ The Separatist perspective was neatly expressed in Ainsworth's conviction that the "congregation of saints, when it is the greatest, is but a little flock and a small remnant."³⁵ Membership should remain small enough, the congregationally minded Separatists insisted, for the entire congregation to meet in one room, so that members would have an intimate and personal knowledge of one another in order to be able to exercise all the corporate duties of a congregational ministry.³⁶ "Each member of the church mutually ought to know one another," Thomas Helwys wrote, "so that they can perform all deeds of brotherly love to one another in a physical and spiritual manner."³⁷

But the size of the congregation was related as much to the concern for spiritual discernment of Christ's presence and his intentions for the congregational life as it was for carrying out the demands of the covenant relationship amongst its members. In much the same way that the covenant community was perceived to be the dwelling place of God's Spirit, discerning the will of the Spirit for the church was considered a responsibility and an exercise of the gathered saints. As Roger Hayden of Bristol recently observed about the congregational orientation of Separatist polity, "since Christ's power is given to each Christian . . . the mind of Christ is to be found in the shared fellowship of the covenanted believers."³⁸

3. Congregational Discipline

While the church covenant formally knit individual saints together with their God, and placed Christ's ministerial authority in the hands of the gathered saints, the purpose of Separatist congregational discipline was to strengthen social cohesion and preserve the organic, spiritual life of the covenanted community. Along with the traditional two-mark definition of a true visible church in classical Protestantism, which included the Word rightly preached and the sacraments properly administered, communal discipline duly dispensed became an essential element, a third characteris-

---

³⁴B. R White, *English Separatist Tradition*, 26-27.
³⁵Ainsworth, *Communion of Saints*, 344.
³⁶R. Tudor Jones, *John Robinson's Congregationalism* (London: Congregational Memorial Hall Trust, 1987) 18.
³⁷Article 12 of the Helwys's congregation's "Synopsis fidei," as quoted in Coggins, *John Smyth's Congregation*, 201.
³⁸Roger Hayden, "Baptists, Covenants, and Confessions," in Fiddes et al., *Bound to Love*, 25.

tic mark of a true church in Separatist ecclesiology.[39] Robert Browne explained that the significance of congregational discipline was derived from its role in preserving the living presence of Christ within the covenanted community. The exercise of congregational discipline ensured that "Christ is the life and essence of the Church," without which he becomes "but a dead Christ," diminished to a meaningless, incomprehensible symbol at the center of a spiritually lifeless institution.[40] In this way, then, Separatists understood communal discipline as a sign of Christ's real spiritual presence in the community, as "a ceaseless manifestation of the Spirit of life," to use the words of John S. Coolidge, "working to overcome what is not life."[41] Thus, John Robinson characterized congregational discipline as a display of Christ's own participation in church affairs, "for the use whereof Christ shows his judgement . . . and promises his joint assent in their public assembly."[42] Negatively, congregational censures provided the means by which, in the typically colorful language of Separatist rhetoric, "the body of Christ is disburdened of noisome, rotten members." Positively, congregational discipline was considered to be "a duty of love" to be carried out as a joint action of the church assembled, in which action "the redeemer will come until them . . . [and] live in the midst of them."[43]

Perhaps more than any other feature of Separatist ecclesiology, congregational discipline also revealed the collective, corporate shape of their polity. When it came to matters of spiritual discipline. Separatist ecclesiology gave priority to the communal conscience over that of the individual. For example, if an individual Separatist was convinced that another member of the congregation had violated the covenant relationship in such a way that warranted church censure, he/she was nevertheless obliged to maintain full communion with the offending party and assume their fidelity to the covenant as long as the congregation judged the offender innocent of wrongdoing. Conversely, individual members were required to refrain from all spiritual communion with anyone under the

---

[39]George, *John Robinson*, 136-39.
[40]Browne, *Writings*, 460-61.
[41]John S. Coolidge, *The Pauline Renaissance in England* (London: Oxford University Press, 1970) 60-61. See also Timothy George's exploration of this theme as the motive for separation in *John Robinson*, 105-15.
[42]John Robinson, *Of Religious Communion Private and Publique* (Amsterdam, 1614) 24.
[43]Ainsworth, *Communion of Saints*, 453, 459, 478.

censure of the community—even if they were convinced that the community had, in its collective judgement, erred in the matter.[44]

Ideally, church discipline functioned as the means through which, as Ainsworth wrote, "the saints are most nearly united together in one body."[45] In this way, congregational discipline held the potential of spiritually unifying disparate members of a gathered church, each of whom struggled with their own infirmities and sinful inclinations that could—and, at times, *did*—erupt into public quarrels, factionalism, and mutually bitter recriminations among the saints. But Ainsworth was also aware that congregational discipline, with its emphasis on the will of the collective conscience, had the potential to become oppressive and unduly harsh in its judgement of opinions, practices, and beliefs that deviated from the accepted norm.[46] An irenic and moderate voice within the Separatist tradition, Ainsworth urged caution in carrying out the disciplinary mandate of congregational life.[47] He encouraged Separatists to treat one another with tenderness and loving-kindness out of an acknowledgement that all members were equally subject to the corruption of the flesh: "so in the bowels of love and mercy, they are to tender each one his neighbor as himself," because each one has "their burden of sins and infirmities."[48]

Central to these convictions about the communal bond of church discipline was the social dimension that Separatists acknowledged concerning the presence of the Holy Spirit. They were convinced, as Henry Barrow explained, that mutual discernment among the gathered saints signified the Spirit's active presence and blessing in their corporate lives. Barrow was equally confident that in the event of disagreements within the gathered community, the presence of Christ's Spirit that had

---

[44] John Robinson, *The Works of John Robinson*, ed. Robert Ashton (London: John Snow, 1851) 3:87.

[45] Ainsworth, *Communion of Saints*, 436.

[46] Ainsworth himself became the center of a controversy in Johnson's congregation over the issue of whether or not his apostacy from Separatism during the early years of his Separatist career disqualified him from holding the office of teaching minister. The controversy eventually caused one of several splits the Ancient Church would suffer, leading in this instance to the formation of a new congregation of Separatist "moderates" under Ainsworth's leadership. See Moody, "The Apostacy of Henry Ainsworth," 15-31.

[47] Michael Moody has highlighted the conciliatory, noncombative spirit of Ainsworth's personal character in " 'A Man of a Thousand': The Reputation and Character of Henry Ainsworth 1569/70–1622," *Huntington Library Quarterly* 45 (1982): 200-14.

[48] Ainsworth, *Communion of Saints*, 436.

initially moved a majority in the congregation to a common understanding in matters of faith and practice would eventually move all of the elect into harmonious understanding of biblical truth.[49] It was this same strong commitment to congregational solidarity and communal conscience which underlay the communitarian advice that John Robinson offered in a letter, written in July, 1620 to the Pilgrims who were about to set sail from Southampton for North America. Robinson has, of course, gained considerable notoriety for his celebrated "Farewell Address" given to the departing Pilgrims some months earlier at Delftshaven, in which he indicated that he was "very confident the Lord had more truth and light yet to break forth out of his holy word."[50] But he also urged those same Pilgrims in his July letter to beware of individual aspirations and personal ambitions which so easily become, he said, "a deadly plague" to the well-being of their life together in Christian community. In words that are perhaps not so easily agreeable to the individualistic sensibilities of most modern, western Christianity, as Robinson's "further light" advice so often, is, his July correspondence admonished the Pilgrims to "let every man repress in himself and the whole body in each person, as so many rebels against the common good, all private respects of men's selves, not sorting with the general convenience."[51]

Conclusion

The Separatists believed that the life they embraced together in the gospel possessed a spiritually dynamic quality, as the further light clause of Robinson's farewell and numerous other Separatist church covenants attested.[52] They were convinced that, just as the Spirit of God had led them in the past out of the darkness of popery, episcopacy, and the duplicities of Puritan compromises with a corrupt established church, into the clearer light of Separatist ecclesial practice, God's Spirit would in future years bear them further along the road of Protestant reform, on which they had covenanted to walk together. They fully expected that the Spirit which united them through the covenant would also guide them, as Bradford had expressed it in the Gainsborough-Scrooby covenant, "in the

---

[49] Henry Barrow, *The Writing of Henry Barrow 1590–1591*, ed. Leland H. Carlson (London: George Allen & Unwin, 1966) 257.
[50] Edward Winslow, *Hypocrisie Unmasked* (London, 1646) 98.
[51] John Robinson, "Certain Useful Advertisements," in *Mourts Relations* (1622), ed. H. M. Dexter (New York: Garrett Press, 1969) xlv.
[52] Coggins, *John Symth's Congregation*, 117-19.

fellowship of the gospel to walk in all God's ways, made known, or to be made known unto them."[53]

James Coggins, a Canadian Mennonite Brethren editor, has observed, however, that in the act of covenanting as a gathered congregation, the Separatists rarely acknowledged the possibility of conflict between the two sides of the church covenant relationship, i.e. between their covenant with God and the one they made with each other as members of a congregation.[54] The assumption was, of course, that those two sides would always function in concert as a single work of the same Spirit.[55] But the frequent schisms that fragmented Separatist congregations suggest that the two sides often clashed, especially when individual Separatists believed they had discovered further light in Scripture that had not as yet been "made known" to the rest of the congregation.

While there appeared serious, often irreparable, cracks in the practice of Separatist communal ideals, this did not minimize the powerful attraction of those ideals for many alienated English Puritans who found themselves repelled by the mixed and polluted company of the parish churches and drawn toward the strong spiritual bond that sometimes also characterized life together in exiled Separatist congregations.[56] This, at least, was the very reason William Bradford assumed that Robinson's Leyden congregation prospered so in the years leading up to the Mayflower journey. According to the then-aging governor of Plimoth Plantation, "many came unto them from diverse parts of England, so as they grew a great congregation," all because, as Bradford put it, they had "lived together in peace and love and holiness." And whenever disputes arose among them, "as it cannot be but some time there will, even amongst the best of men," they were, in Bradford's quaint expression, "ever met with and nipped in the head betimes, or otherwise so well composed as still love, peace, and communion was continued."[57] Bradford went on to say,

> Such was the true piety, the humble zeal and fervent love of this people (whilst they thus lived together) towards God and His ways, and the single-

---

[53]Bradford, *Of Plymouth Plantation*, 9.
[54]Coggins, *John Smyth's Congregation*, 120.
[55]See the discussion of this in Moody, "Thomas Settle," 11-12.
[56]Patrick Collinson, "The Cohabitation of the Faithful with the Unfaithful," *From Persecution to Toleration: The Glorious Revolution and Religion in England*, ed. Ole Petre Grell, Jonathan I. Israel, and Nicholas Tyacke (Oxford: Clarendon Press, 1991) 58-59.
[57]Bradford, *Of Plymouth Plantation*, 18.

heartedness and sincere affection one towards another that they came as near the primitive pattern of the first churches as any other church of these later times have done.[58]

Obviously, the experience of social cohesion and spiritual rapport in Separatist congregational life at times proved to be in this way a palpable one for many within the fold. Forced separation from the communal life of gathered Separatist churches by imprisonment could prove, as it did for Henry Barrow, a painful experience. Writing from a London prison cell in the early 1590s, Barrow said, "So sweet is the harmony of God's grace unto me in the congregation, and the conversation of the saints at all times, as I think myself as a sparrow on the housetop when I am exiled from them."[59] While the polemical tone of Separatist writings often obscured this communal dimension of the Separatist experience, B. R. White observed that the personal testimony of Separatists like Barrow

> provides a useful reminder that [they] were not merely seeking an outward conformity to what they believed to be the divine pattern for the church: they believed that in the fellowship of the covenanted community they experienced the communion of saints with an intimacy and a reality utterly unknown to the casual and undisciplined assemblies which met for worship in the parish churches around them.[60]

The communal ideal of Separatism thus worked in two directions. As long as a Separatist congregation experienced the kind of harmony described by Bradford and Barrow, that experience confirmed the communitarian aspirations of Separatist polity, and also justified the enormous personal sacrifice of normal ties to extended family and English society which the act of separation often involved. When, however, these same communal aspirations were undermined by discord and factionalism within exiled Separatist congregations, the dissonance individual Separatists must have felt between expectation and experience often led to profound disenchantment and a seemingly inevitable collapse of the corporate life that the exiled Separatist saints so wished to embrace in the fellowship of the gospel.[61] The many Separatist failures to realize fully

---

[58]Ibid., 19.

[59]Henry Barrow, *The Writings of John Greenwood and Henry Barrow 1591–1593* (London: Allen and Unwin, 1966) 143.

[60]White, *English Separatist Tradition*, 83.

[61]The disenchantment was often deeply felt. Patrick Collinson cites Thomas White's bitter complaint about his sojourn with Johnson's Amsterdam congregation: "I thought . . . that they had been all saints, but I found them all devils." See Collinson, "Sects and

their communal ideals may lead modern heirs of the Separatist dissenting tradition to dismiss their ecclesial experiments from any serious consideration as informative models for congregational life in the contemporary church today. But in an age of radically shifting values, and an increasingly fragmented, isolated, and alienated modern society, the Separatist quest for what recently has been characterized as an "authentic Christian community over against the environing culture,"[62] remains an alluring one for study for those who seek to learn in our time what it may mean to be a community of faith, as Bradford put it, "in the fellowship of the gospel," a community that attempts to walk together "in all God's ways, made known, or to be made known unto them."[63]

---

the Evolution of Puritanism" in *Puritanism: Transatlantic Perspectives on a Seventeenth-Century Anglo-American Faith*, edited by Francis J. Bremer (Boston MA: Massachusetts Historical Society, 1993) 161.

[62]Timothy George, " 'Mt. Sion in a Wilderness': A Profile of Pilgrim Spirituality," *This Sacred History: Anglican Reflections for John Booty*, ed. Donald S. Armentrout (Cambridge MA: Cowley Publications, 1990) 73.

[63]Bradford, *Of Plymouth Plantation*, 9.

"Sing Side by Side": John Rippon and Baptist Hymnody[1]

Ken R. Manley

> It has afforded me no small Pleasure to unite, as far as I could, here below different Denominations of ministers and Christians, in the same noble Work which shall for ever employ them above. My enquiry has not been, whose Hymns shall I choose, but what Hymns; and hence it will be seen, that Churchmen and Dissenters, Watts and Tate, Wesley and Toplady, England and America, sing side by side.[2]

Few issues are as contentious in many parts of the Baptist world today as changes in worship, especially the introduction of new kinds of songs. Baptists have a long history of controversy over hymn singing: whether to sing at all, what to sing and how to sing. But it seems that eras of spiritual renewal, especially among evangelicals, are marked by new outbursts of praise in song. The vision and labor of one leading Baptist at a time of great renewal among English Baptists casts an important light on the place of hymnody in such renewal.

John Rippon (1751–1836) was a leading English Nonconformist, especially among Particular Baptists. His leadership of London Baptists as pastor of Carter Lane, Southwark from 1773 until his death, his *Baptist Annual Register* (1790–1802), his central role in the promotion of a vigorous evangelical Calvinism and in the formation of the Baptist Union all suggest his importance.[3] But the clearest indication of Rippon's desire

---

[1] I wish to record my deep gratitude to B. R. White, under whose guidance an interest in Rippon and his significance was first stimulated many years ago. Rippon's interest in renewal, ecumenical relations, Baptist church life witness, especially its worship and mission, are also themes of central importance for Dr. White's scholarly and church work. This study is dedicated with respect and affection to my friend, Dr. White.

[2] J. Rippon, editor, *A Selection of Hymns*, viii. (In these notes, the place of publication is London, unless otherwise indicated.)

[3] For Rippon, see K. R. Manley, "The Making of an Evangelical Baptist Leader: John Rippon's Early Years, 1751–1773," *Baptist Quarterly* (hereafter *BQ*) 26 (1976): 254-74; K. R. Manley "John Rippon and Baptist Historiography," *BQ* 28 (1979): 109-25; K. R. Manley, "Pattern of a Pastorate: John Rippon at Carter Lane, Southward (1773–1836)," *Journal of Religious History* 11 (1980): 169-88; K. R. Manley, "John Rippon and American Baptists," *Quarterly Review* 41 (1980): 52-61. These studies draw on my thesis: "John Rippon, D.D. (1751–1836) and the Particular Baptists" (D.Phil. dissertation, Oxford University, 1967).

to serve the wider community of Baptists and that which made his name a household word among Baptists in both Britain and America was the publication of *A Selection of Hymns from the Best Authors* . . . (hereinafter *Selection*) (1787), which, with his related books, constituted a highly significant contribution to Baptist hymnody. Rippon consciously strove to unite all Christians, at least as they sang "side by side."

Rippon lived in a time of remarkable development in English hymnody. Isaac Watts and those of his "school," notably Phillip Doddridge (1702–1751), dominated all Dissenting hymnody. The songs of the Wesleyan Revival, slowly and not without occasional doctrinal alterations, began to be sung by Dissenters. The Calvinistic wing of the Revival produced Augustus Toplady, and the *Olney Hymns* (1779) of John Newton and William Cowper.

Baptists too were in what has been called "the golden age" of their hymnody (1760–1800).[4] The controversies over the legitimacy of congregational singing had virtually ceased, and many of the most prolific hymn-writers Baptists ever produced were active: Daniel Turner, Anne Steele, Benjamin Beddome, Samuel Stennett, Robert Robinson, Samuel Medley, John Fawcett, and Benjamin Francis. Rippon's editorial work was of cardinal significance in the promotion and preservation of the best of this Baptist hymnody, as well as influencing the use of the best hymns from all sources.

Three reasons for an analysis of Rippon's hymnodic work may be suggested. First, hymns help us to recover the worshipping life of an earlier generation. The distinguished hymnologist, L. F. Benson has suggested that

> A hymn may or may not happen to be literature; in any case it is something more. Its sphere, its motive, its canons and its uses are different. It belongs with the things of the Spirit, in the sphere of religious experience and

---

[4]L. F. Benson, *The English Hymn, Its Development and Use in Worship* (New York, 1915) 215. A still useful review of Baptist hymnody is R. H. Young, "The History of Baptist Hymnody in England from 1612 to 1800" (D.Mus. dissertation, University of Southern California, 1959). Although Young's treatment of Rippon is generalized, his comments on the tunes published by Rippon are helpful. There is valuable material on Baptist hymnody in Raymond Brown, *The English Baptists of the Eighteenth Century* (1986) and J. H. Y. Briggs, *The English Baptists of the Nineteenth Century* (1994). For Rippon and other connections with Bristol Academy, see E. Sharpe, "Bristol Baptist College and the Church's Hymnody," *BQ* 28 (1979): 7-16.

communion with God. Its special sphere is worship, and its fundamental relations are not literary but liturgical.[5]

Similarly, Ernest A. Payne commented that the hymnbook took the place for dissenters which the Prayer Book traditionally enjoyed in the devotional life, public and private, of the Anglican.[6] Hence a study of Rippon's books suggests the devotional content of Baptist worship during his lifetime and is a valuable pointer to Baptist spirituality for the period.

Secondly, hymns (as the Prayer Book again) are invaluable for the preservation and communication of theology. "We write no Creed, because our hymns are full of the form of sound words," B. L. Manning claimed for Nonconformists.[7] John Wesley described his 1780 hymnbook as a "body of practical and experimental divinity,"[8] and as such he utilized it. The widespread use of Rippon's book among Baptists was a theologically unifying force of almost incalculable significance. Few ordinary Baptists would read John Gill's tedious tomes,[9] but most of them sang from Rippon's book. As Raymond Brown rightly stressed, "A newly liberated Calvinism had found expression in song."[10] this was a responsibility Rippon fully recognized. Accordingly, some attempt is made here to demonstrate how Rippon's book promoted the orthodox but moderate Calvinism he espoused.

Finally, Rippon's careful collection, frequent improvement, and wide distribution of many Baptist hymns were important in the development of Baptist hymnody. Rippon's hymnbooks were: (1) the *Selection* (1787) greatly enlarged in the tenth (1800) and twenty-seventh (1828) editions; (2) *A Selection of Psalm and Hymn Tunes* . . . , (hereinafter *Tune Book*) (ca. 1791); (3) *An Arrangement of the Psalms, Hymns, and Spiritual Songs of the Rev Isaac Watts* (hereinafter Rippon's *Watts*) (1801).

1. The Selection

(i) *Preparations, Sources, and Editing*. Rippon's *Selection* enjoyed a phenomenal success. The principal explanation is simply that he satisfied

---

[5]Benson, *The English Hymn*, viii.
[6]*The Free Church Tradition in the Life of England*, 3rd ed. (1951) 95.
[7]*The Hymns of Wesley and Watts* (1942) 133.
[8]*A Collection of Hymns, for the Use of the People Called Methodists* (1780).
[9]John Gill (1697–1771) had been Rippon's predecessor at Carter Lane and a major theological influence among Particular Baptists. For details see Brown, *English Baptists of the Eighteenth Century*.
[10]R. Brown, *The English Baptists of the Eighteenth Century*, 93.

a deep need for a good hymn collection. The hymns most commonly in use were those of Watts, from his *Hymns and Spiritual Songs* (1707) and *Psalms of David* (1719), frequently republished and known as Watts's *Hymns and Psalms*. Baptists found the hymns of Watts eminently suitable: they were doctrinally orthodox, objective in tone, and free from frivolities. One result of Watts' ascendancy was a bias toward homiletical hymnody among Baptists.

The only specifically Baptist general collection available before 1787 was *A Collection of Hymns Adapted to Public Worship*, popularly known as the Bristol Collection (1769), edited by C. Evans and J. Ash, which contained 412 hymns. Several Baptist writers, notably Anne Steele, but also Beddome, Turner, and Robinson were represented. However this book was inadequate for several reasons; what was needed was a supplement to Watts (such as Rippon produced), not an alternative to Watts. The general usefulness of the book for public services, especially for hymns related to the sermon, was restricted. Certain doctrinal or occasional needs were not provided for: there were no hymns specially designated for the doctrines of election or perseverance (vital Calvinistic themes), and none specifically on the Holy Spirit; only three on baptism, no general hymns for singing "after the sermon," and very few suited to the meetings for prayer, or association gatherings. During the succeeding years many good hymns had gradually found their way into the worship of the Baptists, and many quality original hymns had been restricted to only one or two congregations. The only other Baptist books available were collections of the poems and hymns of individual authors, such as those by Daniel Turner,[11] Benjamin Wallin,[12] Anne Steele,[13] John Needham,[14] John Fellows,[15] and John Fawcett.[16] But these were mostly restricted in scope, and no congregation could be expected to possess all of them. There was an apparent need for one good collection, and this Rippon clearly understood.

As Rippon emphasized, the situation was highly unsatisfactory. Worshippers had no idea who had written many hymns used in their

---

[11]*Divine Songs, Hymns, and Other Poems* (1747).
[12]*Evangelical Hymns and Songs* (1750).
[13]*Poems on Subjects Chiefly Devotional, by Theodosia*, 2 vols. (1760).
[14]*Hymns Devotional and Moral* (1768).
[15]*Hymns on Believer's Baptism* (1773).
[16]*Hymns Adapted to the Circumstances of Public Worship and Private Devotion* (1782).

services, nor where they could read them again for their private devotions. Rippon found that his people continually asked him, "Why could we not have some of the best Hymns in all these Authors put together, and used with Dr. Watts?"[17] Thus the impetus for the *Selection* arose directly out of Rippon's own pastoral experience.

Rippon gradually realized that a similar need existed in America, where Watts also reigned supreme. The first Baptist hymnbook was produced in Newport, Rhode Island, in 1766, *Hymns and Spiritual Songs, Collected from Several Authors*. But there was a need for good specifically Baptist hymns, especially for baptismal services. The success of the *Selection* on both sides of the Atlantic demonstrated the urgent need for just such a book.

Rippon aimed to complement Watts suggesting that he did not have many "whole" hymns on

> the Characters of Christ—the Work of the Spirit—the Christian Graces and Tempers—the Parables of the New Testament—the Ordinance of Baptism—and but few suited to Associations and General Meetings of Churches and Ministers—Ordinations—Church meetings—Meetings of Prayer—Annual Sermons to Young People, &c.[18]

These aspects Rippon strengthened in his book. He also aimed to provide a greater variety of hymns on specific themes and a variety of meters.

Rippon confessed that the materials he utilized might well have "appeared to greater advantage" had others handled them. He hoped that it would not deemed presumptuous, for "a Junior Brother," to "walk abroad and gather up the Golden Ears which have long lain scattered in the Fields of Piety and Genius, that so a Sheaf of Gratitude might be presented by an affectionate Pastor to his affectional People."[19] Certainly Rippon brought to the task a capacity for hard work, a patience with detail, a discriminating poetic taste, and usually an unerring assessment of the Baptists' hymnodic needs.

In selecting suitable hymns Rippon examined "more than *Ninety* printed Volumes of Hymn-Books, Hymns, Psalms, &c attentively perusing all the Collections I could obtain in this Country and from America."[20] Thus he had to select from literally thousands of available

---

[17]*Selection*, ii.
[18]Ibid., iv.
[19]Ibid., viii.
[20]Ibid., v. More than sixty books probably used by Rippon have been examined in the

hymns. In fact, the only American hymns used were those by Samuel Davies,[21] published by Thomas Gibbons in 1769.[22] Rippon confidently claimed that this book "ought to contain a greater variety of Subjects and Metres, than either of the Collections extant."[23]

Some hymns, of course, had to be included because of their popularity. Hence, some 110 hymns from the Bristol Collection also in Rippon's book. Then there were "more than *Three Hundred* others," which had been previously printed, but had not appeared in a general collection. For example, Rippon used 101 hymns by Doddridge,[24] about twice as many as other hymnals ("Bristol" had 41); 53 by Anne Steele; 39 by Watts from other than his *Hymns and Psalms*;[25] 34 from the *Gospel Magazine* (1774–1784), although of these only ten had not appeared in other Collections; 32 from the *Olney Collection*; 25 by Thomas Gibbons.[26]

About "one-fourth part of the Whole," or as Rippon claimed in the preface to the tenth edition, about "one hundred and fifty" hymns, had not been published previously. Two-thirds of these original hymns may be readily identified: 38 by Samuel Stennett, who had given Rippon "more than 70 hymns";[27] 42 by Beddome, who had given Rippon "above 500" hymns[28] (although 13 had been in the "Bristol Collection"); 8 by Turner, 5 by Francis, 4 by Ryland (Junior), 2 by "K,"[29] Robinson's "Mighty God, while angels bless thee," and several anonymous hymns, some of which were by Rippon himself.

Rippon indicated the authorship for 395 hymns. Authors of a further 123 hymns have been traced, so that about 70 remain as anonymous.[30] It may be immediately noted that while 187, or 32%, of the hymns are

---

preparation of this study.

[21] For Davies (1723–1761) see J. Julian ed., *Dictionary of Hymnology* (1907) 280-81 (hereinafter Julian).

[22] T. Gibbons, *Hymns Adapted to Divine Worship* (1769). For Gibbons, see Julian, 420.

[23] *Selection*, vi.

[24] P. Doddridge, *Hymns Founded on Various Texts in the Holy Scriptures*, ed. J. Orton (1755).

[25] For a list of Watts's other works, see Julian, 1237.

[26] A second volume of *Hymns Adapted to Divine Worship* was issued in 1784.

[27] J. Rippon to T. Ustick (Philadelphia), 18 August 1786 (Archives, American Baptist Historical Society).

[28] Ibid.

[29] "K" has been suggested as: (1) George Keith, for which there is no real evidence; and (2) Robert Keene. See Julian, 537. For Keene, see below.

[30] For a full list of all authors and known denominational links in all editions, see Manley thesis, 227-29.

known to be by Baptists (in the first edition), Rippon was not unduly influenced by the denominational allegiances of the authors.

The most popular hymn-writer in the *Selection* was Doddridge with 105 hymns by the 27th edition (101 in the first edition). Baptist writers most frequently utilized were Anne Steele, Benjamin Beddome, and Samuel Stennett. Eighteen Baptist poets had hymns in the first edition. Rippon wrote some hymns himself, although these are not generally identified.[31] Non-Baptists most often employed were Watts, Gibbons, the Wesleys, John Newton, William Cowper, August Toplady, John Cennick and Samuel Davies. Clearly the Dissenting hymn-writers dominated. But the inclusion of some 24 Wesleyan hymns in 1787 is significant. Alexander Knox later suggested that one of the signs of the decline of Calvinism among Dissenters was the increasing use made of the Wesleys' hymns.[32] By contrast, the "Bristol Collection" had only three hymns by the Wesleys, so Rippon may fairly be claimed to have introduced many of their hymns to the general body of Baptists.

To alter hymns was almost an axiomatic task for any self-respecting hymn editor. John Wesley's famous complaint[33] about the treatment that Charles' and his hymns received was largely ignored. Rippon freely altered several hymns, and was helped in his "corrections" by Stennett, Turner, Francis, Beddome, and Dunscombe.[34] Clearly, however, the bulk of the "corrections" were his responsibility. After the careful examination of as many alterations as have been discovered the general impression of R. H. Young may be confirmed, that Rippon's tampering "seems to some extent defensible in that his alterations, for the most part, tend to improve the flow of verse rather than alter theological meaning."[35]

Rippon's "corrections" fall into two broad types. Some are altered for poetic style or literary improvement and others (relatively few) for doctrinal reasons. Most frequently verses were simply omitted since hymns of ten or more verses were not generally suitable for congregational purposes. In several cases there is a suspicion that the omission was not merely for brevity's sake, but because of poor poetry or theology: but

---

[31] For examples of hymns by Rippon, see Manley thesis, 230-33.
[32] *Remains of Alexander Knox, Esq.*, III (1837) 181, quoted in J. D. Walsh, "Methodism at the End of the Eighteenth Century," in *A History of the Methodist Church in Great Britain*, ed. Rupert Davies and Gordon Rupp (London: Epworth Press, 1965) 229.
[33] J. Wesley, op. cit., preface, vi. See B. L. Manning, *Dissenting Deputies*, 118.
[34] J. Rippon to T. Ustick, 18 August 1786 (see n. 27).
[35] Op. cit., 131.

this, of course, cannot be proved. One illustration, however, is the third verse of Hymn 200 which Rippon omitted after his first edition. Based on the imagery of the Vine and the Branches (John 15), Toplady's hymn became ridiculous:

> Grafted in thee, by Grace alone,
> In Growth I daily rise,
> And rais'd on this Foundation-stone
> My Top shall reach the Skies.

Again, many of Rippon's transpositions of verses have passed into popular usage. Often Rippon rearranged a hymn to conclude with a note of praise.

Perhaps Rippon's chief merit as an editor was the skill shown in more extensive revisions. In at least twenty hymns one or more verses, presumably by Rippon, were added to the original version. Most of these centos passed into common use: to take only the examples listed in Julian, some twenty-four centos by Rippon were widely adopted. The most famous is Rippon's extensive alteration of Edward Perronet's "All Hail the Power of Jesus' Name!" This hymn, found in most modern hymnals, is usually correctly designated, "Edward Perronet, altered John Rippon" and is the outstanding illustration of Rippon's facility for improving a hymn.[36]

There are several examples of an unfortunate expression or poor rhyme being altered. Although not averse to the description of sinners as "worms" ("vermicular hymns" as Canon Dearmer called them),[37] Rippon did alter one hymn on the Lord's Supper, substituting "unworthy guests" for "unworthy worms."[38] Again, Wesley's "Ye that pass by, behold the man!" (Hymn 136) was altered probably for aesthetic motives. In Rippon's first edition, it read as the original:[39]

> O thou dear suffering Son of God,
> How doth thy Heart to Sinners move!
> Help us to catch thy precious Blood,
> Help us to taste the dying Love!

---

[36] For details, see Manley thesis, 158-60. For Perronet's original version, see *Gospel Magazine* 7 (1780): 185; cf. E. Perronet, *Occasional Verses, Moral and Sacred* (1785) 22.
[37] Quoted by H. W. Foote, *Three Centuries of American Hymnody* (Hamden CT: Shoe String Press, 1961) 359.
[38] Hymn 472, vs. 5, 1.4; cf. I. Watts, *Horae Lyricae* (1834) 104.
[39] Op. cit., hymn 24.

The image of the third line was altered in the second edition:

> Sprinkle on us thy precious blood,
> And melt us with thy dying Love!

Possibly, of course, the change of emphasis from the activity of the sinner ("Help us to catch") to that of God ("Sprinkle on us") reflects a theological distinction.

Other poor phrases altered include: the tear "that secret wets the widow's bed";[40] Wesley's "slaughtered Hecatombs";[41] Toplady's "pouring eyesight on our eyes."[42]

Rippon was duly concerned with sound theology in his hymnal:

> I trust it will be found, that the Hymns in this *Selection* are truly evangelical; but if any Sentiment or Expression has escaped me that is contrary to the sacred Oracles I hope I shall be willing to correct it whenever an opportunity may offer. It would pain me beyond Expression if there were any Hymn in the Book that might give just Reason for offence, to any serious Mind. I hope no Line, nor even Syllable, will be found tending to make the Breaches between good Men wider than they are already."[43]

Rippon accordingly avoided all polemical hymns, such as one Toplady had included in his *Psalms and Hymns* (1776):[44]

> In vain do blind Arminians try
> By works themselves to justify:
> Thy righteousness, O God, exceeds
> Men's dutys and their brightest deeds.

But concern with theological accuracy is known to have produced alterations in about twenty hymns, although some of these are on minor uncertain points. Rippon also utilized already "corrected" versions of hymns, as when he used Toplady's version of Wesley's "Blow ye the trumpet, blow";[45] but did designate it as "altered by Toplady" (hymn 57). One hymn by Charles Wesley was certainly altered because of its

---

[40]Hymn 33, vs. 5, 1.4; changed in 2nd ed. This hymn was probably by S. Colett, see Julian, 1593.
[41]Hymn 83, vs. 2, 1.4; cf. J. Wesley, op. cit., hymn 123.
[42]Hymn 182, vs. 1, 1.8; cf. A. Toplady, op. cit., 21.
[43]*Selection*, vi-vii.
[44]Hymn 79.
[45]Cf. Julian, 151. Toplady had altered "all-atoning Lamb" to "sin-atoning Lamb."

Arminian tendency, "Father of faithful Abra'm hear," a prayer for the conversion of the Jews. Originally the fourth verse read:[46]

> Come, then, thou great Deliverer, come,
> The veil from Jacob's heart remove;
> Receive thy ancient people home,
> That quicken'd by thy dying love,
> The world may their reception find,
> Life from the dead for all mankind.

The last two lines were altered (hymn 422):

> Thy world may their reception view,
> And shout to God, the glory due.

Again, another Wesleyan hymn, "Thou God of Glorious Majesty" (hymn 549), verse 5 originally commenced:[47]

> Be this my one great business here,
> With serious industry and fear,
> Eternal bliss to insure . . .

This emphasis on man's ability to "insure" was altered:

> Be this my one great business here,
> With holy trembling, holy fear,
> To make my calling sure!

Indeed Rippon's concern with theological accuracy prompted him, in one instance, to add an explanatory note. In the first edition, hymn 109 (of two verses), began:

> Salvation thro' our dying God
> Is finish'd and complete . . .

But in the tenth edition, Rippon added two new verses (probably of his own composition) which emphasized the regenerating influence of the Holy Spirit and added this comment:

> Christ has made a complete atonement for the sins of his people, in that sense his work is finished: The work of the Spirit, which at present, in some of the saints, is only begun, in due time shall be completed also; (and then salvation will be finished, but not before).

---

[46] J. Wesley, op. cit., hymn 439.
[47] Ibid., hymn 58.

(The words in brackets were added in the twenty-seventh edition). This note is eloquent comment on Rippon's concern with theological orthodoxy, especially with a full statement of the work of the Holy Spirit.

Another fear of Rippon, and of orthodox Calvinists, was that distortion of their faith which issued in Antinomian practices. One example of an alteration because of this fear, was given in Hymn 350, which Rippon took from the "Bristol Collection."[48] The second verse originally read:

> Accept our faint attempts to love,
> Our frailties, Lord, forgive;
> We would be like thy saints above,
> Unlike them as we live.

The last line was changed by Rippon: "And praise thee while we live."

There are very few changes in the sacramental hymns. One hymn (230) which Rippon adapted was by Thomas Gibbons. The fifth verse originally read:[49]

> Now spread the banner of thy love,
> And let us know that we are thine;
> Cheer us with blessings from above,
> With heav'nly Bread, and heav'nly Wine.

Rippon elected to place this hymn under "Christian Graces—Hope," and deleted the sacramental reference in the fourth line: "With all the joys of hope divine."

One baptismal hymn (450), by Joseph Stennett, originally read in verse three:[50]

> O sacred rite! by this the name
> Of Jesus we to own begin;
> And seals the pardon of our sin.

Rippon avoided any reference to baptism as a "seal" with the disclaimer: "Pledge of the pardon of our sin." The other theological

---

[48]Op. cit., hymn 312.
[49]T. Gibbons, op. cit. (1769) bk. ii, hymn 50.
[50]J. Stennett, *Hymns Composed for the Celebration of the Holy Ordinance of Baptism* (1712) hymn 12.

changes are minor, such as Providence providing not "all they want,"[51] but "all they need" (hymn 288, verse 3, line 4).

(ii) *Arrangement and Contents*. Rippon's *Selection* not only contained more hymns than other contemporary collections ("Bristol" with 412 and Toplady's with 419 were the nearest to Rippon's 588 hymns) but was better organized. He arranged the book into seventeen distinct subjects, and gave various subheadings to each page. The pages were numbered so as to agree with the numbers of the hymns on each page, a simple device which greatly speeded up the location of hymns. He added four general indices including "A Table of Scriptures," an index to suitable hymns for various texts.

The number of hymns Rippon allocated to each section is of interest. A large number of hymns, 86 or 15%, are devoted to the Scriptures; 87 or 15% to the Holy Spirit; and 77 or 14% to Christ (This last figure is misleading, since obviously many hymns in other sections have a strong Christological significance.).

R. H. Young has claimed to trace a connection between the arrangement of the *Selection* and the 1677 Particular Baptist Confession of Faith (reaffirmed in 1689)[52], but whether Rippon consciously followed it is uncertain. The parallels are only to be expected. Most of the thirty-two "chapters" or sections of the Confession may be illustrated from the *Selection*, although Rippon began with "God," not with "the Holy Scriptures," as did the Confession. What is certainly true is that the *Selection* evidenced a distinctly orthodox Calvinist theology, but a strong evangelistic spirit is also traced. A brief survey of the book reveals the theology and piety which Baptists, according to Rippon, found helpful.

After hymns on God, Praise and Creation the fall of man is stressed:

Adam, our Father and our head
Transgress'd, and justice doom'd us dead;
The fiery law speaks all despair,
There's no reprieve or pardon there. (Watts)

The section on the Scripture includes the familiar Calvinist emphasis on the necessity of the Law for due appreciation of the Gospel as in hymn 50 (probably by J. Maxwell)[53]:

---

[51]B. Beddome, op. cit., hymn 549.
[52]Op. cit., 162.
[53]See J. Gadsby, *Memoirs of the Principal Hymn-Writers and Compilers of the 17th and 18th Centuries*, 2nd ed. (1855) 156.

> Here, Lord, my soul convicted stands
> Of breaking all thy ten commands:
> And on my justly might'st thou pour
> Thy wrath in one eternal shower.

There are 52 hymns on "Scripture Doctrines and Blessings." This major subsection does demonstrate many parallels with the 1677 Confession, and Rippon clearly tried to balance the number of hymns given to each doctrine.

The characteristically Calvinistic tenet of election was not given undue prominence, but is clearly present (Hymn 62, verse 1):

> How happy are we
> Our election who see,
> And venture, O Lord, for salvation on thee!
> In Jesus approv'd,
> Eternally lov'd
> Upheld by the power we cannot be moved. (Toplady)

The doctrine of Christ's substitutionary atonement is clearly taught in Hymn 74, verse 2:

> And wast thou punish'd in my stead
> Didst thou without the city bleed,
> To expiate my stain? . . . (Toplady)

Similarly justification was presented in two hymns, both from the Wesleys, notably John's translation from Count von Zinzendorf, "Jesus, thy blood and righteousness" (no. 84). Perseverance, another Calvinist emphasis, was presented in four hymns. Salvation was well summarized in Doddridge's "Grace! 'tis a charming sound" (no. 41).

The section on "Scripture Invitations and Promises" (15 hymns) offered clear indication of Rippon's evangelical concern, with direct appeals to the consciences of sinners. Toplady's adaptation of Hart's "Come, yet sinners, poor and wretched" (no. 115) may be taken as typical. Verse 4 reads:

> Come, ye weary, heavy laden,
> Lost and ruin'd by the fall!
> If you tarry till you're better,
> You will never come at all;
> Not the righteous,
> Sinners Jesus came to call.

Rippon was able to employ three Baptist writers in this section, Stennett (no. 114), Fawcett (116), and Anne Steele (nos. 117, 120), the last of which was "The Saviour calls—let every ear."

Under the heading CHRIST were 77 hymns.

(a) Incarnation and Ministry (7 hymns). Dissenters were not concerned with the Christian Year, but Wesley's "Hark, the herald Angels sing" (no. 130), Robinson's "Mighty God while angels bless thee" (No. 132), Doddridge's "Hark, the glad sound the Saviour comes" (no. 134), are well-known Advent hymns. There were only three hymns on the life and ministry of Christ.

(b) Suffering and Death (4 hymns). These were to be supplemented, Rippon noted, from the hymns on Redemption and the Lord's Supper.

(c) Resurrection and Ascension (7 hymns), of which the most popular still is Wesley's "Christ, the Lord is risen today" (no. 141).

(d) Exaltation, Kingly Rule, and Intercession of Christ (50 hymns). This was one subject in which Rippon thought Watts deficient. The "characters" of Christ were all based on biblical images which were held to foretell or represent Christ. Listed in alphabetical order, these included Christ as Advocate, the Brazen Serpent, a Fountain, a Kinsman, Melchizidek, the Rock ("Rock of ages," no. 195). The exegesis underlying these hymns may not have been satisfactory, but suggested a Christocentric emphasis in Baptist preaching.

The HOLY SPIRIT with 88 hymns was another doctrine Rippon felt needed supplementing, and for which he had a special concern. He provided for the first time a good section of hymns on this theme for Baptists ("Bristol" had none).

(i) Influences of the Holy Spirit (11 hymns). These describe the work of the Spirit in biblical images, such as the Comforter (no. 206). But Rippon's adaptation of a ten-verse hymn by Toplady to produce the following poor hymn (212), revealed Rippon's love of expressive imagery:

1. At anchor laid, remove from home,
   Toiling, I cry, SWEET SPIRIT, come!
   Celestial breeze, no longer stay,
   But swell my sails, and speed my way!

2. Fain would I mount, fain would I glow,
   And loose my cable from below;
   But I can only spread my sail;
   THOU, THOU must breathe th'auspicious gale!

(ii) Graces of the Holy Spirit (77 hymns). These "Christian Graces and Tempers" were placed alphabetically. What is theologically significant is that Rippon placed all these hymns in the section devoted to the Holy Spirit. Numbers in brackets indicate the number of hymns devoted to each theme: Faith (9), Fear (2), Fortitude (1), Gravity (1). This last hymn, by Watts, included the following somber verse (229, verse 4):

> What if we wear the richest vest!
> Peacocks and flies are better drest;
> This flesh, with all its gaudy forms,
> Must drop to dust, and feed the worms.

Hope (4), Humility (4), Joy (4), Justice (1), Knowledge (3), Liberality (1), Love to God and Christ (7), Love to the Brethren (3), including Fawcett's "Blest be the tie that binds," Love to Neighbor (1), Love to Enemies (2), Meekness (1), Moderation (2), Patience (2), Peace (1), Rest (1), Repentance (9). This large number again suggests Rippon's evangelistic note, although some, as Stennett's (270, verses 6 and 7), are excessively sentimental:

> May I round thee cling and twine,
> Call myself a child of thine,
> And presume to claim a part
> In a tender Father's heart . . .
>
> Yes I may, for I espy
> Pity trickling from thine eye;
> 'Tis a Father's bowels move,
> Move with pardon and with love.

Resignation (4), yet another Calvinistic theme (no. 276, verse 4):

> What is the world with all its store?
> 'Tis but a bettersweet;
> When I attempt to pluck the rose,
> A prickling thorn I meet. (Beddome)

Self-Denial (2), Serenity (3), Trust (6), Wisdom (1), Zeal for Christ (2).

THE CHRISTIAN LIFE with 35 hymns also suggested significant features of Baptist piety. This section was reminiscent of Wesley's 1780 book with its emphasis on "the experience of real Christians."[54] Rippon

---

[54]For a discussion of the arrangement of Wesley's book, see B. L. Manning, *Dissenting Deputies*, 11-12. This is the only instance of Wesley's arrangement possibly influ-

included hymns for various experiences of the Christian, ranging from first awakenings to faith, to his times of backsliding or persecution, and to his death. One hymn, by Stennett, evidences an angelology[55] (307, verse 4):

> Hither, at his command they fly,
> To guard the beds on which we lie
> To shield our persons, night and day;
> And scatter all our fears away.

WORSHIP (69 hymns). The various contexts of worship for contemporary Baptists were reflected in the arrangement.

(a) Private Worship (4 hymns), designed to help the Christian in his prayer and Bible reading.

(b) Family Worship (5 hymns), including a hymn to be sung on moving to a new home (no. 333) and two "prayers for children." These could be used in a way comparable to a "Dedication" service: (336, verse 4):

> May they receive thy word,
> Confess the Saviour's name,
> Then follow their despised LORD
> Thro' the baptismal stream.

No hymns of this type had been given in the "Bristol" book.

(c) Public Worship (8 hymns). Rippon included three hymns suitable for the opening of a new meetinghouse, one of which (no. 388) was first sung at the opening of Horsley, Gloucs., meeting house in 1774, as Rippon noted.

(d) Lord's Day (7 hymns). The spirit of the day was thus expressed by Joseph Stennett, a Seventh Day Baptist,[56] (no. 348):

> In holy duties let the day
> In holy pleasures, pass away:
> How sweet, a sabbath thus to spend,
> In hope of one that ne'er shall end!

---

encing Rippon's arrangement: in general, Dissenters preferred more doctrinal divisions.

[55] For an interesting discussion of Wesley's angelology, see J. E. Rattenbury, *The Evangelical Doctrines of Charles Wesley's Hymns* (London: Epworth Press, 1942) 325-27. Similarly, for Watts's angelology, see the index to Rippon's *Watts*.

[56] For Stennett (1663-1713), see *Dictionary of National Biography* (hereinafter *DNB*) (1855) 190.

(e) Before Prayer (6 hymns) including Cowper's "What various hindrances we meet," and a paraphrase of the Lord's Prayer by J. Straphan (no. 358) which was first published by Rippon.

(f) Before Sermon (13 hymns). This and the next section emphasized the prominent part assigned to the sermon in Baptist worship. The sermon was expected to be a medium of divine power, producing conviction and conversion (360, verse 2):

> Jesus, the work is wholly thine
> To form the heart anew;
> Now let thy sovereign grace divine
> Each stubborn soul subdue. (adapted from Beddome)[57]

Preaching was likened to casting the "Gospel-net" (hymn 366). The sense of expectancy is again illustrated in this verse by Jonathan Evans:[58]

> Come, thou soul-transforming Spirit,
> Bless the sower and the seed:
> Let each heart they grace inherit,
> Raise the weak, thy hungry feed:
> From the Gospel
> Now supply thy people's need.   (368, verse 1)

(g) After sermon (21 hymns). Once the seed had been sown, only the power of God could "make it spring and grow" (hymns 372, 373). Rippon adapted a Moravian antiphonal hymn by Cennick[59] (no. 384) to emphasize that the glory was God's. Fawcett's "Lord, dismiss us with thy blessing" and paraphrases of three New Testament benedictions concluded this section (nos. 389-92).

(h) Doxologies (5 hymns, all of one verse). Services customarily concluded with a doxology, such as Ken's "Praise God from whom all blessings flow" (no. 395).

Calvinists' attitudes to THE WORLD were reflected in five hymns. The negative aspects were not unduly prominent, but Christians were to renounce all worldly ambitions:

> Begone, for ever, mortal things!
> Thou mighty molehill, earth, farewell!

---

[57] See *Julian*, 567-68.
[58] Ibid., 358.
[59] Ibid., 673.

> Angels aspire on lofty wings,
> And leave the globe for ants to dwell. (402, verse 4: Watts)

Life within the Dissenting chapel was reflected in the section entitled THE GOSPEL CHURCH (39 hymns). These are hymns for the formation of a church, for ordination, including one suitable for a service when a church called one of its members to enter the ministry. The relationship between pastors, deacons and people was seen in ten hymns which refer to events such as the dangerous illness of a pastor; or a pastor's departure from his people, with this solemn warning (414, verses 4, 5):

> But they who heard the word in vain,
> Tho' oft and plainly warn'd,
> Will tremble when they meet again
> The ministers they scorned.
>
> On your own heads your blood will fal,
> If any perish here;
> The preachers who have told you all
> Shall stand approv'd and clear. (Olney Hymns)[60]

Then came a people's prayer for their pastor (415), and a pastor's "wish for his people" (416). One hymn was suitable for the election of deacons, whose ministry was defined (417, verse 3):

> Happy in Jesus, their own LORD,
> May they his sacred table spread,
> The table of their pastor fill,
> And fill the holy poor with bread.[61]

A few missionary hymns should be carefully noted. Hymns 419 and 420 (based on one hymn by Gibbons)[62] evidenced a longing to see the Gospel preached in every land, "to the Jews," "the untutor'd Indian tribes," "Africa's sable sons." One verse became something of a motto for Rippon (419, verse 7):

> Asia and Africa, resound
> From shore to shore his fame:
> And thou, America, in songs
> Redeeming love proclaim.

---

[60] Op. cit., bk. ii, hymn 28.

[61] This emphasis on the deacons' role as "serving tables" illustrates the teaching of John Gill as in *Body of Divinity* (1770) 3:291.

[62] Op. cit. (1769) bk. ii, hymn 69.

(This was quoted in the preface to the *Selection*, and on the cover of every issue of the *Register*). That these hymns were being sung before 1792 and the founding of the missionary society was suggestive of a global vision for the Gospel already present among key Baptists.

Associations, or "General Meetings of Church & Ministers," an important dimension of Baptist life at this time were provided with nine hymns. The emphasis was upon prayer for pastors, and Beddome's fine hymn, "Father of mercies, bow thine ear" (426), was introduced here. There are a few hymns which prayed for revival, such as John Ryland's refrain added to a hymn by John Newton[63] (427):

> Lord revive us
> All our help must come from thee!

Such hymns were doubtless sung in the Midlands, where the influential call to prayer for revival was issued in 1784. Again in this section there was a longing for the spread of the Gospel, as in William Williams'[64] "O'er the gloomy hills of darkness" (428, verse 2):

> Let the Indian, let the Negro
> Let the rude Barbarian see
> That divine and glorious conquest,
> Once obtain'd on Calvary;
> Let the Gospel
> Loud resound from pole to pole.

To what extent such hymns helped to prepare for missionary advance was uncertain, but clearly when the wave of missionary enthusiasm broke over the churches, these hymns helped promote its message. This section was expanded in later editions.

"Collections for Poor Church and Poor Brethren" (5 hymns) was a regular feature. Hymn 434 was a good example.

> The Lord, who rules the world's affairs,
> For me a well-spread board prepares;
> My grateful thanks to him shall rise,
> He knows my wants, those wants supplies.
>
> And shall I grudge to give his poor
> A mite from all my generous store?

---

[63] Julian, 804.
[64] See Julian, 856. Rippon had altered the original.

NO, LORD! the friends of thine and thee,
Shall always find a friend in me.

Hymns for Church Meetings (5 hymns) were intended mainly for praise for converted sinners ("experiences") and regret at the backsliding of a believer (discipline).

Rippon provided a good collection of the best baptismal hymns. "Bristol" had included only three hymns specifically linked with baptism. Daniel Turner, of Abingdon, helped Rippon with this section.[65] There are 13 hymns for singing before baptizing, and 4 afterwards, with 13 single verses to which this note was added:

> As it is now pretty common to sing by the waterside, and as some of our brethren in the country give out a verse or two, while they are administering the ordinance, it is hoped these single verses will be acceptable.

The theology of baptism emphasized baptism as an act of obedience, of following the example of Christ (445, verse 3):

> Plainly here his footsteps tracing
> Follow him without delay;
> Gladly his command embracing,
> Lo! Your captain leads the way:
> View the rite with understanding,
> Jesus' grave before you lies;
> Be interr'd at his commanding,
> After his example rise. (Fawcett)

Baptism is an "emblem" of Christ's passion (449, v. 2), and there are some references to the activity of the Spirit (460):

> Eternal Spirit, heavenly Dove,
> On these baptismal waters move;
> That we, thro' energy divine,
> May have the substance with the sign. (Beddome)

There was a clear progression from baptism to communion (452, v. 5):

> Thus we, dear Saviour, own thy name,
> Receive us rising from the stream;
> Then to thy table let us come,
> And dwell in Zion as our home. (J. Fellows,[66] altered)

---

[65]Note to hymn 442 (in 1st ed. only).
[66]*Hymns on Believer's Baptism* (1773) hymn 43.

Rippon titled some of the 19 hymns on the Lord's Supper as "sacramental hymns," but they are mainly meditations upon the death of Christ, with little reference to the Table. One notable exception was Samuel Stennett's (483, verses 1, 4, 5) which seemed to go beyond a bare "Memorialist" emphasis:

Here at thy table, Lord, we meet,
To feed on food divine:
Thy body is the bread we eat,
Thy precious blood the wine . . .

"His body worn with rudest hands
Becomes the finest bread:
And with the blessing he commands,
Our noblest hopes are fed.

"His blood, that from each op'ning vein
In purpose torrents ran,
Hath fill'd this cup with glorious wine,
That cheers both God and man.

TIMES AND SEASONS (52 hymns) suggests how Baptists celebrated their life together. There were hymns for morning and evening (7), and Seasons of the Year (11). Spring, a sign of God's goodness, was also a parable of the need for God's "warmest beams" to turn "thy winter into Spring" (498). Summer and the harvest had an obvious spiritual application, whilst winter was a picture of the barren soul (507). Other hymns were for: New Year's Day (3), notably Robinson's "Come thou fount of every blessing"; Birthday (1); Wedding (1), by Berridge, to which Rippon added the last verse (Dissenters were not permitted to conduct their own marriage services, but this hymn could be sung as a prayer for a happy couple); Welcome and Farewell of friends (3) and Youth (7). (Two of these were designated for Sunday Schools in 1787, when the movement was in its early days). One was antiphonal in form, verses alternating between "Congregation" and "Children" (522). Old Age (1), and Fast and Thanksgiving Days (12). These days were held either because of the spiritual condition of a local church, or more commonly, as part of a national call. One hymn prayed for success in war (527, verse 4):

With all the boasted pomp of war
In vain we dare the hostile field;
In vain, unless the LORD be there;
Thy arm above is Britain's shield. (Steele)

There were hymns of thanksgiving for victory, and two to be sung on November 5th (the anniversary of the capture of Guy Fawkes and the failure of the Gunpowder Plot):

> When hell and Rome combin'd their power,
> And doom'd these isles their certain prey,
> They hand forbade the fatal hour,
> Their impious plots in ruin lay! (534, verse 3: Steele)

"Sickness and Suffering" (6 hymns) reflected upon the brevity of life, the necessity of redeeming time, and the frailty of man. Hymn 548, verse 1 is typical:

> Eternity is just at hand;
> And shall I waste my ebbing sand,
> And careless view departing day,
> And throw my inch of time away!

DEATH AND RESURRECTION featured 20 hymns. A pathetic feature was the need for hymns specifically referring to the death of children, or offering comfort to bereaved parents. From numerous "dying testimonies," this section was known to have been widely used.[67] There were two hymns on the resurrection of the body, in which the biblical statement was interpreted quite literally (as in hymn 569, verse 5).

DAY OF JUDGMENT (10 hymns) and HELL AND HEAVEN (9 hymns) were the last sections. There was, again, no undue emphasis upon the negative. Only three were about hell, in general terms, and one is simply a paraphrase of the parable of the Rich Man and Lazarus (582). Stennett's "On Jordan's stormy banks I stand" (584) was long popular, but Isaac Watts had the honor of the last hymn, "Earth has engross'd my love too long" (588).

(iii) *Editions of the Selection*. Rippon's commitment to producing the best possible hymnal was evidenced by this careful attention to improving the *Selection* in successive editions so that his book was widely used for more than two generations. At the same time an analysis of these editions reveals the developing life and needs of the churches. Indeed, the *Selection* became an agent for consolidating those developments in church life.

---

[67]Cf. *Baptist Annual Register* (hereafter *Register*) iii.101, 389, 409; iv.1144.

(a) *In England.* Before the book was published, Rippon was assured of support "from one End of the Kingdom to the other"[68] Others who had been contemplating a hymnbook gave way to Rippon's project.[69] Rippon gained the support of the associations, as he wrote to Manning in 1787, "You will be glad to hear that it has met with a respect at each of our Associations superior to any Baptist publication in my time."[70] Accordingly the *Selection* was advertised in association Circular Letters,[71] and used at association meetings.[72]

The first edition, of which three thousand copies were printed by June 1787, had been sold out by February 1788 when Rippon prepared a second edition of three thousand.[73] The second edition had been sold by September 1789,[74] and Rippon could claim that his book had been "introduced into about one half of our Baptist churches all thro' England."[75] By the end of 1792 at least fifteen thousand copies had been sold within five years.[76]

For the fifth edition (1793) Rippon made a few minor alterations in the preface, and included a suitable tune, indicated by the number from his *Tune Book*, for every hymn. Rippon thus made an important advance in hymnody, for this close association of words and tunes does not appear to have been so fully adopted in earlier hymnals.[77]

The first major enlargement was made for the tenth edition, for which Rippon added sixty-two new hymns, "the far greater part of these are

---

[68] *Selection*, v.

[69] Ibid. Cf. (anon.) to Rippon, Newcastle, 28 June 1786, B.M. Add. MSS. 25389, F. 568. (British Library, London; microfilm of Rippon's correspondence is in the Angus Library, Regent's Park College, Oxford).

[70] Rippon to J. Manning, 29 June 1787. (Special Collections, Brown University, Providence RI.)

[71] E.g., see Northampton letters of 1787, 1788, 1789.

[72] Cf. *Register*, i.450; ii.33, 324, 480, etc.

[73] Rippon to Manning, 28 June 1787 (original at Brown University) and Rippon to T. Ustick, 13 Feb. 1788 (original in possession of Roger Hayden).

[74] Rippon to Manning, 21 Sept. 1789 (original at Brown University).

[75] Rippon to Manning, 28 Oct. 1788 (original at Brown University).

[76] Rippon to J. Morse, 28 Feb. 1793 (original at Historical Society of Pennsylvania, Philadelphia) refers to 4,000 sold in 1792. Note that in his *Tune Book*, p. iii, Rippon claimed nearly 20,000 copies had been sold. The preface to this was written between 1794 and 1797 (see discussion below).

[77] For details of the various editions, see Manley thesis, 184-85.

entirely ORIGINALS, and are duly placed under the protection of the law"[78] Rippon commented:

> A few are inserted on the Trinity, on the Divinity of Christ, and on the Work of the Holy Spirit. . . . But the greater part of the additions consist of Hymns adapted to Village Worship to Monthly Prayer Meetings for the Spread of the Gospel to Missionary Meetings, and to the chapter of Hymns before and after Sermon; a chapter this, which there was but little danger of protracting to an undesirable length. The sections on Affliction, Death and Judgment have also received some enlargement; and so have the Indexes, both of Scriptures and of subjects.

These additions provide an interesting commentary on the development of Baptist interest in evangelism, both in the villages of Britain and abroad. For example, five of the six hymns added to the "Scripture" section were "Scripture invitations," and Rippon added this note: "As the few Hymns in the former editions of this Volume, entitled *Scripture Invitations and Promises* have been found peculiarly acceptable and encouraging, the Section is *now* considerably enlarged."[79] Evidently the practice of accompanying sermons with invitation hymns was growing, as was the evangelistic fervor of the Baptists. A further four hymns added to the "After Sermon" section were similar in emphasis.

But the section most enlarged was *The Church*. . . . Indeed one subsection was altered from "Church—Associations of Churches" to "Church—Associations and Missions," and a further subsection was entitled "Monthly and Missionary Prayer Meetings." Fourteen missionary hymns were added. Typical of the new attitude was Hymn 418 (4th, part verses 1 and 4):

> Go, favour'd Britons and proclaim
> The kind Redeemer you have found;
> Publish his ever-precious name
> To all the wond'ring nations round . . .

> Go, tell on India's golden shores,
> The Ganges, Tibet, and Boutan,*
> That to enrich their deathless mind
> You come—the friends of God and Man.

> * (Tibet and Boutan—parts of Asia, Little known to Europeans, but lately mentioned by the Baptist Missionaries!)

---

[78]Op. cit., iv.
[79]Op. cit., note before hymn 114.

Rippon also added nine verses to hymn 420, noting that "Verses 8, 9, and 10, of this Hymn in substance, were written off Margate by Mr. William Ward, one of the Baptist Missionaries, on their departure for India, May 28, 1799."

The succeeding editions were substantially unaltered, although Rippon published them in various sizes. From 1802, when his arrangements of Watts was published, the two were frequently bound together.

Rippon's last major expansion was for the twenty-seventh edition (1828). He was then in his seventies, but three reasons probably suggested an enlarged edition: (1) to protect his copyright; (2) a rival Baptist book was prepared the same year; (3) a genuine desire to improve the book by the inclusion of hymns achieving popularity. The preface claimed that more than 200,000 copies had been sold in Britain, and a further 100,000 in America. Taking only the British figures, between the fourth and twenty-seventh editions about 85,000 copies had been sold, an average of 3,700 per edition.

Rippon added 118 full hymns, as well as 36 doxologies, so that he could justifiably claim to have included more than 150 new hymns. Two further missionary hymns were added, and two hymns suitable for "infant dedication," although not so described, were added.

The range of authors was wide, although Beddome, the Wesleys, Doddridge, Newton, Medley and Cowper were again utilized. New authors included the youthful Henry Kirk White, Rippon's friend W.B. Collyer, Thomas Kelly, Thomas Haweis, and Bishop Heber, including his "From Greenland's Icy Mountains." Baptist authors included John Ryland, and Rippon's nephew, Thomas. One unusual source was Sir John Bowring's *Specimen of the Russian Poets* . . . from which Rippon took Hymn 786, a doxology of two verses. This was originally part of the "Izhe Kheruvimij," or "Song of the Cherubim," the hymn chanted during the procession of the Cup.[80] Most of the original hymns, about three-quarters of the total added, were uniformly poor and none achieved lasting usage. The *Selection* now contained 803 hymns (including the doxologies).

Subsequent editions in Rippon's lifetime were substantially unaltered. (The thirtieth added a few authors' names). The last known edition of his lifetime was the thirty-first, which the British Library dates as c.1830.

---

[80] Op. cit. (2nd ed. 1821), 157. For Bowring (1792–1872) see *DNB*.

Immediately after his death, John Haddon, the London printer who had issued a rival hymnbook in 1828, also produced a new edition (1837) of the *Selection*. Aware that the original hymns of Rippon's 1828 edition were under copyright, Haddon omitted 73 hymns and replaced these with others. This must have only confused the public. After the expiration of the copyright laws, an enlarged *Comprehensive Rippon*, as it became known, was published, first in 1844. This added some four hundred hymns, again interspersed as parts to the original Rippon edition. The total number of hymns was over a thousand. The general arrangement was retained, but one new section for "Dedication of Children" was added. The *Comprehensive Rippon* continued in use well into the second half of the nineteenth century, a new edition appearing in 1861.

(b) *In the United States*. From the beginning of his project, Rippon asked leading American Baptists in the U.S., like James Manning of Providence, Rhode Island, Thomas Ustick of Philadelphia, Pennsylvania and Richard Furman of Charleston, South Carolina to help distribute his *Selection*. Rippon hoped to meet the demand from England, and of the first six thousand copies printed, about eight hundred went to America. He considered printing an edition in the U.S., but decided to supply books from England, offering a discount of 25% to any who would sell them for him.[81]

But the success of the *Selection* was so immediate, and shipments from England so delayed[82] that two unauthorized editions were printed in 1792, one in New York by William Durell,[83] and the other in Elizabethtown, New Jersey by Shepard Kollock.[84] The latter was identical with the London edition, except that the Preface was omitted. John Bowen, a member of Carter Lane Church who emigrated to America in 1799, acted as an agent for Rippon but commented, "the English Labors and the American enjoys the sweets of labour with little troble [sic]. . . ."[85]

While details of these transactions need not concern us, the production of these editions was expressive of the demand for the *Selection*. The

---

[81]Rippon to Manning, 21 Sept. 21, 1789 (original in Brown University).
[82]The European war caused extensive dislocation of Atlantic trade in 1793. See J. S. Watson, *The Reign of George III (1760–1820)* (Oxford: Clarendon Press, 1960) 181.
[83]So C. Evans, *American Bibliography . . .* , Chicago, viii (1914) 348.
[84]Copy in British Library.
[85]Bowen to Rippon, New York, August 15, 1801, in Baptist Historical Society, *Transactions* (1:1908-1909) 72-73.

number of local printings was remarkable.[86] By 1828 Rippon was told that about 100,000 copies had been sold in America.[87] There were also several editions of the *Comprehensive*.

Also of interest was the fact that Rippon was involved in several copyright disputes in both England and the United States.[88]

(iv) *Success of the Selection*. The *Selection* was without an effective rival among British Baptists from 1787 until 1828. The earlier books retained, however, some local or personal loyalties. The "Bristol Collection" was reprinted several times, an eighth edition in 1801, and a tenth in 1827. But its use was restricted, and as late as 1803 Thomas Berry was surprised to find the Tewkesbury Church was still using the "Bristol Collection," and expressed regret that reverence for the memory of Caleb Evans prompted the use of such "a little, little thing."[89] But Rippon's book became widely adopted, and despite a few smaller books of exclusively local use, Rippon's enjoyed a virtual monopoly—with Watts—of Baptist praise.

The *Selection* also enjoyed a measure of popular usage among non-Baptists. The main obstacle to its widespread use was, of course, the group of baptismal hymns. Rippon overcame this by the following procedure which he explained to Jedidiah Morse, a Congregationalist of Boston, "We have so modified the Sheet on Baptism that by a neat cancel which is accounted for in a note, the book may be Had, with only such Hymns on that ordinance as were composed by Paedobaps."[90] This surprised some of Rippon's Baptist friends,[91] but how many adapted versions were sold is unknown, and none has been located. However, T.G. Crippen in a review of Congregational hymnody, described Rippon's book as "probably the most important" of all the supplements to Watts, and added: "The compiler was a Baptist, but the book was used in many

---

[86]For details of the American editions and Rippon's troubles with "pirate" editions, see K. R. Manley, "John Rippon and American Baptists," *Quarterly Review* 4 (1980): 58-61.

[87]*Selection*, 27th ed. (1828) iii.

[88]For details, see Manley thesis, 192-96.

[89]Berry to Rippon, Tewkesbury, 4 Jan. 1803, B.M. Add. MSS. 25386, F.80.

[90]Rippon to Morse, 28 Feb. 1793 (original at Historical Society of Pennsylvania, Philadelphia).

[91]Cf. J. C. Sprague to Rippon, Bovey Tracey, 5 Jan. 1799, B.M. Add. MSS. 25389, F.148.

paedobaptist congregations—in some within the memory of the present writer."[92]

The first serious rival to the *Selection* was *A New Selection of Hymns, especially adapted to Public Worship, and intended as a Supplement to Dr. Watt's Psalms and Hymns* (1828), published by John Haddon, a London Printer. The *Baptist Magazine* gave this new venture a most unsympathetic welcome.[93] The reviewer noted that 260 out of its 581 hymns were already in Rippon, and that Rippon's book, especially after its recent enlargement, was far superior in every way. But the new book made its way; it was slightly cheaper, and all profits were designated for the widows of Baptist pastors. By 1833 over 400 Pounds Sterling had been given to this charity,[94] and by 1837 over 60,000 copies had been sold.[95] The charitable aims led to the formation, in 1860, of the Psalms and Hymns Trust, which devoted all the profits of Baptist hymnbooks to the same ends.[96] But the *Comprehensive Rippon*, it was noted, continued well into the second half of the nineteenth century.

The reasons for the long monopoly by the *Selection* may be summarized:[97]

(1) Comprehensiveness. The *Selection* offered a wide range of subjects, and more hymns, than its rivals. It was nicely calculated to meet the homiletical and devotional needs of the Baptist congregations.

(2) Metrical variety.

(3) Facility of reference. The indexes were more detailed, and often more accurate, than others. This was invaluable for preachers seeking hymns relevant to their sermons.

(4) Price. Universally available, at reasonable prices, the *Selection* was offered at a discount to ministers, who would be encouraged to introduce it into their churches.

(5) Theological orthodoxy. Rippon was aware of this responsibility and, as has been shown, was scrupulously concerned with orthodoxy.

(6) Intrinsic merit of the hymns. Rippon's literary taste and judgment of what the churches needed, especially the new missionary hymns, were vital factors in its long success.

(7) Catholicity of choice. Rippon was stately concerned with the quality of hymns, not their origins. Hence by 1828 he included not only

---

[92]T. G. Crippen, "Congregational Hymnody," *TCHS* VII (1916–1918) 227.
[93]Op. cit., xx, 1828, 468-69.
[94]Ibid, xxv (1833) 331.
[95]Ibid., xxix (1837) 412.
[96]See R. W. Thomson, *The Psalms and Hymns Trust*, 1960.
[97]The first four reasons were suggested in the *Comprehensive Rippon*, (1844) preface.

Wesleyan hymns, but as noted earlier, a translation of a small part of the liturgy of the Russian Orthodox Church.

(8) Association of hymns and tunes. This was a new feature, and of great significance in the improvement of Baptist singing.

In short, the *Selection* fully met specific pastoral and devotional needs of the Baptists; this was the main secret of its success. In addition, the *Tune Book* and arrangement of Watts, both successful in their own right, materially promoted the *Selection* with which they were both directly connected.

2. Tune Book

Full consideration of Rippon's *Tune Book* is not possible in this study,[98] but it is important briefly to trace ways in which this production extended the influence of the *Selection*.

Rippon felt strongly about the poor quality of contemporary hymn singing by Dissenters. He disapproved of lining-out of hymns and noted that the removal of lining-out was "gaining Ground in some Congregations of the first Note in London, at Bristol, and elsewhere." But still Rippon lamented that although most congregations were sensitive to "seriousness in *prayer* and soundness in *preaching*" few were concerned about good hymn singing, which was "often most shamefully prostituted."[99]

Rippon made a characteristically dramatic statement of his concern for good singing:

> [A]nd were my own head bound round with weeping willows, and my harp to lie neglected on the ground, I would, nevertheless, make a single effort to glorify God, and if it were but one, it should be this—to encourage all the thousands of Israel to *sing in the ways of the Lord*.[100]

The need for the book was well illustrated by Rippon:

> *Any tune*, by any *incompetent person*, is sung with but very little regard to the subject of the Hymn. This inattention is extremely mischievous in tunes which have a repeat. By a misapplication of these the congregation may be forced not only to stop in the midst of a line, and to go back, before they have pronounced any distinct idea; but also to stop in the very midst of a word, and to retreat, leaving a syllable or two behind, till they advance again, and perhaps oftener than once, to meet the forlorn termination.

---

[98]For details, see Manley thesis, 202-16.
[99]*Tune Book*, iii.
[100]*Tune Book*, iv.

Circumstances of this description amuse the trifling, pain the sensible and serious, and rob whole auditories of their devotion.[101]

Rippon was assisted by Robert Keene[102] and Thomas Walker.[103] Six of Keene's tunes were included in the *Tune Book*. Keene has been suggested as possibly the mysterious "K," author of "How Firm a Foundation."[104]

The assistance of Thomas Walker (1764–1827), an alto vocalist of the metropolis, is more significant. By the fifth edition of the *Tune Book* (1808), thirty-three of the tunes were by Walker, double the number by any other composer. John Dyer thought Walker was formerly a member of the Prescott Street Church, "but his tuneful propensities proved a snare to him—his domestic life was eminently unhappy—and he died in a state of derangement"![105]

It may be noted, however, that, although Rippon was responsible for the enterprise and the risk (and presumably the profits), most of the actual musical work was probably done by the two musicians. (The identification of him with the "John Rippon" who composed an oratorio, *The Crucifixion*, appears to be false.)[106]

The first edition of the *Tune Book* is usually dated as circa 1791.[107] This edition was smaller than later editions, with only 256 tunes, and had no preface, nor indices, but simply a few unexplained musical examples.

---

[101] J. Rippon, *Watts*, ix.

[102] Robert Keene must be distinguished from the man of the same name who was a close friend of George Whitefield and who died on 30 January 1793. Rippon's Keene was a member and precentor at Carter Lane although he was dismissed from the church because of drunkenness and a "breach of trust" on May 20, 1793.

[103] W. T. Whitley, "The Tune Book of 1791," *BQ* 10 (1940–1941): 434.

[104] The evidence is reviewed in Julian, 537; it was first suggested in 1822 by Dr. Fletcher, a friend of Thomas Walker's. But compare William J. Reynolds, *Hymns of our Faith. A Handbook for the Baptist Hymnal* (Nashville TN: Broadman Press, 1964) 70.

[105] E. A. Payne, ed., "The Necrologies of John Dyer," *BQ* 13 (1949–1950): 306. For Dyer (1784–1841), secretary of the BMS (1818–1841), see E. A. Payne, *The First Generation* (1936) 120-26, and B. Stanley, *The History of the Baptist Missionary Society 1792–1992* (Edinburgh: T.&T. Clark, 1992) 208-12.

[106] As by O. A. Mansfield, "Rippon's Tunes," *BQ* 8 (1936–1937): 39; E. Sharpe, op. cit., 11. The oratorio, copies of which are in the British Museum and the Bedleian Library, is dated ca. 1837 (after Rippon's death). It has been suggested (*DNB*) that it was by Rippon's nephew John, but no references to a nephew of that name have been located. Rippon did have a son named John.

[107] So British Library *Catalogue*. Rippon is described as "A.M." and not "D.D." (received in 1792), and see *Register* i. 326, where Rippon lists it in the publications of "1791 &c," (this list was in fact published in May 1792).

The second edition, dated between 1794 and 1797 (probably the latter),[108] was much improved. For the third and fourth (1802) editions, additional tunes were added. These were entirely the work of Walker, as the additions were published separately with his name as editor.[109] By the fifth edition (1808)[110] the final expansion to 320 "tunes and odes" was completed. Walker claimed in 1811 that Rippon's book had met with "universal acceptance" and that "many thousand copies" had been sold.[111]

Four distinctions may be claimed for the *Tune Book*. First, it was the largest hymn tunebook yet produced by any churchman in England. R. H. Young calls it, "the most complete and far-reaching book of the century."[112]

Secondly, it was the first to add, systematically, marks of expression, such as *p*, *f*, *ff*, *cresc.*, etc., and tempo indications such as "grave," "lively," "solemn," "brisk," etc. O. A. Mansfield complains that the expression marks are "somewhat mechanical" and occasionally vary from modern ideas.[113]

Thirdly, the *Tune Book* became the most extensive companion to one particular hymnbook. The custom of suggesting a specific tune for each hymn was an advance in Baptist hymnody, for earlier Baptist hymnbooks had been very sporadic in this.[114]

Fourthly, the Tune Book is the best example of contemporary Dissenting psalmody. Rippon explained in his preface that numerous requests for suitable tunes for some hymns with peculiar measures, had necessitated references to several different tunebooks and thus the need for one volume became obvious. Rippon's book, therefore, "codified the best of the tunes in nonconformist use up to that date, and added a

---

[108] Advertisement for 2nd ed. on cover *Register* no. xiii (August 1796), although was given in list of books for 1797 (op. cit., ii 475); but in 1794 it was advertised in *Baptist Catechism* (1794), although perhaps only then in preparation.

[109] T. Walker, *Appendix to Dr. Rippon's Selection of Tunes*; T. Walker, *Second Appendix to Dr. Rippon's Selection of Tunes*. The first contained tunes numbered 257 to 278; the second, tunes 279 to 294.

[110] Cf. *Supplement to the Fifth Edition of Dr. Rippon's Tune Book* (1808).

[111] *Walker's Companion to Dr. Rippon's Tune Book* . . . (1811) preface.

[112] Op. cit., 101.

[113] Op. cit., 39.

[114] Cf. R. H. Young, op. cit., 99-100.

number of new ones."[115] With Walker's *Companions* it represented the "normal hymnody" of the Dissenters of the period.[116]

Remembering the difficult task Rippon and his helpers set themselves it is not surprising that several mistakes occurred, and that a greater knowledge of musical history and theory has underlined these.[117] Opinions may differ as to the propriety of adapting "popular airs." Mansfield called it "ecclesiastical inconsistency."[118] Certain of Rippon's contemporaries thought the same as the following anecdote will illustrate:

> After a funeral sermon for a venerable and pious lady the minister gave out Dr. Watts's excellent hymn, "There is a land of pure delight," &c. And the clerk set it to an old convivial glee, beginning "Drink to me only with thine eyes" &c. A lady in the congregation, who had long renounced these levities, was extremely pained by the recollections this occasioned, and bitterly assailed by the ridicule of some gay acquaintants who happened to be present. The next day she stated the fact to the minister; and on complaint being made to the clerk, he pointed to the tune called "Prospect" in Dr. Rippon's book, and pleaded that there were many more of the same class in that collection![119]

"Prospect" was set to that very hymn of Watts' in Rippon's book. Walker's defense for introducing classical airs was that it was analogous to students for the ministry being required to read Homer and Virgil.[120]

Clearly it would be an anachronism to judge the *Tune Book* by modern standards. Admittedly many of the tunes were inferior, but there were several noteworthy ones. W. T. Whitley claimed in 1941 that 97 of the tunes were still in use.[121] Well over thirty tunes appeared in both the Baptist (1962) and Congregational (1953) books. There is little doubt that the progress of Baptist hymnody was advanced by the production of this substantial volume of tunes to accompany his highly acceptable *Selection*.

---

[115]M. Frost, ed., *Historical Companion to Hymns Ancient and Modern* (1962) 110.

[116]Ibid. This is confirmed by R. H. Young, op. cit., table 2, "Psalms and Hymn Tunes most Frequently Found in Ten leading English Tune Books of the Eighteenth Century," which shows that of 47 tunes found in four or more of these books, Rippon had 33; while he omitted none of those which were in extensive use in the second half of the century.

[117]See O. A. Mansfield, op. cit., 43; and R. H. Young, op. cit., 111.

[118]Ibid.

[119]*Baptist Magazine*, xxii (1830) 57.

[120]R. W. Thomson, op. cit., 4.

[121]Op. cit., 434.

3. Rippon's Watts

Rippon's third hymnodic project added to the total impact of both the *Selection* and the *Tune Book*. By his arrangement of *Watts*, Rippon demonstrated his faithfulness to the traditional loyalties of Dissent associated with Watts. When both the *Selection* and *Watts* were bound together—and Rippon printed them in the same sizes—they comprised the complete Dissenters' hymnbook. Rippon now had virtually a complete monopoly of the hymns most Baptists were singing. Inevitably, the general popularity of the *Selection* was assisted by his *Watts*, as it was by the *Tune Book*.

4. Influence of Rippon's Hymnody

Because of the huge success of the *Selection*, and of the related *Tune Book* and *Watts*, Rippon was able to exert the most wide-ranging influence, both on the Baptists as a denomination and on the history of hymnody.

The various congregations were drawn together as they united in their hymn singing. Members moving from one church to another found the same book in use. In the most subtle of ways, the general pattern of worship and theology of the *Selection* was impressed upon the churches, an invaluable unifying influence. For nearly fifty years, the *Selection* was the only Baptist book in common use.

The main use of the *Selection* was, obviously, for local church services. It was, for example, officially adopted at Tenterden in 1798[122] and Watford in 1799,[123] but few church records in fact stipulate the hymnal used. Missionary meetings used the *Selection*[124] and the missionaries in India sang from it. For example, when John Fountain arrived in Serampore, Carey, Thomas, and he sang in three parts, a hymn from the *Selection*.[125] Again, it provided a collection of hymns suitable for translation, as when Carey told Rippon of a baptismal service: "We sang a Bengal translation of the 451st hymn of your *Selection*, Jesus, and shall it ever be & c after which I prayed and descended into the water."[126] The

---

[122]W. S. Davies, *In Pleasant Places, Story of Tenterden Baptist Church over Two Centuries* (1967) 15.
[123]J. Stuart, *Beechen Grove Baptist Church, Watford* (1907) 46.
[124]E.g., see *Register*, iv. 948.
[125]Ibid., iii, 73.
[126]Ibid., iv, 900.

Selection was used by black congregations in Jamaica and Sierra Leone,[127] and by some British prisoners in at least one center in France during the long war.[128]

Perhaps the most important aspect of the unifying influence of Rippon's hymnody was its theological impact. On the one hand it preserved the orthodoxy of the 1689 Confession; indeed unlike the "Bristol Collection" it had hymns on important Calvinistic doctrines such as election and perseverance of the saints. There was a healthy Christological and Trinitarian emphasis, while the necessity of the Holy Spirit for regeneration and sanctification was strongly underlined. Indeed, in 1828 the *Selection* was preferred to its new rival because it included sections on "Effectual Calling," "Moral and Ceremonial Law," "Justification" and "other important doctrines."[129] However, even more important was the manner in which the *Selection* embodied an evangelistic Calvinism. As T. G. Crippen wrote of the *Selection*, "hymns embodying the Gospel Call are as clear as any Arminian could desire."[130] Like any good hymnbook, Rippon's work helped to define and interpret the Christian faith for its own generation. Not the least of the influences shaping the new evangelistic Calvinism of the Baptists, was the regular singing of hymns which taught this theology. As has been shown, sermons were expected, according to the hymns in the *Selection*, to be a powerful means of bringing sinners to conversion. Hymns on the spread of the Gospel, especially in the work of foreign missions, were included in generous numbers, while hymns longing for the revival—such as could be sung in the monthly services—were also provided. In each of these ways, the *Selection* helped advance the general spread of "Fullerism" and the genuine missionary and evangelistic concern of the Baptists.

Less easily defined, but still important, was the liturgical influence of the *Selection*. Its arrangement reflected the desire of the ablest Baptist ministers for a proper ordering of services. But in a period when many new congregations were formed, and numerous small gatherings were held in villages, often led by untrained laymen, the influence of the *Selection* in shaping the worship of the Baptists may be assumed. There were hymns suitable for the general praise of God found in the front of

---

[127] For details see Manley thesis: 299-306.
[128] *Baptist Magazine* 5 (1813): 264.
[129] *Baptist Magazine* 20 (1828): 468-69.
[130] "Congregational Hymnody," *TCHS* 7 (1916–1918): 228.

the book, there were hymns suitable for before prayer, before and after a sermon, and doxologies with which to conclude the services. Hymns for baptism, especially those for before and after the service were also provided, as were hymns for the Lord's Supper. Indeed, as has been shown, one of the principal uses of the *Selection* was that it catered for almost every conceivable situation in the life of a church—seeking a pastor, election of deacons, funerals, etc. The *Selection* not only reflected but stimulated the homiletical bias of Baptist worship, and suggested an ordered sequence for the whole service.

Another related aspect was the devotional influence of the *Selection*. The piety of its generation was both represented and encouraged. As H. W. Foote has shown,[131] it is easy to select lines or verses from old hymns which amuse or appall us, and to caricature the worship it suggests. But it is more important to attempt an understanding of the genuine religious emotions they represent, and to recognize the uninterrupted stream of faith and idealism which flows from generation to generation. The sections designed for use in sickness are known to have been widely used. But in an age when many people possessed very few books—perhaps only a bible and hymnbook—the devotional use of the hymnbook in both private and family prayers is perhaps far beyond much modern imagination.

Numerous obituaries refer to the comfort of its hymns. For example, Mrs. Leeks had Hymn 550, ("Ah', I shall soon be dying") read to her, with the following results: "She felt the power of these verses, and with her hands clasped, her eyes fixed upwards, the tears trickling down her cheeks, she seemed in fervent prayer, and said, Ah, that is what I want."[132]

Andrew Fuller read over some of the hymns in the *Selection* and shed tears of joy while he sang, as he thought of his fellow Christians in various parts of England and India.[133] Such references are invariably to Rippon's book: it had become the Baptist collection.

But more easily demonstrated is the influence of the *Selection* in the history of hymnody, especially of Baptist hymnody. Four features may be noted. The *Selection* promoted the trend, begun by the "Bristol Collection," toward a comprehensive hymnal among Baptists; it replaced

---

[131]*Three Centuries of American Hymnody* (1961) 349-50.
[132]*Register*, iv, 759.
[133]A. Fuller to T. Stevens, Olney, 5 Oct. 1793, *Baptist Magazine* 8 (1816): 494-95.

the more literary or devotional writings of individuals. The *Selection* also provided a standard for Baptist hymnody. As M. Frost observed, the Independents had Watts as the basis of their hymnody, and the Methodists had the Wesleys' or Whitefield's collections; but that only with Rippon's *Selection* did the Baptists have a "commanding nucleus round which to group their hymnody."[134] Many notable hymns, such as "How Firm a Foundation" were first introduced by Rippon, whose *Selection* was without doubt the single greatest factor in the extensive circulation of the best of Baptist hymnody created in one of their most productive periods.

Rippon's *Selection* became an unrivalled source book for succeeding editors, Baptists and other denominations, so that Rippon "has permanently impressed himself upon the churches as having influenced their choice of hymns."[135] This cannot be overemphasized. For example, some 86 hymns are described by Julian as being first published by Rippon and as being "in common use" (Julian's first edition was 1892). A further 24 centos by Rippon are similarly described. In addition, other hymns, published previously, were given a wide circulation by Rippon's book. As H.W. Foote commented about the hymns of Samuel Davies, that although Gibbons first published them, they "owe their circulation to Dr. Rippon."[136] The *New Selection* of 1828 had 260 hymns from Rippon's book, and when C. H. Spurgeon produced *Our Own Hymn Book* in 1866, at which time Rippon's book ceased to be used in his old congregation, he included 195 hymns from Rippon's book. Changing taste has reduced the number of hymns still in use, but 34 appeared in the *Baptist Hymn Book* (1962) and 21 are in *Baptist Praise and Worship* (1991).

The influence of Rippon's book was even more pronounced in the United States, so that one historian of Baptist hymnody in America has included a section, "The Influence of John Rippon."[137] Rival books relied heavily on the *Selection*.[138] Dr. Benson rightly observed that the *Selection* was also "a link of connection between Baptist hymnody in England and America."[139] While this is true and significant, it must be noted that the influence was all one way: Rippon is not known to have included any

---

[134]M. Frost, ed., op. cit., 110.
[135]L. F. Benson, op. cit., 145.
[136]Op. cit., 151.
[137]W. J. Reynolds, *Hymns of our Faith* (Nashville TN: Broadman Press, 1964) xvii-xviii.
[138]For details, see L. F. Benson, op. cit.
[139]Ibid., 145.

American Baptist writers (indeed only Samuel Davies of America was used).

Thus Rippon's importance for Baptist hymnody has been shown. He demonstrated an accurate judgment and literary taste, collected numerous worthy originals, and by his editorial discretion and skill, he produced a book which attained an unqualified success. He secured for himself "a permanent place in the history of hymn singing."[140] As they used Rippon's books, Baptists for two generations at last fulfilled his vision of "Churchmen and Dissenters," England and the United States, singing side by side.

---

[140]Ibid., 144.

The Covenant Life of Some Eighteenth-Century Calvinistic Baptists in Hampshire and Wiltshire

Karen Smith

> I thank God that I was bro't up in the Baptist denomination. The more I know of religion either as doctrine or the experience and practical part of it the better I am satisfied with my own sect. Not that I wish to put any undue stress on that but I have no temptation to alter my sentiments as I think the particular baptist is very constant with the word of God.[1]

This comment found in Jane Attwater's[2] diary in November 1785 seems to suggest that she believed there was only one way to express Baptist life and faith, that is, using the approach to faith that she believed was generally accepted by Baptists in Hampshire and Wiltshire in the latter part of the eighteenth century. Like many others, she believed that there was only one true Baptist way.

Studies of the life and faith of Baptists have highlighted the difficulty of uniting them around one particular set of doctrines or approaches to worship. Frequently it is suggested that certain "principles," such as the belief in the authority of Scripture, freedom of conscience, or the priesthood of believers, should be the starting point for research of Baptist spirituality.[3] However, even these fundamental elements of faith are open to wide and varied interpretation by Baptists.

In spite of the diversity of views held among Baptists on biblical, ethical, and doctrinal matters, there is one central tenet which has united

---

[1] Diaries of Jane Attwater (1779–1789) Angus Library, Regent's Park College, Oxford.

[2] Jane Attwater was born in 1753. Her parents lived in Bodenham. She was a younger member of a literary circle that gathered around Anne Steele, the hymn writer, and a contemporary of Anne Steele's niece, Mary. Jane's mother was a cousin of William Steele's second wife, Anne (Cater) Steele. She married Joseph Blatch of Bratton in November 1790. Marjorie Reeves, *Sheep Bell and Plough Share* (Wiltshire, 1978) 33.

[3] See Ernest Payne, *The Fellowship of Believers* (London: Kingsgate Press, 1944). Stephen Winward pointed out the difficulties of defining Baptist spirituality when he suggested that it is preferable to speak of five characteristic marks of Baptist spirituality: a personal response in faith, freedom in prayer, the reading of Scripture, preaching, and a zeal for evangelism. See "Baptist Spirituality" in *A Dictionary of Christian Spirituality*, ed. Gordon S. Wakefield (London: SCM, 1983) 36-38.

Baptists of every theological persuasion: the idea that an individual's experience of faith is nurtured and shared within the context of the wider covenant community. The basis of Baptist life has always been the principle that believers are never believers alone, but bound together in a covenant community. Hence, Baptist devotion may best be considered by examining the way personal individual faith has found expression *within* the context of covenant community.

This essay will focus primarily on a group of Baptists living in Hampshire and Wiltshire in the eighteenth century, especially the church in Broughton, of which the hymn writer Anne Steele[4] was a member.[5] There is, however, no suggestion that their approach to devotion was or should be understood as necessarily normative among all Baptists in the eighteenth century. Findings from local and regional studies may not necessarily be applied to larger groups of Baptists. However, it is suggested that by examining this group of Baptists, one may explore devotion within the context of covenant life.

1. Walking Together: The Congregational Way

As children of the Protestant Reformed tradition, English Calvinistic Baptists founded their doctrine and polity on the belief that Scripture alone was authoritative for faith and practice. From the beginning, they affirmed that the principles of the Christian life, as well as the pattern of church life, were to be based on biblical teaching. For them, the Christian life began with divine initiative, as God opened his heart to the world through the death and resurrection of His Son. Personal salvation came through faith alone. In other words, they believed salvation depended on the direct response of a believer to the grace offered by God in Christ—a gift of God made possible through the work of the Holy Spirit.

---

[4]Anne Steele was born in 1717 to William and Anne (Froud) Steele. She was baptized on 19 July 1732 and joined the church in Broughton where her father was the minister. Her first volume of poetry, *Poems on Subjects Chiefly Devotional*, was published in 1760 and reprinted in 1780 with a third volume, *Miscellaneous Pieces*. See the Broughton Church Books and the Steele family Papers, Angus Library.

[5]Attention will be given to the ministers who served churches in the area as well as diaries, papers, and sermons relating to the Steele family. The Steele family has an important place in the history and growth of the churches in Hampshire and Wilshire. Henry Steele (1654–1739) served as pastor of the congregation from 1699 until his death in 1739. His nephew, William Steele, then served as pastor from 1739 to 1769. After his first wife died, he married Anne Cater Steele. His daughter was Anne Steele (1717–1778), the hymn writer.

Although they believed salvation was extended to those who by faith accepted the forgiveness offered to them in Christ, those who accepted Calvinist doctrine never presumed that everyone would be saved. Only those who were "effectually called" could by faith and through the work of the Holy Spirit be drawn unto Christ and experience union with him. The 1689 *Confession* stated:

> Those whom God hath predestined unto Life, he is pleased, in his appointed, and accepted time, effectually to call by his word, and Spirit, out of that state of sin, and death, in which they are by nature, to grace and Salvation by Jesus Christ.[6]

Union or participation in the death and resurrection of Christ was reserved only for the elect, those known only to God and chosen by him to be unified in Christ. Moreover, while personal faith was essential, union with Christ was not simply an individual experience, but a corporate one which united believers as members of the body of Christ—the Church.

Like others in the Reformed tradition, Calvinistic Baptists never equated the church with any institution. Far from recognizable as a particular group, the "true church," was the church "invisible" or the universal church, which included all the "elect." Since election was known perfectly only to God, however, the church on earth, or the "visible" community of faith, included both the elect and the nonelect.[7] Unlike those who identified the "visible" body of believers with the state church, Baptists, as well as Independents, believed it was best represented as a "gathered community," or a voluntary association of believers who acknowledged their faith in Christ, covenanting with God and each other in order to separate from the world and walk in his way—those already revealed as well as those yet to be discerned.[8] The "congregational way" held that the church was a society or fellowship of believers who

---

[6] W. L. Lumpkin, *Baptist Confessions of Faith* (Philadelphia PA: Judson Press, 1959) 264.

[7] Ibid., 285.

[8] In spite of the fact that the Independents did not adequately represent their theology in every instance, E. A. Payne noted that Baptists in some periods have accepted the writings of Congregationalists on questions of church and ministry. He cited the influence of the writings of John Owen, such as *The True Nature of the Gospel Church* (1689), on Baptists in the seventeenth century and, in the closing decades of the nineteenth century, the wide acceptance of R. W. Dale, *Manual of Congregational Principles* (1884). Payne, *Fellowship of Believers*, 16.

professed a willingness to "give themselves to the Lord and to one another," and joined together with Scripture as a guide to faith and practice.[9] As a "gathered community" of saints, they joined together by mutual agreement, pledging their desire to live in the world and, yet, to be not of the world. As members of Christ's body, they each were expected to demonstrate their faith and commitment by both word and deed. The 1689 *Confession* described the members of local churches as

> Saints by calling, visibly manifesting and evidencing (in and by their profession and walking) their obedience unto that call of Christ; and do willingly consent to walk together according to the appointment of Christ; giving up themselves to the Lord and one another by the will of God, in professed subjection to the Ordinances of the Gospel.[10]

As a means of expressing their plan to "walk together," congregations usually drew up covenant agreements that stated the desire of believers to unite by mutual consent in order to live together as a community of faith.[11] Although the wording of covenant agreements varied, they each began by signifying that the believers who entered into fellowship with one another did so because they believed they had been drawn together by God. In other words, they were made a covenant community by the will of God. God alone had made the covenant relationship possible as he "freely offereth to sinners Life and Salvation by Jesus Christ requiring of them Faith in him, that they may be saved."[12]

Generally, covenant agreements included statements that set forth the duties of those who joined in this "spiritual relation." These articles usually placed more emphasis on the practical issues of living together than on doctrinal unanimity. Their purpose was to emphasize that the members had been called out to be a visible community of saints, and by joining together, they were pledging to embrace both the duties and privileges of church membership, including worship, prayer for one

---

[9]The "congregational way" as G. F. Nuttall has written, is not to be taken on all points as identical with what is now known as Congregationalism, but it is to be seen as an interpretation of the Gospel and a doctrine of the church which is much larger than any denomination in the modern sense. See *Visible Saints* (1957) vii.

[10]Lumpkin, *Baptist Confessions of Faith*, 286. The *Confession* was modification of the Independent Savoy Confession (1658).

[11]For a discussion of the significance of the covenants to seventeenth-century Dissent, see G. F. Nuttall, *Visible Saints*, 77-78.

[12]Lumpkin, *Baptist Confessions of Faith*, 259.

another, attendance for the ordinances, and participation in the discipline and government of the congregation.[13]

The earliest evidence of a covenant statement for Calvinistic Baptists in Hampshire and Wiltshire was signed by those who attended a meeting on June 3, 1655, at Porton in Wiltshire,[14] "brethren and sisters from Wallop, Sarum, Stowford (Stoford), Chalke (Broad Chalke) and parts adjasent" who

> there with one accord declared theire resolutions for ye future through Christ wch strengtheneth them soo (sic) to walke as becometh saints according to ye Gospell of Our Lord Jesus Christ in all obedience of his commands and in love towards each other brethren and sisters ptakers of ye same God through Jesus Christ our Lord.[15]

On the same day, nine believers were baptized and it was agreed that monthly meetings would be held in rotation at Amesbury, Stowford, Chalke, and Porton.[16] One hundred and eleven people representing at least twenty villages which were within a twelve mile radius of Porton, signed the statement.[17]

Covenant agreements like this one had an important place in Baptist life and faith in the eighteenth century. As the Porton fellowship grew and other village congregations were formed, many others drew up covenant statements as well. Many appear to have based their covenants

---

[13] William Steele, sermon on Psalm 27:40 (18 July 1720).

[14] A copy of a document describing the first meeting may be found in the first Broughton Church Book (BCB I) in the Angus Library. In addition, there is an article by Arthur Tucker, "Porton Baptist Church, 1655–1685," *Transactions of the Baptist Historical Society* I (1908–1910) 58-61, which was based on the record of this meeting in a Salisbury Church Book. Unfortunately, the records used by Tucker were lost from the church some years ago, but from the partial transcript of the meeting provided in the article, it is possible to establish that the account of the meeting in the BCB I and the Salisbury book from which the transcript was made were similar. Ivimey too gives a similar account of the meeting that he says was taken from extracts from the Salisbury Church book. Joseph Ivimey, *History of the English Baptists*, 4 vols. (London: Burditt, Button, Hamilton, Baynes, 1811–1830) 2:582. Moreover, there is a pamphlet written by John Toone, *A Short Account of an Ancient Nonconformist Church Once Existing at Porton, Near Salisbury* (1865) 2, which cited the same account that he said was in the Salisbury Church Book, then extant.

[15] BCB I, the Angus Library.

[16] Ibid.

[17] The places represented at the meeting were Stowford, Salisbury, Stoke, Broad Chalke, Bodenham, Endford, Wetherhaven, Allington, Bulford, Ivingford, Amesbury, Winterbourne, Edmington, Pitton, Farlie, Glimsford, Porton, Wallop, Charlton, and Fovant. BCB I.

on one included in Benjamin Keach's treatise, *The Glory of a True Church and Its Discipline Display'd* (1679). As the title suggests, Keach attempted to lay down guidelines for what he described as "an orderly and true church."[18] For him, a church should be a place where people give themselves to the Lord and to one another. He suggested that maintaining order required taking the covenant seriously. In looking at this treatise, it becomes apparent that the twofold emphasis on personal faith and mutual agreement was believed to be the very heart of the covenant community.

2. Examining Experience: The Testimony of Believers

Membership in a particular "gathered community" of believers was not a matter of merely giving verbal assent to a covenant agreement, but rather was dependent upon the individual's ability to demonstrate a sincere commitment to the Lord Jesus based on his or her knowledge and experience of Christ in Scripture. In other words, membership was an integral part of discipleship—of "right walking" with Christ.

Those seeking fellowship with a group of believers were required to express their commitment and trust by giving a testimony of their "experience" to members of the congregation. While entrance into the church was regarded as distinct from baptism, in practice they were usually combined. However, no one was to be baptized and received into church membership without having first made a public profession of an "experience of grace," or without showing clear signs of living in obedience to the commands set forth in Scripture and exemplified in the life of Christ.

Although the practice of both men and women giving an extemporaneous testimony to the congregation before being accepted in the covenant community was normative among Calvinistic Baptists in the eighteenth century, the point at which congregations began to expect applicants for church membership to "give evidence of their faith" is a matter of dispute. Those who have studied the modification of English Calvinism, especially among the Puritans in the seventeenth century, have noted that one of the distinctive marks of their faith and practice was the link they made between churchmanship and soteriology, particularly as it related to the idea of assurance.[19] Unlike John Calvin, who described

---

[18]Benjamin Keach, *The Glory of the True Church* (1679) 5.
[19]Stephen Brachlow discusses the background to the way Puritan churchmanship was

saving faith as something that was passively received from God, many Puritans asserted that giving signs of an "effectual calling" could be regarded as an indication that one was assuredly one of the elect.[20] Believing that the church was properly made up of the elect, the ability to identify particular marks of salvation, naturally, came to be associated with entry into a community of faith.

Precisely when and how this practice developed is not known. It has been argued by some that the early Separatists did not require applicants for membership to be "tested," but rather merely to give confessions demonstrative of their intellectual understanding of faith. Edmund S. Morgan at Yale University argued that the idea of requiring members to give an account of their experience developed among nonseparating Puritans in Massachusetts before spreading back to England.[21] Clearly, the practice of requiring individuals to "give in their experience" to the congregation was practised among dissenters in England in the 1650s, since two collections of the accounts of members of Independent congregations were then printed.[22]

Although they vary in length and style, the surviving written conversion narratives[23] generally seem to follow the pattern set out by the Puritan divine, William Perkins.[24] Perkins' "morphology" outlined conversion

---

linked to soteriology in his article, "Puritan Theology and General Baptist Origins," *Baptist Quarterly* (hereafter *BQ*) 31 (1985): 183. See also R. T. Kendall, *Calvin and English Calvinism to 1649* (Oxford: Oxford University Press, 1979).

[20]Brachlow, "Puritan Theology and General Baptist Origins," 184.

[21]Edmund S. Morgan, *Visible Saints* (New York, 1963) 58-63, 92-105, 109-10. He claimed that reformed churches required nothing more of prospective members than an outward "profession of faith," an understanding of basic doctrine, and visibly "godly conversation," and that the "test" of experience only emerged in New England probably about 1634 under John Cotton, and then was taken back to England.

[22][H. Walker] *Spiritual Experiences of Sundry Believers* (1652); J. Rogers, *Ohel or Beth-Shemesh, a Tabernacle for the Sun* (1653).

[23]Some attention has been given to conversion narratives among Puritans in England and New England in the seventeenth century, e.g., Owen C. Watkins, *The Puritan Experience* (1972), Patricia Caldwell, *The Puritan Conversion Narrative, the Beginnings of American Expression* (Cambridge: 1983), and Charles Lloyd Cohen, *God's Caress, The Psychology of the Puritan Religious Experience* (Oxford: 1986). However, apart from studies which have attempted to apply modern psychological theory, little has been done by way of comparing and analyzing those which exist in the eighteenth century. Cf. F. W. B. Bullock, *Evangelical Conversion in Great Britain, 1696-1845*, (1959) and Sydney G. Dimond, *The Psychology of the Methodist Revival, An Empirical and Descriptive Study* (London: Oxford University Press, 1926).

[24]Michael Watts says that "the process of conversion expounded by Perkins was upheld by English Evangelicals for three centuries as normative of Christian experience."

in progressive stages, which included the acknowledgment of sin, preparation and assurance, conviction, compunction and submission, fear, sorrow, and faith. Moreover, nearly all the narratives emphasize the significance of the Word as the primary means through which believers were brought to recognize their total depravity before God. Often, for instance, there were references to having been "struck" or "impressed" by a verse of Scripture heard in a sermon, which led to a period of self-examination, and then to repentance. It follows, then, that for Calvinistic Baptists—as for the Puritans, as Owen Watkins has described them—"the spoken word was the one agency by which, on a plane of nature, the innermost faculties could be reached, and this was why the sermon was regarded as the most effective channel of grace."[25] Often believers recorded having heard the Word read and preached, sometimes over a period of one or more years, before they entered a period of doubt and trial which led to a true and sorrowful repentance.

Since acceptance into a congregation was dependent on the individual's ability to give a sure testimony, efforts were made to ensure that the testimony of those received was real and genuine, and that the person was of sound character. After the testimony was "given in" to the congregation, neighbors and relatives gave statements regarding the character of the individual. Then following discussion, a vote was taken by church members to decide whether the person should be accepted.

Those speaking on behalf of a person seeking membership took their responsibility seriously. In August 1730, for instance, Anne Cater Steele accompanied one of her servants, Mary Strong, to see Henry Steele, and afterwards wrote in her diary that she was pleased because the girl "talked better than expected."[26] The next day, however, before the matter was to come before the church, she began to have misgivings, unsure if she should submit the girl's name for membership. Later, she wrote in her diary, "I know the Lord he knows that I would never put forward any name but such whom I have good grounds to hope are believers in Christ."[27]

However, doubt over the authenticity of believers' experiences could lead church members to postpone their decision until the person had

---

The Dissenters (Oxford: Clarendon Press, 1978) 174.
[25] Watkins, *The Puritan Experience*, 6.
[26] 2 August 1730, ACS Diary, microfilm, Angus Library.
[27] 3 August 1730, ACS Diary.

undergone a waiting period. On one occasion, for example, Mrs. Steele reported talking to a woman who wished to be baptized, and while she hoped God had "been at work upon her soul" she had advised the woman to

> wait a little longer and be constant in prayer for more knowledge and faith and also to count the cost of a profession of religion then if it appears to be a work of grace upon her heart it will be no grief of mind to her to wait God's time.[28]

Despite the fact that much attention was given to the need for a clear testimony of an experience of grace upon acceptance into a community of faith, the need to look for evidence of faith did not stop here. In other words, even after they had testified to their faith and been accepted into the church, believers were expected to continue looking for signs of their election and calling. This did not mean, of course, that even the knowledge of salvation could be attained by one's own merits. "The grace of faith," as the 1689 Confession stated, "whereby the Elect are enabled to believe to the saving of their souls is the work of the Spirit of Christ in their Hearts.[29] However, while assurance was not the essence of faith, those who diligently searched, acquired knowledge of it. As the *Confession* remarked,

> This infallible assurance doth not belong to the essence of faith, but that a true believer, may wait long and conflict with many difficulties before he be partaker of it; yet being enabled by the spirit to know the things which are freely given of God, he may without extraordinary revelation in the right use of means attaine there unto: and therefore it is the duty of everyone to give all diligence to make their Calling and Election sure. . . .[30]

The idea that assurance was to be sought after was the theme of a sermon by William Steele on Psalm 39:5, in which he described three aspects of faith: credence, reliance, and assurance. Faith of credence and reliance, according to him, meant that one gave credit to the truth of what is revealed in Scripture and relied on Christ for salvation.[31] Faith of assurance, on the other hand, meant that one had a "well grounded and full persuasion" of an interest in Christ.[32] While the first two were by far

---

[28] 4 January 1755, ACS Diary.
[29] Lumpkin, *Baptist Confessions*, 268.
[30] Ibid., 275.
[31] William Steele, sermon on Psalm 39:5, n.d., Angus Library.
[32] Ibid.

the most important, he nevertheless urged listeners to strive to attain the latter. All believers, he wrote,

> Must labor to get our evidences clear for heaven, we should not only labor to be sure we have faith of relyance and dependence on Christ, but indever [*sic*] to improve it to the faith of assurance.[33]

The need for assurance continued to dominate the devotional lives of many of these eighteenth-century Baptists. In November of 1733, Anne Cater Steele wrote in her diary of her efforts to find this faith of assurance:

> That was on my mind tis God that worketh in us to will and to do his owne good pleasure I find myself often taking a view of my own ways and actions and then compare them with reason and the word of God and that came to mind and herein do I exercise myself to have always a conscience void of offence especially toward God when I know I do justly offend everyday.... I tho't what if my hope of salvation should be but dreams and at last appear to be chaf how dreadfully then shall I have been mistaken. This stir'd me up to cry earnestly to the Lord and I hope I was enabled to act in faith and was truly senceable [*sic*] of my own nothingness.[34]

Like her stepmother, Anne Steele also expressed doubts at times over the assurance of her salvation. In 1763 Caleb Ashworth[35] wrote to Anne Steele and mentioned that when he was visiting her in Broughton, she had expressed "doubt and suspicion as to her spiritual interests." He claimed that a precious few could have complete and uninterrupted assurance, and that doubts should simply send her "to the blood of Jesus and teach her to pant more fervently after the Holy Spirit."[36]

Throughout most of the eighteenth century, even women—who generally were admonished to "keep silent" in church meetings—were expected to stand before the congregation and give evidence of an "experimental work of grace" on their hearts. Moreover, it was understood that they would spend time "examining their experience" before coming to the Lord's Table. As time went on, however, if the person concerned felt unable to speak freely before the congregation, some

---

[33] Ibid.

[34] 14 November 1733, ACS Diary.

[35] Caleb Ashworth was the successor to Philip Doddridge as the tutor formerly at the academy at Northampton, but then in Daventry. See James Hardeman, "Caleb Ashworth of Cloughfield and Daventry," *BQ* (1936–1937): 200-206. See also the *DNB*.

[36] Microfilm III, Steele Family papers, Angus Library.

congregations gave the believer permission to read a written statement of personal confession.[37] In 1751 Mrs. Steele noted that her niece was "desiring to offer her experience in writting [sic], she being very subject to be surprized."[38] The church agreed and she was received. The fact that the experiences of believers was evaluated and judged by themselves and church members, points again to the delicate balance between individual confession and incorporation into a visible community of faith.

3. Baptized into Christ: The Confession of a Community

From the beginning, Baptists were distinguished from other dissenters as to the proper subject and mode of baptism. Unlike those who baptized infants by sprinkling as a sign of admission into the visible community of saints, both Calvinistic and General Baptists in Britain maintained that baptism for believers should be carried out by immersion only.

Throughout the seventeenth and eighteenth centuries, Baptists engaged in a number of "pamphlet controversies," in which they tried to defend and clarify their stance on baptism.[39] While acknowledging their belief that only adult believers who gave evidence of an experiential faith are proper candidates for baptism, Calvinistic Baptists also maintained that baptism was linked to the experience of regeneration. However, what they always vigorously affirmed was that the waters of baptism were not in themselves efficacious for salvation, but rather *signified* that the person had already been regenerated. Moreover, while they emphasized that baptism was never to be seen as merely a rite of initiation or a means of entry into membership of the church, it was accepted nevertheless as a real sign of fellowship with Christ and with his body, the Church.

In 1741 John Lacy[40] took up the issue of baptismal regeneration in

---

[37]Salisbury Church Book.

[38]7 July 1751, ACS Diary.

[39]One of the most well-known attacks on Baptists was made by Daniel Featley in a tract, which was published in 1646 and underwent seven editions by 1660, entitled:*The Dippers Dipt. Or Anabaptists Duck'd and Plung'd Over Head and Eares*. Another important treatise in the eighteenth century was Joseph Stennett's pamphlet on baptism entitled *An Answer to Mr. David Ruffen's Book Entitl'd Fundamentals without a Foundation or a True Picture of the Anabaptists Together with Some Brief Remarks on Mr. James Broome's Letter Annex'd to the Treatise* (1704). For a synopsis of some of the more important public disputations on baptism, see J. J. Goadby, *Bye-Paths in Baptist History* (1871) 139-79. A. S. Langley, *Transactions of the Baptist Historical Society* VI (1918–1919) 216-43, lists twenty-six disputations in which Baptists were involved.

[40]John Lacy (1700–1781) was born at Clatford near Andover on 22 May 1700 and

his *Remarks on a Pamphlet Call'd a Conference about Infant Baptism*.[41] in which he questioned whether infant baptism led the "covenant of grace" into a "covenant of works," since it seemed to "lay the foundation of security with parents."[42] For Lacy, what mattered most was that the person who was baptized be overcome with "a new nature." Baptists, he wrote, "say tarry till a new nature is given and suitable conversation produced, and then baptize them; otherwise baptism can be of no signification."[43]

Baptism was an individual witness and testimony of faith, but at the same time early Baptists contended that it was a sign of incorporation into the body of Christ, a sign of fellowship with him in his death and resurrection. Early Baptists believed that, through the waters of baptism, they were not only professing their personal faith in Christ and indicating their desire to "live and walk in newness of life," but they were also joining Christ and his body in a unique way. As with every act of worship, baptism, for these Calvinistic Baptists, was both a corporate and an individual act, signifying the believer's obedience, faith, and desire to follow in the example set by Christ and taught in the New Testament, and fur-

---

moved with his family to Portsea in 1704. He married in 1728 and afterwards joined the Meetinghouse Alley Church. He was called out by the congregation to preach in March 1732 and in July 1733 he was given pastoral charge of the congregation. He published *Conference about Infant Baptism* (1741), *An Answer to a Late Anonymous Pamphlet Entitled a Treatise on the Subject and Mode of Baptism* (1743), *Divine Hymns* (Portsea: 1747), a translation of *Bull Unigenitus with Its Rise and Progress* (1753), *The Universal System: or Mechanical Cause of All the Appearances and Movements of the Visible Heavens with a Dissertation on Comets* (1779), and according to Ivimey, who was for some time a member of his church, he left a paper entitled "The Duty and Office of Deacons." See Samuel Rowles, *The Christian Soldier Waiting For His Crown* (1781); Joseph Ivimey, *History of the English Baptists* 4:486-89; Edward C. Starr, *A Baptist Bibliography, Being a Register of Printed Materials by and about the Baptists, Inluding Work against the Baptists*, vol. 13 (Rochester NY: American Baptist Historical Society, 1968) 166-67.

[41]*Remarks on a Pamphlet Call'd a Conference about Infant Baptism Wherein the Mistakes of the Author Are Set in a Clear Light, Believers Proved to be the Only Proper Subjects of Baptism and Immersion or Plunging Essential to It in a Letter to a Paedobaptist Friend* (1741). Although it was published anonymously, Joseph Ivimey who was at one time a member of Lacy's church at Portsea, credited Lacy with this pamphlet: Ivimey, *A History of the English Baptists* 4:489. Further evidence for Lacy's authorship may be found in a copy of this treatise in the Angus Library which is inscribed with the signature of Isaac Keene and dated 17 January 1741-1742, and noted to be have been written by "Mr. Lacy of Portsmouth."

[42]J. Lacy, *Remarks on a Pamphlet*, 19.
[43]Ibid., 45.

thermore, marking the believer's incorporation into the body of Christ. Charles Cole,[44] for instance, wrote a hymn which emphasized baptism as an act of obedience on the part of the believer, based on the pattern set by Jesus. Just as Jesus obeyed the Father's will, so those who follow him should also be obedient and enter the "baptismal tomb." A hymn based on Matthew 3:13-15 urged the believers to heed Jesus as the ultimate example:

> Thus he obey'd his father's will
> Fulfilled his righteousness,
> Shew'd his duty's comely path to all
> The subjects of his grace.
>
> Come then Ye friends of Jesus come,
> By his example led,
> Enter the baptismal tomb
> As members of the Head.[45]

The imagery of baptism as a "tomb" highlights a second important aspect of baptism for Calvinistic Baptists during this period, namely, that it symbolized the remission of sin and signified fellowship with Christ in his death and resurrection. In another hymn based on Romans 6:3-4, for instance, he spoke of baptism as a "solemn sign" which not only symbolized a desire to submit to sin, but also Christ's death and resurrection:

> As Jesus dy'd to save
> The sinful sons of men
> And from the Prison of the grave
> Arose to life again
>
> So we should die to sin
> And live to righteousness

---

[44]Charles Cole (1733–1813) was born at Wellow in Somerset. His parents died when he was six and left him in the care of relatives. He took up the trade of a cloth weaver and in 1756 was baptized and received into membership by the church at Bradford in Wiltshire under the care of Richard Haines. In 1759 he was called to serve as pastor to the church in Whitchurch, Hampshire. A hymn writer, Cole published a collection of hymns in 1789 entitled *A Threefold Alphabet of New Hymns: (1) On the Public Ministry of the Word, (2) On Baptism, (3) On the Lord's Supper*. See *Baptist Magazine* 6 (1814): 222. See also a letter dismissing Charles and Jane Cole from the church at Bradford in Wiltshire to the Church in Whitchurch, 14 April 1759, Whitchurch Papers, Angus Library.

[45]Cole, *A Threefold Alphabet of New Hymns*, 76.

> Who in the liquid grave have been,
>   The Saviour to confess
>
> The Saviour's death to shew,
>   When buried in the flood
> And in that solemn sign we view
>   the risen son of God.[46]

As the 1689 *Confession* declared, through baptism believers are "ingrafted into" Christ, and hence, uniquely joined to other believers as well.[47] Baptism was never merely an individual confession of faith, but a corporate act that signified a deeper union between the individual, Christ, and other believers.

4. United in Suffering: The Shared Life of the Community

In examining the life of early Baptists, it becomes clear that the very core of early Baptist devotion urges believers to confess Christ through testimony and baptism, submitting not only to Christ, but also to one another. The sense of mutual agreement and responsibility was not simply about keeping the rules of the church or having a proper sense of order or discipline—though these were considered necessary. Rather, sharing together in the truest sense meant uniting in both the suffering of Christ and of others who are part of his body. As the covenant document of one congregation put it,

> We do purpose to bear one anothers burdens to cleave to one another and to have a fellow feeling with one another in all conditions both outward and inward as God in its Providence shall cast any of us into. We do purpose to bear one anothers weaknesses and failings and infirmities with much tenderness not discovering to any without the church nor within unless according to Christ's rule, and the order of the Gospel provided in that case.[48]

The ordinances of baptism and the Lord's Supper naturally provided a focus for their understanding of unity in suffering. As already noted, baptism into the suffering and death of Christ was a means by which men and women were joined to Christ and to one another. The Lord's Supper, on the other hand, allowed believers to regularly renew baptismal vows and to join in the sufferings of Christ and of one another.

---

[46]Ibid., 77.
[47]Lumpkin, *Baptist Confessions of Faith*, 291.
[48]Whitchurch Church Covenant, 1714.

At no time was the Baptists' emphasis on covenant theology more apparent than at the celebration of the Lord's Supper. Observed once a month, like baptism, the Lord's Supper was an ordinance of the church, as well as a graphic reminder of Christ's love and sacrifice for their salvation. Likewise, it also provided an opportunity to share in communion with Christ and in fellowship with other believers. Like the Puritans before them, Calvinistic Baptists related the Lord's Supper to redemption rather than to creation, and therefore, they emphasized God's gracious act of love and the forgiveness of sin rather than self-offering. It was believed that participating in the Supper provided one with guidance and strength for true Christian living. Judging from the sermons and hymns of Baptists in the area during this period, it appears that the Supper was both an opportunity to reflect upon Christ's death, as well as a time for real communion with Christ.

Speaking of the church as the "banqueting house of God," William Steele described the Word and the ordinances as a "means of grace when Christ is manifest and entertains the believer with Grace." On another occasion he wrote that "Christ himself is the feast and persons by faith spiritually feed on him." In a sermon on John 10:11, he described Christ as the food which one may feed on at the Supper. "Christ," he wrote, "feeds his sheep with himself . . . the flesh and blood which he gives is food for our nourishment and life for our souls."[49]

The concept of the Lord's Supper as both an opportunity for reflection upon the saving work of Christ and also a time of real communion with him is illustrated in Anne Steele's hymn "Communion with Christ at His Table," which was copied by her stepmother into her diary on Sunday March 10, 1750, and later published in *Poems on Subjects Chiefly Devotional*. While the verses call to mind the believer's own unworthiness and Christ's sacrificial love, they simultaneously express a desire for real communion with him:

> To Jesus our exalted Lord
> (Dear name, by heaven and earth ador'd!)
> Fain would our hearts and voices raise
> A cheerful song of sacred praise.
>
> But all the notes which mortals know
> Are weak and languishing and low;

---

[49] William Steele, sermon on John 10:11, n.d., Angus Library.

Far, far above our humble songs
The theme of immortal tongues.

Yet while around this board we meet,
And worship at his glorious feet;
O let our warm affections move
In glad returns of grateful love.

Yes, Lord we love and we adore,
but long to know and love thee more;
And while we taste the bread and wine,
Desire to feed on joys divine.

Let faith our feeble senses aid
To see thy wondrous love display'd
Thy broken flesh, thy bleeding veins
Thy dreadful agonizing pains.

Let humble penitential woe,
with painful, pleasing anguish flow
And thy forgiving smiles impart
Life, hope and joy to every heart.[50]

Charles Cole—pastor at Whitchurch from 1759 to 1813, and author of *A Threefold Alphabet of New Hymns* (1789)—expressed similar views of the ordinance. For instance, in a hymn based on John 6:35, he encouraged believers to see with "believing eyes" and taste the living bread:

Fullness of grace in Christ doth dwell
   Enough to save from sin and hell
And his rich mercy we adore
   Divinely free an endless store.

He is the true and living bread,
   With which believing souls are fed
On him they feast with great delight
   And so increased their inward light.

The manna in the wilderness,
   Was but a fading sign of this,
That was the Isr'elites supply,
   and yet the Isr'elites must die.

But Jews and Gentiles that receive
   This heavenly bread shall ever live

---

[50] 10 March 1750, ACS Diary.

> With this their wants are ere supply'd
>   and hungry souls are satisfy'd.
>
> This bread of life we have in view
>   When the redeemers death we show
> When at this table we appear
>   To see and taste the Symbols there.
>
> Beyond these Signs of bread and wine
>   We see the substance all divine
> We see with our believing eyes
>   The lamb of God, a sacrifice.[51]

Since the Lord's Supper offered the opportunity both to remember Christ's sacrificial love and to experience communion with him, during the eighteenth century, there was a great deal of emphasis on "preparing" before approaching the Lord's Table. As individuals reflected upon the sacrificial love of Christ, they were to consider their own unworthiness merely to seek communion with him. Personal preparation before the Supper was to be taken seriously by the believers. On many occasions, Mrs. Steele recorded both her time of preparation and her actual experience at the ordinance. In one instance she remarked,

> I read my experience since my last sitting down at the Lord's table and find and know I have been in a poor and barren frame a great part of the time I now beg I may be prepar'd for the ensueing day and I may be refreshed and quickened by the holy ordinances of God's house. I was sweetly drawn out in my evening duty in love and thankfulness. . . . I heard Mr. Eastman pretty diligently from "and this is my commandment that we should believe on the name of his son Jesus Christ and love one another" . . . my desires ran out to God in the ordinance both for my comfort for myself and for others that came with power so he that eateth me so shall he live and I hope I have been fed on Christ.[52]

Preparation and participation in the Lord's Supper was both a time of remembrance and a time of communion with Christ. John Lacy's "For the Lord's Supper" exclaims:

> Now let my thankful tongue repeat,
>   In songs of sacred peace
> How heav'n did all my foes defeat
>   And gave me a release.

---

[51] Cole, *A Threefold Alphabet of New Hymns*, 98.
[52] 1 April 1733, ACS Diary, Angus Library.

> Let Christ my gracious King arise
>   And rule my stubborn heart:
> Descend dear Jesus from the skies
>   And never let us part.
>
> Open the fountain of thy blood
>   Where all my love begins
> Give me to plunge into that flood
>   To wash away my sins.
>
> Then come my friends here let us join
>   Since Jesus is so nigh
> Supported by this bread and wine
>   Till we are called on high.[53]

The conception that following in the way of Christ was in some sense *real participation* in the sufferings of Christ and others would appear to have been an important part of devotion for these eighteenth century Baptists. In her diary, Mrs. Steele refers incessantly to her desire to share in the joy, as well as the sorrow, of those within her community, often crying out in her prayers on behalf of others. In fact, Mrs. Steele noted the significance of bearing one another's burdens when on one occasion, as she prepared to go to the Lord's Table, she wrote:

> I find that the concerns of others go very near my soul such as I hope have an interest in Christ when I know their temptations their afflictions or their consolations. I seem to bear an equal share in either[:] how can it be otherwise when I look upon them together with myself as part of the purchase of Christ's suffering and so a part of the real body of whom Christ is the head.[54]

Like baptism and the Lord's Supper, prayer was also a means of communion with Christ. William Steele preached on the bounden duty and peculiar privilege of prayer;[55] moreover, he pointed out what he believed to be "the insofishency [*sic*] of precomposed and stented forms of prayer," labeling the neglect of daily prayer as "fatal."[56]

While it is difficult to understand the place of suffering in Christian faith, these early Baptists seemed to recognize that it was part of their life together. At the same time, they realized that deep suffering was often

---

[53] J[ohn] L[acy], *Divine Hymns Made Most Important Points of Christianity* (1747).
[54] ACD Diary, 1 April 1734, Angus Library.
[55] William Steele, sermon on Matthew 6:9, 7 February 1725.
[56] William Steele, sermon on Matthew 6:11, 28 November 1725.

something which isolated and separated individuals from each other. Anne Steele often expressed her pain to God in ways suggestive of her loneliness and suffering. For instance, she wrote,

> My God, to thee I call—
>   Must I for ever mourn?
> So far from thee, my life, my all?
>   O when wilt thou return!
>
> Dark as the shades of night
>   my gloomy sorrows rise,
> And hide they soul-reviving light
>   From these desiring eyes.
>
> My comforts all decay
>   My inward foes prevail;
> If thou withhold thy healing ray,
>   Expiring hope will fail.[57]

Even early Baptists acknowledged that one can never completely enter into the suffering of another. Yet they seem to have understood that even as they shared in the sufferings of Christ— particularly by way of baptism, the Lord's Supper, and prayer—so they were united with others who together with them composed Christ's body, the church. Devotion for them was not simply keeping the rules of the church, attending meetings, or even attending worship services. Instead, it involved *real sharing* in Christ. Perhaps we can discern that through this unified suffering, the many expressions of Baptist faith come together. In covenant commitment, the varieties of expressions of faith are gathered into the oneness of the suffering of Christ.

---

[57]Hymn LXXIX, "Mourning the Absence of God, and Longing for His Gracious Presence." *Hymns by Anne Steele* (London: Gospel Standard Baptist Trust, 1967) 88.

Another Baptist Ejection (1662): The Case of John Norcott

Geoffrey F. Nuttall

John Norcott's name is now forgotten, but for a long time it was well known—at least among Baptists—thanks to his book, *Baptism discovered plainly and faithfully according to the word of God. Wherein is set forth the glorious pattern of our blessed Saviour, Jesus Christ, the pattern of all believers in their subjection to baptism*, published in 1672 and again in 1675, with a preface by William Kiffin and Richard Claridge. Later editions appeared in 1694 and 1700; in 1709, 1721, 1722, 1723, and 1740; and in 1801 and 1878, this last one "corrected and altered" by C. H. Spurgeon.[1]

Baptism discovered appears to have been Norcott's only book, but in 1674 he contributed with Benjamin Keach a commendatory epistle to a piece by Josia Bonham of Priors Marston, Warwickshire, *The churches glory: or, the becoming ornament: being a seasonable word, tending to the provoking, encouraging and perfecting of holiness in believers*.[2] When Norcott died on March 24, 1676, Keach preached his funeral sermon, *A summons to the grave*,[3] including an elegy he wrote (which was also published separately),[4] as well as other tributes, for which there is unfortunately no biographical information.

A colleague of Kiffin and Keach, Norcott was clearly a man of note; however, little is known of him, save that from 1670 to 1676[5] he served as minister of the church at Wapping, where he succeeded John Spils-

---

[1] See Wing N1227-1227A; W. T. Whitley, *Baptist Bibliography* i.28-670; Regent's Park College, the Angus Library Cat. (1908), 229; Dexter, nos. 2253, 2289. For Claridge, who in 1691 became a Baptist and in 1697 a Quaker, see *D.N.B.*; Whitley, index to authors; *Descr. Cat. of Friends' Books* (1867), ed. J. Smith, i.409-17.

[2] Wing B 3592, without location here noted by the unlisted symbol LA; there is a copy in the Angus Library (Cat., 33).

[3] Wing K 95, without location in this country; Whitley, 20-676 (copy at Dr. Williams's Library).

[4] Wing K 61; Whitley, 19-676.

[5] For the church at Wapping, see E. F. Kevan, *London's Oldest Baptist Church* (London: Kingsgate Press, 1933) 62-64, reprinting passages from Keach's funeral sermon and elegy.

bury,[6] leader who was a signatory of both the *Confession of Faith* of 1644 and the *Declaration of several of the people called Anabaptists* of 1659,[7] and who, like Norcott, had written a *Treatise*[8] in defence of believer's baptism. Norcott's career before he came to Wapping has remained obscure.

It is thus of interest to find that in 1657 Norcott was put in charge of a parish in Hertfordshire, and in 1662 was ejected from it, adding another to the small number of Baptists who suffered in this way.[9] His name is not included in Edward Calamy's volumes on the ejected ministers, nor is it among the names added in A. G. Matthews's *Calamy Revised* (Oxford, 1934). It is, however, recorded in William Urwick's massive work *Nonconformity in Herts* (1884).[10] The parish was Stanstead Thele (from the manor), also called Stanstead St. Margaret's (from the dedication of the church), but was—and still is—commonly known simply as St. Margaret's.

Norcott was not a common name, but is there any evidence that John Norcott of St. Margaret's and the Baptist John Norcott were one and the same? There is only indirect evidence, but it is convincing. For the man who in 1657 inherited the manor of Thele, and in 1664 died there and was buried at St. Margaret's, was none other than the Baptist Lord President, Henry Lawrence.[11]

Henry Lawrence held a number of important political posts before becoming Lord President (a title conferred on him by Oliver Cromwell) of Cromwell's Council of State, which made him in effect its Chairman, and later he was a member of Cromwell's House of Lords. Lawrence, however, remained true to Hertfordshire. He was a Member for the county in the Barebones Parliament of 1653, and again in 1654, and after the Restoration, lived at Thele. His Baptist convictions were strong and

---

[6]For Spilsbury and his importance, see Kevan; and *Association Records* (1971–1974), ed. B. R. White, 208n.29.

[7]Wing C 5789-94; Whitley, 24-644; and Wing D 619; Whitley, 64-659.

[8]Wing B S 4976-77 (1643, 1653), without location in this country for either edition; Whitley, 42-644, with location for each.

[9]For six Baptists ejected, see B. R. White, *The English Baptists of the Seventeenth Century* (London: Baptist Historical Society, 1983) 88-91, 102-103; see also G. F Nuttall, "Another Baptist Vicar? Edmund Skipp of Bodenham," *Baptist Quarterly* 33/7 (July 1996): 331-34.

[10]P.552. Urwick's own copy of his work, with occasional additions in his own hand, is in my possession.

[11]See *D.N.B.*; *V.C.H. Herts*. iii.474.

renowned. In 1646 he published *Of Baptisme*, and in 1649 another piece on the same subject. The title "Lord President" was said to have been given to him in order to gain favour with "the Baptized people, himself being under that ordinance."[12] What could have been more natural than placing a Baptist in the parish church? Since St. Margaret's was a donative,[13] free from any requirement for permission or confirmation, to do this presented no difficulties.[14] William Graves, Norcott's predecessor at St. Margaret's, is recorded as having been chosen by the parishioners.[15] Graves removed to another Hertfordshire living, Little Munden, from which he, too, was ejected in 1662.[16]

The historians of Hertfordshire recorded the burial at St. Margaret's in 1665 (or 1663) of "Edward Cresset, of this parish, Esq.,"[17] and Cresset again was a Baptist, who moved in the same circles as Henry Lawrence. A number of his friends in the church worshiping in Glaziers' Hall, to which he belonged, were cosignatories with Spilsbury and Kiffin of the *Confession of faith* and other manifestos.[18] Cresset himself was one of those appointed commissioner for the approbation of public preachers ("Triers") in 1654.[19] In 1655 he sat with Kiffin on the Committee set up to collect monies for poor Protestants.[20] In the same year, when a Conference was convened to consider the readmission of the Jews, the selection of participants was in the hands of Henry Lawrence as Lord

---

[12] See *D.N.B.*; Tai Liu, *Discord in Zion: the Puritan Divines and the Puritan Revolution* (The Hague, 1973), 139. Lawrence's wife Amy, a woman "of extraordinary piety," was the daughter of Sir Edward Peyton, 2nd, bt. (1588?–1657), "a staunch Puritan" with Fifth-Monarchist leanings (*D.N.B.*).

[13] Urwick, *Nonconformity in Herts*, 551.

[14] *V.C.H. Herts.*, iii.476 records that the history of the advowson at this time is "very obscure."

[15] Urwick, *Nonconformity in Herts*, 551.

[16] See *Calamy Revised*; Urwick, *Nonconformity in Herts*, 599.

[17] Urwick, *Nonconformity in Herts*, 551n.2, noting the Hertfordshire historians' variation in the date of Cresset's death. Both *V.C.H. Herts.* and *Roy. Comm. Hist. Mon. Herts.* note seventeenth-century inscribed slabs in memory of the Lawrence and Cresset families. Cresset's wife Mary, was the daughter of James Marshall, of London, esq., presumably the James Marshall in Friday Street at the Half Moon who was a son-in-law of the Baptists Thomas and Barbara Lambe (see *Cal. Of Corresp. Of Richard Baxter*, Oxford, 1991), edited by N. H. Keeble and G. F. Nuttall, letter 473.

[18] E.g., William Consett, Edward Roberts and Samuel Tull (*Association Records* 122n.20, 123n.48, and 209n.38).

[19] For a complete list see Tai Liu, 164-65.

[20] Whitley, Addenda (204) 30-655.

President.[21] Cresset, again with Kiffin, and along with Henry Jessey, was one whom he chose.[22]

Two Baptists do not make a church, but there seems no reason to doubt that until his ejection in 1662, John Norcott of St. Margaret's *was* the Baptist John Norcott.

---

[21]R. L. Greaves and R. Zaller, eds., *Biographical Dictionary of British Radicals in the Seventeenth Century* (Brighton, 1982–1984) 2:175-76.

[22]B. R. White, in *Reformation, Conformity, and Dissent. Essays in Honor of Geoffrey Nuttall*, ed. R. Buick Knox (London: Epworth Press, 1977) 148n.26; also 138, 143, for important links between Cresset and Jessey.

The Contribution of Bernard Foskett

Roger Hayden

One of the significant contributions of B. R. White to Baptist history has been his willingness to explore significant Baptist lives to set them in context. His review of Baptist historians at the opening of his volume on seventeenth-century Baptists is typical: placed alongside other significant monographs, like those dealing with Hanserd Knollys and William Kiffin, it represents a continuing need in Baptist historiography for critical assessment of key figures.

One such person who was influential among eighteenth-century Baptists, and has never been properly evaluated by Baptist historians is the subject of this study: Bernard Foskett. Foskett was the pastor at Broadmead, Bristol; the principal of the Bristol Baptist Academy; and a significant leader in the Western Association of Baptist churches. It is almost impossible to overestimate the influence of Bernard Foskett on the development of Baptist life in the eighteenth century. Not only did he make his own individual contribution through Broadmead Baptist Church and the Western Association of Baptist Churches, but he also significantly influenced wider Baptist church life by providing the only training available for Baptist ministers in England and Wales during this period. Individual ministers might train certain students in their own homes, but even in London it was one of Foskett's trained Welsh students, Thomas Llewellyn, who provided that expertise for the London Education Society.

It was Foskett's insistence upon the 1689 Confession as a basis for church and Association life which enabled churches to resist the influence of Socinian and Arian incursions, as well as provide an evangelical alternative to the arid, noninvitation preaching of the hyper-Calvinists who dominated London Baptist life at this time. He encouraged the development of congregational hymn singing in Baptist churches, even writing some of his own hymns for use in worship at Broadmead. The occasional hymn writing of Foskett and others—such as Joseph Stennett, Benjamin Wallin, and Foskett's protégé, Benjamin Beddome—in turn encouraged John Ash and Caleb Evans, students at Bristol Academy, to produce the first Baptist hymnbook in 1769 as an alternative to Watts's, a collection supplemented with many hymns by Baptist authors. His impact remained substantial even after his death, since the pastors and tutors who succeeded him until 1791 were the Welsh father and son,

Hugh and Caleb Evans, whom Foskett himself had trained for Baptist ministry.

1. Foskett's Early Years

Bernard was the third of seven children of William Foskett, a Justice of the Peace at North Crawley, Buckinghamshire, born March 10, 1685. Bernard, like his brothers, William and Caleb, remained single all his life. He received a private education and trained to be a physician. It was in London that he was baptized at Little Wild Street Church on 7 October 1708, then under the ministry of John Piggott.[1]

An opportunity for ministerial service was taken by Foskett in 1711 and on 29 April, when he became pastor of the Henley-in-Arden church in Warwickshire. It was said of him at this time that

> though he had spent a considerable time in qualifying himself to do good to the bodies of men, he rather chose now to serve them in a more important way by doing good to their souls; preferring the character of an able Minister to that of a skilful Physician.[2]

Henley-in-Arden was part of the Baptist church in Alcester, which also had a branch at Bengeworth, near Evesham. John Beddome (1674–1757) had gone as an assistant minister to John Willis (d. 1705) on 19 September 1697, having earlier been in membership at Horsley Down, London, the church where Benjamin Keach served as minister. Beddome had bought a large house, formerly an old inn, at Henley-in-Arden, half of which he turned into a place of worship and the half into his home.[3]

When John Willis died, Beddome took over the pastoral charge of all the Alcester churches, but continued to live in Henley-in-Arden. Joshua Thomas wrote privately to John Rippon on 19 March 1795:

> Mr F. had contracted an uncommon intimacy with Mr. Beddome. In July 1711 the former actually removed to his friend at Henley. He had been a member at Mr Piggot's 8 or 9 years, and probably exercised his ministerial talents to the greater part of that time. After that removal he continued to exercise, so that the two intimates were fellow labourers in the work, but Mr

---

[1] According to a note on a deed of gift made by Foskett on 16 November 1728, entered in his own hand, he was baptized on 7 October 1708.

[2] Caleb Evans, *Elisha's Exclamation* (Bristol, 1781) 22.

[3] Alcester Church Book; J. Rippon, *Baptist Annual Register*, iii.422-31. The house still stands next to the chapel in Alcester.

B. was the senior by 9 or 10 years, and the actual pastor of the Church at Alcester and Henley since the death of Mr Willis. Mr B. seems to have been the beginning of the Baptists at Henley, but they were members at Alcester. These two worthy ministers were both single then. . . .

Mr. Foskett being thus come to settle in the country they both consulted now to spread the tent wider, lengthen the cords and strengthen the stakes, in 1712 the Alcester church consisted of about 100 members but they lay wide. . . .

Regarding the talents of these two worthy ministers this account is given. "Mr B. the most acceptable preacher; Mr F. the most learned man: the former remarkable for his spiritual winning discourse, especially to young converts and enquirers; the latter for exemplariness and great regularity of his life and conversation: the former more owned in the work of conversion, tho' both had many seals to their ministry. . . ."[4]

With Foskett's arrival, the two men began a complete reorganization of the widespread congregation. First, the faith of the church was clearly drawn up in a Confession of Faith, followed by—and linked to—a Covenant, to which all members subscribed by signature when joining the church. The Confession is a closely argued, biblically attested statement of orthodox Christian belief in a Calvinistic form. It was noted that

In order to an enjoyment of these glorious privileges there is an absolute necessity of a change of heart and nature, which change we believe is the result of mear grace for it is of his own will that he hath begotten us.[5]

The Covenant held thirteen specific items which delineate the nature of Christian fellowship in a gathered church. Unity and truth are central, as is a determination to live as a reconciled community. It concluded with an affirmation to be subscribed by all the members which brought the Confession and the *Covenant* together in the closest relationship: "In testimony that we do own and firmly believe all the aforementioned articles of faith, and that we do desire and design (by the assistance of grace) to practise according to this our mutual agreement, we have put our hands."[6]

Beddome and Foskett were influenced by links with Benjamin Keach, who had constructed his own covenant document for Horsley Down.

---

[4]Letter E. 16 (28) Angus Library, Regent's Park College, Oxford.
[5]See appendix 1 of Roger Hayden, "Evangelical Calvinism among Eighteenth-Century Baptists, with Particular Reference to Bernard Foskett, Hugh and Caleb Evans, and the Bristol Baptist Academy, 1690–1791" (Ph.D. dissertation, University of Keele, 1991).
[6]Broadmead Baptist Church Book, 168-70.

Always concerned about confessional statements, Foskett considered their formulation important for sustaining the faith of individual believers, the unity of the local church, and the churches' being bound together in Association.

Another Keach influence emerged as the two ministers began working together: the development of hymn singing in public worship. John Piggott (d. 1713), the Little Wild Street minister during Foskett's membership, supported those in favor of hymn singing in the violent pamphlet war that raged over the issue among London Baptists at the beginning of the eighteenth century. The Church Book noted:

> Aug 20, 1712 began by the consent of all concerned to sing the praises of God in the publick worship at the weekly meeting on Wednesday. Four months later, on December 25, "resolved to sing the praises of God in the publick worship every Lord's Day at Alceste." Within a few weeks, on 18 January 1713/4 it was "resolved the same at Benjworth by the members on that side. . . ."[7]

The strengthening of the community at the Lord's Table was the next concern. It was decided to hold a communion service six times a year at Henley and Bengeworth, alternately. To strengthen the sense of fellowship, the Alcester church minuted in May 1713

> that such of the members that live here as could conveniently should go to Henley and to Benjworth to visit and sit down at the Lord's Table with each respective Branch and that all distant members from each part should come to Alcester that there might been an annual general meeting of the whole church. All this being esteemed a good method to keep up communion with one another and to demonstrate to the world our unity and peace.[8]

In 1714 John Beddome, then age forty, married Rachel Brandon of London, a wealthy descendent of the Duke of Suffolk. It was a happy marriage which produced five children: Benjamin, Joseph, Samuel, Mary, and Foskett. Five years later Bernard Foskett "came to Town" in response to a request from Broadmead, Bristol, to preach on two Sundays in the city. Broadmead wished him to succeed Caleb Jope as the minister responsible for training students for the ministry. They prevailed upon Foskett to preach an additional four Sundays in March–April 1720, on a second visit to Broadmead. At this point the church issued a call to

---

[7]Ibid.
[8]Alcester Church Book.

ministry among them "in persuance of the Design of Mr. Edw. Terrill."[9] Two months later Foskett "was at a great distress in his own mind about it" and urged the church to reconsider. They immediately reaffirmed their call and a prayer meeting was held each Sunday morning at 8 am to help clarify the situation. It required a further six Sundays in Bristol to convince Foskett that he should accept the invitation. He did so on 7 October 1720, succeeding as pastor when Kitterell died in 1724, and remaining pastor and President of the Academy until his death in 1758.

This decision, as others in Foskett's life, had been made only after consultation with John Beddome. On 7 April the Broadmead letter of invitation was given personally to Foskett "in the presence of Mr Jn. Beddome, another minister and friend of his." Beddome was in Bristol, because when Emmanuel Gifford—minister at the Pithay, Bristol—died in 1721, an invitation was given to John Beddome to become the minister, which he accepted. Beddome followed "his friend to Bristol, so both were settled at the head of two reputable Societies there. After removal Mr Foskett would board with his friend again. They were together at Henley and Bristol above, or near, 40 years."[9]

2. Foskett and the Western Association

There were doctrinal tensions within the Western Association following the London Salters' Hall Conference in 1719, which addressed a dispute about Trinitarian beliefs among Presbyterian ministers in Exeter. Both Baptist and Congregationalist ministers attended, and John Sharp of Frome reported to the Western Association when it met at Trowbridge that he was glad "none of the churches, or ministers belonging to this Association, hold any such pernicious doctrine."

This was far from true. The Congire Church, Trowbridge, under John Davisson became Unitarian by 1727. Joseph Jeffries, who succeeded Thomas Whinnel at Taunton in 1717, brought that church to a General Baptist Unitarian stance by 1734. When Baptists in Wellington, part of the Taunton church, had to replace their pastor in 1738, a small group of Particular Baptists formed themselves into an independent congregation and called Robert Day of the Bristol Academy to be their pastor.

The root of the doctrinal issue in the Western Association was that associating churches were not required to affirm an agreed statement of

---

[9] Joshua Thomas to John Rippon, see n. 4 above.
[9] J. G. Fuller, *Dissent in Bristol* (Bristol, 1840) 30.

faith as a basis for their individual and interchurch fellowship. The so-called *Preliminaries* carried no doctrinal affirmation. It was Broadmead, Bristol, under Foskett's leadership, which proposed an additional article at the 1723 Association meeting, which read:

> That, seeing many errors have been broached, and ancient heresies revived, of late, in the world, no messenger shall be received from any church whose letter don't every year express, either in the preamble, or body of it, that they of the Church do approve the Confession of Faith put forth by above a hundred Baptist churches, (Edit. 3d. A.D. 1699) and do maintain the principles contained therein; such a letter being signed at a church meeting, in the name and by the consent of the whole church.[10]

Broadmead was unsuccessful in securing this addition, and in May 1724 instructed their messengers to insist again upon the *Confession* inclusion and affirmation. All that was agreed was that each church affirm, on its own terms, belief in a Trinitarian understanding of the Godhead. The tensions over an adequate *Confession of Faith* for churches in association grew until 1732. Caleb Evans's judgment on what happened next is given in his handwritten account of the Western Association's origin, at the front of its minute book for that year:

> The Western Baptist Association was for many years kept up by the *Baptists* as such, without any regard to their different principles in other respects. The consequence of this was, these annual meetings were found to be rather pernicious than *useful*; as there was scarcely a meeting of the kind, but some unhappy differences arose betwixt the *Calvinistic* and *Armin'n* Ministers. In the year 1731 their annual meeting was to have been held at *Tiverton* but an awful Fire abt. That time, which consum'd most of the Town, prevented it. The next year it was not reviv'd. But in the follow:g year, an Invitation was sent to the respective Churches by the Church in *Broadmead, Bris:l*, desir:g them to renew their former annual Meeting upon the foot of their agreement in the Baptist Confessn: of 1689.[11]

The new "Preliminaries" drawn up for the reformed Association now significantly omitted the Preliminary which had allowed Baptists—General or Particular, with either antinomian, hyper-Calvinist tendencies or Arian views—to share in the one Association, now read:

---

[10] Ibid.
[11] *Records of the Baptist Western Association, 1733–1812*. This is a MS book held at Bristol Baptist College, England, which has Caleb Evans's address in the front cover. The first 176 pages give a transcript of each year's Western Association meeting since its reformation in 1734.

> That we join together in Association as agreeing in the Confession of Faith put forth by the Elders and Brethren of our Denomination in the City of *London* in year 1689 as being we think agreeable to the Scriptures. And we expect that every Associating Church do in their Letter every year, signify their approbation of the said Confession. N.B. They who differ from the Confession of Faith with respect to the Time in which the Sabbath is to be observed, are not to be understood by this subscription to contradict their particular judgment in this matter.[12]

A letter from Broadmead inviting churches to form a new Association dated 22 October 1732, was signed by Foskett and his associate minister, Hugh Evans, and makes Foskett's key role in this decisive intervention very clear:

> We believe you are not insensible of the advantage of the associate meetings of the churches, and the happy tendencies those assemblies, when well regulated, have, to secure the truths of the Gospel, what our affections to one another, and, by mutual christian offices, to promote spiritual and most valuable interests. . . .
>
> An agreement in judgement and practice concerning baptism, has always been thought necessary to our comfortable walking together; and we are still of opinion, with our forefathers, that harmony in the other great doctrines of the Gospel is of no less consequence than this. You cannot, we believe, be insensible of the revival and growth the dangerous errors of Arius and Arminius, and others; and are we not therefore obliged, in conscience, at this juncture, to make a public stand against them, and for the most sacred and important truths of the Gospel, and for that end declare our hearty Amen with the Confession of Faith put forth by the elders and brethren of our denomination, the third edition, 1699? That being so good a system of principles, and so agreeable to the Holy Scriptures we think it proper that every associating church, should, every year, either in the preamble or body of their letter, signify their approbation of it; and upon this foundation, we propose a revival of the Assembly, which an awful providence prevented the last year, and has been neglected this year also. This we hope, with the divine blessing, may answer the great and good ends proposed by such a meeting. We hope that those that are not acquainted with this Confession, will procure and read it, that they may know the sentiments of their pious forefathers in the matters of greatest importance. We allow for different sentiments about singing the praises of God, and the time in which the Sabbath is to be observed; but in all other things we expect an agreement in that confession; and, hoping you will deal plainly and faithfully with us on that foundation only, dear brethren, we invite you to join with us in the

---

[12]Ibid., 7.

> Lord, and to meet us at the meeting house in Broadmead, Bristol, on Wednesday in the Whitsun week next ensuing, by your messengers if you can. . . . And now, brethren, desiring that both you and we may be preserved stedfast in 'the faith once delivered to the saints', we subscribe ourselves."[13]

Foskett and John Beddome drew up the Association Letter to be read in the churches, in which the doctrinal issue was made the reason for the meeting:

> We find the churches generally approve of the revival of the Association upon the Bottom of the Confession of Faith mentioned in the Letter of Invitation . . . willing heartily to concur in an Association founded in order to give a public testimony against the growing errors of the day, . . . because they apprehend they sap the very foundation of Christianity . . . to contend . . . with a single eye to God's glory, notwithstanding the opposition of Satan, corrupt reason and carnal interests . . . laying aside all personal and private Pique, . . . being encouraged by many examples of the pious and learned Confessors and Martyrs, the first Reformers and Protestant Divines of diverse nations. . . .
>
> Brethren, we cannot but recommend to your perusal and study the Confession of Faith mentioned in ye letter of invitation and desire that such persons in the church as have it not would procure it and diligently read it. . . .
>
> And in the meantime . . . particularly desire that the Lord would pour down his spirit to qualify persons for the sake of the Ministry. . . .[14]

The letter goes on to urge familiar Foskett themes which he put into practice in Broadmead, suggesting that heads of family catechize their children and servants and then bring them to "public catechizing," so they can be guarded from "the dangerous errors of the Day." Congregations are advised to "set aside times for Conference" to discuss Christian truth and life, and to "have meetings of Prayer, especially on First Day Mornings preparatory to the Public Exercise of the Day." The "regular discipline in the churches" according to Scriptural direction, constant attendance upon "their duty at the Lord's Table and preparatory meetings for it," are commended. Members are urged to take care "to keep the business proper to each Church within themselves, remembering each should be as a Garden enclosed and a fountain sealed."

---

[13] Broadmead Baptist Church Book, under the date 22 October 1732.
[14] Ibid.

At the Association meeting at Exeter in 1733, Joseph Stennett, a good friend of Foskett, preached from Philippians 2:27 "with one mind, striving together for the faith of the gospel," and commented:

> The most grievous wounds the gospel has received, have been in the house of its pretended friends. And, a little reflection will convince us that the absurd and blasphemous reasons of the Deists did but little execution, comparatively, till a set of men arose, among ourselves, who have paved the way for that amazing success, which these sworn enemies of Jesus Christ have of late years obtained. It is, indeed, most shocking to consider that some, under the character of Christian ministers, instead of contending earnestly for the faith of Christ, are industriously sapping the fundamental principles of it.[15]

Stennett urged again that the Association be based on a *Confession of Faith*:

> I freely own . . . my text obliges us to make a public and explicit confession, as proper occasion offers of every doctrine which we believe to be contained in the word of God. The simplicity of the gospel, I think, naturally requires this, and without it no communion can be secured from a mixture of persons of the most corrupt principles that have ever been advanced in the world.[16]

Stennett encouraged Christians to strive for the whole counsel of God in Scripture, as well as for every particular gospel doctrine, and believed "the doctrine of the ever blessed Trinity, is of the greatest importance to his glory."[17]

Stennett returned to the issue when he wrote his *Letter* to the churches in 1734 from Exeter, a primary center of Unitarian influence. The basis for Association life is developed under seven headings. The first recognizes the need for a statement of faith since "no Christian society can usefully and comfortably subsist without some fundamental agreement of this kind." The second reason for Association was because

> we think we act according to the divine rule declared in the word of God . . . [we think this is such a Confession as our Dear Lord expects from us before men (Matt. 10:33) which we dare not be ashamed to acknowledge with our lips (Ps. 199:46) and subscribe with our hands (Is. 44:5) since we believe it with our hearts (Rom. 10:9-10)].

---

[15] Joseph Stennett, *The Christian Strife for the Faith of the Gospel* (1738) 78.
[16] Ibid., 16.
[17] Ibid. 21.

Third, the Association was convened upon the "declared principles" of the Christian faith, and the *Confession* also expressed a unity with "others of the Reformed Churches." Finally, Baptists are separated from the other Reformed churches on account of baptism, but unity on the central doctrines of Christian faith must be affirmed. Next, the Western Association had "always professed itself to be on the Particular principle," evidenced by those of its ministers who signed the 1689 *Confession* in London, a position reaffirmed in 1723 when the new title was agreed. Finally, the larger *Confession* was used, "because by sad experience we have observed that some have artfully found means to evade those shorter Declarations."[18]

Between 1689 and 1734, the Western Association remained loyal to its fundamental understanding of Evangelical Calvinism. Whereas London Baptists—wrongly thought by later historians to be typical of Baptists generally in the eighteenth century—failed, the Western Association was successful. London Baptists were able to sustain neither a national General Assembly, nor an Association, and regional Baptist life degenerated into a ministerially led group gathering in various London coffeehouses. The result was a lack of any sustained program for an educated Baptist ministry, despite pleas for such, and the opportunity for the hyper-Calvinism typified by John Gill to get a substantial hold on many churches countrywide.

Under the leadership of Bernard Foskett and the Broadmead church in the early part of the eighteenth century, the Western Association continued the evangelical Calvinism of the previous century. Foskett successfully introduced the *1689 Confession* as the doctrinal basis for individual churches and the Association between 1722 and 1734. His initiative in calling an Association meeting at Broadmead after the Tiverton fire in 1732 was critical. The doctrinal standard agreed upon excluded General Baptist churches and kept both Arminians and Unitarians out of the churches, also directly affecting the development of other Associations in the Midlands, Wales, and Ireland, and linked it with a similar stance in the Northern Baptist Association. Once the doctrinal matters were resolved, Foskett turned his attention to the training of an educated Baptist ministry under the provisions of Edward Terill's request

---

[18]Fuller, *Dissent in Bristol*, 35-36; *Records of the Baptist Western Association*, 29-30, provides the material in square brackets, which was omitted by Fuller.

at Broadmead. The Academy really began to function after 1734, with Foskett training the majority of his over seventy students in equal numbers, from Wales and England, until his death in 1758.

3. Foskett as Pastor and Tutor

As Baptists entered the eighteenth century, the fierce denominational opposition to "human learning" was declining, particularly in the West of England and Wales, though not in London, where formal theological education amongst Baptists was spasmodic.

Foskett's first task as Kitterell's assistant under the Terrill trust was to gather all the books together. A catalogue of the books had been made on 23 November 1685. John Philips (d. 1761), Foskett's second student, was made responsible for checking this list against the books held by Mr. Browne, Mr. Evans, and Mrs. Warrin. They produced 198 books, which Philips brought to the Broadmead vestry on 18 December 1722, with 43 still unaccounted for. Foskett added a further nine volumes to the collection, all of which suggests that John had done very little—if anything at all—by way of teaching students.[19]

Among the books listed were a number of old Bibles and copies of the Apocrypha, Hebrew and Greek Bibles, grammars and lexicons, and concordances—plus English, French, and Latin grammars and dictionaries. Most numerous were the thirty-four copies of the *1689 Confession of Faith* and a number of catechisms from Anglican and Dissenting sources: Perkins on *The Ministry*, Luther on *Galatians*, Calvin's *Institutes* and *Harmony*, Hooker's *Survey of the Church*, Ames's *Cases of Conscience*, and Cartwright's *Reply*. There were also copies of Cox's *The Covenant*, as well as Thomas Collier's *Distinction of the Covenant*. Several disputes on baptism and against the Quakers gave the collection a contemporary dimension. One other strand, which probably derived from Foskett's medical training, included such volumes as *The Vocal Organs and Read, On the Muscles*.

Thomas Rogers was Foskett's first student. "A member of Mr Gifford's church," he was accepted as "a student under the direction of Mr. Foskett according to Mr Terrill's deed," receiving "the 10 Pounds Sterling given by Mr Edward Terrill for the ensuing year." Though Rogers came from the Pithay Baptist Church in Bristol, he was originally

---

[19]This list of books is held at Bristol Baptist College.

a member of a Baptist church in Pontypool, South Wales. The next student, John Philips, was also a Welshman, from Rhydwilim. On 5 August 1721, "Bro Jn Philips came to be instructed in the Hebrew language by Bro. Foskett" and was recommended by the Fundees as "a person proper to have the 10 Pounds Sterling for one year accordingly to Mr Terrill's Direction." In the summer of 1723, there was a conference at Broadmead when

> the Brethren consider'd Mr Terril's Deed respecting students and concluded that his design was to take such as live in or near this City and not those that come here only occasionally for that purpose. And he seems to intend such that have had some learning in their youth, for they thought he design'd to have them learn Greek or Hebrew and that the other Literature should be such as they might take in at the same time such as Logic, History, Divinity. Some thought he meant only single persons; but others suppos'd he Design'd Young Men whether single or married. All concluded he intended gifted persons who might by this means be rendered capable of searching the Original Texts.[20]

This decision affected the distribution of the Terrill money, and no student is noted until Daniel Garnon (1702–1777) arrived from Carmarthenshire, in November 1727. Other Broadmead members with preaching abilities were also being encouraged. Joseph Gaube, for example, began preaching with Kitterell's encouragement in November 1724, and by April 1725, the church book minuted that he had permission to preach on "our Days of Prayer whenever either of our Pastours desire it."[21] Gaube is the first of a number of Broadmead members who were called to the work of the ministry, but were not regarded as "students." Yet it is difficult to believe that they received no training from Foskett as their pastor.

After Kitterell's death, Foskett's position as pastor appointed under Terrill's will did not change, but he was now the senior minister of the church. A search for a new colleague proved difficult, and no students were given instruction until the issue was resolved. Andrew Gifford (1700–1784) was the first to be employed in a while, but he had not been there long before he accepted a call to be the minister at Little Wild Street, London.[22] In 1730 George Braithwaite (1681–1748) of Bridlington, Yorkshire, spent time at Broadmead, but indicated his refusal of the call

---

[20]Broadmead Baptist Church Book, 171-75.
[21]Ibid., under the date 19 July 1723, 178.
[22]Ibid., 182-85; L. G. Champion, *Farthing Rushlight: A Life of Andrew Gifford, 1700–1784* (1961) 31-33.

on 2 May 1731.[23] In October 1731 the church invited Edward Harrison, who had been supplying at Newbury, Berkshire, to become Broadmead's "stated assistant in the Ministry."[24] Earlier in the year he had preached on two Sundays, followed by a spell of five Sundays and midweek meetings, and though all *seemed* positive, his stay was brief and unhappy.

Edward Harrison's membership had been at Devonshire Square, London, a Particular Baptist church from which he transferred to Broadmead in March 1731/2. Within twelve months, Foskett was to lead Broadmead in the refounding of the Western Association upon the doctrinal basis of the *1689 Confession*. It appeared that Harrison would be a good colleague, but at the height of the Western Association debate, Harrison's soundness on the matter of particular redemption was called into question. He declared to the church his decision "to remove from us on act of his having sentiments in Matters of Faith diffring from the Church, the dropping of whc in sermons, has given uneasiness to several Brethren of late. He said he had no other reason for leaving us." Three weeks later, a private meeting of male members—held so "that the matter might be more fully and freely talkt over," and dealt with ascribing "less prejudice to Mr Harrison"—decided unanimously that Harrison should leave on 29 September 1733.[25]

When this decision was reported to members on 16 October, the female members endorsed the motion also unanimously. Out of consideration for Harrison's family, the deacons were empowered to give any "subscription money" in their hands to Mr. Harrison, and members might add as they thought fit."[26] However, the matter did not end there, and at a church meeting in January 1733/4, "a narrative of Mr Harrison's case" was read by Thomas Page, snr., which "a considerable majority" of the members did not accept. This was because on 28 December 1733, Foskett had asked the members

> to stay and then took out a Waste Book wherein he said he had drawn out Mr Harrison's case in order to be transcribed among the Records of the Church; which he then read out but it was observed that his Narrative ran chiefly in some general terms, lightly touching or glossing over some Material Circumstances and wholly passing by others which were absolutely

---

[23]C. E. Shipley, *Baptists of Yorkshire* (London, 1912) 54-56; Broadmead Baptist Church Book, 186, 188.
[24]Broadmead Baptist Church Book, 190.
[25]Ibid., 191.
[26]Ibid., 192.

necessary for putting the affair in a clear light and much in Mr Harrison's favour.[27]

On 12 February Foskett faced a censure motion from those supporting Harrison who charged him with being "guilty of falsifying his word," and as a consequence, refused to accept his ministry. The church meeting agreed almost without exception that Foskett was not guilty, appointed members to meet the Harrison supporters, and sent two deacons to tell Harrison "the Ch: resents his Conduct, in showing the Narrative to those out of the Church," and summoned him to answer this at the next church meeting.

It was nearly two years before Harrison gave Broadmead satisfaction, when the church meeting noted and agreed to "a letter to dismiss Mr Edw: Harrison to Newbury he having by ye 31st Decr past made some acknowledgment of past errors as by the Original on the file may be seen, the copy of the Letter sign'd by the Ch: 11th inst is also on file."[28]

Set in the context of the wider discussion of doctrinal issues in Broadmead and the Western Association at this time, it is not surprising that Foskett would not tolerate any theological divergence in his assistant. More important, there was a replacement ready in the wings. It was on 6 September 1733, that Hugh Evans first exercised his preaching gift before the church members. Once the matter with Harrison was resolved, it is no surprise that on 7 March 1733/4, "the Ch: unanimously gave Bro. Hugh Evans a Call to the Ministry or Mission to preach the Gospel, where the Providence of God should call him." Broadmead lost no time in calling him to be Foskett's assistant, a position he accepted on 9 January 1734/5. He was ordained five years later on 7 February 1739/40, as a "Teaching Elder by the imposition of the hands,"[29] such a delay in ordination being common among Baptist churches in the eighteenth century.

Once Hugh Evans was installed, Foskett's work with the students increased significantly. The four who had come in the 1720s soon became 16 in the 1730s, 29 in the 1740s, and 24 in the 1750s. There were 33 English students and 31 Welsh students during this particular period. In addition, there was at least one from Ireland and eight others whose ethnic origins are unknown. Twenty-one of the forty-five churches which

---

[27]Ibid., 192, 195.
[28]Ibid., 192.
[29]Thomas Wright, *Augustus Toplady and Contemporary Hymnwriters* (1911) 76-77.

comprised the Western Baptist Association between 1734 and 1791 were served by ministers trained at Bristol. Twenty-two of the ministers trained at Bristol in Foskett's time (1720–1758) served in churches of the Western Association; the remaining fifty-one served in churches predominantly in the west of England, Wales, and Ireland.

4. Foskett and the Welsh Baptist Churches

The close ties between Bristol and Welsh Baptists precede the eighteenth century, going back at least as far as the 1640s, as the *Broadmead Records* testify. By the 1690s, Welsh Baptists—though small in number—were sharing in the London Assembly, which agreed with the *1689 Confession*, and when the national body divided its meetings between London and Bristol in the mid-1690s, Welsh Messengers attended the Western Association until they reformed their own Welsh Association at Llanwenarth in 1700. Even then, a number of Welsh churches attended both Association gatherings each year, retaining the strong personal links between the Welsh and English ministers well into the middle of the eighteenth century.

The most consistent contact was sustained by Miles Harry (1700–1776), who personally attended the Western Association for most of his ministerial life on an annual basis, his last visit being noted in 1764. This was not surprising, bearing in mind his close association with Foskett and Hugh Evans in the work of the Bristol Academy, to which he sent students from the school at Trosnant.

An examination of the lists of Broadmead members during the century reveals the presence of Hugh Evans (1712–1781) from 1729 as member, and then copastor with Foskett; and the further contact through Caleb Evans (1737–1791), Hugh's son, makes it abundantly evident that Broadmead had a significant Welsh community within it during the whole period. Hugh Evans, for example, was introduced into the Broadmead congregation as a result of being sent to live with his aunt, Mary Evans, a member there. He was baptized by Foskett on 7 August 1730 and after a short period back in Wales, returned to Bristol, becoming Foskett's assistant in 1734 and his successor in 1758. It is from this time that the Bristol Academy really began to flourish, and at first, it was largely the teaching of Welsh students that got the Academy under way. In the 1730s, six of the sixteen students were Welsh, four of them starting in Bristol in 1736. In the 1740s, twelve of the twenty-nine students in training came from the Principality. In the 1750s, eleven of the twenty-four students receiving training came from Wales.

Hugh Evans came from the Pentre Church, Newbridge-on-Wye, Radnorshire, and he was the first of seven students from that church who trained at Bristol during Foskett's time. Over the eighteenth century, at least eighty-seven Welsh students from twenty-five different Welsh churches entered Bristol. Most of the Welsh students came from four Welsh churches: Pen-y-garn, Pentre-newydd, Pen-y-vai, and Llangloffan. The contacts were in both directions. Foskett, Hugh Evans, and later Caleb, were often at the Welsh Association meetings, and in fact, frequently preached at them. While Foskett was in charge at Bristol, Hugh Evans visited the Welsh Association gatherings, preaching in English, on no less than ten occasions. The invitation to do this, which was repeated so regularly in these years, originated with Foskett's visit to the Welsh Association in 1733, when it was held for the first time at Pen-y-garn, where Miles Harry was the energetic, educated, and evangelical minister. Joshua Thomas described the event in these terms: "This year the truly renowned Mr Foskett of Bristol attended Penygarn. Mr Enoch Francis preached according to appointment, then Mr Foskett was desired to preach and he was pleased to comply; so they had an additional sermon that year."[30]

The 1733 Assembly was significant in that the Welsh Association became exclusively and consciously a Particular Baptist community. The Welsh Messengers adopted Western Association practices and principles which aligned them clearly with the Evangelical Calvinism of the churches and the Academy under Foskett's leadership. It was more than a decision to have an Association Book in which the Preliminaries would be recorded and the Breviates sent to the churches together with a copy of the circular Letter in a permanent form; it was a conscious adopting of the specific doctrines and practice of English Particular Baptists. The 1689 *Confession* was reaffirmed as the unifying doctrinal statement upon which Welsh Baptists associated. "The Preliminaries of the Western Association were written in the Welsh book, but in English, and they were read in Welsh annually." It was in 1752 that the Preliminaries were translated into Welsh by Timothy Thomas, pastor at Aberduar, and

---

[30] Joshua Thomas, *Materials for the History of the Baptist Churches in Wales*, MS volume (1782) 271. Original now in National Library of Wales, Aberystwyth; photocopy at Bristol Baptist College, Bristol.

inserted into the Association Book. The Preliminaries were printed in Welsh for the first time in 1776, when a copy was sent to each of the Association's churches.

5. Conclusion

The impact of the Evangelical Revival seeped into the English Baptist tradition via some of the Welsh students who comprised half the total number trained by Foskett in this period. As the Academy moved into the 1750s, the influence of the Revival became evident not only through the writings of Jonathan Edwards, but also by the presence of those who had experienced it for themselves and who, in the first instance, came from Wales.

Bernard Foskett was a seminal figure in Welsh Baptist life. He chose a Welshman to share the training with him at Broadmead, making for a vital contact between English and Welsh Baptists in the eighteenth century, since it was the only place of training available for Baptist student ministers. Foskett brought his own evangelical Calvinist tradition to the life of the Welsh Baptist Association, and secured it doctrinally upon the *1689 Confession*. He and Hugh Evans regularly visited and preached at the Welsh Baptist Association and encouraged Miles Harry to be present at the Western Association gatherings when he could. His influence was most profound upon the Welsh students who trained with him at Bristol in the middle years of the eighteenth century. Not all were influenced by the Revival, but they were all profoundly indebted to the ethos and training provided at Bristol.

Hugh Evans, who worked with Foskett as pupil and colleague for over thirty years, knew him better than most:

> His natural abilities were sound and good; and his acquired furniture, of which he never affected making a great show, was very considerable. He had a clear understanding, a penetrating judgment, and a retentive memory. His application to study was constant and severe: but though he was of a retired and contemplative disposition, yet he was not so detached from the world, as to be wholly unpractised in the duties of social life. In the management of his temporal concerns, he was inflexibly just and honest; his counsels prudent and faithful; in his friendships sincere and steady. . . . His conduct as a Christian . . . was most exemplary and ornamental . . . serious and regular . . . in his private devotions, in his attendance on family and public worship. . . . Nor was his religion confined to the closet, the family or the house of God, but happily diffused its sacred influence through his whole life. . . . I must not however omit to mention what he was always so careful to conceal, his disinterested and extensive benevolence . . . the

necessitous and deserving without distinction partook his bounty: but the pious poor he ever considered as the special objects of his regard. And while he often judiciously prescribed to the indigent sick, he generously supplied them with the means of obtaining what was necessary for their relief . . . poor ministers shared very largely in his compassionate regards. . . .

In the character of a minister, he approved himself judicious, prudent, faithful and laborious. His religious principles, which were those commonly called Calvinistical . . . but though he was strenuous for what he apprehended to be the truth, yet he was fond of no extreme. While he strongly asserted the honours of free grace, he earnestly contended for the necessity of good works; preaching duty as well as privilege, and recommending holiness as the only way to happiness. . . . To all which I may add, that in the office of a Tutor he failed not to pursue the same ends which animated his profession as a Christian, and his public labours as a minister. He was always studious to promote the real advantages of those under his care, endeavouring to lead their minds into a general knowledge of the most beneficial and important branches of literature. And though he judged a superficial education best suited to the years and capacities of some, yet he encouraged and assisted others to the pursuit of a more finished one; conforming himself in the whole to the professed design of the founder of the Institution. And it is remarkable most of those that were under his care that they approved themselves truly serious, and do at this time with great reputation fill many of our churches.[31]

---

[31] John Rippon, *Baptist Annual Register*, i.128-35.

Jane Attwater's Diaries

Marjorie Reeves

Introduction

The writings which have come down to us present two faces of Jane Attwater. On the one hand, in her letters, we meet a sociable, communicative young woman who enjoyed excursions, was attentive to her family, and poured out her feelings to her close friend, Mary Steele, to whom she wrote as "Myrtilla to Silvia." It is true that in some of these letters she portrayed herself as introspective and shy, but the general impression they leave is of a lively correspondent who loved to share her experiences and feelings. On the other hand, her voluminous diaries are intensely private. At certain crucial moments she lapsed into shorthand or, revising later, blocked out what she felt had been written too freely. At times her narrative is so oblique that it is difficult to determine the actual emotional crisis that had upset her. The diaries are in no sense a record of daily events. Spanning a large part of her long life—from 1767, when she was fourteen, to April 1834—the entries generally move from Sunday to Sunday, chronicling the services she attended, the preachers, their texts, and a sermon précis which is often remarkably full. Weekday entries usually concern either religious gatherings (Association meetings, "conferences," prayer meetings, public fast days and so on) or journeys to visit family or friends. Much space is devoted to reflections on her inner state of mind and spiritual aspirations.

Jane was born into a family living at Bodenham, near Salisbury, which already had Baptist affiliations. Little is known about her father, Thomas Waters—later Attwater—but her mother, Anna, came from a Baptist family, the Gays, living at Haycombe on the outskirts of Bath. The Attwaters also developed close connections with the Steeles of Broughton, just across the Hampshire border, who were the leading family in the Broughton Baptist Church. Anna's mother was Jane Cator Gay, whose sister, Anne Cator, became the second wife of William Steele senior. Therefore, Jane Attwater's aunt was Mrs. Steele, while her closest friend became her cousin, Mary, daughter of William Steele junior.[1] Her

---

[1]For a fuller account of this family network, see Marjorie Reeves, *Pursuing the*

brother, Gay Thomas (born 1736), was considerably older, while she was the youngest of three sisters: Marianna, born in 1742; Caroline, born in 1745; and Jane, born 1753. Until her mother's death in 1786 they lived together presumably in the family home at Bodenham. After that it would seem that she lived sometimes by herself and other times with her brother, who had married Mary Drewitt of Bratton. However, she paid long visits to her married sisters: Marianna, now Mrs. George Head of Bradford-on-Avon, and Caroline, now Mrs. Thomas Whitaker in Bratton. She also often went to the Steele family at Broughton.

Apart from these longer visits, Jane regularly made the five-mile trip to Salisbury on Sundays—sometimes twice a day. She also went frequently to services at Downton, and sometimes at Nunton, close to Bodenham. She did not often specify her means of transport, but it is fairly clear that, as a rule, she either walked or rode to Salisbury. When the whole family accompanied her, they went by chaise. We know from other references that she rode horseback, but she seldom told how she made the journeys to Bratton and Bradford, although on one occasion at least, her brother sent a man with horses to fetch her home from Bratton. However she traveled, these longer journeys were always accompanied by some apprehension on her part. Almost all are recorded in some such statement as: "Nov 2nd 1776 I am now through ye goodness of my God arrived in safety in Bradford. I have been preserved from many dangers." Why was she so apprehensive? Was she afraid—as once indicated in a letter—of an accident with a frisky pony? Or could she have feared encountering robbers while crossing the Plain?

One could conclude from the diaries alone that her chief concern in life was attending religious meetings. She was certainly an addicted sermoniser, with an appetite for three every Sunday, with any available weekday religious gatherings thrown in. Her memory must have been prodigious, for her sermon outlines often cover several pages in the diary, although it is sometimes difficult to tell exactly where the notes pass into her own reflections. Occasionally she records an attack of inattention or restlessness: "May ye 23 1773 at Bratton H^d Mr Francis p^{ch} . . . I was in a dead stupid lifeless frame this day could not attend to ye preaching of ye word with right diligence . . . ," Oct. 23 1774 . . . "I am like ye door

---

Muses: Female Education and Nonconformist Culture 1700–1900 (Cassell, 1997) family tree and 2-7. For Jane Attwater's letters (pen name "Myrtilla") and her friendship with Mary Steele (pen name "Silvia"), see ibid., 98-101, 108-22.

on its hinges going from one privilege and Advantage to Another and still receiving little or no benefit." Expressing her state of indecision, two metaphors of the roving fool's eye and the swinging door are favourites in Jane's early writings. Later, after committing herself, she wrote in a different vein: "those little Golden spots of time our Sabbath's are delightful, those Emblems of ye Eternal Sabbath notwithstanding there is imperfection mixed with our duty's enjoyment" (30/3/77).

Nurtured in a strong Baptist tradition, her main allegiance is to "meetinghouses," particularly Brown Street Baptist Meeting in Salisbury, and during visits, the Baptist meetings in Broughton, Bratton, and Bradford.[2] But she also worshiped at other Nonconformist meetings: in Salisbury at the Independent meetinghouse known as Scots Lane,[3] and in Bradford at several different ones, including "Mr. Wesley's." Occasionally she records going "to Church" at Britford, Nunton, etc. The context shows that "Church" always means the parish church. She was also several times "at the cathedral at Sarum," once to hear a performance of Handel's *Messiah*. Thus she looks beyond the sectarian view, clearly voicing an ecumenical outlook on several occasions, as in the following: "April ye 30th 1780 . . . alas w^n shall I see all good people United w^t pity is it y^t little distinctions should separate members of one body O for a more Extensive Chariety O for more of y^t Benevolence wch was manifested in our Lord. . . . "

This careful chronicling has left scholars a mine of information about the preachers who were circulating in this area in the later eighteenth century, their texts, and the contents of their sermons.[4] Jane was usually receptive to the preaching of the Word, and in fact, often recorded her gratitude. But she has a mind of her own and can be sharply critical, both on theological grounds and suitability for the congregation. She will give a quite kind assessment young aspiring preachers, such as "a young Gent. Of the Huntingdon connection,"[5] but she can argue vigorously with an established lay preacher such as John Collins of Devizes[6] about the suitability of singing in worship: "June 25: 1775 at Sarum, in ye Evening Mr

---

[2] For Bradford, Bratton, and Brown Street (Salisbury) Baptist Churches, see appendix.
[3] For Scots Lane Independent Meetinghouse (Salisbury), see appendix.
[4] See appendix.
[5] On Selina, Countess of Huntingdon and the Methodist preachers of her "Connexion," see *The Oxford Dictionary of the Christian Church*, 3rd ed. (Oxford: Oxford University Press, 1997) 806.
[6] On John Collins, see appendix.

Collins returned with us spoke of singing several things wch much disgusted me whether to owing to his narrow way of thinking or my own perverse will I know not but I cannot but think ye praise is a part of worship in wch all may join for has not the vilest numerous mercies to be thankful for . . . in a lively noble tune where there is ye true Spirit of Musick free from a light and foolish air, I think such a sort of Musick tends to exalt the mind to a delightful Extesy . . . [it] may well be term'd ye noblest part of Worship. . . . " She even criticized John Wesley's preaching at Bradford:

> Sept 21st (1774) at ye Methodist room heard Mr. John Wesley in ye Eve . . . spoke of justifying Grace said yet it had been unknown to him till about 3 years [ago] whether converting grace or justifying grace was first but on reading Mr. Haliburton's dissertation on y^t subject he was y^n convinced y^t sinners are born again first . . . on ye whole I thought he spoke many good things but in my humble opinion many of his sentiments could not be agreeable to scripture . . . Tuesday ye 25 at ye room at Bradford heard Mr. John Wesley . . . I could not approve of this discourse. May he be delivered from all Error both in principle and practice Led and guided into all truths.

Attending a prayer meeting at the same place she approves of a woman who took part: "her petitions were truly regular—well-worded and such as I could heartily say Amen to. I thought she performed this duty much better y^n most of ye men . . . " (8/10/77).

Jane's praise can be clear and succinct. "This was an Excellent judicious and practical discourse," she writes in September 1778, when Mr. Jimison of Warminster preached at Scots Lane at "a meeting of ministers." In all her comments on sermons, we glimpse an independent and perceptive mind struggling for air, while still held within a tradition of piety which she wishes to accept with humility.

Two separate, but connected themes run through the diaries until 1790. One is Jane Attwater's long spiritual pilgrimage toward the assurance of salvation. From her earliest spiritual wanderings, through her commitment in adult baptism and onward, she was constantly analyzing her inner state of mind and agonizing over her shortcomings. It is possible here to give only a few short extracts from many pages of spiritual autobiography. She discloses on a different level the long courtship of a mysterious "Mr. B," reflecting in her changing moods the conflict between her desire to discern the will of God for her in the "affair," and the natural reactions of a strong personality, partly attracted to and partly repelled by the attentions of this importunate lover. As she grew older, the pressures in a male-dominated society for the spinster daughter to get married grew stronger, but it is clear that, although willing herself not to "kick against the pricks," Jane really wanted an independent life.

Introductory Note to the Diaries

Jane Attwater/Blatch's diaries were written mostly in booklets of varying sizes made of double sheets of paper sewn together, but loose pages were inserted at random and there are also larger single sheets. In general, they run chronologically, but out of order entries do occasionally appear. The handwriting varies considerably in size, but is usually legible. Standard abbreviations are used throughout. This selection covers only to 1790, spanning less than half of the recorded years and necessarily omitting much that is of interest. The diaries are particularly valuable as a resource for both the names of ministers and other preachers and leaders in the group of meetinghouses frequented by Jane, and also Nonconformist sermon material. When Jane and her husband moved to Bratton, obviously she took her diaries with her. Her only child, Anna Jane, died young, so she had no direct heirs and her diaries passed at an unknown date into the hands of her sister Caroline Whitaker's heirs and hence to the present author. They have now been deposited in the Angus Library of Regent's Park College in Oxford.

Selections from the Diaries

March ye 7 1773 [at Bradford] heard Mr Marshman[7] of Westbury . . . I think his manner was very particular one moment his odd way of expressing himself made me smile and another his striking thre [*sic*] things fill me with trembling horror I think I was never affected in such a manner before May prejudice be banish^d from my breast and I through divine grace be inabled to aply the Word home to my heart. . . . 'Tis true he spoke many good things . . . but I cannot but think upon Mature deliberation that he rather shock'^{d} than convinced the sinners In short whether its oweing to my Evil h^t or whether there is some fault in him I know not but it was really disagreeable. . . .

March 21 [1773] In the afternoon heard Mr. Walleer p^{ch} a funeral sermon. . . . My heart felt a shock at another instance of mortality being presented to my view . . . 'tis a confirmation that I too am mortal and soon must sink into death's cold shade and bid a final adieu to all those shining glittring toys which now

---

[7]For Marshman, see appendix.

attract my Notice nor do I know how soon the fatal dart may strike . . . tho' now in vigorous youth in health and Ease . . . may I walk as a pilgrim and sojourner here knowing that here I have no continuing city . . . how is my heart and thought like ye fools Eye moving to the end of the Earth even in the most solemn performances. . . .

August ye 4th 1773 at Sarum Wednesday morning at a meeting of ye ministers [names 5] Mr Ashbourne of pool p^{chd} [on Apostolic preaching]. . . . We are to suppose they were good linguists but a fine flowery stile were not theirs the Glorious truth they taught needed not ye faint decoration of flowing language it had beauties enough in itself without ye borrowed Tinsel of humane acquirement spoke much of his dislike to the manner in wch some of our Modern Ministers preach . . . [date lost] the Ordinance of the Lord's Supper was administered at ye sight of another of these ordinances how hard was my adamantine heart I seem unsusceptible to any divine impressions . . . 'tis almighty power alone can soften my rocky heart . . . how dreadful [to be] thus separated from ye people of God where if I am not fit to join ye Society on Earth how much less shall I be to join ye Society above of ye Saints. . . .

Nov 21 1773 [ines with Mr. Phillips[8] where meets Mr. B—conversation on the state of her soul]. . . he [Mr B.] Told me . . . he had singled me out as one who was on the Inquiry w^t I must do to be saved and he thought I was not a stranger to ye new birth but was by divine grace inabled to see my own sinfulness and insufficiency . . . he ask'd me what I thought of Baptistm . . . I said I thought it was ye duty of all those who think themselves worthy of partaking this ordinance he said as to worthyness none of them could pretend to it was a common notion y^t people must be Eminent Christians . . . before they join with ye people of God. . . .

Feby 6th 1774 at Sarum . . . My heart like ye fool Eye was moving to ye Ends of ye Earth the numerous triffling follys that ingag'd my attention took off my thoughts from attending to ye sermon. . . . I staid whilst ye Ordinance was administered how was my desire to be made like ye children of God . . . was I worthy to be a member I should sincerely rejoice and I hope joyfully embrace what I should then think a duty incumbent on me . . . my sincere desire is to have some Clear Evidence of my being born again. . . . I know not what conclusion to make.

[*no date 1775*] My thoughts are now much ingaged about a particular thing y^t has lately happened [i.e. Mr. B's attentions]. . . . I desire to cheerfully resign myself to ye will of him who fixeth Bonds of our Habitation . . . teach me what to do . . . Many things are for and many against My own Insufficiency to

---

[8]For Henry Phillips, see appendix.

perform incumbent duties makes me shudder at ye thought of Extricating myself ... tho' my mind is utterly averse to any Connexion of this kind yet I w^d desire to have my mind intirely subservient to thine. ...

1775 Feby 5 My mind is now greatly perflex'd the affair goes on ... my mind is totally averse to a union of y^t kind with any one my heart shudders and recoils at ye thought of Entrying into such a connection ... many reasons there are for and against I w^d wish to set y^m in a balance to see wch preponderates but my will is averse to w^t I know must be ye End of repeated visits of this sort ... I can by no means let Mr B's visits be continued if my heart does not Echo to ye words of my mouth My Friends are all for it Dorinda^9 tells me how much my hon^d mother will be grieved should I give him a positive denial the consideration of her so much approving of Him ... his being as I trust a real Christian wch last thing will induce him to act in every respect agreeable—these considerations are weighty ... but I think he has formed in his Imagination one perfectly different f^m myself with her he is charm'd but should he ever wake and behold ye reality in its true form disappointment and regrett w^d cloud ye rest of his days ... I know I must not keep him in suspense delays are dangerous ... I must not trifle 'tis a matter of too great important O God ... deliver me from all deception both in temporals and spirituals ... I dread ye Interview it must be decisive It will not do longer to procrastinate.

Feb 7 [1775] ... I recd a Letter this week from my hon^d Friend Mr Phillips wherein he tells me he has some who seem serious with their faces Zionwards he says to me "will my dear Friend come with y^m?" O that I were worthy I should rejoice to accompany [them] ... I fear the levity of my disposition ye vileness of my heart and ye stupor wch seems to benumb my every active power. ...

May 12 ... I went to Mr. Phillips where were several y^g people Mr P told me ye eyes of all was on me expecting me to join with y^m in performing ye Command of Christ spoke very affectionately and agreeably to me. ...

Thursday I have gave my hon^d Friend a few thoughts wch I wrote out ... but my heart has reproached me since with its being very superficial ... O that I may ever dwell with the people of God in time and in Eternity. ...

Thursday Eve May 24 went to Sarum Mr P. began with examining another candidate for Baptism this done he read those few thoughts wch I wrote wch appeared very superficial & numerous things wch I ought to have said is omited but the members were pleased to think it worthy of their recognition ... we prepared for the sacred Institution may I be indeed cloathed with the perfectly spotless Robe of Christ's Righteousness as I was cloathed now in robes of pure white I had many fears before I came hither least I should not experience the presence

---

^{9}"Dorinda": pen name of Jane's sister, Caroline Whitaker.

of God & the sacred Influence of the Holy Spirit—but wt Reason have I for Gratitude—praise to my kind my Almighty Friend . . . fearless & quite compos'd I descended into the Watery Tomb . . . and my thoughts whilst in the water was set on the baptism of my Glorious Example Christ . . . a calm serious joy seem'd to run thro' my very soul. . . .

Oct ye 5th 1775 at ye Cathedral at Sarum h^d ye Oratorio of ye Messiah perform^d ye Musick was noble the words more so . . . if ye hearts of ye musicians and their auditors where [*sic*] rightly ingaged in it 'twas a Noble performance but as to myself I have too just reason to complain If ye faint sounds wch ye best of mortals can give to his praise is so delightful on Earth . . . to Exalt ye mind what are those anthems wch are sung above where perfect harmony resides and where discord knows no place.

June 24 1776 [her 23rd birthday] Returning days and swift revolving years call on my soul . . . In ye past year many important things I have been ingaged in throu all of which I can say blessed be God . . . as I have [as I trust by Almighty Grace] been inabled this year to take upon me ye name of a Christian so I trust y^t ye same Almight power will inable me to go in ye ways of God. . . .

June ye 30th at Sarum h^d my hon^d Friend Mr Phillips . . . [he] shew'd ye willingness of Christ to save his people . . . this I have often doubted weather Christ was *willing* to save one so unworthy as myself his *Will* now seemed to appear very clear in my views—may I not deceive myself . . . this day I partook of ye ordinance [the Lord's Supper] O y^t it may not be unworthily . . . may I be truly thankful for y^t I have been permitted to enjoy this privilege . . . O how reviving how animating is a small sense of ye pardoning Love of God thro' jesus christ . . . how little do I know of Experimental Religion w^t a large field lies before me.

August 11: 1776 in ye Eve at Sarum heard Mr. Evans[10] [text: ps. 8, v. 'They go from strength to strength. . . . '] ' . . . & shall this strength be given me? Yes if my face is rightly set Sionward . . . this day I was thinking and fearing weather I should have strength to go on my way as I began but I thought ye same god as has brot me hitherto is ye same to support me to ye end . . . I pray God I may not be suffered to look back now I have put my hand to ye gospel plough. . . .

Aug 18th 1776 . . . I know not how the present dilemma wch I am [in] & have been for several weeks past will End may it End for ye Glory of God & ye good of my immortal Soul. I have *seriously* & I hope *conscientiously* desired to act with ye greatest *caution*. I avoided giving an assent to ye proposals wch were made w^h my heart was averse to anything of ye kind . . . the cause of a certain

---

[10] For P. Evans of Downton, see appendix.

persons behaviour wch to me is very misterious is to me perfectly unknown I believe ye affair is intirely over. . . .

Saturday Eve No. 23rd [1776] . . . I have set up a resolution never to say anything against Mr B to anyone but was he to put it in my power to speak to him I would frankly let him know ye just sense I have of his conduct I confess it shocks me it staggers me in many respects w^h I consider of the great Inconsistency there is in it O for a calm fortitude of mind to view all sublunary things in ye light as I ought. . . .

1776 [undated entry] I am happy being brought up in the Baptist denomination as from w^t one little Examination I have been inabled to make I think the Doctrines that those profess are really consistent with the word of God I w^d wish not to be of this persuasion by way of Tradition only but by way of choice not that I think that there is none good but those who adhere to just this particular way of thinking far from it. I hope & trust there are good people amongst all Denominations who worship God in sincerity and truth . . . I w^d wish ever to retain a true Spirit of Charity . . . a narrow Bigotted contracted Spirit is to me no sign of Christianity but rather the reverse.

Sunday ye 6th of April 1777 . . . In ye Evening . . . our kitchen at Bodenham was opened for ye publick Worship of God . . . [11] there were we suppose more y^n 50 people several from Downton, Sarum, some from Britford [and] Nunton . . . the people all behaved well and seemed very attentive & several has said y^t they wish there were service here every Sunday Evening.

[1778 during this year her mother's failing health often keeps her at home and causes much anxiety. She also records Theodosia's death[12] on Nov. 11th.]

Feby 14: 1779 [records a meeting at her home when Mr. Phillips spoke] . . . this discourse was not at all calculated for those who attended as it was explaining things they knew nothing of nor could it influence their practice . . . I wish my Good friend would better adapt his discourse to those to whom he preaches by telling them the state their in by nature making ye way of salvation by Christ clear to y^m inserting more on ye shortness & uncertainty of Life. . . .

May ye 6th Wednesday at Bradford Church heard a young gentleman . . . Mr Crouch spoke very pithily of the depravity of human nature and the superiority of divine wisdom. . . .

---

[11]For the establishment of a Baptist meetinghouse in Bodenham, see appendix.
[12]"Theodosia": pen name of the poet, Anne Steele, see appendix.

Bath May ye 23rd . . . In ye evening at Lady Huntingdon's Chappell[13] heard Mr Shepherd . . . their singing here was very good . . . I much admired it their manner of Chaunting their prayers, was to me new. . . .

April ye 30 1780 . . . In ye afternoon [Sunday] . . . the members were desired to stop to consult about some [matters] . . . I had before intimated to Mr Phillips that it was ye desire of Mr & Mrs Baily to sit down with us as occasional members—Mr P. mentioned this request but ye people seemed rather to reject it wch affords me concern alas w^n shall I see all good people United wt pity is it yt little distinctions should separate members of one body O for a more Extensive Chariety O for more of y^t Benevolence wch was manifested in our Lord. . . .

March ye 4 1781 [Mr B. appears on the scene again and her mother pressurises her on his behalf] . . . my dear parent's solemn reasonings and persuasions has great weight with me . . . various are the pathetick sentences she daily makes . . . if I behave ill to him tells me if I do she thinks it will shorten her days . . . that she may never live to see me married to anyone else on ye other hand my dear Bro^{r}[14] whom I esteem and love as a Father is absolutely averse to it and speaks in ye strongest terms wch show his aversion even to such a thought. . . .

May 17 [following a gap in the diary] [complains that she had had] a mind unfitted . . . to set anything down But I do not find myself better by this omission . . . I find the utility of Writing these texts . . . it tends to cause that reflection wch otherwise perhaps w^d not exist . . . My diary is a kind of repository wch reminds me of past experiences and the various dispensations of providence . . . how strange it is that I can give up my all as to eternal things into his hands and yet be so anxious about temporal concerns.

Dec 31 I have been reading of ye History of England wherein I discover much of Human Nature in uncultivated ages many barbarous and Inhuman actions were performed [but she also finds examples of] Heroic fortitude & Beauty of Virtue, the overthrow of aspiring ambition & mercenary meanness and by comparing past with present time have ye greater reason for Gratitude for ye Innumerable privileges we enjoy. . . .

[She writes very little during 1782 and 1783, because her mother's last illness overshadowed everything. Her mother died on 11 April 1784, at which point many pages were devoted to mourning.]

July 20 1785 [at Broughton] I have on this visit to my dear Broughton Friends enjoyed ye pleasure of as an agreeable society as I suppose the world can produce the pleasure of Friendship & ye still hearing ye word of God explain'd in

---

[13] For Lady Huntingdon, see above, n. 5.
[14] Gay Thomas Attwater.

an Experimental judicious manner I mourn my own Unworthiness of these blessings . . . & my Insufficiency to give that pleasure or profit I have recd from others. . . .

March 5 1786 [Mr B. appeared on the scene again and she weighed up points for and against him] [He is] reported to be a person of good fortune reported to be worth Twenty Thousand pounds

a good fortune)
his age & person well enough) but his mind uncultivated
a dissenter seems to have) but his manners low and mean
ye power of religion)

With these advantages and disadvantages I don't find my Inclination or think it my duty to alter my situation . . . the Gent^n pleaded much of my being capable of instructing him in religion . . . I referred him to God as the best and ever present Teacher. . . .

July 11 [at Bradford hears a sermon which prompts reflections] my mind & heart seems more expanded in universal benevolence O my God & heavenly father grant me to increase in this divine phylanthropy . . . I have thought much of late what is ye reason for their [*sic*] being so many sects and partyes in ye religious world . . . I want to see all party spirit abolish^d & all y^t love ye Lord jesus in sincerity united in ye strictest bonds of Friendship.

Nov 5th 1786 Yesterday through ye goodness of God came safe to Bristol to visit Mr Evans (Caleb)[15] & family after long repeated invitations from that pious & erminent servant of God I met with a most friendly reception from my Good Friend . . . in ye morning at Broadmead meetinghouse . . . I left a little Heaven below highly delighted with my excursion. . . .

May 18th [1788] in ye afternoon h^d Mr. Ripon of London[16] In ye Eve I drank tea in company with Mr Ripon. In conversation he was speaking of ye Celebrated Dr Priestly[17] [Mr R. told an anecdote to show Priestly's errors. Jane commented that it was] dreadful y^t Error should reign amongst sensible people Dr Priestly I have heard is a most amiable man as to character & behaviour . . . yet suffered to deny the divinity of our Saviour Mr Ripon spoke very well in ye Eve against ye Arian & Socinian notion . . . a good discourse many striking solemn things he

---

[15] For Caleb Evans, see appendix. As a preacher in the whole area, he figures often in the diaries and was a family friend of the Attwaters and Whitakers.

[16] For Dr. Ripon, see appendix.

[17] Dr. Joseph Priestly (1733–1804) originally a Presbyterian minister, moved to Arian and Socinian views, becoming a founder of the Unitarian Society (1791). He was notorious for his scientific thinking. From 1773 to 1780 he was a resident at Bowood, mid-Wilts as librarian to the Earl of Shelburne. Jane could well have heard him discussed when visiting Bradford. See *Dictionary of National Biography* entry.

said and his manner tends greatly to rouse & affect the passions but I can't say it is so lastingly useful or makes so much impression on my Mind as a more calm & moderate way of Speaking but it may be more so to some therefore its a mercy to have a variety of talents. . . .

1790 [In this year John Saffery[18] becomes the minister at Brown Street] Sunday Jany 19th Mr J B came home with me he read a sermon improved time in prayer I trust he is a partaker of ye grace of God In truth did I not think so I should have no Inclination to give any Encouragement to his addresses. . . .

Feby 7th 1790 . . . Mr J B still persists in his visits and increases his earnest Importunities . . . I do not find my mind now averse to it to all appearances matters seem to be drawing to a conclusion.

April . . . I have at last determined to show him wt I have written concerning my future settlement of affairs of fortune etc. In wch I have been very Explicit as in Everything I endeavour to be perfectly Honest and free as to speaking my sentiments before I am bound should it be ye will of God to obedience . . . I wish not to triffle with his happiness . . . My heart reproaches me that I have been too anxiously concerned about this matter tho' it is of ye greatest importance of any Earthly concern yet w^n brot in competition with Eternal [things] it ought to be kept in subjection . . . Especially it has engaged too much of my thoughts of a Sabbath Day . . . I w^d leave all temporal concerns at ye foot of ye Mount . . . [She is upset by her Brother's opposition &, on the other hand, old Mr Burgess's advocacy for Mr B's suit].

[*Undated*] . . . what Inference am I to draw? I seem at a loss absolutely . . . things must now take their course and if my Heavenly Father has ordered this to be ye path where in I should walk I pray it may be made plain before me. . . .

Aug 1st 1790 [cannot even find peace at worship] . . . It seems too much for feeble patience to bear My dear Brothers' pathetic sentences one way & Mr B's another . . . I have certainly been here long enough to answer ye calls of fraternal duty and now if providence points out a path where I think I can promote my own happiness and ye happiness of my Friends shall I not walk therein? But I fear my heart being too fondly attached to creature Comfort and if not finding an Equal return was ye least slight indifference to be paid after I was united it w^d make me totally miserable . . . I am often ready to doubt his sincerity . . . between every perplexity I feel myself very unhappy . . . O my God extricate me.

October 24th 1790 . . . I have at last told him ye terms I wish for him to comply with concerning settling of our affair with wch he readily & generously complied wch I esteem as an additional proof of his affection. . . . Should the intended

---

[18]For John Saffery, see appendix.

Union take place I pray God to make me a real Blessing to him as well as him to me. . . . I trust thou hast not permitted things to be brot thus far to have all our hopes blasted. I pray we may be inabled to view Each other as Gifts of Thine having our supreme love fix'd on thee as ye fountain of very delight.

Nov 14th . . . my dear Bro^r is so softened y^t he is not only willing but desirous to see ye connection take place.

Nov 18th 1790 This day I went to Church with Mr Blatch[19] and was united by the solemnities of Matrimony. . . . I gave myself to Mr B and I trust the events of Thursday will ever be remembered with gratitude.

Appendix.
Meetinghouses and Preachers in the Diaries

Sources

i. J. H. Chandler, *Wiltshire Dissenters' Meeting House Certificates and Registrations 1689–1852* (Devizes Wiltshire Record Society, 1985) (Ch.).

ii. M. E. Reeves, "Protestant Nonconformity," *Victoria County History* iii (London: Oxford University Press, 1956) 99-149 (*VCH*).

Meetinghouses

Bodenham (near Salisbury)	Baptist, house of Mrs. Anna Attwater, widow, 1776; house of Mr. Thomas Attwater, 1780 (Ch. 345, 362)
Bradford-on-Avon	(a) Baptist meetinghouse 1689 (Ch. 14). (b) Presbyterian 1692, 1695 (2), 1699 (Ch. 29, 48, 49, 84); Independent 1739 (Ch. 273); Presbyterian/Independent, the Grove meetinghouse 1793 (Ch. 445; *VCH*, 125); Congregational (split from the Grove), Morgan's Hill 1741 (Ch. 279; *VCH*, 125). (c) Quaker 1701 (2), 170 (Ch. 105, 106, 124). (d) Methodist 1756 (Ch. 309).

---

[19]"Mr. B," i.e., Joseph Goodenough Blatch: The Blatch family appears to have originated in Bratton. They were Baptists, already linked by marriage with the Whitakers and figuring several times in Jeffery Whitaker's mid-eighteenth-century diary. They owned property in the surrounding district and a younger branch had settled in Amesbury. Hence, at the time of his marriage JGB was coming into Salisbury from Amesbury. But he had close links with Bratton and in August 1793, he and Jane moved to Bratton, perhaps to "Tinkers Tenement"—now Ivy Cottate. He died in 1840 when the Church Minute Book recorded the death of "Our excellent and valued Deacon." Jane died in November 1843.

North Bradley	Baptist, connected with Southwick, 1689, 1702, 1709, 1774, 1780 (New meetinghouse) (Ch. 16, 130, 178, 339).
Bratton	Baptist, connected with Erlestoke, 1698, 1701, 1734 (meetinghouse) (Ch. 70, 123, 261)
Broughton	Baptist, first at Porton, ca. 1655, moves to Broughton 1710 (*VCH*, 102-103, 112-13, 119).
Downton	General and Particular Baptist churches, licenses, 1698 (2), 1705, 1706, 1715, 1754, 1775 (Ch. 63, 67, 148, 151, 200, 307, 344), early group General Baptists, but seceding group of Particular Baptists formed in 1734 (*VCH*, 113-14, 126). This is the church which figures in the Diaries.
Salisbury	(a) Baptist, ca. 1630 group of Anabaptists form General Baptist Church; ca. 1655 John Rede from Porton forms Particular Baptist Church, origins of Brown Street, licensed 1751. (*VCH*, 102-103, 113-14, 120, 134; Ch. 306). (b) Independent, 1767 Scots Lane new meetinghouse (Ch. 319). (c) another Independent group, 1756, Shoemakers' Hall, Hogg Lane (Ch. 310).
Trowbridge	Baptist, 1689 (2), 1708 (Ch. 6, 19, 167). Presbyterian, 1692 (2), 1703, 1723 (Ch. 33, 34, 35, 138, 237).
Westbury	Baptist, 1689 , 1693, 1714, 1723 (Ch. 7, 37, 196, 236).

Preachers

Adams, John, at Scots Lane 1778; witness, enlargement of meetinghouse 1790 (Ch. 426).

Bishop, "Mr. Bishop's meetinghouse in Westbury" (diaries 1773, 1774).

Button, William, at Brown Street 1773 (Diaries); witness, enlargement of Scots Lane meetinghouse 1790 (Ch. 426).

Clark, John "of Trowbridge," at Bratton 1784 (Diaries); 1st minister of the Tabernacle Congregational Church from 1767 (*VCH*, 131n, 130-33).

Collins, John, of Devizes, at Bratton 1774, at Brown Street 1775 (NB critical account), at Bradford 1779, 1785, at Broughton (2) 1786 (Diaries).

Cooper, minister, Bratton Baptist Church, at Brown Street (2) 1777, Bodenham 1780, Beckington (opening of new Baptist meeting) 1788 (Diaries).

Coward, "young Gent[n] from Plymouth," at Brown Street 1776, 1777 (2), 1779 (Diaries).

Day, "of Wellington," at Association Meetings, Brown Street 1782 (Diaries).

Dure?, During, Richard, at Bratton 1774 (Diaries); Westbury Leigh 1797 (Ch. 483).

Dyer, "of Whitchurch," at Brown Street 1781, Bradford 1788 (Diaries).

Evans, Caleb, of Bristol, key Baptist leader in the southwest. He and his students preach continuously in the whole area, recorded frequently in the Diaries, e.g. Bratton 1767, Brown Street 1776, 1781, 1782, 1788, 1790, Bradford 1788, Beckington 1788, see M. Reeves, *Pursuing the Muses* (London: Cassell, 1997), p. 44, n. 52; N. Moon, "Caleb Evans, Founder of the Bristol Baptist Education Society" *Baptist Quarterly, xxiv,* 4 (1971) 175-90.

Evans, "of Downton," at Brown Street 1776, 1777, 1778 (Diaries).

Samuel, witnesses new Baptist meetinghouse, Downton 1775 (Ch. 344).

Hors(e)y, leader in the Baptist Church, Portsmouth, frequent preacher in the Salisbury area, e.g. Brown Street 1774, 1775, 1776, 1778, 1779; Downton 1775, 1777, 1778; Bodenham 1777.

Jameson (Jimison), William, Independent of Warminster, at "a meeting at Mr. Phenes," Bradford 1774, at "a meeting of ministers," Scots Lane 1778 (Diaries), witnesses licences, Longbridge Deverill 1777, Imber 1779 (Ch. 354, 359).

Kent, at Broughton Baptist Church 1770, 1777, 1778; Brown Street 1773, 1775 (Diaries), NB John Kent, elder of the Porton Church 1675.

Marshman, "Mr. Marshman of Westbury" at Bradford Baptist Church 1773 (Diaries, see above, Jas. Reason, alias Marshman witnesses licence, Baptist Westbury Leigh Church 1693 (Ch. 37); John, ditto 1797 (Ch. 483): Joshua sails to join Carey in India 1799 (*VCH,* 137, 148)

Mercer, "yg Gent^n from Gloucestershire come to reside in Romsey," at Broughton 1778, at a meeting of ministers, Scots Lane, 1778 (Diaries).

Munston, "a young academic from Hommerton academy," at Brown Street 1790 (Diaries).

Nike, "From Romsey," Baptist, at Downton Baptist meeting 1770, at Brown Street 1773, 1775, 1776, 1779, at Scots Lane Independent 1774 (Diaries).

Pearce, Methodist, Bradford 1773 (Diaries), innkeeper, an early Methodist leader in Bradford (*VCH*, p. 129 n.).

Phene, leader of unidentified meetinghouse, Bradford, (?) Independent, 1774, 1776, 1777, 1779, 1786 (Diaries).

Phillips, Henry, minister, Brown Street Baptist Church from at least 1768, occurs continuously in the Diaries, preaches also at Downton and Bodenham (Diaries, 1773, 1775, 1781, 1782), witnesses licences at Bodenham 1776, 1780 (Ch. 345, 362), kept a school at Brown Street (*VCH)*, 123 n. died 1789.

Rawlings, 'from Trowbridge', Baptist, at Broughton 1770, 1775, 1777; Wallop 1770; Brown Street 1776 (Diaries).

Rippon, Dr. John, (1751-1836), well-known London Baptist minister, hymnologist and editor of *The Baptist Annual Register* (1790-1805). He was born into a Baptist family at Tiverton, Devon, so his West country roots may account for his visit to Salisbury in 1788. Educated at the British Academy, he was obviously the type of scholarly minister with whom Jane would enjoy a theological discussion about Priestley's views (see *Dictionary of National Biography*).

Saffery, John, (1763-1825), Baptist minister, Brown Street (see Diaries), noted for evangelical tours and money-raising activites for the Baptist Missionary Society (see *VCH*, 137, 148; Reeves, *Pursuing the Muses*, 149-51, 157, 173;

his voluminous correspondence and collecting books are in the Angus Library, Regent's Park College, Oxford.

Shrapnell, head of a Sunday School, Bradford 1785 (Diaries). Henry, Anabaptist, 1662 licensed as Baptist teacher 1672 (*VCH*, 111). Richard, Presbyterian, Trowbridge 1692 (Ch. 34).

Slooper (Sloper), family in Devizes area, "Mr. Slooper of Devizes at Beckington" 1788 (Diaries).
    John, Devizes 1773 (Ch. 338).
    John, junior, Market Lanington 1723 (Ch. 238).
    (?) Independent, Urchfont 1775 (Ch. 343).
    John, Independent, Devizes 1777 (Ch. 352).
    John, trustee, Congregational Chapel, Hilperton 1777 (*VCH*. 131 n.).

Stedman, Dr. William Steadman, (1764–1837) at Brown Street 1790 (Diaries); entered the "network" of western Baptists in 1784 when training for the ministry under Caleb Evans at Bristol; pastor of the Broughton Baptist Church 1791–1798, where Jane met him. His chief distinction was as a preacher, first in the surrounding countryside and then with his friend John Saffery on wider evangelical tours which combined home mission with enthusiastic collecting for the nascent Baptist Missionary Society (see *Baptist Magazine*, June 1837, 229-39; *VCH*, 137).

Steele, Anne (1717–1778), poet (Theodosia), daughter of William Steele, see Reeves, *Pursuing the Muses*, 25-29, 61-84, 89-92.

Steele, William, 1689–1769, minister, Broughton Baptist Church, mentioned often in Dairies, see also Reeves, *Pursing the Muses,* 2, 4, 26-27; witnesses Baptist licences for Winterslow 1749, 1754 (Ch. 305, 308).

Taylor, "of Calne," "a favourite preacher of mine," at Brown Street 1790 (Diaries).
    Charles, Chippenham 1709 (Ch. 174).
    Isaac, minister at Calne and village preacher, interested in schools and records history of Calne meetinghouse (*VCH*, 114, 137, 145-46).

Walker, at Bradford Baptist Church 1773, 1774, 1776, 1777, 1779; at Brown Street 1776 (Diaries).

Webb, Captain, 'at Mr. Wesley's room', Bradford, 1786 (Diaries). See John Wesley's *Journal,* vi. 452, quoted *VCH*, 129, n. 54.

Weiler (Wheeler), John, Independent, "at his meeting," Sarum 1773 (Diaries). 1767 minister, Scots Lane new meetinghouse (Ch. 319).

Winter, "from Marlborough," at Scots Lane 1778 (Diaries) probably Cornelius, convert of Whitefield's, ordained 1767, involved in revival of Congregationalism started by Cennick, Whitefield and Rowland Hill, brought the old Independent Church at Marlborough into the new movement and started an academy there. (*VCH*, 131-34).

Yerbury, Joseph, at Mr. Wesley's room 1774 (Diaries).
    Francis, witnesses licence for (?) Quaker meeting 1692 (Ch. 29).
    John, clothier of Melksham, 17th c. Quaker (*VCH*, 119, n. 45).

"Active, Busy, Zealous": The Reverend Dr. Cox of Hackney[1]

John H. Y. Briggs

1. Early Life[2]

This study offers an account of the interrelating activities of an early nineteenth-century Baptist minister, who—by reason of his polymath interests—provides interesting insight into the history of the whole denomination. The integration of different and disparate themes in the life of one London pastor, discussed here, reflects a bundle of concerns that occupied Baptist energies more generally throughout this vital period of expansion and consolidation. It is a fitting subject for B. R. White's *Festschrift*, insofar as Cox was a most distinguished figure who only just escaped being Stepney's first principal, but as both tutor and neighboring minister played an important part in the early history of what has become Regent's Park College.

"The only son of pious parents," Francis Augustus Cox was born in Leighton Buzzard in March 1783, inheriting considerable local property from his Baptist grandparents. The young Cox demonstrated a precocious interest in matters of religion. Well into his reading of Bunyan's *Pilgrim's Progress* at the age of nine, he was soon found gathering friends for prayer meetings at the Mr. Cornfield's Academy[3] in Northampton. He preached his first sermon in Leighton Buzzard at the age of fifteen, thereafter training for the Christian ministry at Bristol Baptist College. He soon became one of that distinguished group of students who

---

[1]These are the adjectives used by Skeats and Miall to describe Cox. H. S. Skeats and C. S. Miall, *History of the Free Churches of England, 1688–1891* (London: A. Miall, 1891) 471-72.

[2]Cox's early life is reconstructed from material contained in Daniel Katterns's two funeral/memorial sermons, *Maturity in Death Exemplified* and *Ripe for Harvest*, and H. Gamble's *Fidelity Recognized and Rewarded*, all three of which were published in 1853 and are available at the Dr. Williams's Library in London which also holds a rich collection of Cox's publications. Further copies are to be found in the Angus Collection of Regent's Park College, Oxford.

[3]Cornfield was identified by Katterns as "a respected member of the Baptist denomination."

went on from Bristol to complete their studies at a Scottish university, which in Cox's case was Edinburgh.

Cox was ordained to his pastoral charge, that of the historic congregation at Clipstone, in 1804, a congregation which included Andrew Fuller, John Sutcliffe, and Robert Hall. Very soon he was affirmed by the *Baptist Magazine* and other local records as he assumed a full part in the life of the association. Upon the failure of Robert Hall's health, Cox was invited to supply the pulpit at Cambridge on secondment from Clipstone, and in fact, he did well enough in the initial assignment to be offered a call to the pastorate, which he accepted.

The relationship between the young Cox and the Cambridge Church proved, however, to be an unhappy one, probably because his Calvinism was too overt for Cambridge. A letter in St. Andrew's Church Book from Cox to the church's senior deacon confessed, "A variety of unhappy circumstances have conspired to render my situation unpleasant and every way undesirable." In a letter to John Ryland, Robert Hall explained that the subsequent division in the church was not substantially doctrinal. It did not originate "in a difference of principle" or in disapproval of Mr. Coxe [sic] for his attachment to evangelical doctrines, but merely a dissatisfaction . . . with his abilities and manner of preaching as "superficial and declamatory." The legacy of Robert Robinson's uncertain Christology had obviously not altogether left the Cambridge congregation. Thus Hall added, "There are not I am confident above two members of the church who would not greatly prefer a moderate Calvinist to a socinian or an arian."[4]

Thus, when Cox's preaching, for whatever reason, failed to satisfy the expectations of the Cambridge congregation, he resigned in April 1808 and returned to Clipstone, which had apparently remained vacant. However, Cox soon found that, after the episode in Cambridge, he could not settle there, thus withdrawing from the pastorate and leaving behind a large and united people. This he did even though he did not have any other paid office in view.[5] Shortly afterwards in 1811, he began to serve the Hackney Church on a strictly temporary basis, explicitly emphasizing his hope for the possibility of a call to the pastorate. Hackney was, however, to become his life's work, sustaining a pulpit ministry of some

---

[4] G. F Nuttall, "Letters from Robert Hall to John Ryland, 1791–1824," *Baptist Quarterly* (hereafter *BQ*) (1991): 127-28.

[5] Ibid., Hall to Ryland, November 1810.

forty-two years, and increasing the membership sixfold during the period in which he served as sole pastor. Sharing in his induction were William Newman, John Rippon, and Joseph Hughes. Dr. Pye Smith of Homerton was prevented at the last minute from participating in what was described as a "highly interesting service" which the *Baptist Magazine*'s reporter found difficult—if not impossible—to characterize. For the record, Cox himself was, interestingly, described as "late of Cambridge."[6] Daniel Katterns, who was for nine years his associate in the pastorate, believed that in this chain of events which brought Cox to Hackney "the overruling providence of God" was operating, for clearly Cox was the right person for the area, then an emerging suburb of some potential prosperity.

A man of prayer, Cox proved himself a careful preacher, precise in his use of language and never commonplace in his thinking. Not a "colloquial" preacher, he was "evangelical, simple, clear, earnest, affectionate." His favorite topics were those relating to "the character of God, to the benefits of the true religion, to the kingdom of Christ and to the joys of immortality." Only rarely and reluctantly did he allude to divine penalties, preferring instead to secure conviction by the powers of clear biblical exposition and "conclusive reasoning." "You never heard the wrath of God fulminating from his lips as though it were a congenial and delightful topic, but it was always touched with reluctance, and with an evident desire for the salvation of his hearers." Katterns believed that all the expositions of his senior colleague were the work of "a scholar of the highest reputation." His publications were those "of a well-founded biblical critic," an area in which Cox displayed extensive learning. They were of a kind which, though rejecting the approaches of Phillip Doddridge and other figures of the past century, were not yet alert to the findings of the higher critics. Katterns above all affirmed that Cox was "always a preacher of the gospel, yet more richly evangelical as he proceeded."

Cox collected the largest—but certainly not the wealthiest—congregation in the neighborhood, which called for an early move from Shore Place to Mare Street, as well as the extension of the chapel on the latter site on two occasions. Notwithstanding Cox's scholarly sermonic style and his eschewing of a popular style of preaching, "the common people heard him gladly." By a miracle of sanctified intellect, profound truth "was not vulgarized but levelled to everyone's capacity."

---

[6]*Baptist Magazine* (hereafter *BM*) November 1811.

"In the religious world, Dr. Cox was preeminently a public man. . . . No public movements took place in the cause of Christ that did not solicit his cooperation which he delighted to give." Indeed, it would be difficult to list all the organizations for which he served as secretary, and certainly all the committees on which he sat. For example, he took a lead in orchestrating the campaign that finally secured the abolition of the Test and Corporation Acts in 1829. Both activist and scholar, he was, however, never a narrow denominationalist, rather "belonging to the whole church of God."

The year 1841 found him particularly busy. At the Baptist Union Assembly, he proposed resolutions on Bible publishing monopolies and the financial support of the Union, chaired a subcommittee to find a new treasurer, and was himself elected to serve on the Union's committee. Immediately thereafter, he presided over the meetings of the Baptist Colonial Missionary Society, serving also on the Baptist Board on Colonial Apprenticeships. In November he chaired a meeting in London to secure support of the persecuted Baptists of Denmark, having earlier served as secretary of both the Baptist Continental Society and the of the interdenominational Society for Diffusing the Gospel through the Continent of Europe. At the end of the year he was the only London—and the only Baptist—signatory of the Address issued by the Manchester Conference seeking popular support for the repeal of the Corn Laws. He was later to be termed virtually "an agent of the League" in East London.[7]

Within a year of settling at Hackney—that is, in 1813—he was serving on the committee that was responsible for setting up the first Baptist Union. He took the chair on some occasions, though was later less active in those debates. This was probably because he sided with the open-communion views of his fellow Bristol student, Robert Hall, in the communion controversy, as over against the closed-communion views of Joseph Ivimey, the first secretary of the infant Baptist Union.[8]

Three times president of the Baptist Union, Cox helped found the Baptist Magazine, providing some of its initial capital as well as frequent submissions. He helped establish beyond the denomination the wider nonconformist paper, the *Patriot*, and edited the interdenominational

---

[7]K. R. M. Short, "Benjamin Evans and the Radical Press," *BQ* (1962): 247. For Cox's association with the Corn Law dispute, see the same author's "Baptist and the Corn Laws" *BQ* (1966): 309-20.

[8]Seymour Price, "The Early Years of the Baptist Union," *BQ* (1928): 57-60, 121-22.

Missionary World (1849). Not surprisingly, writing about heaven and about Sunday—which, in the language of the day, was seen as an antetype of heaven—created some difficulty for an activist like Cox. However, predeceased by two of his three wives and four of his seven children, it was a topic he could scarcely escape. To be sure, paradise *was* a place of rest, but this was never to be construed as "a state of drowsy lassitude or indifference"; rather, it was a state in which all were engaged in the service of Almighty God.[9]

Cox's two doctorates, an LL.D from Glasgow (1824) and a D.D. from Waterville College (1838), were perceived as "well deserved." He was fluent enough in French to offer himself for missionary service in France, and probably would have needed fairly extensive German to complete his pioneering study of Melanchthon, "whose spirit it has been truly said that he imbibed."

2. The Stepney Context

Joseph Gutteridge—deacon of Abraham Booth's church at Little Prescott Street and treasurer of the Baptist Education Society—was very much the moving force in the establishment of Stepney College. To him fell the task in 1810 of appointing a first principal. His first notion was to secure the services of the learned Joseph Kinghorn of Norwich, "whose prudence, moderation and good sense," it was hoped, "would form a connecting link between the higher and lower classes of our Calvinistic friends." Kinghorn, however, could not be persuaded to leave East Anglia, notwithstanding a pressing correspondence from Gutteridge that stretched from April 4 until Kinghorn's final reply on 23 July after he had had the opportunity to meet with the committee in London.[10] In the summer of 1810, Cox's name was strongly canvassed for the position, more on the basis of potential than achievement, for he was still relatively young and not yet established as either pastor or scholar. He was, however, already known as "a zealous advocate for an educated ministry, at a time when much prejudice prevailed upon the subject."[11]

---

[9]*The Religious Character of the Weekly Rest, a Sermon Preached at Bloomsbury Chapel, Feb 14, 1849*, 177.

[10]For the details, see Edward Steane, *Memoir of the Life of Joseph Gutteridge* (London: Jackson and Walford, 1850).

[11]Katterns, 25. "Selections from the Diary of William Newman," ed. R. E. Cooper, *BQ* (1959): 85: "Dore tole me that Cox was the person now in view."

The invitation to lead the new institution at Stepney went to William Newman, the pastor of the church at Bow, who accepted the offer in January 1811, combining college work alongside his existing pastorate. Cox's many gifts were not, however, wholly lost to Stepney, for the College was to enjoy "not only his counsels but his instructions," for from 1813 to 1822, he taught mathematics at the College on a part-time basis.[12] As a tutor he was influential in the ministerial formation of many a member of the College during this time. This, however, led to some difficulty, for Cox—unlike Newman—had the benefit of formal theological training. Beyond that the issue of open communion divided them, for Cox was a fervent supporter of Robert Hall, whereas Newman was a passionate strict communionist. Not surprisingly, the student body, likewise, became divided on the issue, with nearly all of them supporting Cox and Hall rather than Newman, who nevertheless resolutely campaigned for the closed-communion position in the lecture theater. Gutteridge was not well pleased. Newman noted in his diary, "I have committed two offences never to be forgiven. One, strict communion; and other is, I have not bowed sufficiently to the Treasurer."

Tensions in the College did not diminish either "willingly or unwillingly" with Cox, described as Newman's "turbulent" colleague, provoking the rallying point for the malcontents.[13] By this time, however, the cause of contention was not just the communion issue but the radicalism of the students as over against the conservatism of the President. Newman was a loyal Hanoverian, even though he was so delighted at the acquittal of Queen Caroline that he sent the students a bottle of Madeira with which to celebrate. But that was an exception arising out of his sense of justice and fair play. In political matters he was generally a traditionalist. As early as 1820, there is recorded a note of his regret: "The young men in several instances infected with a spirit of Radicalism." When Newman chose an eminently monarchist hymn,

---

[12]For the account in this and the following paragraphs, I am indebted to R. E. Cooper, *From Stepney to St. Giles', The Story of Regent's Park College, 1810–1960* (London: Carey Kingsgate Press, 1960).

[13]"Newman Diaries," *BQ* (1960): 280, 31.10.21, "The three rebels went over yesterday to Mr. Cox. He gave them no encouragement," but 282, 16.6.26, "F.A.C. was in the second rebellion and said 'Be firm' yet voted against the three. Keen remonstrated and got out by saying 'You went too far'. J. Groser said he had perfect contempt for F.A.C. I remember that Wayland charged him with aiding and abetting in the grand rebellion of 1820; and Tomkins a few weeks age acknowledged this to Mr. Young, whose wife spoke of Cox's 'forwardness' to take Newman's place."

"The Crowns of British Princes Shine," he noted that one man refused to sing: "He was afterwards as surly as a bear." Things went from bad to worse. Newman spoke of "a tendency to discontent and insubordination among some of [Stepney's] inmates, which was, at length discovered, in a form least equivocal, and attended by circumstances which left nothing to conjecture as to the animus by which it was dictated." According to him, only prompt actions limited this "unholy flame." This is the language he uses to refer to what was, in fact, a minor rebellion in 1821, which both led to the expulsion of three students, and made a serious and injurious impact on Newman's health.

In 1825 Newman's diaries suggest that Cox was harboring notions of establishing a separate college. Thus, in January of 1825, Newman wrote of a "Rumor of a new Baptist college near London." An informant identified Joseph Hughes of the British and Foreign Bible Society; Benjamin Shaw, MP and Treasurer of the BMS; and Henry Waymouth, occasional chairman of the Dissenting Deputies as collaborators in the scheme, men with whom Cox worked closely on other projects. Newman considered the whole affair a mere "castle in the air," and seems to have been sufficiently troubled to have challenged Cox on the matter, for on 1 February he wrote, "FAC defended himself concerning the new college." By 28 January 1826, a further dimension to the dispute was revealed, for Newman wrote, "The cause is now perhaps, not the cause of the an individual tutor, but the cause of vital religion against a mere heartless form with the decorations of literature and philosophy." This was, of course, not very different from another controversy endured in the same period at Serampore, on which Cox seems to have taken the more narrow, rather than the more liberal position. It seems more than likely that what set Newman's besieged mind into a spin was, in fact, Cox's preliminary work to secure support for the founding of London University, as opposed to a second Baptist theological college.

The 1821 crisis had already caused Newman to resign from "the superintendence of the domestic arrangements of the institution," while remaining theological tutor and president.[14] Five years later things had gotten so bad that a committee of inquiry was set up to hear student complaints.[15] Feeling that he no longer possessed the confidence of either

---

[14]George Pritchard, *Memoir of the Rev'd William Newman, D.D.* (London: T. Ward, 1837) 295-97. See also 327-34.

[15]It is significant that one of the ring leaders of the students opposed to Newman was

committee or student body, Newman resigned at the end of 1826. Cooper, confessing that he found it difficult to assess Cox's part in the decline of Newman's effectiveness wrote, "It was believed that he would succeed Newman. That he hoped as much was well known. But he did not."[16]

3. Involvement in Founding London University

By the time of Newman's resignation, Cox was involved in wider educational enterprises. As early as May 1820, a sketch had appeared in the *Baptist Magazine* titled "Protestant Dissenting Academy." This was almost certainly the output of Cox's pen, qualifying him to have equal status with the poet William Campbell, as initiating the idea that came to fruition in the founding of London University. Indeed, not long after, in 1830, Professor Lardner bore testimony: "The first notion of a university is said to have been suggested by a dissenting clergyman named Rev. Mr. Cox"[17]

There were good reasons to establish a new "nonconfessional" institution. In fact, the enrollment of Jewish students was considered from the beginning. The exclusion for Jews and nonconformists from Oxford and Cambridge, then England's only universities, led to the inconvenience of conscientious dissenting students having to undertake their higher education in either Holland or Scotland. The new college, which was to provide "no abode for idlers," was not intended to create competition with the work of the seminaries. Rather, it was to offer such a liberal education as to prepare its graduates for entering into one of the professions or as should "adorn private life with literary pursuits in the hours of leisure from business." The scope of its curriculum was to be comparable with that of "any of the most celebrated universities in Christendom," through Glasgow was singled out as the more precise

---

W. D. Jones, of whose academic abilities Newman had no high opinion, but who was not so academically feeble but that the college thought it worth sending him to Edinburgh in a Ward Scholarship. After a twenty-year pastorate at Sheppard's Barton, Frome, he returned to Stepney as President in 1848, only to resign mysteriously the following year. Cooper, *Stepney*, 42, 53-54.

[16]Ibid, 43.

[17]C. W. New, *The Life of Henry Brougham to 1830* (1961) 362. Even earlier, in his *History of the Dissenters*, 1812, David Bogue had written, "Were an institution established in a central part of England upon a liberal plan, open to all denominations, Christian and Jews, and were the incomes of the professors to arise, like those of Scotland, in great measure from the students, whom their celebrity would attract, it would find sufficient support."

model to be followed.[18] Northampton and Reading were early on considered potential locations, though the focus of concern soon moved to London.

An initial committee of Baptists was soon enlarged to include other dissenters, as well as Scotsmen resident in England. This enlarged group met in April of 1825 at the King's Head Tavern in the Poultry, a hostelry which witnessed the birth of a number of dissenting initiatives. Aware that a secular group led by Lord Brougham and Thomas Campbell had similar interests, a delegation was sent to see if the two groups might not combine their energies.[19]. Among those representing the religious interest were Benjamin Shaw; Cox; and the charismatic luminary, Edward Irving, of Regent Square Scots' Church. An immediate concern was whether or not to include theology chairs in the new institution. Brougham and friends wrote to Campbell, "We think with you that the introduction of Divinity will be mischievous; but we must yield to the Dissenters with Irving at their head. We must have a theological college."

The immediate reaction of Anglican subscribers was predictable: the theology was to be Church of England, or else there should be no theology at all! To its credit, the dissenting interest was apparently flexible. Presented with the Anglican response, the reply was, "Enough, enough. We are convinced and concede the point that the University shall be without religious rivalship." Irving, however, had his doubts and confided to Carlyle, "It will be unreligious, secretly antireligious, all the same," the origin of the popular designation of the new university as "godless Gower Street." The issue of the inclusion or the exclusion of theology was to rumble on for several years.[20]

Cox's counsel was particularly important as one of the few amongst the planners of the new institution who had experience teaching in higher education, and this by virtue of his tutorship at Stepney.[21] Accordingly, he was appointed honorary secretary of the provisional committee of the new university, and it was he who presented the plan at the first public meeting, chaired by the Lord Mayor and called for the establishment of

---

[18]*BM* (May 1820): 205-207.
[19]H. H. Bellot, *University College, London, 1826–1929* (1929): 21; New, *The Life of Henry Brougham*, 362; Seymour Price, "The Centenary of the Baptist Building Fund," *BQ* 3 (1926): 81ff.
[20]Bellot, *University College, London*, 22-23.
[21]New, *The Life of Henry Brougham*, 367. This was not wholly fair as Gregory held a chair at the Military Academy at Woolwich.

"a palace for genius." The support of the London dissenters was crucial to the success of the new venture. They offered the new project a well-developed connexion not only in London, but the provinces as well. In addition, their wealth was needed for the new institution to get off the ground. Beyond that, there was their experience of the old dissenting academies—with their modern curricula of studies, together with their close ties with the Scottish universities—who had an historic role in training a nonconformist elite. Together with some North American institutions, Scottish universities played an important role in giving dignity to dissent, sometimes only reluctantly received, by the recognition of nonconformist scholars and leaders through the award of honorary doctorates.

Ironically, cautions as to the secular nature of the new institution led to the exclusion of all clergy from the Council of the College, and therefore of Cox (though he continued to serve as clerk and secretary until September 1828). Instead, Baptist interests were represented on the Council by Olinthus Gregory, Professor of Mathematics at the Royal Military Academy at Woolwich, evidence theologian, and biographer of Robert Hall—who sat on the education committee, and whose name is to be found on the foundation stone of University College. Gregory was supported by Benjamin Shaw, Treasurer of the Baptist Missionary Society (1821–1826), and sometimes MP for Westbury.[22] Along with John Smith and I. L. Goldsmid, Shaw underwrote the purchase of the site for the University College at his own risk, until the new institution had accumulated sufficient funds actually to restore it. The conglomeration of individuals is an interesting one, considering it was made up of a liberal Whig MP, a Jewish emancipationist, and a Baptist man-of-the-city. Indeed, the whole enterprise involved a remarkable interplay of interest. For his part, Cox became increasingly intimate with Lord Brougham, who used his rectorship of Glasgow University in 1824 to confer on Cox an

---

[22]Westbury was an infamous pocket borough, the nomination to which at this time belonged to Sir Manasseh Masseh Lopez, a financier largely in East India Stock which may well be the association with Shaw's financial interests. Benjamin Shaw, as a Lloyd's underwriter, spoke in the house mainly on commercial topics. He was a major patron of dissenting philanthropy and of Baptist causes in particular, including Stepney College. He is not listed in David Bebbington's "Baptist MPs in the Nineteenth Century," *BQ* 2 (1981), but is of particular interest in serving as an MP prior to the repeal of the Test and Corporation Acts. See my entry on him in *The Blackwell Dictionary of Evangelical Biography*, ed. Donald Lewis (1995) 1002.

honorary LL.D. At Gower Street, perhaps as a substitute for not being a member of Council, Cox was in 1827 appointed Librarian, Brougham having suggested it as a possibility two years earlier. His salary was 200 pounds sterling per year, out of which it was supposed he would fund an assistant. However, financial exigencies led to his appointment being terminated in 1831.

The funds for the new institution were to be secured by the sale of 1,500 shares of a nominal value of 100 pounds sterling each, with Cox as a foremost advocate and fundraiser. One of the principal purchasers was the Duke of Bedford, for many years president of the noncredal British and Foreign Schools Society of which he regarded Brougham as the founder. The religious issue still obstructed the project. As Irving's comments earlier indicated, while conscientious dissenters could convince themselves without difficulty of the necessity of proceeding on a purely secular, noncredal, basis, Evangelical opinion, represented on the Council by Zachary Macaulay, was less certain. Regretfully declining an invitation to Brougham Hall, Cox wrote with regard to the sale of the shares, "Some of our Evangelicals, however, are at work in another way, and I or you or some of us may expect an attack (besides the caricatures shop) of which I am by no means sorry." He encouraged Brougham to support the idea of launching the sale of a further thousand shares when most of the first issue were secured, and also supported Joseph Hume's recommendation that large shareholders be encouraged to split their holdings to increase the number of sympathizers for the new venture.[23]

Religion remained a problem. Profession New notes that, whereas Evangelicals were troubled by a University that did not teach religion, High Churchman were shocked at the thought of a University that did not teach specifically the religion of the Church of England. Wilberforce suggested "a separate endowment for lectures on the Evidences of Christianity," begging Brougham to "reflect seriously on the consequences of imparting to so influential a body of men . . . all branches of philosophical knowledge, leaving them wholly ignorant of the grounds and basis of Christian truth."

Fundamental questions were being raised in the debate about the nature of the new world's being ushered in by the "industrial revolution" and associated changes. On the one hand, the established church stood for

---

[23]New, *The Life of Henry Brougham*, 364; Brougham Mss (2 August 1825) cited in New, *The Life of Henry Brougham*, 365.

a Christendom view of society with only one legally permitted exposition of Christian truth. Dissent, to be true to its own fundamental principles, could not agree to that, and was even at this early date moving to a pluralist position, necessitated by its cooperation with the establishment men, a powerful Jewish financial interest, those of no religious commitment at all, as well as both orthodox and heterodox dissenters. A long history of disabilities coupled with the insistence of the established church on total control of educational institutions made secularists out of pious dissenters—in other words, made them supporters of an educational institution which itself would be deliberately detached from the advocacy of religious values.[24]

The coalitioning involved in such a process was not unfamiliar to Evangelicals. Of their protest against slavery, the historian Elie Halevy had this to say:

> By a strange paradox men who were Protestant to the backbone, zealots of the dogma of justification by faith, were so devoted to philanthropy that on the common ground of good works they were reconciled with the most lukewarm Christians, even with declared enemies of Christianity.

Indeed, both Brougham and Goldsmid had both been involved in the antislavery campaign, and in that struggle won the confidence of many Evangelicals. Apparently, however, education was another matter, though a younger Macaulay—that is, the historian—came to the defense of the new college in the pages of the *Edinburgh Review*: "We entertain a firm conviction that the principals of liberty, as in government and trade, so also in education, are all important to the happiness of mankind. We do in our souls believe that they are strong with the strength and quick with the vitality of truth."[25]

Brougham went on record as retorting, "It was not because they disregarded religious education that the Council had omitted theological lectureships, but because they deemed the subject too important to be approached lightly or inconsiderately. Their object was to leave the religious instruction of the students to their parents and clergymen."[26]

This statement may have been the spur which led three Anglican clergy who held chairs at the college to announce in the *Times* that, with

---

[24]New, *The Life of Henry Brougham*, 365.
[25]Elie Halevy, *A History of the English People in 1815* (London: Ark, 1949) 383; *Edinburgh Review* (February 1820) cited in New, *The Life of Henry Brougham*, 370-71.
[26]The *Times* (28 February 1828) cited in New, *The Life of Henry Brougham*, 379.

the approbation of the Council, they had made some provision for theological instruction, and that at a place near the University, "a course of divinity lectures will be delivered during the academic session." The Dissenters could hardly stand by, so Cox and the Congregational Joseph Fletcher announced that they would run a similar course outside the University in a former Episcopal Chapel which they purchased for the purpose. The lectures were to be on the Evidences of Christianity, Biblical Literature, and Church History.

The Council disclaimed approval of either, whereupon church and dissent joined forces to try and secure the Council's blessing, with Cox nominated privately to secure Brougham's support for such extracurricular activity. This he did by arguing that such a way of proceeding would disarm the opponents of the college of the frequently uttered charges of godless secularism. Apparently, they were right, for Lord Althorpe was soon indicating that the additional lectures had quite satisfied his qualms about the venture, curious as to how he could become a shareholder.

For the committed Anglican, however, an alternative was soon provided with the establishment of the credally based King's College in 1828. Brougham was quite sanguine about the competition which he likened to that betwixt "British and Foreign," and "National" Schools. Thereafter, what had originally been called London University adopted the title of University College, which—with King's College—subsequently became a part of the federal University of London upon its incorporation in November 1836. The degrees of the new university were to be open "to persons of all religious persuasions, without distinction and without the imposition of any test or disqualification whatsoever."[27]

4. Champion of Religious Liberty

In many ways, Cox personified the activism of nineteenth century dissent, and nowhere was he more active than in the cause of religious freedom. Foremost amongst Baptists in seeking through his own personal energies to champion the cause of religious liberty, he labored without stint to secure recognition for dissenting principles in national life. For three years he was secretary of one of the older bodies, the General Body of Dissenting Ministers, to represent dissenting interests. In fact, in the days

---

[27]University College correspondence no. 647 of September 1828, cited in New, *The Life of Henry Brougham*, 382; S. W. Green, "Sketch of the History of the Faculty" in *London Theological Studies* (1911).

prior to the founding of the Liberation Society, his was one of the names that link a number of independent initiatives. Thus, together with William Newman, he early served on the committee of the Protestant Society for the Protection of Religious Liberty. Founded in 1811 by John Wilks, the radical MP for Boston, this society was set up when it seemed that Lord Sidmouth, as Home Secretary, was set upon further restricting the toleration allowed to dissenters to license their chapels for worship.[28]

Cox was also involved with the Society for Promoting Ecclesiastical Knowledge (1820), which published some of his early work. He was later to become the most active of the three secretaries of the Evangelical Voluntary Association (1839),[29] which sought to raise a "banner against the worldly alliance of the Church with the State, the totalitarian principles of the Roman Church and the Puseyite pretensions of the English Church." This task claimed to be guided by Scripture in which, it was believed, voluntary principles for the propagation of the Gospel were clearly articulated. At the society's first meeting, Cox declared "that the struggle was not for a particular government and administration, but for the emancipation of the religion from secular ties." This was a more modest aim than that of Edward Miall, who urged a radical change in the composition of government as a precondition to church reform. A methodology of "calm investigation and prayerful seeking" was also different from Miall's "tumultuous cry for agitation."[30]

With other Baptists—such as Giles, G. H. Murch, Thomas, Joseph Angus, and Pewtress—Cox served on the committee of the British Voluntary Church Society, also known as the Voluntary Church Association, founded in 1834. Its four secretaries were T. Morrell of Coward College, fellow Baptist Charles Stovel, Thomas Archer, and Joshua Wilson. At its opening meeting, Cox proposed a motion seeking the support of those in the Established Church willing to accept the voluntary principle. Favoring complete candor between voluntary and established-church Christians, Cox was wary of any compromise that would sacrifice principle for the sake of false harmony. Straining the common use of language, he claimed that he was not against the notion of "established"

---

[28] *BM* (June 1818): 235-36; (June 1819): 260; (August 1821): 356.

[29] W. H. Mackintosh, *Disestablishment and Liberation: The Movement for the Separation of the Anglican Church from State Control* (London: Epworth Press, 1972) 8, indicates "the bulk of the business was handled by three secretaries headed by Dr. F. A. Cox."

[30] Ibid, 6-9.

religion, but that the governors of a country could best "establish" religion by their example, by setting religion entirely free rather than advancing it by protective measures which perpetuated the privileges of the Church of England. Church and corn seemed to be protected by like measures, and those who opposed the one used the same or similar arguments to contest the other. While legal measures might secure "forms" of religion, they could not command personal commitment, which had to be nurtured by love, not coerced by law. The unification of all supporters of the voluntary principle was most desirable. If Anglicans would abandon the principles of state support, there would be no need for dissent, for episcopalianism as an ecclesiological system was quite separate form established religion *per se*. Unpersuaded by arguments of "The Church in Danger," Cox argued that if religion were freed to be itself, it would soon establish *itself* in the hearts and minds of the people. Like so many of his colleagues, he argued that the modern history of the United States of America offered ample evidence for this. The seconder of his motion was John Angell James.[31]

At the end of July of the same year, Cox addressed the identical theme when addressing the Liverpool Young Men's Voluntary Church Association on State Establishments of Christianity Injurious to Religion. In his attempt to push "the issue of grievances to the ultimatum of principles," he categorically denied "the authority of governments to prescribe, provide, or in any way interfere with the religion of individuals; which is an affair between conscience and God." National establishments at best could merely secure nominal Christianity, in itself a dangerous commodity. A commitment of the heart must always lie beyond the competence of legislation to deliver.

Governments and monarchs argued that if they had a responsibility to secure the material welfare of their subjects, then *a fortiori*, they must have an obligation to seek the spiritual welfare of their subjects. But Cox believed that this was false reasoning, for in the latter case, the most they could do was set the conditions within which spiritual defense could freely occur. Even Toleration Acts were objectionable. The Act of 1689 may have ameliorated the condition of society and limited in some degree the spirit of ecclesiastical oppression, but with all its limitations it still exemplified the principle of intolerance. "Never can truth be satisfied, or

---

[31]"Report of the Speeches delivered at the Public Meetings of the British Voluntary Church Society, May 19th and 26th, 1834," 26-30.

religion be free, till the Dissenters shall be delivered, alike from the oppression of an establishment, and the mockery of a toleration." State authorities were blasphemous in their abrogation of the sovereignty of Christ in His Church. "The alliance of church and State," it was noted, "is opposed to the Saviour's representation of the spirituality of his dominion." It was a matter of straightforward observation that, where there were strong religious establishments—as in Europe—religion languished, but that it flourished in the United States where the establishment principle was absent.[32]

Along with fellow Baptists Thomas Price and J. Howard Hinton, Cox served on the Council of the Religious Freedom Society, inaugurated in May 1839, following a resolution passed by that Baptist Union which declared state establishments "a palpable departure from the laws of Christ, a gross reflection on his wisdom and power, and the most formidable obstacle in the land to the diffusion of true piety."[33] Cox's engagement was practical, and thus his name (together with those of Murch, Price, Howard Hinton, and Samuel Green) will be found in a petition on behalf of the Chelmsford shoemaker, John Thorogood, imprisoned that year for nonpayment of church rate.[34]

His most significant work, however, was done with the Anti-State Church Association, (1844) which later became the Liberation Society. With Thomas Price and Edward Miall, he was one of the small three-man steering committee appointed by the Leicester Conference of the previous year to set up the London Conference at which the new society was to be launched. Arthur Miall indeed labeled him as one of the few London ministers prepared to take up the state church issue.[35] The Baptist Union was the only general group to send delegates to this conference. After a successful rallying of dissenting sentiment, at the end of the conference, Cox—with Miall and J. M. Hare of the *Patriot*—was appointed as one of the three secretaries of the new body. The following year, along with J. P. Mursell of Leicester, he led the liberationist secession from the Anti-Maynooth Council, for the main body grounded their object to the grant to the Roman Catholic College at Maynooth simply on a common

---

[32]"State Establishments of Christianity Injurious to Religion" (30 July 1839), Crescent Chapel, Everton.
[33]Baptist Union Minutes, 11 May 1839.
[34]*BM* (1839): 627.
[35]Arthur Miall, *Life of Edward Miall* (1884) 91.

Protestantism, whereas the seceders based their protest on their general objection to ecclesiastical endowments. Accordingly they set up a parallel conference of their own of some numerical strength.

Cox also shared with his fellow secretaries in presenting a petition against the Regium Donum, the personal payment which had been paid out of the monarch's private purse for the relief of poor dissenting ministers and their widows. Such funds were made available in recognition of the loyalty of Dissenters to the Hanoverian regime. However, in 1804, when the expenditure was transferred from the royal purse to a parliamentary vote, this was perceived as challenging, even if in a small way, the integrity of the voluntary principle. Accordingly, in 1845 he was one of those who penned an "Address to the Distributors and Recipients of the Parliamentary Grant for the Poor Dissenting Ministers in England and Wales," "to remove this foul blot from the fair fame of their consistency," even though he had earlier been a distributor of the grant. Cox was also involved with C. J. Foster, Professor of Jurisprudence at London University, who like Cox was one of the founders of that institution in drawing up proposals for the amalgamation of the Liberation Society and the Dissenting Deputies. The plan was not, however, implemented because of the Deputies' objections to Miall's belligerent sensationalism.[36]

Cox also exploited every occasion that came his way to rehearse dissenting claims for religious liberty. As early as 1818, he had taken the initiative under the patronage of the Duke of Sussex to found an East London Auxiliary of the British and Foreign Schools society, which he thought more important than even the work of the British and Foreign Bible Society. After all, what was the use of distributing the Scriptures if the poor could not read them? "Knowledge," he argued, "was connected with and sustained industrious habits, and industry promoted individual improvement and national prosperity."[37] As one who had campaigned for the repeal of the Test and Corporation Acts, it was he who was asked at the celebratory dinner, graced by the presence of the Duke of Sussex, to propose the toast of the Archbishops, Bishops, and other members of the Established Church. In 1834 he was the spokesman for the Body of Dissenting Ministers when they claimed their right to address the throne, and was for three years their secretary.[38] B. R.

---

[36]Mackintosh, *Disestablishment and Liberation*, 55.
[37]*BM* (1818): 156-57.
[38]B. L. Manning, *The Protestant Dissenting Deputies* (Cambridge: Cambridge Univer-

Haydon's large canvas, depicting the great Anti-Slavery Convention of 1840, showed Cox present alongside other engaged Baptists such as William Brock, John Howard Hinton, and William Knibb.[39]

In the same year he chaired a meeting of London dissenting ministers campaigning for "that Secular Education concerning which all are agreed and not that Education in Religion on which we are so much divided."[40] Even education was priceless. In 1843 he published *No Modifications: a letter addressed to the Rt Hon Lord John Russell, respecting resolutions presented to him by the House of Commons on the subject of education, occasioned by the proposed bill of Sir James Graham*. This legislation was seen by Baptists as introducing objectional proposals for essentially Anglican education, and thereby the extension of the authority and influence of the established church, under the guise of clauses within a more general Factory Bill. Since the bill was moved at a time when the Church of England appeared to be capitulating to Catholic influence, the dissenting chorus of hostility was shrill, but a generation of England's children were the ones deprived of opportunity when the educational clauses in Graham's legislation were dropped.

By nature a rather reflective and scholarly man, Cox can be properly represented as being essentially coerced into activism by his acute dissenting conscience. Though he clearly achieved high status within his own community, he retained an alert ear for dissenting disabilities which weighed more heavily upon the dissenting body as the nineteenth century progressed. The argument for confessional privilege seemed more and more fraught with difficulty the more the years passed by. The attack upon dissenting disabilities was not, however, special pleading. Cox was equally active in opposing unjust Corn Laws, the legal manifestation of an unjustifiable protection of aristocratic agriculture, as in combating that system of black slavery which underpinned the economy of Jamaica and so bitterly divided society in North America. The exclusiveness of the established church's control of university education was to be amended by the development of new free institutions alongside the old citadels of privilege. At the same time, schooling was not be allowed to become a new monopoly of church power and privilege. This new educational free-

---

sity Press, 1952) 247-47, 461-62.

[39] For further information on Cox and Slavery including his North American visit of 1835, see K. R. M. Short, "English Baptists and American Slavery," *BQ* (1964): 243-62.

[40] *BM* (1840) 198-201.

dom was not created simply to aid personal development. A denomination which failed to exploit such new opportunities for the benefit of the training of its ministry, was guilty of shortchanging its own missionary vocation, for a better educated society put a new premium upon an educated pulpit.[41]

---

[41] A forthcoming article in *BQ*, complementary to this present study, will explore Cox's contribution to Baptist life in apologetics, scholarship and intellectual controversy.

The Evangelical Revival and the Baptists

W. Morgan Patterson

One of the most fascinating and far-reaching events in the post-Reformation period of Christian history was the religious stirring that occurred in England in the eighteenth century. Usually referred to as the Evangelical Revival or the Wesleyan Awakening, it focuses primarily on the distinctive ministry of two men: George Whitefield (1714–1770) and John Wesley (1703–1791).

The Revival their energetic labors spawned had a wholesome, invigorating, and positive impact on the religious scene in particular, and on English society in general. It played a major role in shaping the contours of English life in the latter half of the 18th century and well into the nineteenth century. Its broad influence on England and, to a considerable extent, on the American scene, can hardly be exaggerated.

Although the Evangelical Revival involved the work and ministry of a number of clergymen and other sympathizers, its genius and inspiration centered mainly in the activities of Whitefield and Wesley. It was their vision of the Christian faith and life, their boundless energy and courage, and their unique gifts which sparked and defined the religious fervor that followed.

Both men were Oxford graduates; both were Anglican clergymen; both were evangelical in their preaching and convictions; both were indefatigable itinerants; and both were examples of an unrelenting witness to the Christian gospel. Still, there were marked differences between them. Theologically, Whitefield was a Calvinist, and Wesley leaned towards Arminianism. Whitefield was decidedly more ecumenical in his relations with Christians in other denominations than was Wesley. And Whitefield was the unquestioned popular preacher while Wesley was the consummate organizer.

It was this diversity of gifts, undergirded by a common goal and zeal, that enabled them to touch tens of thousands of people with a decisive, life-changing effect. Also, despite their differences, they were friends, their ministries complemented each other, and they affirmed the efforts of each other. They were colleagues in a common venture, but they were very different in their styles of ministry and in some of their doctrinal convictions.

The aim of this essay is not merely to pay tribute to two remarkable Christian leaders and spokesmen of an earlier century, but rather to try to identify, describe, and assess the substantial impact and influence which they had on Baptists in eighteenth century England. For example, there were dozens of young men (perhaps most notably, Dan Taylor and John Fawcett) who were awakened spiritually by Whitefield, Wesley, and their associates but who eventually became strong Baptists and men of influence and leadership in their denomination and in the communities where they ministered.

Not only individuals, but there were also entire congregations or groups, initially touched by Methodism, who became Baptists. There were numerous examples of interaction between Baptists and Methodists involving debate and discussion, the polemical exchange of pamphlets between Wesley and Baptist pastors, and the castigation of Baptists by both John and Charles Wesley. Yet, at other times, there were friendly comments of appreciation by Baptists for Wesley and for the salutary effects of his ministry throughout England. In a few instances, some Baptists became Methodists, and there occurred the frequent use or purchase of each other's chapels.

Dan Taylor

Probably the most-often-cited example of Methodist influence on the Baptists is Dan Taylor (1738–1816). From being the leader of Methodist prayer meetings to becoming the founder and pastor of the Baptist church in Wadsworth, he later was the major force in the creation of the New Connection of General Baptists in 1770. His natural abilities and strongly held convictions enabled him to provide dynamic leadership for the Baptist cause.

As a teenager, young Taylor was converted and soon began to lead Methodist prayer meetings and to visit the sick in the neighborhood of Halifax. He was encouraged by friends to preach, and he did so in September, 1761. Because his efforts in ministry were laudable, he was urged to obtain the endorsement of John Wesley to become a "traveling preacher." However, Taylor had developed serious reservations about some of Wesley's doctrinal views and "the scheme of discipline which that gentleman had imposed on his followers."

Indeed, Taylor's biographer states that "his independent spirit was not formed to submit to that dictatorship which Mr. Wesley then assumed over the conduct and faith of his preachers."[1] Instead, Taylor withdrew from the Methodists in 1762.

About the same time, four others left the Methodists, and they invited Taylor to preach for them. He consented and "delivered his first discourse for them, in the open air, at a place called *The Nook*, in Wadsworth."[2] Not long afterwards, it became "necessary to determine upon some plan of church order, and some principles of doctrine."[3] In such a circumstance, baptism "became the subject of enquiry," and he concluded "that believers' baptism by immersion was the appointment of Christ"[4] and that he "was himself an unbaptized person."[5]

Thereupon, he applied to several Particular Baptist pastors for baptism,[6] but they all declined to administer it because of Taylor's view that "Jesus tasted death for every man, and made a propitiation for the sins of the whole world."[7]

Ultimately, Taylor was put in touch with a Mr. Jeffries of the General Baptist church in Gamston who baptized him and his friend, John Slater, in a river near Gamston on 16 February 1763.

Taylor then returned to Wadsworth and proceeded to baptize a number of persons. In May, he attended the Lincolnshire Association and thereafter became a part of it. Mr. William Thompson, the General Baptist pastor at Boston, was instrumental in organizing Taylor's friends and disciples into a General Baptist church, the first in Yorkshire. Taylor

---

[1] Adam Taylor, *Memoirs of the Rev. Dan Taylor* (London: printed for the author, 1820) 9. Taylor, the historian of the General Baptists, has virtually outlined the sequence of events in Dan Taylor's shift from Methodists to Baptists. See *The History of the General Baptists* (London: T. Bore, 1818) 2:70-72.

[2] Ibid.

[3] Adam Taylor, *The History of the English General Baptists* (London: printed for the author by T. Bore, 1818) 2:72.

[4] Ibid.

[5] *Memoirs*, 9.

[6] W. T. Whitley listed ten Calvinist Baptist ministers in the general area of Taylor's home who presumably would not baptize him. See *Minutes of the General Assembly of the General Baptists in England*, II (London: Kingsgate Press, 1910) 128. Incidentally, among those Particular Baptist ministers listed are Richard Smith at Wainsgate, William Crabtree at Bradford, and James Hartley at Haworth, all of whom were also products of the Wesleyan Revival.

[7] Taylor, *History*, 2:72.

was formally called as pastor and was ordained in the Autumn of 1763 under the leadership of Gilbert Boyce of Coningsby.

Subsequently, Taylor served churches in Halifax and London, but he is best known as the driving force behind the formation of the New Connection of General Baptists in 1770 over questions of Christology. He gave vigorous, creative, and unstinting leadership to this new group of Baptists. His energy and tirelessness seemed almost unlimited. It might also be noted that in these respects he reflected the characteristics of the peripatetic Wesley, devoted to a ministry of preaching, evangelizing, organizing converts, and providing assistance to the churches. Like Wesley, Taylor was a study in "perpetual motion." As a result, the New Connection under his leadership grew in numbers, vitality, and influence to become a viable denomination in the early nineteenth century.

John Fawcett

John Fawcett (1740–1817) was a second major Baptist figure in the north of England touched by the preaching of the Revival. He was converted in 1755 through a sermon preached by George Whitefield at Bradford. Then, after attending the ministry of William Grimshaw of Haworth for two years, he was baptized in 1758 by William Crabtree, Baptist pastor in Bradford, who himself was a convert of Grimshaw.

Fawcett's influence on Baptists in the years ahead was far-reaching. In 1764, he became pastor of a small congregation at Wainsgate, and then at Hebden Bridge in 1777. Though self-taught, he read voraciously and acquired a broad knowledge of religious subjects and issues.

About 1773, he founded a small school which provided a basic education for many young men who went into the Baptist ministry. At one point, he was offered the leadership of Bristol Academy but declined, and he is regarded as one of the founders of Horton Academy in 1804.

Fawcett was also mentor and friend of John Sutcliff (1752–1814) of Olney, who was one of the founders of the first Baptist missionary society in 1792, and pastor of the church which sent William Carey into the ministry. Sutcliff had been baptized by Fawcett in 1769.

Others who studied with Fawcett included John Foster (1770–1843), for a time a Baptist pastor who later distinguished himself as an essayist.

Also, William Ward of Serampore, early Baptist missionary to India and colleague of William Carey.[8]

Fawcett was a published author of, among other works, the two-volume Devotional Family Bible. Among his most lasting contributions was the hymn "Blest Be the Tie That Binds Our Hearts in Christian Love," a testimony to his commitment to his flock, and now sung by Baptists and others for more than two hundred years. He was a strong supporter of associational life among Baptists and is credited with being one of the founders of the Lancashire and Yorkshire Baptist Association in 1787.[9] One other interesting connection of Fawcett with the Wesleyan Revival involved his father-in-law, John Skirrow, and the church at Bingley. Skirrow was excluded from the Methodists because of his Calvinism and was subsequently baptized by Fawcett along with nine others. As a result, a church was formed, and a chapel was erected in 1764. John Wesley, who visited Bingley in 1766, complained "with a heavy heart that so many Methodists here have gone over to the Anabaptists."[10]

William Grimshaw

William Grimshaw (1708–1763), the Anglican vicar of Haworth from 1742 until his death, was known for his fervent evangelical preaching, his energetic ministry, his tolerant attitude towards all Christians, and his friendship with Whitefield and both John and Charles Wesley.

Clearly regarded as supportive of the Methodist revival, Grimshaw welcomed Whitefield and the Wesleys into his parish and pulpit on numerous occasions, and they carried on a correspondence which indicated mutual affection and respect. In several instances, Grimshaw and Whitefield even travelled together on brief preaching excursions. As for Grimshaw's commitment to John Wesley, one biographer repeatedly refers to him as Wesley's "lieutenant in the North,"[11] and he imitated

---

[8]It was Ward who on 6 September 1812, in Calcutta, baptized Adoniram Judson and Anne Judson, and then Luther Rice in November. Sent to India as Congregational missionaries, they became the first Baptist missionaries from America. The Judsons proceeded to have an impressive ministry in Burma, and Rice returned to the United States to help organize the Triennial Convention in 1814, the first national body of Baptists in America.

[9]*The Baptists of Yorkshire: Being the Centenary Memorial Volume of the Yorkshire Baptist Association* (London: Kingsgate Press, 1912) 101.

[10]Ibid., 186.

[11]Frank Baker, *John Wesley and the Church of England*, 59, 115, 165. Baker's major work on Grimshaw is *William Grimshaw 1708–1763* (London: Epworth Press, 1963).

Wesley in engaging in some itinerant preaching in the parishes of Yorkshire.

Grimshaw's personality, piety, and catholicity led him to appreciate and to interact with Christians of all types: Methodists, Independents, Presbyterians, Quakers, and others. But it was the Baptists on whom he probably had the greatest and widest influence. Baker, emphasizing this point, states that his "direct impact on Baptist history is considerable," even "incalculable . . . in the immediate area" of his parish.[12]

Under Grimshaw's preaching at least four young men were converted who eventually became Baptist ministers. They were James Hartley, William Crabtree, Richard Smith, and John Parker. Also, his influence on Fawcett and Taylor can be seen as well.

James Hartley (1722–1780) became the first Baptist pastor in Haworth after attending the ministry of Grimshaw for several years. He became a Baptist by 1748 and soon gathered others in Haworth to form a Baptist congregation in 1752. He served the church until his death in 1780.

The success of his efforts might be indicated by the enlargement of the chapel in 1775. Also, Grimshaw's half-humorous comment is probably evidence of Hartley's effectiveness in Haworth, "The worst of it is, that so many of my chickens turn ducks."[13] Yet, the two men remained good friends with Grimshaw "officiating at his two marriages and at his first wife's funeral."[14]

Fawcett, who knew Hartley quite well, comments in his Memoirs on Hartley's diligent study of the Scriptures, his abilities as pastor and preacher, and the high esteem in which he was held by all who knew him.[15]

As a young man, William Crabtree, by his own confession, lived a rowdy life of drunkenness, cursing, and swearing. However, he had occasion to hear Grimshaw preach in his neighborhood of Wadsworth. Grimshaw spoke on the Prodigal Son, and Crabtree said that it struck him to the heart. Thereafter, he began to attend Grimshaw's services regularly.[16]

---

[12]Frank Baker, "The Rev. William Grimshaw (1708–1763) and the Eighteenth Century Revival of Religion in England" (Ph.D. dissertation, University of Nottingham, 1961) 470.
[13]Ibid., 243.
[14]Ibid., 244.
[15]Quoted by Joseph Ivimey, *A History of the English Baptists*, IV (London: Isaac Taylor Hinton, 1830) 579-82.
[16]Isaac Mann, *Memoirs of the Late Rev. Wm. Crabtree* (London: Button and Son,

Nevertheless, by 1750 he had become a member of the Baptist church at nearby Wainsgate where Richard Smith was pastor at that time and where Crabtree was eventually elected to the office of deacon.

Then, in 1753, he was ordained to the pastoral office by James Hartley and Richard Smith, and he began his ministry at Bradford to the little congregation of twenty-three members. Smith had recommended him to the people in Bradford saying that "brother Crabtree [was] one whom he thought the Lord had cut out for a minister," and so Crabtree was invited "to come over and exercise once amongst us upon trial."[17] He served that church until his death in 1803.

Besides having baptized Fawcett in 1758, Crabtree extended his influence in founding other Baptist churches, ordaining young men for the ministry, and participating actively in the Baptist cause. For example, in the initial effort to raise money on behalf of the Baptist Missionary Society to send William Carey to India in 1793, Crabtree, then in his seventies, raised more than £40—"going even to the vicar and curate, who each gave cheerfully a guinea."[18]

Richard Smith, after attending the ministry of Grimshaw as a young man, gave evidence of "sincere piety" and a "steady attachment to the interests of religion."[19] It became the opinion of his friends that he possessed gifts for ministry, and he was urged "to give a word of exhortation, or to expound some portion of Scripture." Before long, he was preaching in Wadsworth in private houses and barns and enjoying a good response.

About 1750, a meetinghouse was erected at nearby Wainsgate, and Smith became pastor of a small congregation. His ministry there continued until his death in 1763 in his fifty-fourth year. He was succeeded by John Fawcett.

The influence of Smith on James Hartley and William Crabtree was weighty. They were "raised up" by the Wainsgate church and subsequently sent into the ministry of the Baptist interests in Haworth and Bradford respectively.

1815) 13-16.

[17]Ibid., 22.

[18]S. Pearce Carey, *William Carey* (London: Hodder and Stoughton, 1923) 111.

[19]"Sketch of the Life and Character of Mr. Richard Smith . . . ," in *The New Theological Repository* 2 (1801): 124. This tribute to Smith was written by Fawcett and published first in John Rippon's *The Baptist Annual Register* 3:393-96.

In his eulogy of Smith, Fawcett states that the Wainsgate Baptist church led by Smith "may justly be considered as a kind of mother to many religious societies of the same faith and order, in the neighbouring towns and villages."[20]

As a young man, John Parker struggled with spiritual questions and his own sinfulness, and he was urged to hear the eminent Grimshaw. At last he consented to go and was converted under Grimshaw's exposition of the Thirty-Nine Articles. Not long afterward, however, he was baptized by Alvery Jackson, pastor of the Baptist church at Barnoldswick.[21]

In 1753 he entered the ministry and began preaching at Bolland. When Jackson died in 1763, Parker succeeded him at Barnoldswick, and he served that church for twenty-five years. Then, in 1790 he moved to Wainsgate where poor health limited his activities, and he died in 1793.

Grimshaw's influence on each of these men and others was clear and decisive at a critical point in their lives. They attributed to him, in large part, their transformation, and they maintained a friendly relationship with him as long as he lived.

Baker observes that "the Baptists caused Grimshaw the most trouble, but among them he exercised a greater influence than among other dissenters."[22] There was mutual appreciation and genuine affection between them, and the Baptists spoke warmly of his versatile, winsome, and effective ministry. Upon the death of Grimshaw, Dan Taylor composed a lofty ninety-five-line poetic tribute to him and later published it in the *General Baptist Magazine*.[23]

Besides those Baptist ministers named above, whose conversion and early spiritual development was traceable to William Grimshaw, there were many others who attributed their personal awakening to the Methodists and to those evangelical churchmen who were sympathetic to the Revival. Three examples will suffice.

Francis Smith (1719–1796), pastor of the General Baptist church at Melbourne, Derbyshire, tells in his memoirs how he earlier had come

---

[20]Ibid., 2:125-26.
[21]Fawcett wrote a brief biographical essay on Parker, and it was published in *The Baptist Annual Register* 2:100-107.
[22]Baker, 243.
[23]Vol. 2, 129-30.

under the influence of Methodist preachers and was convicted of his sins "in the midst of my wild career."[24]

Joseph Piccop at first preached among the Methodists who presently excluded him because of his Calvinism. He found Baptists at Accrington and was baptized. He introduced believer's baptism at Bolton and then served the church at Bacup from 1744 to 1773. He was known for his energy and wide-ranging influence.[25]

William Hague of Malton and several Methodist friends adopted Calvinist doctrines, became acquainted with members of the church at Bridlington, and were baptized in 1776. A church was founded in Scarborough with Hague as pastor. He served the congregation for forty-eight years, and the chapel was enlarged three times.[26]

Finally, it must be noted that besides Grimshaw, there were other evangelical leaders who had an influence on the Baptists: William Romaine of Blackfriars, Howel Harris of Wales, Henry Venn of Huddersfield, and Selina Hastings, Countess of Huntingdon.

John Wesley and the Baptists

During the course of John Wesley's fifty-year-long ministry he often encountered Baptists for whom he did not have much patience or respect. He resented their effective proselytizing of his converts, their disputatious spirit, and their preoccupation with believer's baptism. He and his brother Charles were often openly critical of the Baptists.

For example, they often referred to the Baptists by using the highly pejorative term "Anabaptist." After preaching at Heptonstall in 1766, he wrote in his Journal: "The renegade Methodists, first turning Calvinists, then Anabaptists, made much confusion here for a season."[27] A few days later he wrote: "At one I preached at Bingley, but with an heavy heart, finding so many of the Methodists here, as well as at Haworth, perverted by the Anabaptists."[28]

---

[24]*The General Baptist Magazine* 1 (1798): 264. See also *Historic Memorials of Barton & Melbourne General Baptist Churches*, by J. R. Godfrey (Leicester: Buck, Winks and Son, 1891) 111-17.

[25]W. T. Whitley, *Baptists of Northwest England 1649–1913* (London: Kingsgate Press, 1913) 101-104, 131-32, 326.

[26]C. E. Shipley, "The Churches of the East and North Ridings District," in *The Baptists of Yorkshire*, 204-205.

[27]*John Wesley's Journal*, 31 July 1766.

[28]Ibid., 4 August 1766.

In a letter to Thomas Wride, dated June 23, 1771, Wesley wrote: "I desire that neither any preacher of ours nor any member of our Society would on any pretense go to an Anabaptist meeting. It is the way to destroy the Society. This we have experienced over and over."[29]

In a sermon at Sevenoaks in 1788, Wesley is alleged to have said:

> When a Sinner is just awakened to see his state as a Sinner, the people called Anabaptists, begin to trouble him about outward forms and modes of Worship, and that of Baptism; but they had better cut his throat, for it is sending of him to Hell and perdition.[30]

Several ministers signed a statement confirming the accuracy of the words and sent the information to Mr. William Kingsford. Kingsford then published a sixteen-page tract entitled *A Vindication of the Baptists*, and it went through at least five editions. It also began a polemical exchange between Kingsford and a Methodist defender identified as "T. C."

There were other episodes in which Wesley and Baptists aired their differing convictions on various subjects. In the Summer of 1748, Wesley visited Coningsby where the beloved Gilbert Boyce was the General Baptist minister. Wesley claimed that Boyce had "begged" him to lodge with him whenever he came to town. So, he called on Boyce, and afterwards Wesley wrote:

> I was scarce set down in his house, before he fell upon the point of baptism. I waived the dispute for some time; but finding there was no remedy, I came close to the question, and we kept to it for about an hour and half. From that time we let the matter rest, and confirmed our love towards each other.[31]

Thereafter, Boyce and Wesley exchanged letters in which they continued to debate their views of baptism and other subjects.[32] Then, in 1770, Boyce published *A Serious Reply to the Rev. Mr. John Wesley in particular, and to the people called Methodists in general*. In it he carefully articulated his appreciation for the good work Wesley had done, but he also outlined their disagreements. Boyce was plain-spoken and cogent in his rebuttal of Wesley, but his spirit was irenic.

---

[29]*The Letters of the Rev. John Wesley, A.M.*, ed. John Telford (London: Epworth Press, 1931) 5:260.

[30]William Kingsford, *A Vindication of the Baptists, from the Criminality of a Charge Exhibited against Them by the Rev. Mr. Wesley* (Canterbury: J. Grove, 1788) 3.

[31]*John Wesley's Journal*, 5 July 1748.

[32]See Wesley's letter to Boyce, 22 May 1750, ibid., 3:35-37.

In 1752, a published exchange of views occurred between Wesley and John Gill, the high Calvinist Baptist theologian and longtime pastor in London. In the preceding year, Wesley had written *Serious Thoughts upon the Perseverance of the Saints* in which he stated that "a saint may fall away" and "perish everlastingly."

Gill replied with a fifty-nine page essay entitled *The Doctrine of the Saints Final Perseverance, Asserted and Vindicated*. In it he forcefully asserted that it is a doctrine "fully expressed in the sacred scripture." In response to this pamphlet, Wesley published *Predestination Calmly Considered* in which he sought to refute the Calvinist doctrine of election.

Once more, Gill published *The Doctrine of Predestination Stated, and Set in the Scripture—Light* (1752). The subtitle identifies the author's aim: "In Opposition to Mr. Wesley's Predestination calmly Consider'd."

This dispute between the two men seems to have ended with a twelve-page tract by Wesley entitled *An Answer To All which the Revd. Dr. Gill Has Printed on the Final Perseverance of the Saints* (1754). It is a poem of thirty-seven stanzas of eight lines each, and it has been described as "scorchingly sarcastic."[33]

One other exchange with a Baptist needs to be noted. In 1775, Wesley published *A Calm Address to Our American Colonies* in which he took the side of Britain and taxation, against the position espoused by the colonies. His views precipitated numerous replies including some from English Baptists. Caleb Evans, respected Baptist minister in Bristol, wrote *A Letter to the Rev. John Wesley, Occasioned by his "Calm Address to the American Colonies"* (1775). In it Evans strongly contradicts Wesley stating that those who are taxed without representation are, in effect, slaves. Evans went on to answer other Methodist writers who had sided with Wesley.

Charles Wesley (1707–1788)

Charles Wesley, the notable and popular hymn writer, shared his brother's distaste for the "bigoted Baptists," and he sometimes spoke harshly of them. In his *Journal* he described a meeting at Gawksholm where he preached. He wrote:

---

[33]Luke Tyerman, *The Life and Times of the Rev. John Wesley, M.A., Founder of the Methodists* (London: Hodder and Stoughton, 1840) 2:191.

> Several Baptists were present, a carnal, cavilling, contentious sect, always watching to steal away our children, and make them as dead as themselves. Mr. Allen informed me that they have carried off no less than fifty out of one Society, and that several Baptist meetings are wholly made out of old Methodists.[34]

In a stanza composed by Charles Wesley, he defended infant baptism and railed against the "sect" that opposed it as he wrote:

> Partisans of a narrow sect
> Your cruelty confess
> Nor still inhumanly reject
> Whom Jesus would embrace.
> Your little ones preclude them not
> From the baptismal flood brought
> But let them now to Christ be saved
> And join the Church of God.[35]

George Whitefield and the Baptists

The interaction of Baptists with George Whitefield was very different from their relations with the Wesleys. The comments of contemporary Baptists, both in England and America, were uniformly laudatory. Whitefield was admired and loved, and he was looked upon as a friend of Baptists. He was always welcomed in Baptists pulpits and by Baptist auditors. Even General Baptists, whose theology differed from the Calvinism of Whitefield, were often drawn to the charisma of Whitefield and his electrifying sermons.

Several Baptist leaders besides Fawcett and Taylor were deeply affected by the preaching of Whitefield, including Robert Robinson of Cambridge, Samuel Medley of Liverpool, Andrew Gifford of Bristol, Benjamin Randall of New Hampshire who founded the denomination of Free Will Baptists, and Shubael Stearns of America, a leader of the Separate Baptists. Each had a different story to tell, but all expressed their spiritual indebtedness to the ministry of George Whitefield.[36]

---

[34]*Charles Wesley's Journal*, 18 October 1756, 2:128.
[35]From C. Wesley MSS, Cambridge University Library, cited by Olin C. Robison, "The Particular Baptists in England 1760–1820" (D.Phil. diss., Oxford University, 1963) 144.
[36]A good brief survey of several Baptist leaders influenced by Whitefield is found in *The English Baptists of the Eighteenth Century*, by Raymond Brown (London: Baptist Historical Society, 1986) 66-82 et passim. See also "The Influence of Whitefield on

Joseph Ivimey, Baptist historian and pastor in London in the early nineteenth century, had high praise for Whitefield's evangelistic labors, his selfless spirit, and his Calvinist views. It is a singular tribute he paid to Whitefield when he said:

> It is probable, but for the rise of such a preacher as Whitefield, both as to his principles, spirit, and manner of address . . . that infidelity would, in this country, have triumphed over Christianity.[37]

Other Instances of Wesleyan Influence

Charles Whitfield (1748–1821) was converted under the preaching of John Wesley when Wesley visited Newcastle. He became a Methodist preacher for a time but then adopted Calvinist views. Wesley, upon hearing him pray, stated, "Brother Whitfield has offered up a Calvinistic prayer." Nevertheless, Wesley tried to save the young man for his cause by giving him several volumes of his sermons to read.

By 1770, however, Whitfield changed his view on baptism and joined the Baptist church at Tuthill-stairs. Then, a member of the Baptist church at Hamsterley heard him preach, and he was invited to supply at Hamsterley. In 1771 he accepted their call to become pastor, and he enjoyed a long and active ministry both at Hamsterley and in the denomination.[38]

William Terry was a clock and watchmaker in Bedal who had been "a hearer of the late Rev. and celebrated John Wesley and his connexion." But, as a result of his study of the Bible he became a convinced Calvinist. Then, on 5 January 1793, he was baptized by Charles Whitfield, the Particular Baptist pastor at Hamsterley, and Terry preached that very evening.

Later in the year a Baptist church was organized at Snape, and Mr. Terry became its pastor. The ordination service was

> conducted in a dwelling house, the poor people not having a meeting house; a barn being too dark and cold; and their *friendly* neighbours the Quakers and Methodists at Massam, being so unfriendly as each to deny the use of their respective houses upon this occasion.[39]

Baptists" by W. T. Whitley in *The Baptist Quarterly* 5 (1930–1931): 30-36.
[37]Ivimey, *A History of the English Baptists* 3:280-81.
[38]David Douglas, *History of the Baptist Churches in the North of England, from 1648 to 1845* (London: Houlston and Stoneman, 1846) 199-204 et passim.
[39]Rippon, *The Baptist Annual Register* 2:122. Also, 15-16.

In 1750, John Stephens was called as pastor of the Devonshire Square church in London. Several Baptist ministers were uneasy about assisting in his ordination because of his earlier association with the Methodists. As a consequence, Mr. Stephens was invited to attend a meeting of the ministers, and he "gave an account of his Total Seperation [sic] from the Methodists to the Satisfaction of the Brethren."[40]

The role of the Methodists can be seen among a group of earnest evangelical independents in the Barton area who afterwards became Baptists. Adam Taylor told the story of these Christians by tracing their first impulse to conversion back to Methodist influence. Apparently, the origin of the group was marked by the preaching of David Taylor in 1741. Taylor was in the employ of Selina Hastings, friend and ardent supporter of the Wesleys and Whitefield.

By 1745 the converts had formed a church at Barton, though they were not yet Baptists. First, they concluded that baptism should be by immersion though they continued to baptize infants. Then, by 1755, as the result of further study of the New Testament, they began to practice believer's baptism by immersion. Believing there was no one who would baptize them, they instituted believer's baptism on their own. The record states:

> It was agreed, that Mr. Donisthorpe should first baptize Mr. Kendrick, and then Mr. Kendrick should baptize him: after which, they should unite in administering the ordinance to the rest of their associates.[41]

Eventually, out of this community of Baptists several churches were formed. By 1760 four centers had grown out of the Barton group and, besides Barton, they included Melbourne, Kegworth, Loughborough, and Kirkby Woodhouse. In the years following, out of these churches came more than a dozen others.[42] Prominent among those associated with these Baptists was Samuel Deacon of Ratby, who was converted under the preaching of David Taylor. He later became the pastor of the General

---

[40]"The Baptist Board Minutes," in *Transactions of the Baptist Historical Society* 5 (April 1917): 232.

[41]Taylor, *History* 2:31. One treatment of the evolution of this congregation and its early leaders/pastors appears in *Historic Memorials of Barton & Melbourne General Baptist Churches* (Leicester: Buck, Winks and Son, 1891) 4-5, 14-15, et passim. Another is "Barton-in-the-Beans," by Percy Austin, in *The Baptist Quarterly* 11 (1942–1945): 417-22.

[42]Austin, ibid., 418, 420.

Baptist church at Barton and a founder of the New Connection of General Baptists in 1770.

The obituary of Rev. Joshua Wood of Sallendine Nook indicated that at about the age of fourteen he frequently accompanied his mother "to hear those ministers who are commonly distinguished by the name of Methodists." "It pleased God to make use of their preaching for the awakening of . . . his need of the salvation which is in Jesus Christ." He made a public profession of religion at seventeen "when he joined Mr. Wesley's society at Leeds." However, after hearing Whitefield preach, "he embraced the doctrines commonly called Calvinistic, and . . . left the society above named."

Sometime later, he "was convinced that the baptism of believers by immersion is the one baptism which was instituted by Jesus Christ." He was then baptized in 1760 by James Hartley of Haworth. Not long after that, he began to preach at the Baptist church at Halifax and was ordained pastor. About 1773 he moved to Sallendine Nook where he served until his death in 1794.[43]

One other interesting example of Baptist/Methodist interaction involved the Broadmead Church in Bristol as early as 1742. The congregation appointed representatives to visit three of their members "to reprove them for going frequently to hear John and Charles Wesley." The church wanted to learn "whether they had imbibed their (the Wesleys') corrupt notions." It was reported by the church's "messengers" that the "said members had fallen into the error of general redemption, falling from grace, and sinless perfection in this life."

As a result, "said members" were admonished to read the Scriptures and to attend services regularly at Broadmead. In the meantime, they should not receive communion if they in fact had adopted Methodist doctrines. Two years later, still another incident of this kind occurred.[44]

Friendly Relations between Baptists and Methodists

There were numerous instances in which Baptists and Methodists interacted in a friendly manner, participated in common services, exchanged

---

[43] Rippon, *The Baptist Annual Register* 2:223-28.
[44] J. Jackson Goadby, *Bye-Paths in Baptist History: A Collection of Interesting, Instructive, and Curious Information, Not Generally Known, concerning the Baptist Denomination* (London: Elliot Stock, 1871) 257-58.

pulpits and chapels, spoke well of each other, and, in general, conducted themselves toward each other in a positive and cordial way.

John Wesley recorded in his *Journal* an incident in Boston. Because the wind was blowing too hard for him to preach out of doors, "Thompson, a friendly Anabaptist, offering me the use of his large meetinghouse, I willingly accepted the offer. I preached to most of the chief persons in the town."[45]

At Portsea, under the ministry of John Lacey, pastor from 1733 until his death in 1781, George Whitefield "and his coadjutors" were always "cheerfully received and cordially encouraged." They stayed in the home of one of the members of the church and "every Wednesday evening had the free use of his pulpit." Some fellow ministers "thought him wrong in encouraging the Methodists." However, Lacey replied, "Would to God that Jesus Christ was preached at the corner of every street, I would not care by whom."[46]

During the 1780's, Daniel Miall served as assistant to the pastor at Portsea and later became pastor. It is said of him that he began "preaching, though a Baptist, among Mr. Wesley's people, and the founder of the Methodists showed him much attention" despite his Calvinist views.[47]

Elsewhere, in a note on the Baptist church in Canterbury, served by Samuel Rowles, the comment is made:

> In this town a monthly evening of prayer, for the success of the gospel, is observed in rotation at the three meetings belonging to the Baptists, Lady Huntingdon's, and Mr. Wesley's people.[48]

At a conference of General Baptist ministers held at Hugglescoat in 1779, the following question was raised:

> Is it right for one of the ministers in this Connection to preach amongst the Methodists, the Indipendants [*sic*], the Whitefieldites, Perticular [*sic*] Baptists etc.?

---

[45]*John Wesley's Journal*, 17 June 1780. William Thompson was the General Baptist pastor in Boston from 1762 until his death in 1794. It was he who helped Dan Taylor organize the Wadsworth folk into a church. They became fast friends, and Thompson was one of the founders of the New Connection in 1770.

[46]Ivimey, *A History of the English Baptists* 4:487.

[47]Ibid., 4:492.

[48]Rippon, *The Baptist Annual Register* 3:18-19.

Ansr. Yes! provided, the minister is so far from every place in our Connection that he can nether [sic] hear nor preach at any of them.[49]

In 1796, William Steadman and a fellow minister undertook a ministry of itinerant preaching in the County of Cornwall at the request of the Baptist Missionary Society. He reported that "in some neighbourhoods, the Methodists lent us their place of worship; in others we used private houses."[50]

Steadman's contact with the people of Cornwall led him to state that "the labours and successes of the Methodists have largely contributed to civilize the inhabitants in general, and to bring them into the habits of hearing the word."[51] In a letter to John Rippon, Steadman made other complimentary remarks about the support and interest he found among the Methodists.[52]

In a brief account of the ordination of Thomas Morgan at Birmingham in 1802, led by Dr. Ryland of Bristol and Andrew Fuller of Kettering, it was observed:

> On the morning of the Ordination, the Meeting-house in Cannon-street, appearing too small to contain the congregation expected to assemble, the Methodists very kindly offered the use of their chapel, in Cherry-street, which afforded comfortable accommodation.[53]

A similar incident occurred at the ordination of Moses Fisher as pastor of the Particular Baptist church in New Brentford. The members of his church expressed gratitude for the "kindness of the friends in Mr. Wesley's connection, who gave them the use of their chapel in Old Brentford, for the occasion."[54]

In 1799, the *General Baptist Magazine* printed a fascinating five-page book review. The book's title was *An Address to the Volunteer Corps of Great Britain*, written by Robert Hardy, identified as Curate of Westbourne, Vicar of Stoughton, and Chaplain to his Royal Highness the Prince of Wales.

Apparently, the book's author had targeted the Methodists for severe criticism because of their dissent from the Church of England. At one

---

[49]*Transactions of the Baptist Historical Society* 5 (July 1916): 119.
[50]Rippon, *The Baptist Annual Register* 2:460.
[51]Ibid., 2:461.
[52]Ibid., 3:57.
[53]Ibid., 4:1111.
[54]Ibid., 4:1148.

point, Hardy stated that "the Methodists have not even the appearance of apostolic authority." At the same time, Hardy defended those Anglican ministers who might happen on occasion to have been guilty of "idle, dissolute, and vicious lives."

Then, the reviewer skewers the views, comments, and attitudes of Hardy as the reviewer comes to the defense of the Methodists. The review is a telling refutation of the Curate's criticisms of Methodism and an articulate vindication of Methodism's effectiveness in reforming "more wicked men within these last forty years than all the Curates in the kingdom have."[55]

The reviewer is decidedly supportive of Methodist efforts to advance the gospel. Although the writer is not named, the *General Baptist Magazine* was published in London "for D. Taylor."

Epilogue

The Evangelical Revival had a significant impact on both the General Baptists and the Particular Baptists. The spirit of revival engendered by the Wesleys and Whitefield prompted a new evangelistic spirit among the Baptists, manifested in making new converts and forming new churches. There was also the spiritual awakening of dozens of young men who became active and influential ministers in both denominations of Baptists.

There were instances of entire congregations becoming Baptists, and, in general, the existing churches of Baptists were significantly strengthened by the infusion of new members. The formation of the New Connection of General Baptists is clearly traceable in part to the influence of the Revival on Dan Taylor and others. Without doubt, the Revival helped greatly to revitalize the Baptists who, until mid-century, were languishing and often preoccupied with theological minutiae and set forms of worship.

Most of the superlatives used to describe the work of John Wesley are appropriate. The lingering effects of his incredible labors touched more people than any other religious leader in the eighteenth century. Although George Whitefield enjoyed wide popularity and the genuine affection of multitudes both in England and America, his efforts were not institutionalized as were those of Wesley, and therefore not as long-

---

[55]Vol. 2, 301-305.

lasting or as far-reaching. But Baptists were and are deeply indebted to the indomitable faith and energetic ministries of these two men.

Adam Taylor, the historian of the General Baptists, writing in 1818, dealt with the extraordinary contributions of Whitefield and Wesley. After describing the unhappy and declining character of religion in England in the early eighteenth century, Taylor remarked:

> In this gloomy state, it pleased God to send forth his zealous servants, Messrs. Wesley and Whitfield to rouse our countrymen to an attention to the most important of all concerns, the salvation of their immortal souls. These useful men encountered violent opposition; but were blest with astonishing success.[56]

---

[56]*The History of the English General Baptists*, 2:2-3.

The English Baptist Legacy of Freedom and the American Experience

William R. Estep

Out of the turbulent history of the English Reformation, the English Baptist movement was born. It was not a neat development, as few religious events were in the post-Elizabethan Settlement years. There were underground religious congregations even before 1558, the exact nature of which has been subject to debate, but with the executions of Separatist leaders, Henry Barrowe, John Greenwood, and John Penry in 1593, the centers of Separatism shifted from England to Holland.[1]

Once freed from the Spanish yoke, the Netherlands had begun to enjoy the fresh air of religious toleration. It was a temptation the harassed and persecuted dissenters found increasingly difficult to resist. With the rejection of the Millenary Petition by King James I at the Hampton Court Conference in 1604, other Separatists gave up on reforming the Church of England—or, for that matter, even being allowed to worship in peace, and joined their fellow countrymen on the other side of the English Channel.

Among those who had exhausted all available options in England was John Smyth, an ordained clergyman of the Church of England, and former tutor at Christ's College, Cambridge. Smyth had become a Puritan while at Cambridge, and was identified until he led in the formation of a Separatist church at Gainsborough (ca. 1606). By 1607 he and his congregation had determined to leave England and its oppression behind. Smyth was well aware of some of the risks he and his followers were taking—one being Anabaptism, which some English Separatists had already embraced.[2] He warned his flock, "Wee being Now Come into a

---

[1] For contrasting views on the nature of Separatism in England see Irvin B. Horst, *The Radical Brethren: Anabaptism and the English Reformation to 1558* (Niewwkoop: B. DeGraat, 1972); Michael R. Watts, *The Dissenters*, vol. 1 (Oxford: Clarendon Press, 1978); B. R. White, *The English Separatist Tradition* (Oxford: Oxford University Press, 1971).

[2] Shortly after reaching Holland in 1597, some of Francis Johnson's church were rebaptized at Kampen and Naarden. Few of the names are known, but at least a Thomas Mitchell, one of those who underwent a "second baptism," is known have returned to England to spread the news and share his faith.

place of libertie are in Great danger if wee look not well to our wayes, for wee are like men set upon the iyce and therefore may ezely slyde and fall."[3]

Once the Smyth congregation had arrived in Amsterdam, they discovered that Francis Johnson's church, which had emigrated some ten years before, was roused over yet another controversy. With the arrival of John Robinson and his followers from Scrooby, the situation became even more complicated. Even though the Robinson congregation moved to Leiden within a few months, Robinson could not refrain from involving himself in controversies with Francis Johnson, Henry Ainsworth, John Smyth, and virtually all other Separatists in Holland. Robinson claimed that the French Reformed Church, with the exception of a few nonessentials, was more in agreement with his position than that of any of the English Separatists.[4] He also vigorously defended the decrees of the Synod of Dort.[5] It is not surprising that Smyth found the Mennonites, particularly the Waterlanders, more congenial than his fellow Separatists. Dutch authorities became somewhat exasperated with the factious English, who seemed to be constantly excommunicating one another.[6]

---

[3]William Bradford, *Dialogue*, 137, cited by Keith L. Sprunger, *Dutch Puritanism* (Leiden: E. J. Brill, 1982) 31.

[4]John Robinson, "Correspondence with Sir John Wolstenholme." In this letter, signed by John Robinson and William Brewster, the writers attempt to explain their theological position to enhance their image in the eyes of a very important member of the Virginia Company. It was written on 27 January 1617, from Leyden in preparation for leaving Holland for the American colony. See *The Works of John Robinson, Pastor of the Pilgrim Fathers*, vol. 3, ed. Robert Ashton (London: John Snow, 1851) 487-89.

[5]John Robinson, *A Just and Necessary Apology of Certain Christians*, printed in 1625; in reprint edition: *The Works of John Robinson*, vol. 3, ed. Robert Ashton (London: John Snow, 1851) 488. On 168, Robinson described the institution of baptism by John Smyth, which he claimed to have received from some of the members of the Smyth congregation. "Mr. Smyth, Mr. Helwisse, and the rest, having utterly dissolved and disclaimed their former church state and ministry, came together to erect a new church by baptism; unto which they also ascribe so great virtue, as that they would not so much as pray together before they had it. And after some straining of courtesy who should begin, and that of John Baptist, Matt. iii. 14, misalleged. Mr. Smyth baptized himself, and next Mr. Helwisse, and so the rest, making their particular confessions." Robinson followed the description with a scathing denunciation of Smyth and his self-baptism. Smyth repented of his precipitous action and sought to unite with the Waterlander Mennonites with which church in Amsterdam the majority of his followers united after his death.

[6]Keith L. Sprunger, *Dutch Puritanism* (Leiden: E. J. Brill, 1982) 67. Sprunger describes the state of Separatism in the Netherlands: "From the outside looking in, the world of Amsterdam Separatism was a whirl of motion and scandal." Johnson was accused by Ainsworth; Ainsworth was accused by Johnson; Smyth ("drunken with the

As the English Separatists became more and more intolerant of one another, Smyth became more gentle and kind. As Michael Watts at the University of Nottingham puts it, "Smyth came to learn the virtues not only of toleration, but of tolerance also."[7] Smyth wrote in his last work that differences in "the outward church" would not cause him "to refuse the brotherhood of anie penitent and faithful Christian whatsoever."[8]

1. The First English Baptists

Back in Gainsborough, Smyth's Separatist congregation had been gathered on the basis of a covenant, but once in the Netherlands, the question of how a church should be constituted was raised anew. This was doubtless prompted by new questions regarding the validity of infant baptism. A year or so later, the transplanted church had reached the conclusion that according to the New Testament, only baptized believers constituted a true church. Once this question was settled, another arose: "How to begin?" When Helwys refused to baptize his pastor, Smyth baptized himself by affusion, and then proceeded to baptize the others upon their own personal confessions of faith.[9]

The ridicule heaped upon Smyth by his fellow Separatists virtually obscured his other convictions regarding the church and religious freedom. By 1610 he and the members of his church were living and wor-

---

dregges of error, and strange phantasies') was rejected by both Johnson and Ainsworth; Robinson held Johnson as apostate; Johnson thought Robinson even more apostate. John Paget marvelled at it all; "of those separate from the Church of God, there are many sorts" and "sundry sects." The constant spectacle of excommunications and schisms gave Separatism its ill repute in Amsterdam. Hugh Peter told them: "You are hardly thought on because you have excommunicated so many honest men."

[7]Watts, *The Dissenters* 1:48.

[8]Smyth's last work was published posthumously. It was titled *The Retraction of His Errors and the Confirmation of the Truth*. In this work he did not recant his mature convictions, but the manner in which he formerly argued with his detractors. His final position could be called one of "evangelical ecumenism," in which he recognized all those who acknowledge "That Jesus Christ the sonne of God, and the sonne of Marie, is the anointed king, Priest, and Prophet of the Church, the onlie mediator of the new Testament, and that through true repentance and faith in him who alone is our savior, wee receive remission of sinnes, and the holie ghost in his lyfe, and therewith all the redemption of our bodies, and everlasting life in the resurrection of the bodie: and whosoever walketh according to this rule, I must needs acknowledge him my brother: yea, although he differ from me in divers other particulars." W. T. Whitley, *The Works of John Smyth*. vol. 2 (Cambridge: Cambridge University Press, 1915) 752-55.

[9]John Robinson, *Of Religious Communion, Private and Public* (1614), reprinted in *The Works of John Robinson* 3:168.

shipping in a complex of buildings on the Amstel River owned by Jan Munter, a Mennonite and member of the Waterlander Mennonite Church. Smyth's decision to seek union with the Mennonites led to an exchange of confessions of faith. The last of these, consisting of a hundred articles (in English), was not published until after Smyth's death, but there is little doubt that this confession was largely the work of his pen.[10] It reflects considerable thought in its rejection of the pervasive Calvinism of the Separatists and its acceptance of characteristic Mennonite concepts. The Confession's uniqueness lies in the fact that, for the first, time the principles of religious freedom and the limitations of the magistrate's authority were published in English. These principles are found in article 84, which reads:

> That the magistrate is not by virtue of his office to meddle with religion, or matters of conscience, to force or compel men to this or that form of religion, or doctrine: but leave Christian religion free, to every man's conscience, and to handle only civil transgressions, (Rom. xiii) injuries, and wrongs of man against man, in murder, adultery, theft, etc., for Christ only is the king and lawgiver of the church and conscience (James iv. 12)."[11]

The Separatists, without exception, rejected the principle of religious freedom advocated by Smyth and his church. Two years after Smyth's death, Robinson attacked both articles 84 and 85 as contrary to the teachings of the Bible.[12] Smyth would not have been surprised nor were those who had known him in England—for true to the tradition of the Puritans and the Separatists, he had held that the magistrates' responsibility was to enforce conformity to the true (Puritan) faith. As late as 1605, Smyth took such a position in *A Paterne of True Prayer*:

> When there is a Toleration of many Religions, whereby the kingdom of God is shouldered out a doores by the divel's kingdome; . . . wherefore the Magistrates should cause all men to worship the true God, or else punish them with imprisonment, confiscation of goods, or death as the qualitie of the cause requireth."[13]

---

[10]H. Leon McBeth, *English Baptist Literature on Religious Liberty to 1689* (New York: Arno Press, 1980) 15-16.
[11]William L. Lumpkin, ed., *Baptist Confessions of Faith* (Philadelphia PA: Judson Press, 1959) 140.
[12]*The Works of John Robinson* 3:276-77.
[13]*The Works of John Smyth* 1:166.

The remarkable change in Smyth and the transformation of his theology and ecclesiology were doubtless due to the Mennonite influence, particulary that of Hans de Ries, one of the most able leaders among them, and like Smyth, a physician and a pastor with a classical education. Smyth's adoption of the Mennonite position in the magistracy is undeniable in article 85. In this article, Smyth wrote that, due to the nature of his office, the magistrate could not possibly be a true disciple of Christ. Helwys, along with eight to ten others, who had parted with Smyth over his attempt to unite with the Mennonites, found it impossible to follow their pastor's teaching here. Perhaps Helwys had already begun to plan on returning to England and realized there was no way the English "Anabaptists" could have a viable future with such a Mennonite concept. Therefore, Helwys set forth his position in *A Declaration of Faith of English People Remaining at Amsterdam in Holland* (1611). After asserting that magistrates were ordained by God to exercise their authority in civil matters, he admonished his followers:

> Wee ought to pay tribute, custome and all other duties. That wee are to pray for them, for God would have them saved and come to the knowledg off his truth. I Tim. 2.1.4. And therefore they may bee members off the Church of Christ, reteining their Magistracie, for no Holie Ordinance off GOD debarreth anie from being a member off CHRISTS Church.[14]

Helwys recognized that the concepts of religious freedom and responsible citizenship were not necessarily incompatible. While holding that the magistrate could be a Christian while exercising the duties of his office, he denied his authority in religious matters. This was the central message of his curious little book, *A Short Declaration of the Mistery of Iniquity*. Shortly after his return to England (1611/12), Helwys sent an inscribed copy to King James in which he reminded the king of his mortality and the limitations of his royal authority:

> Heare o king, and dispise not ye counsell of ye poore, and let their complaints come before thee.
> The king is a mortall man, & not God therefore hath no power over ye immortall soules of his subiects, to make lawes & ordinances for them, and to set spiritual Lords over them.
> If the king have authority to make spirituall Lords and Lawes, then he is an immortall God, and not a mortall man.

---

[14] Lumpkin, *Baptist Confessions of Faith*, 122-23.

> O king be not seduced by deceivers to sin so against God whome thou oughtest to obey, nor against thy poore subjects who ought and will obey thee in all thinges with body life and goods, or els let their lives be taken from ye earth.[15]

Within the book itself, Helwys spelled out what he meant by religious freedom. His was not whimpering cry for toleration, but a vigorous advocacy for freedom of conscience for all law-abiding citizens, including those of the "Romish religion, heretikes. Turcks, Jewes or whatsoever," for he argued, "it apperteynes not to the earthly power to punish them in the least measure."[16] In this radical position, he was anticipated by Balthasar Hubmaier, who wrote in *Concerning Heretics and Those Who Burn Them* (1524) "that no one may injure the enemy of God [gotssfind] who wishes nothing for himself other than to forsake the gospel."[17] King James responded by imprisoning Helwys. He apparently died in Newgate Prison sometime before 1616, when his will was probated.

Helwys's significance in Baptist history is that he succeeded in establishing for the first time a Baptist church on English soil by synthesizing elements of the Mennonite faith (believer's baptism, the church, freedom of the will, and religious freedom) with those of certain Puritan concepts, for example, original sin, traditional Christology, and the Sabbath.[18] For the cause of religious freedom, his work was indispensable. Not only did he transmit the distinctive teachings of Smyth to England, he also left an able successor, John Murton, to carry on his work. Murton also gave his life for the cause in the same prison in which Helwys died, but not until he had made his own distinctive contribution.

---

[15]Thomas Helwys, *A Short Declaration of the Mistery of Iniquity* (London: Grayes Inne, 1612) flyleaf. (A copy with the handwritten inscription is in the Bodleian Library.) It was reprinted in facsimile by Carey Kingsgate Press in 1935. It was completely reset and reprinted with a historical-critical introduction as *A Short Declaration of the Mystery of Iniquity*, ed. Richard Groves (Macon GA: Mercer University Press, 1998).

[16]Ibid. (original and 1935 facsimile), 69.

[17]See W. R. Estep, *The Anabaptist Story* (Grand Rapids MI: William B. Eerdmans, 1996) 86, for the complete article and accompanying footnotes.

[18]There is some question regarding Helwys's position on original sin. Watts holds that Helwys accepted the concept, while Coggins says Helwys followed Smyth in rejecting inherited sin, and cites the *Synopsis fides* as evidence. It appears Coggins is correct about Helwys's earlier position, but by 1611 in "A Declaration of Faith of English People Remaining at Amsterdam in Holland," Helwys and his followers affirm man's sinful nature in article 4. Lumpkin, *Baptist Confessions of Faith*, 117-18. See Watts, *The Dissenters*, 49, and James Coggins, *John Smyth's Congregation* (Scottdale PA: Herald Press, 1991) 76-77.

Although he was neither a university graduate nor an ordained minister, John Murton, who had accompanied Smyth and Helwys to the Netherlands, was a man of intelligence and conviction. This is made evident in the three known books he authored, the most influential of which was his prison manuscript, *An Humble Supplication to the King's Majesty*. In his *A Defence of the Doctrine Propounded by the Synod at Dort, against John Murton and His Associates*, Robinson wrote that Murton and his group were "fitter to meddle with a spade and a mattock than with those high mysteries" [the Calvinism of the Synod of Dort].[19] That which irritated Robinson and Ainsworth quite as much as Helwys' and Murton's attack on infant baptism, and predestination was their position on the limitations of the magistrates' authority in religious affairs. While Murton recognized "the authority of earthly magistrates, God's blessed ordinance," he also added, "but all men must let God alone with his right, which is to be lord and lawgiver to the soul, and not command obedience for God where he commandeth none."[20] In this and numerous other passages, Murton reflects the positions of both Smyth and Helwys.

In Robinson's rebuttal to Smyth's position (article 84), he interpreted Smyth's statement to mean that God had given the magistrate's authority to enforce conformity to the true (Robinson's version of Separatism) religion and suppress the false. He was particularly vitriolic in referring to Helwys: "To conclude this point then; both these men, and Mr. H. [Helwys] especially, in his whole discourse about this matter, labours of the common disease of all ignorant men, in pleading against the use of the ordinance by the abuse."[21] "Since Robinson's *Of Religious Communion, Private and Public* did not appear in print until 1614, both Smyth and Helwys were incapable or replying. Since Smyth was dead and Helwys was in prison, Murton took it upon himself to answer Robinson.

Even though he was not university educated, Murton proved to be more than a match for Robinson. His six or seven years of sojourn with John Smyth had not been in vain. It was he more than anyone else who carried the torch in England for religious freedom after the death of Helwys. In fact, not only was Robinson compelled to deal with Murton,

---

[19]*The Works of John Robinson* 1:293.
[20]John Murton, *Persecution for Religion Judg'd and Condemn'd*. Printed in 1615 and 1620, and reprinted in *Tracts on Liberty of Conscience and Persecution, 1614–1661* (London: J. Haddon, Castle Street, Finsbury, 1846) 100.
[21]*The Works of John Robinson* 3:277.

but Henry Ainsworth also picked up the cudgel against him. Ainsworth's work, however, did not appear in print until 1644, when both he and Murton were dead. However, Ainsworth's spirit lived on in Massachusetts' Bay Colony, which outlawed Baptists in the same year. On the other hand, Murton's *An Humble Supplication* found new life when Roger Williams incorporated its major arguments in his *Bloudy Tenent of Persecution* in the same year (1644). But Murton's importance for the English Baptist heritage lies in more than his literary contribution. By the time of his death, there were eight Baptist churches of record in England for which Murton and his followers—as well as his detractors—were responsible. While his detractors helped publicize his views—and those of Smyth and Helwys—among the Puritans and Separatists, they failed to refute them convincingly.

Murton's position on religious freedom received substantial support from another source, Leonard Busher, "a citizen of London" living in The Netherlands, "an exile for conscience sake." His last known residence was Delft, according to a letter written in Dutch (1642) to the Flemish Mennonites in Amsterdam requesting financial assistance.[22] In 1611 he was known by Christopher Lawne, a former Separatist, as pastor of a congregation of English "Anabaptists" distinct from both those of Smyth and Helwys.[23] It is also evident that Busher possessed a knowledge of Latin, Greek, and Dutch. However, the one extant book from his pen, *Religion's Peace, or, A Plea for Liberty of Conscience*, printed in 1614, can be acquired only in a reprint edition.[24] Murton seems not to have been aware of Busher's treatise when he wrote *Persecution for Religion Judg'd and Condemn'd*, but apparently reflected a knowledge of *Religion's Peace* in *An Humble Supplication to the King's Majesty* of 1520.[25]

---

[22]I possess a photocopy of this letter which I made in the Mennonite Archives in the Central Bibliotek in Amsterdam.

[23]Champlin Burrage, *The Early English Dissenters in the Light of Recent Research, 1550–1641*, vol. 1 (Cambridge: Cambridge University Press, 1912; repr.: New York: Russell & Russell, 1967) 243-44. Burrage wrote: "Associated with Busher may have been sent Swithune Grindall, Richard Overton, and John Drew (who later united with the Waterlanders), and probably others with whose names were not familiar today."

[24]*Religion's Peace* was reprinted in 1646 and again in *Tracts on Liberty of Conscience and Persecution, 1614–1661*, ed. Edward Bean Underhill (London: Hanserd Knollys Society, 1846) 1-81.

[25]Not only does Murton's *An Humble Supplication* follow a similar format as that of Busher, but he also addresses this work to both King James and Parliament. While he uses the usual arguments against persecution common to the from Smyth circle, he is

Busher has the distinction of having authored the first book in English given solely to an advocacy of religious liberty. It was also unique in that he used sociological arguments to bolster his position, derived for his soteriological and ecclesiological convictions. He contended that while religious liberty is good for society, persecution, on the other hand, will ultimately destroy any government that practised it: "Therefore persecution for differences in religion is a monstrous and cruel beast, that destroyeth both prince and people, hindereth the gospel of Christ, and scattereth his disciples that witness and profess his name. But permission of conscience in differences of religion, saveth both prince and people."[26]

Busher's arguments for religious freedom were inherently theological, not political. "True religion," he affirmed, "is the natural attribute not of birth but of the new birth," which can never be induced by coercion. "Fire and sword are wholly against the mind and merciful law of Christ, therefore, "no king nor bishop can or is able to command faith."[27] He went on to distinguish between the "temporal kingdom" and the "spiritual kingdom":

> Kings and magistrates are to rule temporal affairs by the swords of their temporal kingdoms, and bishops and ministers are to rule spiritual affairs by the word and Spirit of God, the swords of Christ's spiritual kingdom, and not to intermeddle one with another's authority, office, and function.[28]

Like Smyth, Busher set forth the principle that all "true Christians" born of God are, likewise, children of God. Busher repeatedly cited Matthew 28:19, 20 in emphasizing that only those who voluntarily respond in faith are to be baptized, and then only by immersion.[29] As Leon McBeth at Southwestern Seminary has illustrated, after the 1640s, the concept of religious liberty had found numerous adherents in England, not just among Baptists, but also among Independents, Levelers, and some anonymous writers.[30] Among those who became convinced Baptists were

---

more traditional in his discussion of Jews than Busher. The Jews had been expelled from England in 1290 on dubious charges. Busher argued that they should be readmitted to England, because they would be beneficial to the nation, and such treatment would more likely bring them to a knowledge of Christ than continued exclusion or perpetual exile.

[26]Underhill, ed., *Tracts on Liberty of Conscience and Persecution*, 41.
[27]Ibid., 17.
[28]Ibid., 23.
[29]Ibid., 59-60. Busher was apparently the first among the English Baptists to publish that baptism, according to the New Testament, is by immersion.
[30]McBeth, ed., *Literature on Religious Liberty*, 63-72.

Edward Barber and Christopher Blackwood. Barber identified with the General Baptists—as those who followed the trail blazed by Smyth and Helwys later became known—and Blackwood, a graduate of Cambridge and an Anglican clergyman, aligned with those who were later called Particular Baptists.[31] McBeth points out that Blackwood, even though a Particular Baptist, gave evidence of verbal dependence upon Helwys.

Both Barber and Blackwood expanded earlier Baptist arguments for religious freedom. Barber, for example, argued that persecution can prematurely cut off the opportunity for salvation. Therefore, the need or liberty "that they who are now blind may see; They who now reject the Truth, may receive it; They who are now Tares, may become wheat."[32] Blackwood wrote in *The Storming of Antichrist, in His Two Last and Strongest Garrisons: of Compulsion of Conscience and Infants' Baptisme* (1544), a substantial treatise on religious liberty and baptism. In this work he argued that infant baptism was both a humane tradition and an act of coercion, offering a unique speculation against persecution when he asserted "that forcing magistrates to persecute was a sin against their sensitive consciences as well as against the persecuted."[33] He also deplored the wrangling and disputing among Christians and longed for the day when Christendom would not be "the cockpit of the world, to the great scandal of Christ and Christianity."[34]

2. The Particular Baptists

The familiar history of the beginnings of the Particular Baptists from Henry Jacob's Separatist church in London in 1616 need not be repeated here. It is clear, however, that while Henry Jacob was a Puritan, even a leading voice in the Hampton Court Conference with James I, according to the Gould manuscript, the church that he formed in London was a Separatist church from its beginning.[35]

After two secessions, the last of which was in 1638, it appears that two congregations agreed by 1640 that baptism should not only be

---

[31]Ibid., 72-82. McBeth gives brief biographical sketches of both Barber and Blackwood and incisive analyses on their positions on both baptism and religious liberty.

[32]Cited by McBeth, ibid., 72; This quotation is apparently a paraphrase of one of Busher's arguments against persecution. Busher, *Religious Peace*, 17.

[33]Ibid., 77-78.

[34]Cited by McBeth, ibid., 79.

[35]The relevant sections from the Gould Manuscript are reproduced in Burrage, *The Early English Dissenters* 2:292-308.

administered to believers, but should also be done by immersion. Finally acting together, they agreed to send Richard Blunt, who spoke Dutch, to the Netherlands, where they had learned that immersion was practiced by some Mennonites. Upon his return, Blunt baptized Blacklock and both then baptized all those requesting it.[36]

By 1644 there were seven Particular Baptist churches in and around London, a remarkable development when one realizes that most of those in the two original congregations had already spent time in a number of prisons for their faith. In the same year, they felt compelled to issue, in spite of some misgivings regarding confessions of faith, a public confession of their basic doctrines. The pattern followed that of *A True Confession*, largely the work of Henry Ainsworth of the Ancient Church of English Separatists in Amsterdam. The *First London Confession* reflected in some phrases verbal dependence upon *A True Confession*, but the points at which it varied made it a distinctive Baptist confession.

A point of major departure from the Separatist confession was on the magistrates' authority in religious affairs. *A True Confession* ascribed to the magistrates the responsibility to destroy every vestige of false religions, "And on the other hand to establish & mayntein by their lawes every part of Gods word his pure Relligion and true ministerie to cherish and protect all such as are carefull to worship God according to his word, and to leade a godly lyfe in all peace and loyalltie."[37]

The Baptists devoted five articles to the subject of the magistrates' authority. While they acknowledged that the magistrates were ordained by God to rule in civic affairs, they denied both their authority and that of the state in religious matters. They also indicated (XLIX) that they were ready to suffer the consequences of disobedience for not "actively submitting to some Ecclesiastical Lawes, which might be conceived by them to be their duties to establish which we for the present could not see, nor our consciences could not submit unto." In article LI, the Baptists restated their resolve "to proceed together in Christian commu-

---

[36]Upon the basis of the Gould manuscript, some historians have concluded that Blunt went to the Netherlands only to learn how baptism by immersion was done. As it reads, the Gould manuscript is inconclusive, but the logic of the motivation for seeking to initiate baptism by immersion anew in England in the light of the Smyth experience tends to suggest that Blunt was baptized in the Netherlands.

[37]Article 39, *A True Confession* (1596). The complete texts of both *A True Confession* and the *First London Confession* are reprinted in Lumpkin, *Baptist Confessions of Faith*, 81-97; 153-171.

nion, not daring to give place to suspend our practice, but to walk in obedience to Christ in the profession and holding forth this faith before mentioned, even in the midst of all trialls and afflictions."

Even though they attempted to state their position with humility and courtesy, affirming in no unmistakable terms their recognition of the magistrates' God-given authority, they expressed their determination "to obey God rather than men." A careful reading of the two confessions on the magistrates' authority reveals other differences as well. The Separatist confession supports the position of its framers by citing some twenty Old Testament passages and seven from the New. The Baptists, on the other hand, cited thirty New Testament passages and only three from the Old. The differences in these underlying hermeneutics of the two confessions is even more apparent in the authority claimed for each position. The Separatists appealed to God and His Word. The Baptists appealed to "our Lord and master Jesus Christ and his commandment, commission, and Promise."[38]

The revision of 1646 revealed that the Particular Baptists were still in the process of distancing themselves from the Puritans and Separatists (Presbyterians and Congregationalists). In addition to modifying their Calvinism even further, the ministry of the local church was changed from "Pastors, Teachers, Elders, Deacons" to "Elders and Deacons" (XXXVI). They also clarified and strengthened their stand on religious liberty and the separation of church and state. The phraseology is even more reminiscent of the Smyth and Helwys tradition than it was in 1644, for example, "And concerning the worship of God; there is but one lawgiver,

---

[38] The authorship of the 1644 *First London Confession* ("The Confession of Faith, of those Churches which are commonly [though falsely] called Anabaptist") has been a matter of discussion for sometime, without consensus. It is generally agreed, however, that the framers of this confession were dependent upon A True Confession for the articles on God, Christ, and Holy Spirit, as well as those on soteriology, but the question arises what about those articles, such as, baptism, religious freedom, and the separation of the church and state that make it a distinctive Baptist confession? Any Anabaptist influence has generally been ruled out a priori assumptions. In the light of recent research of Professor Glen Stassen, this appears to have been a premature conclusion. He demonstrates rather convincingly that while approximately half of the confession is taken from A True Confession and William Ames's *The Marrow of Theology*, the remainder comes from Menno Simons's *Foundation of Christian Doctrine*. See Glen Stassen, "Finding the Evidence for Christ-centered Discipleship in Baptist Origins By Opening Menno Simons's *Foundation-Book*" (unpublished paper, Louisville KY, 1996) 2-19.

which is able to save and destroy, James 4:12; which is Jesus Christ, who hath given laws and rules sufficient in His word for His worship."[39]

In the revision of article XLVIII, Baptists made it clear with a footnote that they intended the position on church and state for universal application, for example, "To be applied to the government authority of any land or nation." In article XLIX, they indicated that rather than giving up their faith under threat of imprisonment or death, they intended "to obey God rather than men." In addition to pledging their obedience to the magistrates' authority, the Baptists affirmed in article L the legitimacy of oaths: "It is lawful to take an oath, so it be in truth, and in judgement, and in righteousness, for confirmation of truth, and ending of all strife."[40] to the 1646 edition was added a conclusion that attempted to dispel any misapprehension about their lifestyle or intentions. These Baptists claimed to live by the golden rule under the Lordship of Jesus Christ. In humility, they admitted that they "are ignorant of many things," and were willing to be taught better according to "the word of God," but insist that they would "suffer a thousand deaths"—if that were possible—rather than accept "anything that we see not to be commanded by our Lord Jesus Christ." The Conclusion closed with a ringing declaration:

> And if any shall call what we have said heresy, than we with the Apostle acknowledge, that after the way they call heresy worship we the God of our fathers, disclaiming all heresies (rightly so called) because they are against Christ, and to be steadfast and unmovable, always abounding in obedience to Christ, as knowing our labor shall not be in vain in the Lord.[41]

By 1646, as McBeth indicates in *English Baptist Literature on Religious Liberty to 1689*, numerous Baptists and Baptist sympathizers entered into the ongoing debate over the merits of religious freedom. Among these were Thomas Collier, William Dell, Richard Laurence, Samuel Richardson, and John Tombes. As the Presbyterians attempted to replace the Church of England with a Presbyterian establishment, the paper debate heated up. Personal disputes, which often began with a discussion of the merits of believer's baptism, frequently ended with a battle of words over religious liberty, but no new ground was broken. Although,

---

[39]*The First London Confession of Faith 1646 Edition with an Appendix by Benjamin Cox 1646*. Reprint edition with modernized spelling and punctuation: (Rochester NY: Backus Book Publishers, 1981) 17.
[40]Ibid., 19.
[41]Ibid., 20.

the principles had been already enunciated and widely disseminated by 1646, the task remained to implement them, which was never completely accomplished in England. With the Act of Toleration of 1689, the persecution of dissenters for differences in religion ceased and toleration was granted, but the Church of England remained the state church, and nonconformists were still denied access to certain entitlements available to other citizens. The English Baptist legacy of freedom remained in escrow until the English colonies succeeded in giving birth to a new nation.

3. The American Experience

When the Revolutionary War separated England from her American colonies, it did not succeed in severing the religious and cultural ties that bound the English together on both sides of the Atlantic. Although English jurisprudence provided the basic understanding of law and justice in the American colonies, two profound differences were to create a distinctive American nation: There was no state church, and complete religious liberty was to be guaranteed by law. This remarkable development did not come easily without a price. Indispensable to all else that followed was Roger Williams (1603–1684), a "Prophet in the Wilderness," to use Perry Miller's term:

> For the subsequent history of what became the United States, Roger Williams possesses one indubitable importance, that he stands at the beginning of it. Just as some great experience in the youth of a person is ever afterward a determinant of his personality, so the American character has inevitably been molded by the fact that in the first years of colonization there arose this prophet of religious liberty.[42]

Williams was both brilliant and exasperating. In his opposition to the Puritan theocracy of Massachusetts Bay Colony, he sent John Cotton, its chief exponent, into a "tail spin." Denying the truth of that for which he stood, the colony had no other recourse than to banish him to the wilderness. To the surprise of his adversaries, he not only survived, but suc-

---

[42]Perry Miller, *Roger Williams: His Contribution to the American Tradition* (New York: Atheneum, 1962) 254. Numerous books have been devoted to analyzing and evaluating the contributions of Roger Williams, his life, and political theories. Few have understood that his political contributions were rooted in his understanding of the Christian faith and his ecclesiology. One who does is Edwin S. Gaustad, *Liberty of Conscience: Roger Williams in America* (Grand Rapids MI: Williams B. Eerdmans, 1991). See also William R. Estep, *Revolution within the Revolution: The First Amendment in Historical Context, 1612–1789* (Grand Rapids MI: Eerdmans, 1990) 72-96.

ceeded in establishing at a place he called "Providence Plantations," a colony incorporating his own convictions on religious liberty and the separation of church and state. The world was to learn how deeply those convictions were embedded into the soul of the prophet with the release of *The Bloudy Tenent of Persecution* (1644), in which he gave the cause of religious freedom its most vigorous and thorough apologetic it had yet received.

From the New Testament, Williams derived his concepts regarding the church and the nature of the Christian faith. At the heart of William's view of both the true church and a valid faith was his conviction that neither is the result of coercion. This is a recurring theme throughout all his works:

> Can the sword of steel or arm of flesh make man faithful or loyal to God? Or careth God for the outward loyalty or faithfulness, when the inward man is false and treacherous? Or is there not more danger from a hypocrite, a dissembler, a turncoat in his religion (from the fear or favor of men) than from a resolved Jew, Turk, or papist, who holds firm unto his principles?[43]

Williams added his own opinions to the customary Baptist arguments for religious liberty, and reformulated others in a more striking way. The following quotation is an example: "An enforced uniformity of Religion throughout a Nation or civill state, confounds the Civill and Religious, denies the principles of Christianity and civility, and that Jesus Christ is come in the Flesh." [44] However, Williams' most significant contribution to the English Baptist arguments for religious freedom lay in the fact that, through the crucible of his own experience, he was able for the first time in history to form a truly democratic government that guaranteed complete religious liberty, not mere toleration.[45] By 1644, Williams had been able to secure a charter for Rhode Island, which then consisted of Providence, Portsmouth, Newport, and Warwick, with the guarantee of religious liberty for all its citizens.

When Charles II came to the throne, it became necessary to secure a new charter, which was largely the achievement of John Clarke (1609–

---

[43]Williams, cited by Roland Bainton in *The Travail of Religious Liberty* (New York: Harper & Brothers, 1951) 219-20.

[44]Williams, *The Bloudy Tenent of Persecution*, in *The Complete Writings of Roger Williams*, 7 vols. (New York: Russell & Russell, Inc., 1963) 3:4.

[45]Toleration assumes the state has a right to tolerate those religious expressions it chooses to recognize and withhold it from others, whereas religious liberty is a God-given right, not to be withheld by any government.

1676), a physician and pastor of the Baptist Church in Newport, the second Baptist congregation in Rhode Island. In his *Ill Newes from New England*, Clarke recounted his own experience of imprisonment at the hands of Bay authorities for conducting a prayer service in the home of a blind Baptist in the suburbs of Boston. This tract added momentum to the cause of freedom and support for Williams. At the same time, it further undermined the credibility of John Cotton and the Puritans in New England.

Until the Great Awakening infused new life into the Baptists of New England, Baptists could count only six churches in Massachusetts, eleven in Rhode Island, four in Connecticut after more than a century. In the Middle Colonies and the South, the situation appeared—with few exceptions—just as bleak, but with the advent of the revival, the situation began to change dramatically. Both the Congregationalists and Presbyterians were divided into supporters and opposers of the new (itinerant) evangelism. The Baptists for the most part were skeptical, for how could God bless those who had persecuted them? But the unthinkable happened: Thousands of Congregationalists became Baptists, and a new chapter in Baptist history was written.

Congregationalist Isaac Backus (1724–1806) converted as a result of the Awakening, soon began to feel the opposition that the Baptists had long struggled under in Massachusetts. Though he was a Congregationalist, he was also an advocate of the New Light party. The New Lights began to organize their own churches in order to call pastors of their choosing and continue their support of the new evangelism. Compelled to examine his experience in the light of the New Testament, Backus determined that the Baptists were right on baptism, ecclesiology, and religious liberty. Once convinced, he was baptized and promptly became an ardent champion—as well as a fervent evangelist—of religious liberty. Congregationalists who had been converted during the revivals that flared up all over New England followed his example, and Separate Congregational churches became Separate Baptist churches in droves.

As an agent of the Warren Association, Backus became the most influential spokesperson for religious freedom in New England. Of his forty-four books and pamphlets, seven were devoted to religious freedom. In the process of his own studies, he discovered Roger Williams for himself, and helped the first generation of Americans rediscover Williams and his teachings to the lasting benefit of the American experience.[46] However, as William McLoughlin at Brown University points out, Backus quoted Locke much more extensively than Williams. He did so, not because he agreed more with Locke—as T. B. Maston at Southwestern Seminary suggests—but because Locke was far more palatable to New England theocrats than Williams.[47] It is difficult to overestimate the significance of Isaac Backus to the cause of religious liberty in the revolutionary era. He personified the lasting benefits of the Great Awakening for the American experience. More than anyone else, he was also responsible for the unification of the colonial Baptist movement. Although not as consistent as Williams in his advocacy of the separation of church and state, he was far in advance of Locke. Also, his enormous literary output was unsurpassed by any other colonial Baptist. However, he did not influence the course of the new nation to the extent of the Virginia Baptists and his disciple, John Leland (1754–1841).

One the eve of the Revolutionary War, Leland visited Virginia and determined to cast his lot with the much maligned and persecuted Baptists of the colony in which the Church of England held a virtual religious monopoly. The fires of revival had already ignited a new spirit of evangelism among both the Regular Baptists, who had conformed to the Act of Toleration, and the Presbyterians. But Separate Baptists, who refused to secure licenses to preach, became the objects of legal reprisals and often mob action as well. But every county that saw Baptist preachers imprisoned also witnessed the birth of a Baptist church. Soon dissenters outnumbered adherents to the established church, yet the Anglican Church tenaciously held onto its privileged status. Leland, who had carried on a wide-ranging itinerant ministry for seven years, became a political activist.

A native of Massachusetts, he was well acquainted with Backus's works on religious freedom, the most recent of which, *An Appeal to the Public*, published in 1773, may have been the catalyst that brought him to Virginia, where the outcome of the struggle for religious freedom would likely determine the future of Virginia and, ultimately, the course

---

[46]Stanley Grenz, *Isaac Backus: Puritan and Baptist* (Macon GA: Mercer University Press, 1983) 327.

[47]See T. B. Maston, *Pioneer of Religious Liberty* (Rochester NY: American Baptist Historical Society, 1962) 55-64, and William G. McGloughlin, ed., *Isaac Backus on Church, State, and Calvinism: Pamphlets, 1754–1789* (Cambridge MA: Harvard University Press, 1968) 113.

of the nation as well. After eight years in Virginia, Leland led in the formation of the General Committee, which was made up of representatives from all associations of Regular and Separatist Baptists in the state. Subsequently, the Baptists were able to enlist the support of virtually all the dissenters in Virginia, including the Presbyterians. At crucial times, the Baptist-led dissenters were able to rally the masses to the cause by circulating petitions to the General Assembly (legislature), which had taken the place of the House of Burgesses after 1776. Finally, through the brilliant political strategy of James Madison, the General Assessment Bill was defeated and the Anglican Church was disestablished.

In the process of leading the Baptist forces to a significant victory, Leland had become a personal friend and staunch supporters of Thomas Jefferson, whose "An Act for the Establishing of Religious Freedom" of 1786, was one of the milestones in the struggle for religious liberty in Virginia. But when the proposed Federal constitution, of which their trusted friend James Madison was the chief architect, was made public, the Baptists were keenly disappointed. Even though article VI of the new Constitution forbade any religious test for those "seeking any office or public trust in the United States," they agreed with Leland that "religious liberty was not sufficiently guaranteed." Their concern prompted a series of conferences between Baptist leaders and Madison, which apparently resulted in Madison's promising to introduce a bill into Congress that would address the problem.

True to his word, on 7 June 1789, Madison introduced the first version of an amendment to the Constitution, which after ratification would become the First Amendment to the Federal Constitution. At last the Baptists were satisfied, or so wrote Madison to George Washington on 20 November 1789: "One of the principal leaders of the Baptists lately sent me word that the amendments had entirely satisfied the disaffected of his sect and that it would appear in their subsequent conduct."[48]

---

[48]Joseph Martin Dawson cited this letter in *Baptists and the American Republic* (Nashville TN: Broadman Press, 1956) 115. See also Estep, *Revolution within the Revolution*, 156-79, for more complete discussion of the Virginia Baptist contribution to the implementation of the principles of religious freedom and the separation of church and state in the American experience.

4. Conclusion

The English Baptist legacy of freedom found its fullest expression in the American experience. In the new nation its liberating ideas took root, providing its citizens with freedom of conscience without which all other freedoms are meaningless, if possible at all.

The Planter Motif among Baptists from New England to Nova Scotia, 1760–1850

William H. Brackney

Historians have influence upon each other, either through personal associations or cross-fertilization of ideas. In both ways, B. R. White has had a profound impact on many writing scholars. One of the most significant ways that has happened has been through White's interest in Baptist and Free Church scholarship outside Britain, manifested in his interaction with colleagues; his mentoring of students from North America, Australia, and Europe; and his own involvement in writing and delivering addresses in various contexts beyond his beloved Oxford. In my own case, Dr. White and I several times discussed various commonalities in Baptist life across the Atlantic, and he expressed much interest in "crossing borders" and discovering influences, etc. This essay is, therefore, an attempt to do just that in discovering the influences of an American community upon a Canadian context.[†]

Planting: A Religious Ideal

Historically speaking, "planting" can mean several things to different people. A "planter" can be a seventeenth-century agriculturalist in colonial Virginia, can be used as a general term for those who financed the British colonies of North America and the Caribbean islands. And certainly, thanks to the excellent historical work produced over the last two decades in the Canadian Maritimes community, the term "planter" may be specifically applied to that group of settlers from New England to Nova Scotia and New Brunswick between the expulsion of the Acadians and the coming of the Loyalists. The term "planter" may be used in yet another sense as well, as a motif in the transference of

---

[†] This paper was in large part originally prepared for an address delivered at Acadia University's Center for Anabaptist and Baptist Studies where I was a visiting scholar in 1995. I am grateful to Prof. Jarold K. Zeman, University Archivist Patricia Townsend, Elizabeth Horton, and the staff of the Baptist Archives at Acadia University for their support and assistance in my research. It is here offered in honor of B. R. White, who encouraged the search for ties between Baptist groups.

religious culture and values from one region to another, specifically from New England to Nova Scotia.

Baptists provide an interesting case study of "planting" as they illustrate the powerful forces unleashed by the Great Awakening, because the New England Baptist community took a special interest in Nova Scotia between the 1760s and the 1830s. In the late eighteenth century, Nova Scotia was a pristine fertile garden, nurtured by tidal currents, abundant with wildlife, and easily accessible on all its shores, particularly that bordering the Bay of Fundy. It was a virtual "land flowing with milk and honey," as one Baptist observer put it. The "planter" terminology was used widely during that period to characterize what religious leadership believed they were doing in the new colony. It was also used by a score of religious historians from the eighteenth century to recount the story to later generations of Maritimers. In many ways, the planter motif helps to explain the interdependence of two religious communities: New England and Nova Scotia. This interdependence is a series of relationships with profound cultural implications not only for Baptists, but for Nova Scotia society in general.

New England's religious culture was assertive beyond its geographical borders in the last three decades of the eighteenth century, as well as the first two decades of the next century. Historians like Lois K. Mathews, Charles Cole, and Clifford Griffin—and more recently John Andrew and Lois Banner[1]—have identified the importance of New England culture's missionary role. In many ways the early national period in United States history was a denominational world and religious values were a high priority in the northeastern states.

The planter motif has its origins in New Testament Scripture references. Early Puritan writers recognized its value in rationalizing and interpreting their vision. Passages from the Gospels, like Mark 4:28-30 (containing the parable of the seed), the words of Jesus concerning the plentiful harvest in Matthew 9:37-38, and of course, the Pauline allegory to the

---

[1]Lois K. Mathews, *The Expansion of New England* (Boston MA: Houghton Mifflin, 1909); Charles Cole, *The Social Ideas of the Northern Evangelists 1826–1860* (New York: Columbia University Press, 1954); Clifford Griffin, *Their Brothers' Keepers: Moral Stewardship in the United States, 1800–1865* (New Brunswick NJ: Rutgers University Press, 1960); John Andrew, *Rebuilding the Christian Commonwealth: New England Congregationalists and Foreign Missions 1800–1830* (Lexington: University of Kentucky Press, 1976); Lois Banner, "The Protestant Crusade: Religious Missions, Benevolence, and Reform in the United States, 1790–1840" (Ph.D. dissertation, Columbia University, 1970).

Corinthians (3:6-10 "one plants, another waters . . . ") are laced throughout early American thought in both primary and secondary sources.²

The planter motif and related agricultural terminology were both semantically and theologically relevant to Baptists. From the words of Christ in Matthew's Gospel, as applied through the New Light/Separatist experience, Baptists saw themselves as planters and harvesters of the gospel of Christ. By applying the Gospel parables, they became propagators of seed, and from the metaphor in I Corinthians 3, ministers and missionaries saw themselves as part of a long term process of "planting." Among people who lived in a self-defined milieu of biblical literalism, these were not small connections in the revived world of the Bible.

Three examples of "planting" illustrate how New England Baptist religious culture was transplanted to Maritime Canada: (1) by planting a distinct denominational polity and church order, (2) planting the foundation of a structure for mission, and (3) planting the seeds for a learned ministry.

Planting a Polity and Church Order

As several historians have noted, Ebenezer Moulton (1709–1783) was the first of the New England Baptist planters in Nova Scotia. What he represented in terms of Baptist polity and order is significant, yet not clearly defined in the extant literature.³

Born in Connecticut, Moulton was raised in the village of Brimfield, a portion of what was later the town of Wales in central Massachusetts. In 1736 he and his family helped organize the Baptist church at South Brimfield, one of the first new Calvinistic Baptist congregations in the

---

²See Henry S. Burrage, *A History of Baptists in New England* (Philadelphia: American Baptist Publication Society, 1894) 145-46. For an example of excessive use of metaphorical language, see the Mss. letterbook attributed to Harris Harding in the Baptist Archives, Acadia University. Letters dated 1778 to 1793 illustrate this rich use of biblical language applied to contemporary circumstances.

³The original source on Moulton is Isaac Backus, *A History of New England, with Particular Reference to the Denomination of Christians Called Baptists* (Newton MA: Backus Historical Society, 1871) 1:31, 476. William G. McLoughlin, *New England Dissent, 1630–1833* (Cambridge MA: Harvard University Press, 1971) 1:320ff., 480ff., very helpfully pulls together additional details on Moulton's New England pedigree and pastoral ministry. For the Nova Scotian chapters in Moulton's career, Maurice W. Armstrong, "Elder Moulton and the Nova Scotia Baptists," *Dalhousie Review* 24 (1944): 320-23, in conjunction with J. M. Bumsted, are the beginning points, the latter in view of comments in n. 15 below. An article in *Dictionary of Canadian Biography* 4:565, by Gordon Stewart is a helpful outline.

western portion of the colony. He was ordained in 1741 at the Brimfield church. Also involved in mercantile pursuits, Moulton served that congregation, or its offspring Separate Baptist group, for twenty years until debt-ruined and, hence, moved to Nova Scotia.

Moulton's theological pedigree was transformed in keeping with larger realities in the Bay Colony. At the beginning of his ministry, he accepted the old Five Principle position of the then existing Baptist churches of Massachusetts, otherwise known as the "Old Baptists." When the prospect of his ordination became imminent in 1741, First Baptist Church in Boston (considered the informal Baptist see[4]) was enlisted, and Jeremiah Condy went to Brimfield to chair the proceedings. Condy, a Harvard graduate—slightly Arminian in theology—[5] was active in the central counties of the colony in assisting on matters of church order. Only Baptists were invited to Moulton's ordination council: John Callendar of Newport, Benjamin Marsh of Sutton, Samuel Maxwell of Swansea—doubtless because the Boston church had been severely criticized for involving Congregationalists in a previous ordination.[6]

In 1748 Moulton was swept into the Revival along with a number of his members, and they organized a Separate Baptist church that year in South Brimfield. (The new church was "separate" because it practiced strict closed communion, while the older congregation was probably open communion.)[7] The division between the old and new congregations was deep and included a rift between Moulton and his own father. From 1749 forward, Isaac Backus recorded that Moulton was an evangelistic enthusiast who itinerated frequently amongst Massachusetts churches; Moulton's reputation as a New Light reached even to Boston, where in 1742 he helped ordain Ephraim Bound as the first pastor of Second Baptist Church in that city. That event was a singular twist in Moulton's

---

[4]McLoughlin, *New England Dissent* 2:294.

[5]C. C. Goen, *Revivalism and Separatism in New England 1740–1800* (New Haven CT: Yale University Press, 1962) 237, described Condy as temperamentally phlegmatic, intellectual in approach, and more in keeping with the eastern Congregationalists than the Baptists of his era.

[6]Compare C. C. Goen, *Revivalism and Separatism*, 225, with the record of Moulton's ordination in the Records of the First Baptist Church of Boston for 4 November 1741, which is commented upon in Nathan E. Wood, *The History of the First Baptist Church in Boston, 1665–1899* (Philadelphia: American Baptist Publication Society, 1899) 239ff. The questionable ordination was that of Condy himself in 1738.

[7]For a useful guide to defining Separatism, see Goen, *Revivalism and Separatism*, 224ff.

evolving identity, as he publicly repudiated the theological position of Jeremiah Condy, who had supervised his own ordination the previous year.[8] Considered a New Light "schismatic," Ebenezer often suffered harassment from the ecclesiastical authorities. Five years later in Sturbridge, he likewise drew the wrath of the Standing Order. Clearly for Moulton, sovereign grace, evidence of conversion experience, believer's baptism, and closed communion were signs of one's break with the Standing Order (Congregationalist *or* Baptist!), and fundamental to a unified emerging Baptistic polity and practice.

From 1749 to 1757, Moulton was a leader in four successive petition movements of great relevance to his denomination. In the 1754 petition, of which Moulton was a principal signer and probably an author, he and Thomas Green of Leicester made a case for exemption from taxes based on an argument of clear Baptist identity and solidarity. The petition recounted the history of Baptists and demonstrated remarkable consensus among the Old Six Principle General Baptists and the Separate Baptists who were born of the Awakening. In the assessment of W. G. McLoughlin at Brown University, this placed Moulton among a select group of united Baptists who realized where they stood in the aftermath of the Great Revival and the importance of a denominational order.[9]

Insofar as Moulton's associative links were concerned, some cautious assertions may be made. During Moulton's early life in South Brimfield, the original congregation related to other Baptist congregations to the east. The splinter congregation Moulton helped form in 1748 found fellowship with other New Light churches in the region, Baptist and Separate Congregational. There is, curiously, no surviving record indicating that either Moulton or the South Brimfield Church was involved in the Six Principle Calvinistic Baptist Association, which formed among ten congregations in Massachusetts, New Hampshire, and Rhode Island in 1754,[10] suggesting that he rejected the principle of laying on of hands despite the differing positions on the atonement of Christ

---

[8]The issue was sovereign grace and the correction of Condy and others who were accused of Arminian teachings. Cf. McLoughlin, *New England Dissent* 1:320-22, with Goen, *Revivalism and Separatism*, 239, for details of the events.

[9]McLoughlin, *New England Dissent* 1:480-87. The author identified closed communion, denominational catholicity, and voluntarism as the most important of Baptist characteristics in this era.

[10]William G. McLoughlin, "The First Calvinistic Baptist Association in New England, 1754?–1767" *Church History* 36 (1967): 410-18.

held by his warring Baptist brethren. In matters of ordination and redressing oppressive attempts at taxation, there is clear evidence that he was broadly associative among Baptists in these same colonies. To his credit, Ebenezer Moulton—while definitive in his own theological position—recognized the value of consultation with other churches and became more promotive of Baptist unity as his pastoral career matured.

When Moulton arrived at Yarmouth, Nova Scotia, in 1763/1764, he had no patience with the Standing Order, and instead was entrenched in revivalistic Baptist principles. He emigrated as a legitimate "planter" and received seven hundred fifty acres at Cape Forchue. He was selected a magistrate and helped survey land.[11] At first he preached in homes at Yarmouth, Chebogue (Jebogue), and along the Fundy coast, where—as he had done in Massachusetts—he caused dissension over New Light and baptistic principles.[12] Moulton also preached at Barrington, and up and down the Annapolis Valley at sites such as Cornwallis, Horton, and perhaps even Newport.[13]

---

[11] The official record of Moulton's emigration and settlement is reprinted in *Documents Relating to the Great Awakening in Nova Scotia 1760–1791*, ed. Gordon T. Stewart (Toronto: Champlain Society, 1982) 2, 10. It would appear that Moulton arrived first without his family, who followed in 1764.

[12] Armstrong, "Elder Moulton and the Baptists," 322; Gordon Stewart and George Rawlyk, *A People Highly Favored of God: The Nova Scotia Yankees and the American Revolution* (Toronto: MacMillan, 1972) 28, 39. Among Moulton's hearers in Yarmouth was Jonathan Scott (1744–1819), who appreciated Moulton's New Light message, and requested that the elder officiate at his wedding. Later in 1770, Scott became an adversary of Moulton in the Yarmouth Church split: cf. *The Life of Jonathan Scott*, ed. Charles B. Ferguson (Halifax: Public Archives of Nova Scotia, 1960) 7, 9-12; 20. While useful in establishing Moulton in Yarmouth in the early 1760s, Ferguson is not accurate in his details of Moulton's Massachusetts career, nor was his observation that Moulton was the first pastor of the First Baptist Church at Yarmouth. For a primary account of the Yarmouth (Jebogue) Church, see *The Records of the Church of Jebogue in Yarmouth, Nova Scotia 1766–1851* (Yarmouth NS: Stoneycroft Publishing, 1992) 6-27; for a useful interpretation of the Yarmouth revival, consult Daniel Goodwin, "From Disunity to Integration: Evangelical Religion and Society in Yarmouth, Nova Scotia 1761–1830" in *They Planted Well: New England Planters in Maritime Canada*, ed. Margaret Conrad (Frederickton NB: Acadiensis Press, 1988) 190-201.

[13] Longley surmised that because Alline's preaching at Horton was of such short duration, he did not find permanent sympathizers there. The presence of firmly committed Baptists from Moulton's preaching like Benjamin Kinsman and Peter Bishop, could have accounted for this. See Ronald S. Longley, *The Wolfville United Baptist Church* (Wolfville NS: The Church, 1954) 3-12; George E. Levy, *The Baptists of the Maritime Provinces 1753–1946* (St. John NB: Barnes, Hopkins, 1946) 20ff.

At Horton in 1765, where he had singular success which led to the conversion of several individuals, Moulton facilitated a church covenant within the little group and baptized four or five according to its principles. After about two years in 1767, he was forced to withdraw from Horton, probably due to opposition from either Congregationalists or open communionists.[14] For the next half dozen years, Moulton returned to his landholdings near Yarmouth, as well as his duties as a magistrate and perhaps surveyor. Occasionally he preached and continued to create a stir,[15] until in 1772 he returned to Massachusetts, his debts from the 1760s having been either forgiven or forgotten.[16]

The small congregation at Horton continued as "the Baptist Church of Christ in Horton in Kings County," a familiar title from Separate Baptist experience in New England, and probably suggested by Moulton. At least one of the original covenanting members (Peter Bishop) of the

---

[14]Harris Harding's mother is said to have made the oft-qouted comment, "The Lord sent Mr. Moulton to Horton, but the devil drove him away," quoted in Edward M. Saunders, *History of the Baptists of the Maritime Provinces* (Halifax NS: John Burgoyne Press, 1902) 63.

"Letter of the Baptist Church of Christ in Horton to Elder John Davis of Boston" in Archives, Western Reserve Historical Society, Cleveland, Ohio. The letter was rediscovered by William G. McLoughlin and commented upon by J. M. Bumsted in "Origins of the Maritime Baptists: A New Document," *Dalhousie Review* 39 (1969): 88-93. While the historical and Baptist communities are indebted to Prof. Bumsted for his spadework, he missed several critical points and is seemingly incorrect on other matters. First, while Bumsted acknowledged assistance from McLoughlin in locating the letter, he did not apply any of McLoughlin's published date on Ebenezer Moulton's career in Massachusetts, relying instead upon eighteenth-century published work (only!) of Isaac Backus. Second, he seems disinclined to take the obvious elements of the letter to constitute the organization of a church. Church historians have commonly used less definitive data to establish the origins of a congregation elsewhere in New England. Finally, Bumsted accepted injudiciously the thesis of Edward Manning and later chroniclers that the original Horton church was of mixed communion; this was highly unlikely, given Moulton's past record as a strict closed communionist in Massachusetts and the post-1778 character of the Baptist church in Horton. Bumsted's engagement of the question of which congregation—Sackville or Horton—unfortunately diminished his attention to the details of Horton's reported early ministry in this vital matter.

[15]Stewart, *Documents*, 21-29; Stewart and Rawlyk, *A People Highly Favored of God*, 101-104, draws heavily upon the records of the church at Jebogue for the period in the early 1770s.

[16]Harris Harding credited Moulton with making the first Baptist converts in Yarmouth and afterwards enjoying great success at Horton. See *Account of the Rise and Progress of the First Baptist Church in Yarmouth, Nova Scotia*, by Harris Harding, quoted in *Life and Times of Rev. Harris Harding, Yarmouth, N.S.*, John Davis, comp. (Charlottetown PEI: Davis, 1866) 205-206.

Horton church under Moulton's ministry was present for its reconstituting in 1778. Fifteen years after its first organization[17], this small band continued to adhere to Baptistic principles, notably believer's baptism, religious liberty as a public policy, closed communion, and congregational independency, when they were reconstituted as a church and elected a new pastor.[18] This denominational proclivity greatly distressed evangelist Henry Alline (1748–1784), who desired that the church be built upon full enjoyment of religious (theological) liberty in nonessentials.[19]

Henry Fisk, a Baptist deacon in Sturbridge, Massachusetts, in the 1740s, called Moulton "God's threshing instrument," because he rid that village of infant baptism . . . an interesting and dramatic use of the planter motif which remained with Ebenezer throughout his ministry.[20] Yarmouth, Barrington, and especially Horton, with his preaching stations in Nova Scotia, remain Moulton's enduring legacy, and both the seedbed and threshing floor of Baptist principles in what is now Canada. Although

---

[17]Compare the "Records of The Wolfville, N.S. United Baptist Church, 1778–1819" (transcribed by Patricia Townshend) with the "Records of the Cornwallis, N.S. Congregational (New Light) Church, 1778–1795" (copy) in the Baptist Archives, Acadia University. Nothing is stated concerning mixed communion at Horton; rather the behaviour of this congregation in relation to the Cornwallis Church, which was mixed communion, confirms Horton's consistent closed communion pattern.

[18]The earliest accounts of the establishment of Horton Church were Isaac Chipman's three-part articles in the *Christian Messenger* titled "Historical Sketch Prepared for the Jubilee Celebrations Which Took Place at Horton, Parts of Which Only Were Read" 13 March, 86; 20 March, 93–94; 27 March, 99–100, and John Mockett Cramp's version in "History of Baptists in Nova Scotia," an uncollected series of sketches from the *Christian Messenger*, later bound in the Baptist Archives at Acadia. More recent versions include Ronald S. Longley, *The Wolfville United Baptist Church* (Wolfville NS: the Church, 1954) and Watson Kirkonnell, "The Grandmother of Canadian Baptist Churches" in *Bicentennial Essays: The Wolfville United Baptist Church, 1778–1783* (Hantsport NS: Lancelot Press, 1978) 8–12. (Kirkonnell wrongly identified the leadership of the church as "deacons," when the term "lay preacher" would have been more appropriate.) Henry Alline remarked in his journal that he was distressed by the disputes over "nonessentials" such as water baptism, adult baptism, and immersion, which indicates strong Baptist opinion. Alline preferred to base the church upon full enjoyment of religious liberty. See *The Journal of Henry Alline*, ed. James Beverly and Barry Moody (Hantsport NS: Lancelot Press, 1982) 97 and nn. 100-101, and Maurice W. Armstrong, *The Great Awakening in Nova Scotia 1776–1809* (Hartford CT: American Society of Church History, 1948) 68–73.

[19]Alline remarked in his diary of the establishment of the church at Horton, "O may the time come when Ephraim shall no more vex Judah, nor Judah envy Ephraim, and that there might never more be any disputes about . . . water baptism, the sprinkling of infants, or baptizing of adults by immersion . . . " (ibid., 97).

[20]This is an application of Micah 4:13.

to date he has been denied the formal designation of "planter[21]," Ebenezer Moulton must still be credited with having planted the principles of local Baptist church polity and practice in Nova Scotia.[22]

With the principles of New England local church polity and practice essentially in place by the 1780s—and, hence, reinforced by T. H. Chipman and others—the next step in church order was implementation of the associational principle. The idea of an association in denominational life was common when Baptists reached the Maritimes. English Baptists maintained an associational life from about 1626, and New Englanders had met from the 1690s. The purpose of such groups was to provide fellowship, mutual assistance, and advice on matters such as ordination, church discipline, and new church planting. New England Baptists are said to have come of age in 1760, when representatives of various congregations came together in Warren, Rhode Island, to consider James Manning's proposal for an association. Once constituted, this gathering was to oversee the first college in the North American denomination, addressing the all-important concerns of religious liberty for the New England community.

As previous historians have shown, the roots of associational life in Nova Scotia are located in the Annapolis Valley and were the result of New England influence. As early as 1797, an annual gathering of pastors met at various churches in the region for consultation.[23] This group included both Baptists and Paedo-Baptists—"planters for the most part"— until 1799. That year, in part because of a legal action taken against the Baptist pastor at Digby, concern arose over the matter of identity and a Baptist faction moved to a clearer definition of themselves.

Two strategies were applied, both demonstrating New England dependance. First, T. H. Chipman, pastor at Annapolis, was dispatched to Boston, Massachusetts, to confer with the eminent Samuel Stillman, pastor at First Baptist Church. Stillman was the most respected Baptist

---

[21]Modern scholarly definitions of "planter" include only those who remained permanently in Nova Scotia; cf. Levy, *The Baptists of the Maritime Provinces*, 19-22, with Judith A. Norton, comp., *New England Planters in the Maritime Provinces of Canada 1759–1800* (Toronto: University of Toronto Press, 1993) xi-xii, 372-96. Moulton certainly seems to qualify according to the definition given in *Planter Notes* 1 (1989): 2-3.

[22]The records of the Cornwallis/Horton Church (1778), the Cornwallis/ Upper Canard Church and Jebogue near Yarmouth clearly indicate the emerging patterns of faith and order commonly understood in New England as Regular Baptist.

[23]"Announcement of Agreement to Hold a Yearly Conference to Know Our Minds, 1797," in the Baptist Archives, Acadia University. This was a mixed communion body.

clergyman in New England in the premier pulpit of the denomination, and a wise counsel at that; he was also in regular correspondence with Baptists in England and was well educated in the tradition of Calvinistic Baptist life. Stillman advised the establishment of a Baptist association in Nova Scotia on closed communion principles, and he may even have urged the exclusion of Congregationalists, based upon problems with his own congregation years before.[24]

The second strategy was intriguing. Somehow, Chipman was put in contact with the leaders of the Danbury Association in Connecticut. The churches in this association had been a part of the Warren and/or Stonington associations from the 1770s. The rapid growth of churches in western New England in the late eighties led to a proliferation of new associations in the nineties. The Danbury Association was formed in 1791, composed of congregations from the near vicinity of Hartford. The plan of association adopted was built upon that of the Philadelphia and Warren Associations; it was closed communion and Calvinistic by name. It also acknowledged the English Baptist theological tradition in the Confession of 1688. The Danbury Association was a blend of former New Light (Suffield, Farmington) and old Baptist (Wallingford, Windsor) churches; it also included churches across state boundaries.[25] Early in their history as an association, the Danbury churches developed an interest in aiding destitute churches, which doubtless interested the Nova Scotians.[26]

In Nova Scotia Edward Manning at Cornwallis was asked to present an acceptable plan for an association to the 1800 gathering of churches at Upper Granville.[27] This he did, almost verbatim, from the preamble articles of the 1791 "Plan" of the Danbury Association. Manning's plan was adopted, the name of "Nova Scotia Baptist Association" was chosen, and the messengers agreed to pay the costs of printing the minutes and articles of association, plus setting up a legal defense fund for Enoch

---

[24]*The Journal of John Payzant*, ed. Brian C. Cuthbertson (Hantsport NS: Lancelot Press, 1981) 78-83. Payzant was angered by Chipman's precipitous closed communion action, as was Edward Manning at first.

[25]David Benedict, *A General History of the Baptist Denomination in America and Other Parts of the World* (New York: Lewis Colby, 1848) 472-80. See also Goen, *Revivalism and Separatism*, 266.

[26]Philip F. Evans, *History of the Connecticut Baptist Convention 1823–1907* (Hartford CT: Smith-Linsley, 1909) 11-12.

[27]Mss. "Minutes of the Nova Scotia and New Brunswick Association, 1800," in Baptist Archives, Acadia University.

Towner of Digby.[28] The ostensible reason for organizing an association was the rumour mill which cast aspersions on the principles of the ministers. Stillman in Boston had no doubt suggested that the best defense for the pastor in trouble was a clear sense of organizational identity and solidarity such as an association might convey. T. H. Chipman, Enoch Towner, and James Manning were the leaders in assuring it would be styled according to Baptist principles, although Edward Manning and Joseph Dimock, who joined the Association, represented mixed communion congregations.

The rules of the Association, buttressed by the Circular Letter, specifically stated sovereign grace, sincere profession of faith in Christ, believer's baptism by immersion, congregational worship and discipline, and the independency of the churches.[29] The theological tradition of the Association was clearly in line with the Warren and Philadelphia Associations, moreso the Warren on the matter of stressing the independence of the churches, a New England distinctive. The key New England characters in this creation had been Samuel Stillman and the author of the articles of the Danbury Connecticut Association Plan. The plan for a baptistic, closed communion associative body went very much according to Stillman's advice and Chipman's tenacity. By 1800, then, congregations and a pattern of church order had been transplanted from New England to Nova Scotia.

Propagating the Seed:
Structures for Mission and New England Voluntarism

The most far-reaching transplantation of New England Baptist culture to Nova Scotia involved the Massachusetts Baptist Missionary Society (MBMS). Formed in 1802, the Society was part of the great missionary expansion of American Protestants, and is rightly the parent of the Ameri-

---

[28]Cramp, "History of Baptists in Nova Scotia," 75; Rawlyk, "From New Light to Baptist: Harris Harding and the Second Great Awakening in Nova Scotia," in *Repent and Believe: The Baptist Experience in Maritime Canada* (Hantsport: Lancelot Press, 1980) 21. There was no indication of any operational link or accountability between the Danbury Association and the Nova Scotia Association, as Rawlyk suggests.

[29]Silas T. Rand, *The Jubilee Historical Sketch of the Nova Scotia Baptist Association* (Charlottetown PEI: James Haszard, 1849) 8-11; "Circular Letter, 1800," mss. in Baptist Archives, Acadia University.

can Baptist domestic missions movement.[30] Its missionaries did more to propagate New England Baptist ideals than any other single force.

The Society was the leading element of an emerging voluntary pattern in New England's religious mission. Organized on the basis of individual donations (one dollar per annum), a simple board of trustees—all Bostonian Baptist pastors—superintended the work. The Society articulated its work and nurtured and expanded its constituency through a monthly journal, the *Massachusetts Baptist Missionary Magazine*, first published in 1802, and was highly focused on its domestic mission work, its corporate proceedings being essentially the reports of its field staff.

In founding the MBMS, the leadership desired "to furnish occasional preaching and to promote the knowledge of evangelic truth in the new settlements within the United States . . . or farther if circumstances should render it proper." This meant aid to destitute churches, supply of missionaries in the fields, and setting in order a sense of denominational identity. The Society was both the logical result of the Great Awakening, as well as the response of the New England Baptist community to the growing opportunity for Baptist expansion. At first its "fields" (to use yet another agricultural metaphor) included northern New England, western New York, and Pennsylvania. When it became politically expedient, by 1804 Upper Canada, Nova Scotia, and New Brunswick had been added to the list.[31]

Principally Isaac Case, Henry Hale, and T. H. Chipman were on the payroll from 1806 to 1817. Also worth noting were the names of Joseph Crandall and Daniel Merrill, who received grants and sent infrequent reports to the Society's trustees. The mission of Isaac Case illustrates the nature of the New England influence upon Nova Scotian Baptist life. Upon entering New Brunswick on his first tour to Canada in December of 1806, Case observed, "This place hath been settled twenty years, but they have lived without God until about a year ago." When he reached Nova Scotia on another Maritime tour a year and a half later, he found congenial circumstances: "There is a great call for ministerial labors in

---

[30]William H. Brackney, "Yankee Benevolence in Yorker Lands: The Origins of the American Baptist Home Mission Society," *Foundations* 24 (1981): 293-309.

[31]The trustees admonished the missionaries not to become involved in political matters. Upon entering the British dominions, often a local pastor would facilitate relations with the magistrates. Although permission to preach was granted, missionaries still suffered mild verbal harassment.

this province.... Religious people, especially ministers of the gospel, are here trusted with great respect by all classes."

Not merely revivalist enthusiasts, the Massachusetts missionaries were also advocates of New England Baptist church order. Isaac Case's influence in the Annapolis Valley was felt deeply in the first decades. Edward Manning, pastor at Cornwallis Church, a mixed communion congregation, wrestled with the issue of believer's baptism by immersion beginning around 1796. Soon he was baptized in 1797 at Annapolis by T. H. Chipman, a colleague and cofounder of their Association.[32] Subsequently, several new converts were added to the Cornwallis church and were admitted upon believer's baptism. Manning's personal shift, followed by that of the Cornwallis church, led to a question of the validity of his ordination as a legitimate mixed communionist. Elders Isaac Case and Henry Hale of the Massachusetts Society appeared at Horton in 1808 as part of an evangelistic tour, and worked through the personal transformation with Manning. Within a few days, Case and Hale supervised Manning's reordination as a Regular Baptist clergyman, now recognized by New England brethren. Case wrote to the Society, "God was pleased to give Manning further light and to establish his mind in the order of his house."[33] David Benedict, a New England historian using materials supplied by Manning himself, recorded in his 1813 edition "by the advice and assistance of Case and Hale, a unanimity among them was obtained and his reordination was effected. Since that time they have moved on in order and harmony."[34]

Thomas H. Chipman also worked in harmony with the Society, corresponding regularly with Baptist leaders in Massachusetts until he became a kind of agent for the Society in Nova Scotia. In 1806 he requested twelve subsciptions to the magazine, as the magazines have been blessed of many in these parts."[35] Joseph Crandall, the first regularly ordained minister in the province of New Brunswick, was a Baptist native of

---

[32]In a quotation in Cramp, "History of Baptists in Nova Scotia," 58-59, Manning recounted the story of his struggle. I. E. Bill, *Fifty Years with the Baptist Ministers and Churches of the Maritime Provinces of Canada* (St. John NB: Barnes, 1880) 30, leaves some doubt on the precise date of Manning's baptism.

[33]Isaac Case to the Massachusetts Baptist Missionary Society, May 18, 1808. Printed in MBMS, 75. Presumably the "order of his house" was Regular Baptist polity and practice.

[34]David Benedict, *A General History of the Baptist Denomination in America and Other Parts of the World* (Boston: Lincoln and Edmands, 1813) 285-86.

[35]T. H. Chipman to MBMS, 5 December 1806, 305.

Rhode Island who developed a wide-ranging reputation as a rugged frontiersman and church planter in isolated forest regions whose exploits were in tandem with the Society's New England Baptist itinerants.[36]

Beyond its immediate involvement in providing for traveling preachers, the MBMS also provided a model for mission organization. In the Nova Scotia and New Brunswick Association meeting for 1815, the decision was made to begin a missionary society in conjunction with the Association. Isaac Case of the Massachusetts Society had been seated with the delegates and surely reminded them that this was the precise arrangement in Massachusetts. Thomas H. Chipman (agent for the MBMS, and New England Baptist culture!) wrote in the Corresponding Letter for the meeting, "We rejoice to find that our American brethren shew themselves remarkably spirited in forming so many societies for the advancement of the Redeemer's Kingdom . . . their zeal in the end, will we doubt not, give the American brethren a distinguished rank among the host of nations."[37] This remark spoke boldly in the midst of the Napoleonic Wars.

Similarly, at its Fredericton meeting in 1822, the New Brunswick Association declared itself a missionary society, following the influence of Edward Manning and James Munro of the Nova Scotia Association[38]. In January of 1827 the Nova Scotia and New Brunswick associations jointly published their first issues of the *Baptist Missionary Magazine of Nova Scotia and New Brunswick*, modelled on the plan of the Massachusetts magazine.[39]

The work and organizational model brought to the Maritimes by the MBMS was of lasting significance. A zeal for the gospel and gospel

---

[36] Crandall later recalled his peregrinations as an evangelist; he did not mention being on the roster of the Massachusetts Society. See Rev. Joseph Crandall, "New Brunswick Baptist History" Mss. in the Baptist Archives, Acadia and critiqued in J. M. Bumsted, "The Autobiography of Joseph Crandall" *Acadiensis* 3 (1973): 79-96. For useful biographical detail on Crandall, see I. E. Bill, *The Life of the Departed; A Sermon Occasioned by the Death of the Rev. Joseph Crandall of Salisbury* (St. John NB: Barnes and Co., 1858).

[37] "Corresponding Letter," *Minutes of the Nova Scotia and New Brunswick Association Held at the Baptist Meetinghouse in Cornwallis June 26th and 27th 1815* (Saint John NB: Henry Chubb, 1815) 11.

[38] Joseph Crandall, not present for the first meeting in 1822, was a key figure in 1823 and after. Relationships with New England Baptist associations were approved that year.

[39] The first two issues included intelligence from the *American Baptist Magazine* and a lengthy obituary of Thomas Baldwin, late Boston promoter of the Massachusetts Society and president-elect of Waterville College in Maine.

order, plus a quick, efficient vehicle to propagate the interests of mission, were firmly planted by New Englanders.

Planting a Permanent Seedbed

The third major illustration of the transplantation of Baptist culture from New England to Nova Scotia was seen in the development of a learned ministry for the leadership of the congregations. Here a small, but highly influential group of New Englanders and two institutions were of great influence. The leaders were Irah Chase, Alexis Caswell, Henry Green, and Edmund Crawley, and the institutions Waterville and Newton. There was certainly more than first met the eye regarding the interrelationships.

Well developed by the 1820s, and largely Congregational in design, the Baptists quite energetically emulated a familiar New England pattern. The crowning achievement of the Baptist system was the university or four-year liberal arts college; Baptists had two: the College of Rhode Island or Brown (1764), and Waterville College (1812). The strength of the denomination's intellectual life came from a Brown elite, while Waterville struggled valiantly in its first two decades to survive. These colleges were in turn fed by a series of high-quality academies throughout the region: New London in New Hampshire, Suffield in Connecticut, Ricker and Coburn in Maine, and a smaller school in Warren, Rhode Island. Many Baptist students also attended the academies of other denominations, notably, Phillips Exeter and Andover.

For those students wishing to enter the ministry, the final graduate stage was to be taken at Newton Theological Institution (1825) outside Boston. Newton enjoyed the full patronage of the Massachusetts Baptist Missionary Society, the Massachusetts Baptist Convention, the Baptist conventions of Connecticut and Maine, and the Northern Baptist Education Society. Prominent clergy, like Thomas Baldwin and Samuel Stillman of Boston, as well as Joseph Grafton of Newton Centre, Lucius Bolles of Salem, and Francis Wayland of Providence were religious patrons of Newton when it opened in 1825.

The choice of an inaugural professor for the first Baptist theological seminary in the United States[40] was a momentous one. Irah Chase, a

---

[40]See my article, "Dissenter Religion, Voluntary Associations and the National Vision: Private Education in the Early Republic," in *Voluntary Associations in a Free Society: A Symposium on the Bicentennial of the Birth of Luther Rice*, ed. Robert G. Jones (Washington DC: George Washington University, 1983) 10ff., for an explanation of how

graduate of Middlebury College in Vermont and Andover Theological Seminary, taught at Philadelphia, and later, Columbian College as well (1817–1823). He virtually designed Newton's postgraduate curriculum and influenced the entire Baptist family of schools. Chase had occasion to observe and implement William Staughton's English model at Philadelphia, as well as his own experience as a student under Moses Stuart at Andover. Stuart's emphasis upon critical biblical studies and the Andover postgraduate plan became the most powerful influences upon Chase.

Chase was clever in his strategies for planting the New England model in Newton's interest. He traveled broadly and made friends for Newton in many locales; his chief challenge was to differentiate Newton from Andover, from which many Baptist ministers had graduated. As he travelled in the Maritimes and corresponded with ministers in the region, he advocated first the establishment of academies, then full literary colleges. Those candidates who had the capability and resources for full studies, Chase lured to Newton.

In 1827 the well-traveled Chase was in his third year as president at Newton. He was aware of the Baptist community in the Maritimes and looked at Nova Scotia as a field ripe for student recruitment. When a group of evangelical Anglicans formed a new congregation in Halifax that year, Irah Chase was invited as one of the most eminent of New England Baptists to help constitute the church which became Granville Street Baptist. He also baptized six of the constituting members. In the next decade, Chase continued to be a resource to Maritime Baptists through his publications and correspondence.

Chase planned to stay only briefly in Halifax. His strategy was to hand the leadership of the young congregation over to his most trusted devotee, Alexis Caswell, who proved to be another vital link between New England and Nova Scotia. Caswell, a graduate of Brown, had studied with William Staughton and Chase at Columbian College in Washington, D.C., and served as a tutor on its first faculty. He was barely twenty years old when he arrived in Halifax with Chase in 1828, and Chase believed Caswell needed pastoral experience and recognition as a bonafide clergyman. Caswell acknowledged a call to the pastorate at Granville Street and gladly took on the assignment for almost a year.[41] In

---

Newton deserves this distinction.

[41] The record of Caswell's ministry is preserved in "Records of the First United Baptist Church, Halifax, N.S., Book I, 1827–1832," 1-10, in Baptist Archives, Acadia University.

1828 Caswell returned to Providence to teach at his alma mater, where he remained for thirty-six years. In his critical year at Halifax, he won at least one convert who would be of enduring value to Maritime theological education, Edmund Albern Crawley (1799–1888).

At the time of his formal conversion to the Baptist faith, Crawley was a young evangelical Anglican lawyer much drawn to Caswell (they were the same age). Crawley was a graduate of King's College in Windsor, the oldest Anglican school north of the former American colonies. His education consisted of a British approach to training for the professions: a heavy emphasis upon classical authors in Greek and Latin such as Xenophon, Homer, and Cicero, plus two years of New Testament Greek and at least one year of the Hebrew Bible. While theology courses per se were lacking, Crawley possessed excellent skills in the languages and would be shaped for future ideas of ministerial formation.[42]

Alexis Caswell had a profound influence upon the young lawyer Crawley, and in fact, baptized him. Upon Edmund's decision to enter the ministry, he chose to train at Andover Seminary, where Chase had graduated. After completing two years at Andover, Crawley went to Brown University to pursue advanced studies with Caswell and was eventually ordained there. Crawley's debt to Caswell was large, particularly in the growing area of science and religion. Caswell became one of the preeminent teaching scientists of his era, and Crawley fostered a congenial climate at what became Acadia University for scientific inquiry.

Before pressing on with the New England influence upon the institutions at Horton/Wolfville, mention needs to be made of the last link in the chain of New England Baptist divines: Henry K. Green (1800?–1862). Green, a graduate of Union College, Albany New York, who also took two years at Andover Seminary, taught with Chase and Caswell at Columbian College from 1826 to 1828. When that institution closed due to financial stresses, Green was recommended to the Granville St. Church in Halifax by his former faculty colleagues, particularly Caswell. Green did well at the church, but found himself the object of an intrigue among certain influential members of the church who wanted to open the

---

[42]On the curriculum at Kings College, see C. E. Thomas, "The Early Days of Kings College, Windsor, Nova Scotia 1750–1815," in *Journal of the Canadian Church Historical Society* 6:3 and the older Thomas B. Akins, *A Brief Account of the Origin, Endowment, and Progress of the University of Kings College* (Halifax: McNab and Shaffer, 1865) 73, and Henry Y. Hind, *The Centennial of Kings College* (New York: Church Review Co., 1890).

pastorate to the returning Crawley. Green left his mark on the church's quality of leadership and the Nova Scotia Baptist community before leaving the province in 1831 to return to teaching at Washington College.

The dream of a Baptist theological school in Nova Scotia may be traced to 1817, when Thomas McCulloch (1776–1843) at Pictou Academy invited the Baptists to join in a united dissenter educational effort. Edward Manning, Charles Tupper, and others, however, believed that the Baptist community should secure its own school, and were encouraged in this as they observed the progress of Waterville College in Maine. In 1821 Jeremiah Chaplin, president of Waterville, spoke at the Nova Scotia Association meetings and was well received. Manning had become an advisor to Chaplin on fundraising and an agent in Nova Scotia for the College. Though self-taught, Manning was developing—in both Nova Scotia and Maine—quite a reputation for advocacy of higher education for ministry.[43]

In early 1827, with the prospects of a church being organized out of the schism among Anglicans at Halifax, Manning and Charles Tupper made further efforts to establish a seminary. The young lawyer, Edmund Crawley, close to professing his Baptist sentiments, was dispatched by Tupper and Manning to go to Waterville to induce Chaplin to come to Halifax to constitute a church and lay the foundation for a school; New England prestige and support were highly desirable in the minds of the Fathers.[44] Chaplin, however, declined to make the trip; fortunately, Crawley also visited the new Baptist seminary at Newton and its president, Irah Chase, agreed to come as well. Back in Halifax, expectations of New England leadership were so high that John Ferguson believed he would soon witness "the Lord's anointed when he comes amongst us . . . and the downfall of Satan's kingdom"![45]

Once on the scene in Halifax, Chase and Caswell moved the Nova Scotian dream into a distinctly New England stream. Caswell wrote to

---

[43] Jeremiah Chaplin to Edward Manning, 25 September 1819. Manning Correspondence, Baptist Archives, Acadia University. Chaplin treated Manning like a confidante and believed Manning knew more about fundraising than anyone else in the Maine Baptist associations.

[44] The terminology "Fathers" applied to the first generation of Baptist leaders in Nova Scotia: Edward Manning, Theodore Seth Harding, James Manning, Thomas H. Chipman, Joseph Dimock, Harris Harding, and Joseph Crandall. Most were first- or second-generation emigrants from New England.

[45] John Ferguson to Edward Manning, 10 August 1827. Manning Correspondence, Baptist Archives, Acadia University.

Manning in April of 1828 regarding the need for a "seminary of learning under the patronage of the Baptists." With guidance from Chase and the assistance of members at Granville Street, Caswell recommended not a school to train ministers, but an academy for general instruction "in subjects like arithmetic, geometry, grammar, rhetoric and navigation."[46] Caswell's institution was designed for young men called to the ministry and also of general interest to the provincial legislature. This dramatic shift in planning from a ministerial training school to an academy is most easily explained by the desire of the New England Baptist educators to have another feeder school for their institutions, without allowing competition from the northeast. In their view, New England and the Maritime Provinces were a single region of denominational culture, regardless of political boundaries. New Englanders would support academies financially and recognize their graduates. . . . Newton would benefit, as would Waterville.[47]

The Nova Scotians did not seem to mind the subjugation of their dreams to the New England hegemony. In fact, they met with jubilation at Fowlers Hotel in Horton after the association meeting in 1828, and adopted the plan submitted by Caswell, Crawley, and others in the Halifax circle.[48] In addition to agreeing on the type of school they would have, the "Fathers" also organized a Nova Scotia Baptist Education Society based on the plan which Waterville and Newton followed.[49] Soon thereafter, Crawley declared his intentions for the ministry and left to study at Andover, the school of his founding pastor, Irah Chase. There can be little doubt that Edmund Crawley saw himself as the "well-educated Baptist minister to head the institution" whom Caswell had described to Manning.[50] Bill, and later R. S. Longley, would label Crawley the first Baptist of the Maritimes to obtain a full ministerial education. He was, to all intents and educational purposes, a New Englander.

---

[46] Alexis Caswell to Edward Manning, 4 April 1828. Manning Correspondence, Baptist Archives, Acadia University.

[47] This thesis is born out by Ernst Marriner, the historian of Colby (Waterville) College. He believed that Waterville's reduction from a literary and theological institution to a liberal arts school was in deference to the plans to raise up Newton. See Ernst Cummings Marriner, *The History of Colby College* (Waterville ME: Colby College Press, 1963) 47.

[48] Bill, *Fifty Years*, 67; Saunders, *Maritime Provinces*, 193.

[49] See the Nutting papers in Baptist Archives, Acadia University.

[50] Alexis Caswell to Edward Manning, 4 April 1828. Manning Correspondence, Baptist Archives, Acadia University.

As one looks back from the 1830s and follows the formative period of Nova Scotia's Baptist culture, there can be discerned an unmistakable transplantation of New England's to nascent social and religious institutions in the Maritimes. In a world given much to religious orientation, here was an important application of a planter motif derived from Scripture. Elder Harris Harding, a Nova Scotian whose family was itself from New England, made the connection in one of the first written local church histories of a Baptist congregation in the region:

> Whereunto shall we liken the Kingdom of God? Or with what comparison shall we compare it? It is like a grain of mustard seed, which, when it is sown in the earth, is less than all the seeds that be in the earth. But when it is sown, it groweth up, and becometh greater than all herbs, and shooteth out great branches. . . . (Mark 4:30-32 KJV)[51]

---

[51]"Account of the Rise and Progress of the First Baptist Church in Yarmouth, Nova Scotia" by Elder Harris Harding, quoted in *Life and Times of the Late Harris Harding*, 205. Harding saw himself as a metaphor of the harvest; see his letter to Lavina D'Wolf, 20 August 1791: "I see the fields all white before me and Believe I'm going to reap a Glorious Harvest. . . . I shall Bring my Sheaves with joy." Quoted in *New Light Letters and Songs*, ed. George A. Rawlyk (Hantsport NS: Lancelot Press, 1983), 131.

A. J. Gordon and H. Grattan Guinness: A Case Study of Transatlantic Evangelicalism

Scott M. Gibson

1. Introduction

The transatlantic nature of evangelicalism in the late nineteenth century is perhaps traced best by way of a ship's log. Schooners and passenger liners sailed the Atlantic Ocean carrying within them the luminaries of Victorian evangelicalism. From America's D. L. Moody to Britain's F. B. Meyer, late nineteenth-century evangelical leaders crisscrossed the ocean, all the while building up an elaborate network of relationships and support for their various corners of the evangelical kingdom.

The Victorian era was a period of close cultural relations between Britain and the United States. British religious leaders like C. H. Spurgeon and F. B. Meyer met Americans like A. J. Gordon, D. L. Moody, and Ira D. Sankey, while American authors like Mark Twain and Henry Wadsworth Longfellow were read in Britain, along with Charles Dickens and William Butler Yeats. Evangelical Americans such as Samuel F. B. Morse and Frances Willard contributed to the culture of Victorian Britain. In both Britain and America, Victorian religion was predominantly middle-class Protestant, identified with Western civilization, and was culturally powerful. Churches experienced large numerical increases, due mostly to revivals.[1] The gap between the two countries seemed to diminish as the turn of the century drew near.

2. Transnational Studies

Perhaps one of the earliest studies on the impact of transatlantic exchange between North America and Britain was John Wesley White's 1963 study of the influence of North American evangelism in Britain, for which he concentrated on the impressive transatlantic work of D. L. Moody.[2] Later,

---

[1]See Daniel Walker Howe, "Victorian Culture in America," *Victorian America*, ed. Daniel Walker Howe (Philadelphia PA: University of Pennsylvania Press, 1976).

[2]John Wesley White, "The Influence of North American Evangelism in Great Britain between 1830 and 1914 on the Origin and Development of the Ecumenical Movement"

Richard Carwardine published an extensive study on transatlantic revivalism as well, demonstrating the important influence American revival had in Britain, and exploring the similarities and differences of the effects of revival in both countries. Edith L. Blumhofer and Randall Balmer edited a volume on the various forms that revivals have taken in the modern period and the influences that have accompanied them. These essays underscore the transnational nature of revivalism.[3]

Perhaps more recently, Mark Noll at Wheaton College, David W. Bebbington at University of Stirling, and George Rawlyk at Queens University in Canada edited a significant volume on the interconnections between British, American, and Canadian evangelicals, as also their brothers and sisters in other parts of the world. The book focuses on the transnational contexts that have conditioned evangelical convictions, behavior, patterns of organization, strategies of communication, responses to cultural change, and participation in ideological controversies. Although Ernest R. Sandeen acknowledged the impact of British millenarianism on North America, and George W. Marsden at Notre Dame University added the components of revivalism, holiness movements, and relation to culture, their concerns have been widened by the authors included in this anthology, especially by their intimating the richness of comparative study in the broader movement of evangelicalism.[4]

Similarly, another volume edited by Joel A. Carpenter and Wilbert R. Shenk recounts the story of North American evangelical missions as they grew from being a junior partner in the British enterprise to become the dominant force. Although this collection concentrates on American evangelicalism, it also provides a context for understanding American

---

(D.Phil. dissertation, University of Oxford, 1963).

[3]Richard Carwardine, *Transatlantic Revivalism: Popular Evangelicalism in Britain and America, 1790–1865* (Westport CT: Greenwood Press, 1978). Another important study is Susan Durden, "Transatlantic Communications and Influence during the Great Awakening: A Comparative Study of British and American Revivalism, 1730–1760," (Ph.D. dissertation, University of Hull, 1978). Edith L. Blumhofer and Randall Balmer, eds., *Modern Christian Revivals* (Urbana and Chicago IL: University of Illinois Press, 1993).

[4]Mark A. Noll, David W. Bebbington, and George A. Rawlyk, eds., *Evangelicalism: Comparative Studies of Popular Protestantism in North America, the British Isles, and Beyond, 1700–1990* (New York: Oxford University Press, 1994). Ernest R. Sandeen, *The Roots of Fundamentalism: British and American Millenarianism 1800–1930* (Grand Rapids MI: Baker, 1978); George M. Marsden, *Fundamentalism and American Culture: The Shaping of Twentieth-Century Evangelicalism 1870–1925* (New York: Oxford University Press, 1980).

missions overseas.⁵ All of the volumes mentioned above underscore the nature of transatlantic evangelicalism and suggest a cross-pollination heightened by revivalism, missionary interests, and theological concerns—important factors in appreciating the forces that contributed to the context of late nineteenth century evangelicals like A. J. Gordon.

Adoniram Judson Gordon (1836–1895) was born in New Hampton, New Hampshire; was schooled at the Regular Baptist New London Literary and Scientific Institution in New London, New Hampshire; and did his undergraduate studies at Brown University in Providence, Rhode Island, and his theological study at Newton Theological Institution in Newton Centre, Massachusetts. His first pastorate was the Baptist Church in Jamaica Plain, Massachusetts—outside of Boston—from 1863–1869. From there he became the pastor of the Clarendon Street Baptist Church, Boston. He died at the age of fifty-eight in 1895.

Gordon became one of the leading Evangelicals of his day, recognized in not only the United Status, but Great Britain as well. For twenty-five years he served a large urban congregation, but his influence went beyond the city limits of Boston, Massachusetts. He was a supporter of international revivalist D. L. Moody, who came to Boston to hold revival meetings during the winter of 1877–1878. Gordon was a promoter of foreign missions and, in fact, led his own Baptist denomination's missionary board. He wrote hymns and edited hymnbooks and even authored several books. He became one of the most recognized advocates for premillennial interpretation of prophecy of his day, preaching about the second coming, writing articles and books on the topic, and editing a monthly journal focused on it.

3. The Gordon and Guinness Connection: Missions

Although A. J. Gordon and H. Grattan Guinness intersected in the arena of missions, their relationship was fueled by their common interest in the premillennial return of Christ. Gordon was raised in a devoutly missions-minded Baptist home. His parents named him after the first American Baptist missionary, Adoniram Judson (1788–1850). Even as a theological student at Newton, Gordon had an interest in foreign missions when he became a member of the American Baptist Missionary Union⁶ (and later

---

⁵Joel A. Carpenter and Wilbert R. Shenk, eds., *Earthen Vessels: American Evangelicals and Foreign Missions, 1880–1980* (Grand Rapids MI: Eerdmans, 1990).

⁶"Forty-Seventh Annual Report," *The Missionary Magazine* 41/7 (July 1861): 194.

a life member in 1864), during his first year as a pastor.[7] He studied mission development for the denomination and occasionally presented reports at the annual meetings.[8] In 1871 Gordon was appointed to the highest decision-making body of the Missionary Union—the Executive Committee[9], headquartered in Boston and consisting of about ten members who met biweekly to appoint missionaries, plan strategies for fund-raising, and establish new missions.

Gordon held the position of recording secretary,[10] until in June 1888 he was elected chairman of the committee,[11] proceeding to become especially influential in the 1884 acquisition of the Livingstone Inland Mission in Africa, the mission founded earlier by H. Grattan Guinness.

Harry Grattan Guinness (1835–1910), on the other hand, was an Irish-born evangelist and missions advocate. Born in 1835 near Kingstown, Ireland, Guinness was educated at private schools in Clevedon and Exeter, and went on to spend some time studying at New College, London University. Though he did not complete his second year, during his stay he devoted his energy to evangelistic meetings.[12]

Guinness had a reputation as an evangelist and preacher in London—rivaling even Charles Haddon Spurgeon in popularity—preaching often at Moorfields Tabernacle.[13] Word of his ability as an evangelist spread across the Atlantic to the United States. In light of the 1858–1859 revival that had swept across the United States, he received an invitation to conduct evangelistic meetings in various churches in Philadelphia. He then spent the next several weeks in New York City and other cities in the northeast United States and Canada.[14]

---

[7]"Fifth Annual Meeting Report," *The Missionary Magazine* 44/7 (July 1864): 295.

[8]E.g., "Report on the Assam Mission, *The Missionary Magazine* 48/7 (July 1868) 202, 205-206; Mission to France," *The Missionary Magazine* 66/7 (July 1886): 204.

[9]"Fifty-Seventh Annual Meeting of the Board," *The Missionary Magazine* 51/7 (July 1871): 208.

[10]1874–1878 Minutes of the Executive Committee of the American Baptist Missionary Union, Books G & H, Archives of American Baptist Foreign Mission Society, Valley Forge, PA. Hereafter, ABMU Minutes.

[11]Ibid., 1 June 1888, bk. K.

[12]"In Memorium: H. Grattan Guinness, D.D., F.R.A.S.," *Regions Beyond* 32/1&2 (January–February 1911): 12-13. See also Elizabeth Pritchard, *For Such a Time* (Eastbourne: RBMU and Victory Press, 1973) 1-26.

[13]*Dictionary of National Biography*, supplement January 1901–December 1911, vol. 2 (Oxford: Oxford University Press, 1912) 175-76.

[14]"In Memorium," 16-17.

In 1860 Guinness married Fanny Fitzgerald (1831–1898). On their evangelistic tours they came into contact with the Plymouth Brethren and were introduced to the study of prophecy. Both of the Guinnesses became interested in the Brethren's teaching about the second coming of Christ, and subsequently published in 1861 their first brochure on prophecy.[15]

Grattan Guinness discovered that his evangelistic zeal for bringing people to Christ was not limited to city evangelism, but stretched also to peoples in other countries who had never heard of Christ. At the close of 1865, Guinness was in Dublin and decided to establish a "Training Home for Evangelists and Missionaries." His goal was

> to form them (young men) into a class, and encourage them to study as well as to preach, etc., while still pursuing their secular calling, so as to be well assured, ere he sanctions their abandoning it, that they are really adapted for the work to which they devote themselves.[16]

Guinness persuaded J. Hudson Taylor, who was then speaking in Liverpool, to visit his school in Dublin. Taylor was impressed, and this encounter began a lifelong relationship and mutual interest in missions for the two of them.[17]

Although the life of the school in Dublin was only one year, the seeds were planted for a lifelong interest in the cause of missions. After a short while in Bath, England, the Guinnesses spent two years preaching and establishing churches in France. When Guinness returned to Ireland in 1872, he made plans to establish a missionary college in London. After securing a building in East London, the Guinnesses opened the school with six students in March 1873. The school grew, all the while training its students to become evangelists and foreign missionaries. Branches of the school were opened in Bow and in Derbyshire.[18] Some of the first students to leave the Institute went on to become missionaries in China.[19]

4. The Livingstone Inland Mission, Gordon, and the ABMU

With the opening of Africa by Henry M. Stanley in the 1870s came the challenge to send missionaries to the Congo region. In 1877 the

---

[15]Ibid., 20.
[16]Ibid., 23. The latter is a quote from a letter written by Fanny Guinness.
[17]Ibid., 23-24. See also: Alvyn Austin, "Loved Ones in the Homelands: The Missionary Influence on North America," *Evangelical Studies Bulletin* 14/1 (Spring 1997): 3.
[18]Ibid., 28-29.
[19]Ibid., 31.

Livingstone Inland Mission—named after the missionary-explorer David Livingstone—began as a result of the efforts of Reverend A. Tully of Cardiff, James Irvine of Liverpool, and H. Grattan and Fanny Guinness. In 1878 the committee supporting sending the two graduates of the Guinnesses' institute to the Congo. For three years the original committee attempted to rally support for the mission, but it ultimately became the responsibility of the Guinnesses.[20] From 1880 to 1884, the Guinnesses attempted to raise the necessary money. However, in 1883 they took over the American Baptist Missionary Union (ABMU), giving it the direction and financial stability it needed.[21]

In her 30 April 1883 appeal to the corresponding secretary of the American Baptist Missionary Union, John N. Murdock, Fanny Guinness wrote:

> [T]he thought immediately occurred to me that if the "American Baptist's Union" is wishing to undertake a mission in Africa, we might be glad to resign into their hands our mission on the Congo. For some time past we have been feeling that it is almost too serious an undertaking for individuals like ourselves, & that it would be better to transfer it to some larger & well organized society. We should probably have taken steps to do this before but for the difficulty that lay in the way. As you are aware, the English Baptists have also a mission on the Congo, & it would not, of course, be wise to have a second there which was not Baptist in feeling. Now, though we do not call ourselves Baptists we agree with that denomination on the subject of baptism, & though our mission is undenominational, it works in perfect harmony with the Baptists. We might have surrendered it into their hands, but this, we felt, would simply be halving the amount of benefit now accruing on the Congo, as our giving up our mission to them would not have enabled the Baptists of England to do more than they are already doing. My dear husband had often said, "If the American Baptists were willing to undertake it, I would gladly surrender it to them. They have resources sufficient to enable them to carry it on vigorously, & the English Baptists would probably welcome their cooperation."[22]

At first the AMBU expressed caution in accepting yet another responsibility into their already stretched budget. After months of

---

[20]"The Livingstone Congo Inland Mission: Transfer to American Management," *Regions Beyond* (July 1884) 113.

[21]Ibid., 33-35; Edmund F. Merriam, *The American Baptist Missionary Union and Its Missions* (Boston: American Baptist Missionary Union, 1897) 185-86, 188-89. Mrs. H. Grattan Guinness, "Two Months in America," *Regions Beyond* (December 1884): 174.

[22]Fanny E. Guinness, letter to John N. Murdoch, 30 April 1883, reel 104-12, ABFMS Archives: American Baptist Historical Society.

discussion and special committee reports, however, a recommendation was forwarded to the national gathering.[23] In spite of the Union's large deficit, the Executive Committee voted to take it over.[24]

A. J. Gordon was immediately appointed to the committee of three to determine the future of the mission.[25] A committee of two was, likewise, commissioned to visit the Congo in order to ascertain its condition and needs. The latter committee was to report to the former and decisions would then be made.[26] However, the deputation to the Congo left the United States in the middle of the summer, and unfortunately, reached only England. From there they simply communicated with the missionaries in Africa by letter, while conversing with the Guinnesses.[27] Although inept in its longsighted view, this committee provided the recommendations to Gordon's committee, which then offered two different reports. The majority review reported that the missionaries employed in the Congo were not in general men of sufficient natural capacity to carry on the work; they had "done too much exploring and too little study of the languages and preaching to the natives"; and the labor yet to be done in a widespread field was too massive. They recommended either reduction of the mission or a return of the mission to the Guinnesses.

Gordon authored the other report criticizing the deputation and its vicarious trip to the Congo. He noted sarcastically that the deputation report

> bears the characteristics of inclusiveness & uncertainty which might be expected in a document attempting to formulate the most confident conclusions in regard to climate, population and missionary policy existing on the banks of the Congo, . . . based solely on the inquiries on the banks of the Thames.[28]

---

[23]"Report of the Committee on Missions in Africa," *Baptist Missionary Magazine* 64/7 (July 1884): 190-92.

[24]ABMU Minutes, 9 September 1884, bk. J. See also: Robert G. Torbet, *Venture of Faith* (Philadelphia PA: Judson Press, 1955) 321-30.

[25]Ibid., 19 October 1885, 29 March 1886, 12 April 1886, bk. J.

[26]"The Congo Mission," *The American Baptist Missionary Magazine* 46/7 (July 1886): 295-97. The two appointed as a delegation to the Congo were Edward Judson (1844–1914), president of the Union and A. Loughridge, missionary at Hanamaconda, India, who had asked for reassignment to the Congo.

[27]"The Delegation to the Congo," *The American Baptist Missionary Magazine* 65/8 (August 1885): 323.

[28]ABMU Minutes, 9 November 1885, bk. J; "The Delegation to the Congo," *American Baptist Missionary Magazine* 65/8 (August 1885): 323. Edward Judson did not leave Boston until 20 June and A. Loughridge until a week later.

He recommended that someone else be sent to the Congo to examine the work firsthand, agreeing that the number of stations needed to be reduced, due to financial constraints facing the Union, and suggested that an effort be made through articles, tracts, and other printed material to promote the work in Africa. At the next meeting his recommendations were accepted.[29] In reality, Gordon had saved the mission![30] He made additional appeals to the entire Union at the national meeting the following May where the Livingstone Inland Mission was reconfirmed.[31]

Gordon worked zealously for the mission.[32] He traveled throughout the northeastern United States, gathering financial support from his church and others. He even named his youngest daughter, born in April, 1886, after the mission: Theodora Livingstone Gordon.[33] His devotion to the mission most likely was provoked by his close association with H. Grattan Guinness. Not only was Guinness a missions advocate, but he was the leading contemporary popularizer of historic premillennial thought in Great Britain, the particular interpretation of premillennialism which Gordon himself espoused. It was his blending of missionary interests and premillennial zeal that provided the platform for the founding of the Boston Missionary Training School in 1889.

---

[29]Ibid., 16 Nov. 1885, bk. J. See also A. J. Gordon's letter to Guinness as recorded in "Designation Service in Boston, U.S.A.," *Regions Beyond* (December 1886): 51.

[30]A. Sims, letter to Ernest B. Gordon, 7 April 1895, A. J. Gordon Papers, Jenks Learning Resource Center, Gordon College, Wenham, Massachusetts. Hereafter AJGPJ; For a description of the work continued by Guinness in the Congo region, see Harry Guinness, *Not Unto Us: A Record of Twenty-One Years' Missionary Service* (London: n.p., 1908). The Congo mission, now Zaire, was the largest mission field for the American Baptist Churches, USA.

[31]"Report of the Committee on African Missions," *The American Baptist Missionary Magazine* 46/7 (July 1886): 190; Merriam, *The American Baptist Missionary Union and Its Missions*, 197-99.

[32]Edmund F. Merriam, *A History of American Baptist Missions* (Philadelphia: American Baptist Publication Society, 1990) 183-87.

[33]A. J. Gordon, "First-Fruits of the Congo," *Baptist Missionary Magazine* 66/8 (August 1886): 329-30; A. J. Gordon, "Martyr-Seed and Martyr-Fruit in Africa," *Baptist Missionary Magazine* 69/2 (February 1889): 43-45; A. J. Gordon, "We Are Debtors," *Baptist Missionary Magazine* 72/12 (December 1892): 491; Edward F. Merriam, "The American Baptist Missionary Union," *A Century of Baptist Achievement*, ed. A. J. Newman (Philadelphia PA: American Baptist Publication Society, 1901) 188; Merriam, *The American Baptist Missionary Union and Its Missions*, 192-93.

5. The Boston Missionary Training School: Gordon and Guinness

Both Guinness and Gordon were historic premillennialists, although both were first introduced to premillennialism through the Plymouth Brethren, advocates of futuristic premillennialism. The terms "historicist" and "futurist" refer to broad ways of interpreting biblical apocalyptic materials, especially the biblical books of Daniel and Revelation. Futurists see the events to which the text refers as pending. The historicist, on the other hand, sees the events to which the text refers as having already taken place. Historicism was the method used in the church for centuries, since well before the reformation, gaining special prominence in the seventeenth and eighteenth centuries and falling into decline as the nineteenth century progressed. Futurism emerged in the 1830s with the work of John Nelson Darby (1800–1882), and with the Oxford Movement's rejection of a papal antichrist.[34]

Guinness wrote voluminously on historicism at a time when it was already virtually discredited, when futurism had already come onto the scene. In many ways, Guinness is on the transition between the two systems. He is particularly interesting because he utilized elaborate astronomical and mathematical calculations to support his position.[35]

By 1889 A. J. Gordon had considered establishing a missionary training school. In 1887 he and M. R. Deming (1844–1925) reopened the Bowdoin Square Baptist Church, with Deming serving as pastor. This church did experience growth, but the area around the church building was economically depressed and prostitution was a problem in the neighborhood.[36]

The Church purchased two prostitution houses in the neighborhood and modified their purpose, establishing instead a "Young Men's Institute" in one, which would provide lodging, religious training, and biblical instruction for working men of the city.[37] The plan, much like that in Guinness's school in London, was to train evangelists for city work and

---

[34] See Sandeen 59-80; for the Oxford Movement, e.g. [E. B. Pusey?], "The Times of Antichrist," an Advent sermon preached in 1838, *Tract for the Times* 5/83 (London: Rivington, 1840).

[35] Stanley D. Walters, "The World Will End in 1919: Daniel among the Victorians."

[36] A. J. Gordon letter to Alvah Hovey, 24 May 1889, Alvah Hovey Papers, Andover Newton Theological School, Newton Centre MA. Hereafter, AHPANTS.

[37] Ibid.

lay helpers for foreign missions, especially those for the American Baptist mission in the Congo. Gordon wrote to Alvah Hovey (1820–1903), president of Newton Theological Institution, "I am greatly moved to do something to help meet the crying needs of these fields."[38]

The model for the school came from two sources. First, the evangelical passion of the Moravians, and the work of the German Pietist John Gossner (1773–1858), whose pioneer training of laypeople gave Gordon a vision for missionary training, was a huge contribution.[39] Second, and most importantly, a pattern for the school was found in Guinness's work in London, England.[40] During the summer of 1888—when Gordon was a delegate to the Missionary Centenary in London, and while on business for the Missionary Union—he toured Guinness's missionary training school, the East London Institute for Home and Foreign Missions and Harley House in London.[41]

Although Gordon and Guinness may have considered the founding of a missionary training school in Boston when Gordon was in London in 1888, it was not until Guinness came to the United States for business related to the Congo mission in 1889, that the decision was made.[42] Gordon related the story to Hovey. Apparently, while preaching in Boston at the Bowdoin Square Baptist Church, Guinness said to Deming and him, "Why not make a recruiting station for missionaries out of your Institute?"[43] And that is just what they did.

In addition to the Boston school, Guinness helped to found two others: one in Kansas City, with the help of evangelist George C. Needham and sponsored by the YMCA;[44] the other in Minneapolis, Minnesota, with Henry C. Mabie (1847–1918)—pastor of the Central Baptist

---

[38] Ibid.

[39] A. J. Gordon, *The Holy Spirit in Missions* (Chicago: Revell, 1893) 63-75; cf. W. Hallenberg, Johannes Evangelista Gossner," *The New Schaff-Herzog Encyclopedia of Religious Knowledge*, vol. 5, ed. Samuel McCauley Jackson (New York and London: Funk and Wagnalls) 31-32.

[40] Minutes of the Executive Committee of the ABMU, bks. G & H, ABHS.

[41] A. J. Gordon letters, summer 1888, AJBPJ.

[42] A. J. Gordon letter to Alvah Hovey, 24 May 1889, 4 March 1890, AHPANTS.

[43] Ibid.

[44] Mrs. H. Grattan Guinness, "Our Absent Director and His Work in America," *Regions Beyond* (September/October 1889) 295-97; Mrs. H. Grattan Guinness, "Our Absent Director," *Regions Beyond* (December 1889) 422; W. W. E., "Training Schools for Church Workers," *The Watchman*, (28 November 1889): 2; Henry Clay Mabie, *From Romance to Reality* (Boston: n.p., 1917) 112-14.

Church—as president.[45] Gordon's training school as well as these two others were established on the same principle: "undenominational, broadly evangelical, practical, spiritual, humble, and unworldly, and consecrated to the benefit of 'The Regions Beyond' "[46] and opened on October 2, 1889.[47] Guinness referred to them as "branches" of each other, his own school's "young American cousins."[48]

Both Gordon and Guinness held a similar perspective on missions, but it was their premillennialism that caused the most controversy among the Baptists in the United States. In fact, an editorial in the October 1889 issue of the *Baptist Missionary Magazine* accused Gordon of a "new departure on the doctrine of eschatology."[49]

The Baptist *New York Examiner* called both Gordon's and Mabie's schools a "shortcut method" and a threat to the seminaries.[50] Gordon responded with "Short-cut Methods" in the Boston-based *Watchman*. He defended the founding of his school and claimed that its purpose was for the training of "lay workers," brushing aside the accusation of premillennialism as a new departure, and stating that there had always been many Baptists who embraced this doctrine, that his belief was not out of the ordinary.[51]

Guinness did not manage to escape controversy. However, prior to the launching of the new training school in Boston, he was awarded the honorary Doctor of Divinity degree from Brown University. It is apparent that Guinness's nomination came from Gordon, who served on the board of trustees of the university, but for some reason the vote of confidence came as a surprise to Guinness. He wrote to his wife, Fanny:

> By the way, what do you suppose one of the oldest and most respected Universities here has done, without consulting me, directly or indirectly, or even without letting me know? *They have made me a Doctor of Divinity!* As

---

[45]Ibid., 300; The Minneapolis City Directory contains a listing for Mabie's "Missionary Training Institute" for 1889–1894; cf. Mabie, 112-14; *Celebration of the Twenty-fifth Anniversary of the Central Baptist Church, May 3rd and 5th, 1895* (privately printed) 28-32

[46]Mrs. H. Grattan Guinness, "Our Absent Director and His Work In America," 296.

[47]Ibid.

[48]Ibid., 298.

[49]"Editorial: A Missionary Training School," *Baptist Missionary Magazine* 69/10 (October 1889): 388.

[50]James A. Willmarth, "Short-Cut and Cross-Cut," *The Examiner* (27 March 1890): 1; A. J. Gordon, "Short-Cut Methods," *The Watchman* (7 November 1889): 1.

[51]Ibid.

the people here constantly *call* me "Doctor," it will save me the frequent trouble of correcting them! I only learned the fact yesterday by the enclosed extract, though they took the step on the 13th of June.[52]

Of course, Guinness was named a "coconspirator" of Gordon's.[53] When in St. Louis and Kansas City, Guinness's effort to help establish shortcut schools followed him. One disgruntled western Baptist wrote, "Either Dr. Guinness should prove that the young men in our seminaries having volunteered for missionary service have refused to go, or else he should cease placing this stigma on these young men, and on the seminaries."[54] The three schools prompted by Guinness, in Boston, Minneapolis, and Kansas City were claimed by one writer to be "three schools [that] represent a new scheme of short cuts to missionary and ministerial labor."[55]

To be sure, the critics of the Boston Missionary Training School and the two others were in some measure accurate. Guinness's own East London Institute for Home and Foreign Missions *was* a shortcut college. Reflecting on the East London Institute's purpose, Guinness wrote in the preface of *Light for the Last Days*:

> Yet the ever-growing conviction of the shortness of the time for gospel labor, of which the grounds are here indicated, forbids us to relax effort for the multiplication of missionaries in heathendom, and evangelists in destitute districts of Christendom. . . . That the end alluded to in this promise is *near* this book shows; and hence the supreme importance of doing all that in us lies to publish the gospel of salvation to the still unevangelized nations of the earth.[56]

---

[52]*Historical Catalog of Brown University 1764–1904* (Providence RI: Brown University, 1905) 585. H. Grattan Guinness letter in Mrs. H. Grattan Guinness, "Our Absent Director and His Work in America," 300. Guinness was writing from Kansas on 29 June 1889. There is a possibility that Brown's president, Ezekiel Gilman Robinson, former president of Rochester Theological Seminary and of the American Baptist Missionary Union, who presided at his last commencement in 1889, had some influence on the awarding of the Doctor of Divinity to Guinness. See: Stanley D. Walters, "The World will End in 1919: Daniel Among the Victorians," *The Asbury Theological Journal* 44/1 (1989): 46n.2.

[53]Guinness was also listed to be one of the lecturers for the session in October 1889. See "Home Religious Chronicle," *The Watchman* (22 August 1889): 4.

[54]"From St. Louis," *The Examiner* (26 December 1889) 2.

[55]"The New Ministerial Short Cut," *The Examiner* (24 October 1889) 2.

[56]H. Grattan Guinness, *Light for the Last Days: A Study Historic and Prophetic* (New York: A. C. Armstrong & Son, 1887) xv-xvi.

It was a shortcut to train men and women for the purpose of evangelization in light of Christ's imminent return.

One cannot miss the premillennialist agenda underneath the zealous efforts of Gordon in Boston and Guinness in London. Both men's ministries—and even their friendship—were profoundly influenced by their premillennialist presuppositions.

6. Prophetical Studies and Personal Friendship

Following Gordon's death in February 1895, Guinness reflected on their friendship and common interest in prophetic study:

> While I write these words my eye falls on Dr. Gordon's beautiful little book on the Lord's coming, *Ecce Venit*. Scriptural, spiritual, clear, and conclusive, this work has a special value, not only as setting forth the truth as to the second advent, but as presenting, in a simple and striking form, the central features of the historical interpretation of prophecy. Many a conversation I had with our beloved brother on these themes, for when in Boston his house was always my home. Truly we saw eye to eye on these matters. I thank God for the testimony of his servant, Dr. Gordon, as to the fulfilment of prophecy in the history of the Christian church during the last eighteen centuries.[57]

The appreciation went both ways. H. Grattan Guinness's writings were read by both A. J. and Maria Hale Gordon. Like the Guinnesses, the Gordons were one in their embrace of historic premillennialism. Maria Hale Gordon noted in one of her journal entries:

> Have been reading most of the day in Mr. and Mrs. Guinness's new book, *Divine Programme of the World's History*. It is the most convincing and complete vindication of the inspiration of the Scriptures from the fulfilment of their inspired predictions written in the most glowing style.[58]

H. Grattan Guinness was an historic premillennialist. Like Gordon, he shifted from futurism to historicism. Gordon remarked about his own change from one position in premillennialism to another, "If we turn away from the Futurist interpretation—in which we were "nourished and brought up" so far as our prophetic studies are concerned—and express our firm adherence to the Historical, it is because we believe that the

---

[57]H. Grattan Guinness, "In Memorium: Dr. A. J. Gordon," *Regions Beyond* (April 1895): 161.
[58]Maria Hale Gordon, diary, 13 August 1888, AJGPJ.

latter is more scriptural."[59] He considered the Futurist interpretation to be "lame in its feet,"[60] yet, he avoided the pitfalls of other historicists, like Guinness, who had a penchant for setting dates.[61]

It appears that for Guinness, his shift from futurism to historicism came by way of

> A fuller acquaintance, acquired by personal observation, with the condition of the Greek and other professing Christian Churches of Syria, Egypt, and Turkey, and of the effects of Mohammedan rule in the East, and also the Papal system as developed in France and Spain, and with the Continental infidelity to which it has given rise, subsequently led the author to a careful study of the history of Mohammedan and Papal powers, and of the prophecies of Scripture believed by many to relate to them. This resulted in a deep conviction that those Powers occupy in the Word of God, as prominent a place as they have actually held in the history of the Church.[62]

Coupled with the Bible and a fascination with astronomy, Guinness was led to conclude that "the *epacts* [*sic*] of the prophetic periods of Scripture form a remarkable septiform series." Thus, Guinness understood some passages in the Scripture to refer not to days, but to years.[63]

One can easily become overwhelmed when studying the intricate explanations of the various schools of prophecy. Aside from the complexities and nuances of Guinness's interpretations, his formula appears to be rather simple: "Prophecy is history written in advance."[64] His many books, along with his monthly publication, *Regions Beyond*, assisted him in advancing and articulating his views.

Guinness's several books on prophetic study included *The Approaching End of the Age in the Light of History, Prophecy, and Science* (1878); *Light for the Last Days* (1887); *The Divine Programme of the World's History* (1888); *The Key to the Apocalypse* (1899); and *History Unveiling*

---

[59] A. J. Gordon, *Ecce Venit* (New York: Revell, 1889) v.

[60] A. J. Gordon, "Book Notices," *The Watchword* 11/11 (November 1889): 288.

[61] A. J. Gordon, "Not to be Professed," *The Watchword* 5/11 (August 1883): 243; cf. Robert G. Clouse, "The Danger of Mistaken Hope," *Dreams, Vision and Oracles*, ed. Carl Edwin Armerding and W. Ward Gasque (Grand Rapids MI: Baker, 1977) 27-37; James E. Bear, "Historic Premillennialism," *Union Seminary Review* 40/3 (May 1944): 207; Walters, "The World Will End in 1919: Daniel among the Victorians" passim.

[62] H. Grattan Guinness, *The Approaching End of the Age* (London: Hodder and Stoughton, 1880) vii.

[63] Guinness, *Approaching*, viii.

[64] Guinness, *Divine, Programme* iii.

Prophecy: or Time as an Interpreter (1906).[65] These studies underscore Guinness's own place in British premillennial thought. At the close of the nineteenth century, he was perhaps the last principal popularizer of historic premillennialism in Great Britain, and likewise, A. J. Gordon was the last leading historicist in the United States. In a time when their particular position was fading, both men helped keep historicism alive in their respective countries. A. J. Gordon died soon after in 1889, and not long after Guinness died in 1910, the historic school of interpretation having long since closed its doors. Although they were an ocean apart, Guinness and Gordon served as partners in the task of promoting historic premillennialism.

7. Conclusion

Both Adoniram Judson Gordon and Harry Grattan Guinness had a commitment to missions. They established schools to feed the foreign field. Both were devoted to the premillennial return of Christ, and both had been introduced to premillennialism by way of futurism, but had turned from futurism to historicism. It was historic premillennialism that formed their hermeneutic in missions and in missionary education. Gordon and Guinness witnessed the ocean between them become smaller and smaller. They were transnational friends. Guinness's son observed, "A. J. Gordon of Boston . . . became one of his warmest personal friends."[66] They were truly transatlantic Victorians, evangelicals who participated in the vast exchange between the United States and Great Britain. They were changed because of it. And so was Evangelicalism—then and now.

---

[65]Guinness, *Approaching*, H. Grattan Guinness, *Light for the Last Days* (New York: A. C. Armstrong & Son, 1887), this book went through numerous editions, as many as fourteen in 1912; H. Grattan Guinness, *The Divine Programme of the World's History* (New York: A. C. Armstrong & Son, 1888); H. Grattan Guinness, *Key to the Apocalypse* (London: Hodder & Stoughton, 1899); H. Grattan Guinness, *History Unveiling Prophecy: or Times as an Interpreter* (New York: Fleming H. Revell, 1906).

[66]"In Memorium: H. Grattan Guinness, D.D., F.R.A.S.," 36.

Barrington Raymond White
A Bibliography of Printed Works

Stephen Copson

Key

BHH *Baptist History and Heritage*
  (Journal of the Historical Commission of Southern Baptist Convention and the Southern Baptist Historical Society)
BQ *Baptist Quartely*
JEH *Journal of Ecclesiastical History*
JTS *Journal of Theological Studies*

1959

Articles
  "A Puritan Work by Robert Browne," *BQ* 18.109.

1965

Articles
  "Thomas Crosby, Baptist Historian (1)," *BQ* 21.154.
  "Writing and Preserving Baptist History," *Fraternal* no. 136.4 (Journal of the Baptist Ministers' Fellowship).

Reviews and Short Notices
  Cardinal Bainbridge in the Court of Rome 1509–1514 by D. S. Chambers, *BQ* 21.186.
  Calvin: the Second Epistle of Paul the Apostle to the Corinthians and the Epistles to Timothy, Titus, and Philemon, translated by T. A. Smail, *JTS* 16.276 (SN).

1966

Articles
  "Who Really Wrote the Kiffin Manuscript?" BRH volume 1.
  "Thomas Crosby, Baptist Historian (2)," *BQ* 21.219.
  "The Organization of the Particular Baptists 1644–1646," *JEH* 17.209.

Reviews and Short Notices
  Studies in Church History II, edited by G. J. Cuming, *BQ* 21.283.
  Servants of God: A History of the Baptists of Cefn Mawr and District by G. Vernon Price, *BQ* 21.185.
  The Later Lollards by John A. F. Thomson, *BQ* 21.334.

1967

Articles
"Baptist Beginnings and the Kiffin Manuscript," *BHH* volume 1.
"William Kiffin—Baptist Pioneer and Citizen of London," *BHH* volume 2.
"John Gill in London, 1719–1729 ABiographical Fragment," *BQ* 22.72.

Reviews and Short Notices
A History of Protestantism, volume 1, *The Reformation* by E. G. Leonard, *BQ* 22.42.
The Revolution of the Saints by Michael Wazer, *BQ* 22.92.
The Great Rebellion by Ivan Roots, *BQ* 22.188.
Richard Baxter by G. F. Nuttall, *JTS* 18.276.
A History of the Baptists by R. G. Torbet, *JTS* 18.559 (SN).

1968

Articles
"The Baptists of Reading 1652–1715," *BQ* 22.249.
"The Frontiers of Fellowship between English Baptists 1609–1660," *Foundations* 11.244 (*A Baptist Journal of History, Theology, and Ministry*, published by the American Baptist Historical Society).
"The Doctrine of the Church in the Particular Baptist Confession of 1644," *JTS* 19.570.
"John Traske (1585–1636) and London Puritanism," *Transactions of the Congregational History Society* 20.223.

Reviews and Short Notices
The Community of Kent and the Great Rebellion 1640–1660 by A. M. Everitt, *BQ* 22.331.
A History of Protestantism volume 2 by Emile Leonard, *BQ* 22.332.
The Elizabethan Puritan Movement by Patrick Collinson, *BQ* 22.378.
The Heart Prepared: Grace and Conversion in Puritan Spiritual Life by Norman Petit, *JTS* 19.376.
The Puritan Spirit: Essays and Addresses by G. F. Nuttall, *JTS* 19.442 (SN).

Lectures and Addresses
"The Task of a Baptist Historian," *BQ* 22.398 (delivered to the Baptist Historical Society Summer School, 1968).

1969

Articles
"Why Bother with History?" *BHH* volume 4.
"William Erbery (1604–1654) and the Baptists," *BQ* 23.114.
"Thomas Patient in England and Ireland," *Irish Baptist Historical Society Journal* 2 (1969–1970).

Reviews and Short Notices
Vexed and Troubled Englishmen 1590–1642, *BQ* 23.47.
John Knox by Jasper Ridley, *BQ* 23.93.
Elizabeth and the English Reformation by William P. Haugaard, *BQ* 23.141.
The Emergence of Hyper-Calvinism in English Nonconformity 1689–1765 by Peter Toon, *JEH* 19.18 (SN).

1970
Articles
"Isaac Backus and Baptist History," *BHH* volume 5.
"How Did William Kiffin Join the Baptists?" *BQ* 23.201.
"Daniel Roberts of Reading and the Quakers," *BQ* 23.328.

Reviews and Short Notices
A History of the Reformation in Germany to 1555 by Franz Lau and Ernst Bizer, *BQ* 23.237.
Norfolk in the Civil War by R. W. Ketton-Cremer, *BQ* 23.286.
The Last Days of the Lancashire Monasteries and the Pilgrimage of Grace by Christopher Hugh, *BQ* 23.332.
The Influence of Prophecy in the Later Middle Ages: A Study in Joachimism by Marjorie Reeves, *BQ* 23.382.
The English Presbyterians: from Elizabethan Puritans to Modern Unitarians by C. G. Bolam and others, *JEH* 20.359.
The History of the Kings' Weigh House: A Chapter in the History of London by Elaine Kaye, *JEH* 20.374 (SN).
Isaac Backus on Church, State, and Calvinism: Pamphlets 1754–1779 edited by William G. McLoughlin, *JEH* 20.376 (SN).

1971
Books
Editor. *Association Records of the Particular Baptists ofEngiand, Wales, and Ireland to 1660*, part 1, *South Wales and the Midlands*, London: Baptist Historical Society.
The English Separatist Tradition: From the Marian Martyrs to the Pilgrim Fathers, Oxford University Press.

Articles
"Samuel Eaton (d. 1639) Particular Baptist Pioneer," *BQ* 24.10.
"Thomas Collier and Gangraena Edwards," *BQ* 24.99.
"Two Early Propagandists for Believers' Baptistm," *BQ* 24.167.

Reviews and Short Notices
God's Englishman: Oliver Cromwell and the English Revolution by Christopher Hill, *BQ* 24,44.
The Oxford Martyrs by D. M. Loades, *BQ* 24.90.
Edward VI: The Threshold of Power by W.K. Jordan, *BQ* 24.140.

Pride's Purge by David Underdown, *BQ* 24.191.
The Correspondence of John Owen (1616–1683) with an Account of His Life and Work, edited by Peter Toon, *JEH* 22.380 (SN).
The Writings of John Greenwood and Henry Barrow 1591–1593 by Leland H. Carlson, *JTS* 22.277.
Calvinism and the Amyraut Heresy: Protestant Scholasticism or Humanism in Seventeenth Century France by Brian G. Armstrong, *JTS* 22.278.
Revivalism and Separatism in New England 1740–1820 by C. G. Coen (2nd ed.) *JTS* 22.281.

Lectures and Addresses
St. Andrew's Street Baptist Church: Three Historical Lectures Given on the Occasion of the 250th Anniversary of the Foundation of the Church, edited by K. A. C. Parsons, Cambridge.

1972

Articles
"Open and Closed Membership among English and Welsh Baptists," *BQ* 24.
"Baptists in Barnstaple, Devon 1650–1652," *BQ* 24.385.

Reviews and Short Notices
Religion, Order and Law: A Study in Pre-Revolutionary England by David Little, *BQ* 24.233.
Government in Reformation Europe 1520–1560, edited by By Henry J. Cohn, *BQ* 24.363.
Antichrist in Seventeenth Century England by Christopher Hill, *BQ* 24.364.
The Puritan Lectureships: the Politics of Religious Dissent 1560–1662 by Paul S. Seaver, *JTS* 23.288.
Nihil Pulchrius Ordine: contribution à l'étude de l'etablissement de la discipline ecclésiastique aux Pay-Bas ou Lambert Daneau aux Pays-Bas (1581–1583) by Oliver Fatio, *JTS* 23.290.
The Church and the Secular Order in Reformation Thought by John Tonkin, *JTS* 23.519.

1973

Books
Editor. *Association Records of the Particular Baptists of England, Wales, and, Ireland*, part 2, *The West Country and Ireland*, London: Baptist Historical Society.

Articles
"The English General Baptists and the Great Rebellion," *BHH* vol. 8.

Reviews and Short Notices
Calvin's New Testament Commentaries by T. H. L. Parker, *BQ* 25.95.
The Civil Lawyers in England, 1603–1641: A Political Study, *BQ* 25.188.

Somerset in the Civil War and Interregnum by David Underdown, *BQ* 25.189.
New England Dissent 1630–1833: The Baptists and the Separation of Church and State by William G McLoughlin, *JEH* 24.91.
The Radical Brethren: Anabaptism and the English Reformation to 1558 by I. B. Horst, *JEH* 24.309.
Anabaptism: A Social History 1525–1618: Switzerland, Austria, Moravia, South and Central Germany by Claus-Peter Clasen, *JEH* 24.422.
The Lord's Supper in Early English Dissent by Stephen Mayor, *JTS* 24.615.

Lectures and Addresses
"Henry Jessey, Apastor in Politics," *BQ* 25.98 (1973) (Second Henton Lecture, April 1971).

1974
Books
Editor. *Association Records of the Particular Baptists of England, Wales, and Ireland to 1660*, part 3, *The Abingdon Association*, London.
The Story of Andover Baptist Church 1824–1974 (with Rev. Walter Fancutt), Andover.

Articles
"The English Particular Baptists and the Great Rebellion 1640–1660," *BHH* volume 9.
"Samuel Whitewood, 1794–1860, at Andover," *BQ* 25.232.
"John Pendarves, the Calvinistic Baptists and the Fifth Monarchy," *BQ* 25.251.

Reviews and Short Notices
Freedom, Corruption, and Government in Elizabethan England by Joel Hurstfield, *BQ* 25.239.
Politics, Religion and the English Civil War, edited by Brian Manning, *BQ* 25.331.
Lucy Hutchinson: Memoirs of the Life of Colonel Hutchinson, edited by James Sutherland, *BQ* 25.332.
Knibb, "the Notorious": Slaves' Missionary 1803–1845 by Philip Wright, *BQ* 25.387.
The First Book of Discipline, *JTS* 25.255 (SN).

1975
Reviews and Short Notices
Cheshire 1630–1660: County Government and Society during the English Revolution by J.S. Morrill, *BQ* 26.95.
The Improbably Puritan: A Life of Bulstrode Whitelocke 1605–1675 by Ruth Spalding, *BQ* 26.142.
Familiar to All: William Lilly and Astrology in the Seventeenth Century by Derek Parker, *BQ* 26.193.

1976
Books
Authority: A Baptist View, London.

Articles
"Baptist Beginnings in Watford," *BQ* 26.205.
"John Miles and the Structures of the Particular Baptist Mission to Wales 1649–1660" in *Welsh Baptist Studies*, edited by M. John, Cardiff.

Reviews and Short Notices
Charles I's Lord Treasurer: Sir Richard Weston, Earl of Portland by Michael van Cleave Alexander, *BQ* 26.241.
The Levellers and the English Revolution, edited by G. E. Aylmer, *BQ* 26.242.
New England in the English Nation 1689–1713 by Philip S. Jaffenden, *BQ* 26.291.
The Dissenting Tradition: Essays for Leland H. Carlson, edited by C. Robert Cole and Michael E. Moody, *BQ* 26.329.
The Covenant Sealed: the Development of Puritan Sacramental Theology in Old and New England 1570–1720 by E. Brooks Holifield, *JTS* 27.250.

1977
Articles
"Early Baptist Letters (I)," *BQ* 27.142.
"The Ministerial Tightrope," *Fraternal* no. 180.4.
"Henry Jessey in the Great Rebellion" in *Reformation, Conformity, and Dissent: Essays in Honour of Geoffery Nuttall*, edited by R. Buick Knox, London.

Reviews and Short Notices
The University in Society, edited by Lawrence Stone. Volume 1, *Oxford and Cambridge from the 14th to the Early 19th Century*; volume 2, *Europe, Scotland, and the United States from the 16th to the 20th Century*, *BQ* 27.33.
John Bunyan: The Doctrine of the Law and Grace Unfolded, and, I Will Pray with the Spirit, edited by Richard L. Greaves, *BQ* 27.46.
A Great Expectation: Eschatalogical Thought in English Protestantism to 1660 by Bryan W. Ball, *JTS* 28.241.
Theodore Beza's Doctrine of Predestination by John S. Bray, *JTS* 28.282 (SN).

Lectures and Addresses
Hasserd Knollys and Radical Dissent in the Seventeenth Century, London (Thirty-first lecture of the Friends of Dr. Williams's Library).

1978
Reviews and Short Notices
Mysticism and Dissent: Religious Ideology and Social Protest in the Sixteenth Century by Steven E. Ozment, *JEH* 25.344.
Thomas Hooker: Writings in England and Holland 1626–1633 edited with introductory essays by George H. Williams, Norman Pettit, Winfried Herget, and Sargent Bush Jr., *JTS* 29.273.
Calvin et l'Humanisme by François Wendel, *JTS* 29.315 (SN).

1979
Articles
"The Denominational Enquiry and the Local Church," *Mainstream Newsletter* no. 2.

Reviews and Short Notices
The Re-Establishment of the Church of England 1660–1663 by I. M. Green, *BQ* 28.44.

1980
Lectures and Addresses
"Come Wind, Come Weather!" *BQ* 28.292 (address at Regent's Park College, Oxford, on 21 January, 1980).
"Opening Our Doors to God," Ilkeston (Mainstreun Conference Address).

1981
Articles
"The Crisis of our Worship," *The Theological Educator* 11.2.

Lectures and Addresses
Walter Pope Binns Lectures 1980: (1) *Inaugural Address*; (2) *Honest Religion*; (3) *Honest Education*, Liberty, Missouri.
"Theology of Public Worship" (H. I. Hester lecture) delivered during the Annual Meeting of the Association of Southern Baptist Colleges and Schools, Charleston, S.C.

1982
Reviews and Short Notices
The English Connection: The Puritan Roots of Seventh-Day Adventist Belief by Bryan W. Ball, *BQ* 29.288.
Reformation Principals and Practice: Essays in Honour of A. G. Dickens, edited by P. N. Brooks, *JTS* 33.318.

1983

Books

The English Baplists of the Seventeenth Century, London: Baptist Historical Society.

1984

Articles

"The English Separatists and John Smyth Revisited," *BQ* 30.344.

Reviews and Short Notices

Radical Religion in the English Revolution, edited by J. F. McGregor and B. Reay, *BQ* 31.195.

The Church Book of the Independent Church (New Pound Lane Baptist) Isleham 1693–1803, edited by K. A. C. Parsons, *JEH* 36.327 (SN).

Videotape Interview

"The English Baptist Heritage," an interview with William H. Brackney, executive director of the American Baptist Historical Society. Filmed at the Principal's Lodgings, Regent's Park Coflege, Oxford. 60 minutes in length.

Reviews and Short Notices

Are Southern Baptists "Evangelicals"? by James Lee Garrett Jr., E. Glenn Hinson, and James E. Tull, *BQ* 31.404.

The Reign of Elizabeth I by Christopher Haigh, *JTS* 37.309 (SN).

The Writings of Thomas Hooker: Spiritual Adventures in Two Worlds, *JTS* 37.320 (SN).

Advertissement contre l'Astrologie Judiciaire de Jean Calvin, édition critique par Olivier Millet, *JTS* 37.707 (SN).

1987

Articles

"The Practice of Association" in *A Perspective on Baptist Identity,* Kingsbridge (Mainstream).

"The London Calvinistic Baptist Leadership 1644–1660," in *Faith, Heritage and Witness,* edited by J. H. Y. Briggs, supplement to *BQ* volume 32, published in honour of Reverend Dr. W. M. S. West.

Reviews and Short Notices

Saints: Visible, Orderly, and Catholic: The Congregational Idea of the Church by A. P. F. Sell, *BQ* 32.94.

The Assembly of the Lord by Robert S. Paul, *BQ* 32.150.

International Calvinism 1541–1715, edited by Menna Prestwich, *JTS* 38.568.

Lectures and Addresses
"In Search of the New Testament Church" in *Finding Common Ground for a Many-Splendored Family*, Philadelphia: Eastern Baptist Theological Seminary.

1988

Articles
"The Fellowship of Believers: Bunyan and Puritanism" in *John Bunyan, Conventicle and Parnassus*, edited by N. H. Keeble, Oxford.

Reviews and Short Notices
The Baptist Heritage: Four Centuries of Baptist Witness by H. Leon McBeth, *BQ* 32.254.
International Calvinism 1541–1715 edited by Manna Prestwich, *BQ* 32.304.
The Dawn of the Reformation by Heiko A. Oberman, *BQ* 32.56.
Sussex Believers: Baptist Marriages in the 17th and 18th Centuries, by John Caffyn, *BQ* 32.420.
Calvin and Scottish Theology: the Doctrine of Assurance by Charles Bell, *JEH* 39.308 (SM).
God's Caress: the Psychology of Puritan Religious Experience by C. L. Cohen, *JTS* 39.633.

1989

Articles
"Early Baptist Arguments for Religious Freedom: Their Overlooked Agenda," *BHH* volume 14.

Reviews and Short Notices
The Sources of Swiss Anabaptism edited by Leland Harder, *BQ* 33.98.
The Young Calvin by Alexander Ganoccy, *BQ* 33.152.
The Covenant of Grace in Puritan Thought by John von Rohr, *JTS* 40.305.
John Calvin: A Sixteenth Century Portrait by William J. Bouwsma, *JTS* 40.677.

1990

Articles
"Origins and Convictions of the First Calvinistic Baptists," *BHH* volume 15.
"Anabaptist Studies: A Review Article," *BQ* 34.88.
"John Bunyan and the Context of Persecution 1660–1688" in *John Bunyan and His England 1628–1688* edited by Anne Laurence, W. R. Owens, and Stuart Sim, London.

Reviews and Short Notices
Sabbath and Sectarianism in Seventeenth Century England by David S. Katz, *JTS* 41.295.

A Turbulent, Seditious, and Factious People: John Bunyan and His Church by Christopher Hill, *JTS* 41.759.

1991

Articles

"The Twilight of Puritanism in the Years before and after 1688," in *From Persecution to Toleration: The Glorious Revolution and Religion in England*, edited by Ole Peter Grell, Jonathan I. Israel, and Nicholas Tyacke, Oxford.

"The Call of God and the People of God," *Fraternal* no. 234.7.

Reviews and Short Notices

Perfection Proclaimed: Language and Literature in English Radical Religion 1640–1660, by Nigel Smith *JTS* 42.396.

Holy Time: Moderate Puritans and the Sabbath by John H. Primus, *JTS* 42.470 (SN).

The Will of God and the Cross: A Historical and Theological Study of John Calvin's Doctrine of Limited Redemption by Jonathan H. Rainbow, *JTS* 42.842 (SN).

1992

Reviews and Short Notices

Conscience Taken Captive by Don A. Sanford, *BQ* 34.239.

1993

Reviews and Short Notices

A Choosing People: The History of the Seventh Day Baptists by Don A. Sanford. *BQ* 35.120.

1996

Books

The English Baptists of the Seventeenth Century (2nd edition), London: Baptist Historical Society.